D1010247

Also by Mons Kallentoft in the Malin Fors *series*

Midwinter Sacrifice
Summertime Death
Autumn Killing

SAVAGE SPRING

Mons Kallentoft

Translated from the Swedish by Neil Smith

HODDER

First published in Great Britain in 2013 by Hodder & Stoughton
An Hachette UK company

Originally published in Swedish in 2010 as *Vårlik* by Natur och Kultur

1

A CIP catalogue record for this title is available from the British Library

Paperback ISBN 978 1 444 72167 6

Typeset in Plantin by Palimpsest Book Production Limited,
Falkirk, Stirlingshire

Printed and bound by Clays Ltd, St Ives plc

Hodder & Stoughton policy is to use papers that are natural, renewable and
recyclable products and made from wood grown in sustainable forests. The
logging and manufacturing processes are expected to conform to the
environmental regulations of the country of origin.

Hodder & Stoughton Ltd
338 Euston Road
London NW1 3BH

www.hodder.co.uk

Prologue

May 2010

In the chamber of darkness

Where are you, Daddy?

You're supposed to be here with me.

Where have you gone? Daddy, Daddy, you need to come now.

Little brother's crying.

He's so little. He's lying on the floor, crying, and there's pee on the floor, Daddy. There are spiders here, and can the snakes get in? The lizards, the great big lizards with yellow teeth, is that what's making that scratching noise? It's your fault if we die, Daddy.

He says it's nasty, nasty.

Like in the pool at home, Daddy. He never dared to jump in, not even with armbands on. I dare. I'm brave. I'm braver than him, because I'm six and he's only three, nearly four.

I'm sweating and it's too hot. But only sometimes. I've taken my top off, am I allowed to? Now there's that noise again and I can hear the men coming, Daddy, the light under the door disappears, there's a ticking sound and everything goes completely dark, and now little brother has to keep really quiet, otherwise they might hit us, and I get scared and I shout:

'Don't hit me, don't hit me,' and then the light under the door is back and the men go away, I can hear it, but they'll be back soon, and will I be dead then? Are they going to kill us, Daddy?

We're locked in, and I want them to let us out. They bring us food, we've got a potty, and we've been given crayons so we can draw things on the walls and floor. We can't see what we're drawing, but we carry on anyway.

I'm frightened. Little brother's even more frightened.

What's that ticking sound? Where are those horrid lizards? They shimmer in the dark.

It's horrid being frightened. I give little brother a hug and he's all warm and he's crying, and this is the nightmare I never wanted to talk about. Is that why this is happening now, Daddy, because I never talked about it?

If you're kind, then everyone is kind back.

Like you, Daddy, you're kind, aren't you, you must be kind, and I let go of him and bang on the locked door, shouting:

'Don't come back. I don't want to be dead. We don't want to be dead.'

Hurry up and get here.

Six Years Earlier

My body is screaming to feel unconditional love and forgetfulness bubbling through its veins, that's all it wants.

This feeling of feelings is my only desire, the only thing I want.

You have been taken from me.

That's the way I want it, no one knows about you. I will leave you with what I hope are nice people.

You weren't even supposed to exist, and then there were two of you, and I look around the hospital room, and see how the pale, dead light of the Stockholm spring X-rays its way across the speckled linoleum floor, trying to drive me away from here.

I shall leave you now, forever, I shall give you up, and you will never have any memory of me, and who your father is doesn't matter. Maybe I was raped, lying unconscious in some emergency hostel, or in the steel-blue light of one of the toilets in the central underground station, or perhaps someone decided to help themselves in one of the unknown underground chambers where I fell asleep in the wonderful afterglow.

But one day you were inside me. And now you're in the next room, about to meet your new mother and father, and I feel like screaming, but it has to happen, I want to be somewhere else, love has no place for me and you shall be my great, overpowering secret.

You father could be anyone.

So never ask that question.

Now the door to my room is opening, I see you and you are the only beautiful thing on the planet, never forget that. Now you're crying, is the light too harsh? And you lie in my arms, I get you to sleep, take the time you need, the midwife says, take what you need, and then she takes you again and I cling onto the bed and weep, but it's best this way, best this way. And you're gone, but you should know that Mummy loves you.

The Karolinska University Hospital smells of death and bacteria that no antibiotics can touch, and I tip myself out of bed, pull on the clothes hanging in the cupboard, then shuffle off down the corridor towards the lift, making sure that none of the hospital people see me, because they'd try to stop me. But no one sees, because I know how to make myself invisible.

I don't feel any guilt, or shame.

Do I? There's no point thinking about it.

I miss you so much. And I can't resist, don't want to.

Soon I'm sitting in a taxi, it drops me at Sergels torg in the middle of the city, and, with a crumpled thousand-kronor note in my hand, I pay a visit to a black man I recognise, I know how to make my way down into one of the central underground station's most distant tunnels, I borrow the necessary equipment from one of my peers: a flame and a needle later, and the world becomes what it always ought to be, an open embrace free of jagged emotions.

An hour later I'm standing in Hötorget in the suffocating afternoon light. Surveillance cameras everywhere. Watching me.

I see two girls, maybe seven years old, running across the black-and-white paving towards the windows of Kulturhuset, I see their reflections in the glass but I can't make out their faces. I turn around. Clusters of people, some of them nodding in my direction, as if to say: 'So, you're back.'

I nod.

Turn around again.

The girls are gone.

Swallowed up by their own reflections.

PART I

Avaricious Love

I

Linköping, Monday, 10 May

It's almost possible to see your reflection in the sky, it's so explosively radiant and blue.

It's the same colour as the very core of a welding flame, the mother thinks as she walks across the cobbles of the main square, so closely packed together, fused by thousands and thousands of human footsteps, people wandering back and forth in pursuit of what they want out of life.

The sun is low in the sky, its rays piercing the atmosphere like shining, sharp, steel spears before burning the faces of the people sitting under the huge awnings stretched out above the terrace cafés of Mörners Inn and the Central Hotel. A meagre warmth, with the chill of winter still encapsulated deep in its heart.

The mother looks over at the building containing the estate agent, and can just make out the desperate adverts in the windows. She notes that there's no queue at the cashpoint, and she looks up at the clock beneath the eaves, the steel hands look as if they've been fixed into position, but she knows they can move.

Quarter past ten.

Empty shop windows on all sides of the square. Boutiques and cafés that have had to close in the aftermath of the financial crisis. The signs announcing slashed prices and clearance sales remain, and seem to plead for people's attention through the fine pollen dancing in the air.

There are surprisingly few people about, she thinks, no market stalls today, no farmers in from the plain trying to sell organic vegetables grown under glass, no immigrants trying to sell fruit for cash, no second-hand stalls trying to charge ridiculous prices for knick-knacks that should have gone to the dump years ago.

But the hotdog-seller at the corner is there. He's huddled under his orange, yellow and red parasol, waiting for hungry passersby to stop for a morning snack and fill their stomachs with the low-price alternative he can offer.

Ten kronor for a hotdog. And the flowerstall is there, selling tulips in shades of pink, yellow, red, and orange.

The children, the twins, the girls, are six years old now, running ahead of her, over towards the SEB bank, towards the cashpoint where she usually takes out money before they do whatever chores need doing. Matching pink jackets, matching jeans, white trainers with four red stripes on each side.

There are two of them, but they live, act, and talk as one, in all things they are one and the same. Often strangers can't tell the difference between them, and are astonished at the liveliness, gaiety, and beauty that the girls radiate, as if their whole existence were a hymn of praise to the fact that the world exists and they themselves are allowed to be part of it.

Their blonde hair is ruffled by the wind, their bodies move fluidly, yet simultaneously jerky and slightly awkward, a sign that there is still an endless amount to discover, both in their own bodies and in the whole of the universe, which at this moment, in this square, in this provincial city, belongs to them.

The mother breathes in the spring air.

She can smell the newly opened tulips, a desperate smell, as if the flowers are whispering to her: Why are our lives so short when yours, all of yours, are so long?

You take the present for granted, the mother thinks as she looks at her girls. Her thoughts run on: I don't take anything for granted, I know that everything can be lost.

A man in a black hooded jacket, with the hood up, parks a bicycle next to the cashpoint machine. He doesn't lock the bike, and carefully adjusts a rucksack on the parcel rack with his gloved hands.

The man leaves the rucksack, but doesn't stop to withdraw any money, and carries on across the square towards Bokhållaregatan.

The mother doesn't wonder who the man is. Why he has his hood up in the spring sunshine, why he leaves the bicycle and rucksack.

The girls have reached the cashpoint now. They turn to face her and smile, and she feels like rushing over to them, picking them up, one in each arm, and kissing and hugging them, and making them understand all the love she feels, the love she hopes will make them feel safe and free in the world.

Then they catch sight of the hotdog stand. And habit and hunger make them run past her over to the man under the parasol with his steaming cauldrons and photographs of hotdogs.

They jump up and down in front of the man, and she hurries after them.

Have I got enough change?

There ought to be two ten-kronor coins in her bag. She hunts for her purse, and the man with the black beard has already given the girls a hotdog each by the time she arrives, and he nods to her in recognition.

And drinks, they like the pear flavour, don't they?

Pear. Or apple.

The man has a strong foreign accent. She hunts through the bottom of her black leather handbag and there they are, just as she thought, the coins, cold against her fingers. She hands them to the man behind the hotdog stand, who thanks her, bows his head slightly, and says he hopes to see them again soon.

The girls trot off towards the bollards by the cycle racks outside the Central Hotel, the ones that look like sugar-lumps, next to the canvas sail of the pavement café.

The girls' shadows lengthen and their mother hurries after them, calling to them to take care not to spill ketchup on their new jackets, then she remembers and walks back towards the hotdog stand, and the man is standing with his arm outstretched, holding some napkins out to her.

She shakes her head at her own absent-mindedness, and then she is sitting in the cool sunlight on a sugarlump beside her girls, watching them eat, watching them pull their lips back and chew their way through the fatty sausages with practised movements.

The sun strokes their cheeks, making the blood rise to the surface as if to warm itself.

The people at the pavement café.

Who are you? the mother wonders. Trying to keep her mind from things she can't bear to think about or feel. A neatly dressed pensioner in a blue blazer, beige wool trousers and with water-combed hair. Did he used to be an engineer in Saab's aeronautical division? A professor at the university? Or perhaps a consultant in neurosurgery, or the burns unit at the University Hospital? Or is he just an ordinary old man, a worker in the traditional mould, who enjoys adding a bit of sparkle to old age by dressing smartly? Elevating his own existence in order to cope with the death that is inexorably creeping closer.

She chides herself for her thoughts.

At a table on Mörners' terrace four middle-aged immigrants are playing dice. There are matchsticks on the table, and she assumes they're playing for money. Some high-school kids playing truant are sitting at another table, they must be skipping school, unless they've got a free period? There are people of all ages at the other tables, probably unemployed, having lost their jobs in the thousands of lay-offs that have swept the region's businesses. Resignation in their eyes, anxiety, will I ever get another job? Am I finished, will I be able to support my family, give my children a decent start in life?

A young, heavily made-up woman in a white coat is smoking.

I recognise her, the mother thinks, she works in the beauty parlour down on St Larsgatan.

Three men in dark suits go past Mörners, possibly solicitors from one of the city's four law firms. Or financial wannabees. There are still a few of those, even in Linköping. They adjust their ties, shining in the sun in the cheap way that poor-quality, machine-woven silk does. Maybe they're photocopier or mobile phone salesmen, or work in one of the banks here in the square, or at the provincial insurance office.

Some stereotypical university students are clustered around a table at the Central Hotel; science students, to judge by their awkward yet intelligent appearance. Jeans and knitted sweaters, and very clean trainers. Presumably they have their laptops in their little briefcases. Cups of regular coffee on the table, nothing fancy.

What do I know about the people in this city? the mother thinks as she leans towards her girls and wipes their mouths, the hotdogs are all gone and now her beloved darlings are taking it in turns to slurp up the green, artificial-tasting juice that they're so fond of.

Mons Kallentoft

I don't know anything, really, she goes on to think, except that we all live side by side, all of us so different, and we manage to get on simply because we've decided to tolerate each other. And we're all bound together, no matter how much money we have in our bank accounts, or where we come from, or what we do, by the fact that we share the same basic dream of happiness.

But sometimes we bite each other. Just not now. Not here. Nothing bad can happen on a wonderful spring day like this. At times like this, Linköping is the safest of all safe cocoons for human life.

One of the local bus company's red and orange buses stops beside the statue of Folke Filbyter, the progenitor of Sweden's first royal dynasty. A few people get on before the bus heads off towards the castle. A beggar, a middle-aged woman with greasy hair, sits outside the shopping centre with her hand outstretched.

'Are you feeling full now?'

'We're full, Mummy.'

'Then let's go and get some money out.'

'Can I press the buttons?'

'Me too, I want to press the buttons too.'

'We'll do it together.' And they set off across the square, towards the cashpoint machine, where the bike with the rucksack is still parked.

The mother sees the posters in the bank windows. She recognises them from adverts and flyers, doesn't want to think the name, but can't help herself.

Kurtzon.

Kurtzon Funds.

The SEB bank has allowed its windows to be used by the company owned by the supposedly brilliant but extremely publicity-shy financier. The girls have reached the cashpoint, and beside them the automatic doors to the bank slide open and a man wearing a leather waistcoat, with bare, suntanned arms, comes out with a black briefcase in one hand. He looks around and smiles at the girls before disappearing off in the direction of the old courthouse.

The mother is rapidly catching up with the girls, but she stumbles on a paving stone that is slightly higher than the others and drops her bag.

Her purse tumbles out and falls open.

Her green Visa card shines up at her.

Still plenty in the account. It's a long way from the end of the month, and she hasn't touched the insurance money yet.

She kneels down, feeling her joints creak.

The children are standing at the cashpoint now, and the mother sees them playing as if in slow motion, as they pretend to put a card in, press the buttons and then pull out some huge, magical treasure from the machine.

Her bag.

Back in her hand again, and just as she is about to stand up she hears a hissing sound that turns into a bleep. Like a rattlesnake vibrating so furiously that it starts to whistle.

She sees the girls stiffen and hold their ears, and she realises that the sound is coming from the rucksack on the parcel rack of the bicycle, and she wants to run to them but she can't move, her body is locked in a hopeless posture and she sees the girls' faces change and the sound from the rucksack bites into all three of them, like the teeth of poisonous monitor lizards.

Then the mother screams.

She screams her girls' names, but the names disappear into an icy blue-white lightning, followed by a heat more intense that she ever thought possible, and she is thrown through the air. Then there is nothing but a silence that drowns out the infinitely painful thunder that carries across the whole city and on across the newly awoken forests and sprouting fields, open water, and dwellings of Östergötland.

For the girls it is as if the world disappears, torn to shreds by millions of ravenous, salivating beasts, only to dissolve into an all-encompassing light that shifts into something else, into a frothy white heaven with no beginning and no end.

2

Are you in heaven now, Mum?

As Malin Fors steps towards the coffin containing her mother, she feels the ground tremble slightly beneath her feet. She hears a dull rumble, but neither the vibration nor the sound manage to make the windows of the Chapel of the Resurrection rattle.

They're blasting at the roadworks out in Lambohov, Malin thinks, and looks down at the lacy hem of her long, black dress from H&M.

There's a lot of construction work in Linköping, because of the government's investment in infrastructure designed to counteract the impact of the financial crisis, and there's a lot of blasting going on. Unless this is something else, is it you, Mum, trying to say something, trying to crack the world open with the concentrated power of denial?

It's a long time since the last of the snow melted, uncovering the muddy surfaces where grass was waiting impatiently to break through, when Malin had stood in the living-room window watching the bare, apparently dead branches of the trees sway in the tremulous spring wind, and she could almost hear the life flowing through the branches, trying to turn the stiff blackness into green, turning it into something new. Yes, maybe it was life itself singing in the tree's branches, and Malin could sense that something was about to happen, that this spring was going to uncover things that had been hidden in dark and chilly souls.

She had taken a deep breath by that window. Watching the arrival of spring with confidence after seeing out the winter's unquenchable longing for alcohol, struggling against it in isolation, and sure enough, something seemed to have happened, the spring had lived up to the promise it made that day.

A red rose in her hand now.

She looks at the distempered walls of the chapel, placating shades of orange and pale blue, and the raised platform holding the white coffin, positioned beneath the highest point of the roof to maximise the impression of sanctity.

The vibrations and thunder have gone. She is standing with her back to the congregation and thinking that it can't have been thunder, because the sky outside is blue, free from any smudges of white, and the trees and bushes and ground are sculpting forth life one more time after the winter, hoping to show their vitality.

The rose's stem has been stripped free of thorns, safe and comfortable to hold. All pain removed, and was that what you wanted, Mum, was that your secret?

Malin stops beside the coffin. She can hear the silence, the other people breathing.

Not many people there, Mum mourned by Dad, by me, by her granddaughter Tove. But do we really miss you, Mum, Tove and I? The fact that I'm even whispering the question when I'm standing by your coffin is a sort of blasphemy, isn't it?

I can't hear anyone sniffing behind me, no sobbing. Instead I can smell the musty scent of the chapel, and the heat as the sun forces its way through the delicate curtains is warming the whole room, but not this moment, and I close my eyes, see your face, Mum, those hard, downward-pointing wrinkles around your mouth, and the look in your eyes that never dared to meet mine.

I see you, Mum, as I turn to face the others sitting in the pews, and I wish I could say that I feel grief, but I don't feel anything at all.

The call had come on a rainy Saturday morning three weeks before, when she was alone in the flat making vegetable mash, one of the therapeutic tasks she did these days to keep the longing for tequila at bay. Or for any damn alcohol at all, come to that.

Dad sounded upset at the other end of the line, fretful but still together, factual yet sad, but Malin still imagined she could detect a note of relief somewhere in his voice.

He began to cry after the first words, then he pulled himself together, and said that he and her mother had been at the Abama golf course, and that at the third – or was it the fourth? – hole she had hit a ball over the edge of the cliff and watched it disappear into the waves of the Atlantic, and he could see that she was in a bad mood, but trying not to show it. And then, on the next stroke, she cracked when she sliced the ball and it flew off into the bushes under some palm trees. 'And I saw her face turn red. Then she clutched at her throat, as if she couldn't breathe, and fell to the grass, it had just been cut, and she didn't move, Malin, she didn't move, and she wasn't breathing, do you understand what I'm saying, do you understand, Malin?'

She had understood.

'Dad, where are you now?'

'Tenerife Hospital. They brought her here by ambulance.'

She asked the question, even though she knew, she'd heard it in the peculiar tone of her father's voice, a tone she recognised from the dozens of next-of-kin she had informed of deaths in the course of her work as a detective inspector.

'How is she now?'

'She's dead, Malin. She was dead by the time they put her in the ambulance.'

Dad.

His lanky, uncertain figure alone on a bench in some waiting room in a Spanish hospital. His hand moving restlessly over the grey-black hair on his head.

She had wished he was with her, so she could comfort him, and then, as she stirred the saucepan of bubbling root vegetables, she realised that she wasn't worried, scared, or even sad. In fact, it felt more like a huge mountain of practical difficulties was rising up in front of her. She was holding the phone in one hand, stirring the pan with the spoon she was holding in the other.

Tove. Janne. My ex-husband.

I have to tell them. Will Tove be upset? Malin had stared at the Ikea clock in the kitchen, and saw her ever-healthier thin face reflected in the window, her blonde bob framing her prominent cheekbones, and wondered about her appointment with the hairdresser later that week.

'Malin, she's dead. Do you understand?'

'Have you got anyone with you?'

'Malin.'

'Who can you get to be with you?'

'Hasse and Kajsa Ekvall are on their way. They can drive me home.'

'I'll book a flight. I can be there tomorrow.'

'Don't, Malin, don't do that. I can take care of this.'

And she heard it again, the relief in her father's voice. It seemed to contain a promise that she would be able to regain something, that she would one day be able to turn around, look herself in the mirror, and maybe know her own innermost secret.

* * *

The mourners at the funeral are sitting slumped in the pews of the chapel.

The closest family on the first row.

Mum's body brought here by plane from Tenerife.

Malin has stopped behind the coffin and can see Dad crying, a soundless, gentle crying. Tove, wearing a beautiful black dress with little white flowers on it, mostly just looks bored. They decided beforehand that Malin would step up to the coffin first, and that Tove would go after her grandfather.

A white rose in Tove's hand, she chose it herself. And Malin feels a pang of guilt as she looks at her sixteen-year-old daughter. Guilt at having so often been such a bad mother, putting her job and then the drink ahead of her child.

Janne is sitting next to Tove, in a badly fitting blue suit he must have bought specially for the occasion from Dressman. In the seats behind them there are perhaps ten people, all dressed in dark clothes. Couples of Dad's age. She recognises a few of them from Sturefors, people her parents used to socialise with when she was little.

No brothers or sisters. She doesn't have any.

No other family either.

The coffin is simple, no ornamentation, and arranged around it are a number of wreaths from Tenerife. Malin doesn't recognise the names on the wreaths, and it occurs to her that she will never be able to put faces to the names, and that she really doesn't care.

She closes her eyes.

Her mum is there again, but she's only an image, nothing to do with humanity or flesh and blood and feelings. Malin opens her eyes, tries to squeeze out a tear for Dad's sake, but no matter how hard she tries nothing comes out.

The priest, a woman in her fifties, smiles gently from

her chair over by one of the windows. She has just given the standard speech about what a fine person Mum was, and about her talent for interior decorating and golf.

And secrets, Malin felt like adding. She had a talent for secrets, and above all maintaining a façade and making herself seem important, special, as if nothing, and least of all me, was ever good enough for her.

While the priest was talking Malin got the feeling that it was all too late now, that something had been lost, that there had still been some sort of chance for her and her mum to sit down at a table and talk to each other like grown-ups.

She could have asked the question, straight out: 'Mum, why haven't you ever cared about me? About Tove?'

Or, even more pertinently: 'Have you ever loved me, Mum? Loved us?'

She puts the rose on the coffin.

Then Malin moves her lips. Whispers to her mother inside the white coffin: 'Did you ever love me, Mum? God knows, I loved you. Didn't I?'

Five hundred and forty-two days.

That's how long Malin has been sober. How long she and Janne have managed to get along, how long she has managed to withstand her body and soul's howl for alcohol, how desperately fucking long she has managed to keep her boredom locked away.

Her colleagues in the Linköping Police, with Zacharias 'Zeke' Martinsson and Superintendent Sven Sjöman in the vanguard, were worried that she might suffer a relapse when they heard about her mother, about her sudden heart attack, and that Margaretha Fors was being brought home for the funeral, and that Åke Fors would probably be selling his flat in Tenerife and moving back home again.

Losing your mother is hard on everyone, her colleagues reasoned, but for a sober alcoholic an event of that sort could mean that frames of reference collapse, a bottle is opened and leads at the very least to helpless intoxication, and possibly something much worse.

But Malin had told them not to worry when they asked how she was.

She was more than capable of coping with the grief, if she actually felt any at all.

Practical matters gave her something to do, it turned out, and kept her wretched restlessness as bay: talking to Dad over the phone, managing the funeral directors, cleaning up her parents' flat before Dad got back, talking to the priest . . . Things to do, things to organise.

When she told Tove that Grandma was dead, over the phone an hour after she got the call herself, Tove was as indifferent as only a teenager could be. She too had reacted in a practical way, asking if they would be going to Tenerife. Then Malin had heard the fear in her voice.

'You haven't got anything to drink in the flat, have you, Mum?'

'Water and Coca-Cola, Tove.'

'It's not a joke.'

'I promise I'm not going to drink, Tove.'

'You promise? You need to do more than promise.'

'I promise,' Malin had replied, realising that her mother's death was an opportunity for her to win back some of the trust she had lost.

She had felt ashamed.

In her work she got job satisfaction from extreme violence and murder, from other people's misfortunes. She knew that, and had accepted it. But someone who instinctively wonders how to gain any sort of advantage from their own mother's death, what sort of person is that?

Then the longing for tequila returned.

The longing or the thundering power of alcohol. For the senselessness of intoxication. The longing could come at any time, always without warning. She had tried to find a logic in its attacks, a structure, so that she could avoid situations that made her feel thirsty, but she hadn't managed to find any logic in it.

A sickness. A parasite. An unpredictable virus that strikes as it pleases, on a whim. Learning to live with it, like an invisible handicap.

But just then, after her phone conversations with her dad and Tove, the pull had been stronger than ever. So she did what she sometimes did. She exposed herself to pain, and stuck the fingers of one hand into the bubbling, freshly mashed vegetables, feeling them sting and burn, but aware that it wasn't hot enough to harm her skin.

Tove's face is close to Malin's as they sit in the chapel. Her skin is completely smooth, free from the blemishes and spots that almost all other sixteen-year-old girls have. Tove toys with the rose, and mother and daughter exchange a quick glance, not quite sure what to say with their eyes.

Up at the front lies Grandma, Mum, in her coffin. They can see Grandad, Dad, in his black suit, walking up to the coffin. They see him turn around, hesitate, take a deep breath, sob, then whisper something and lay a red rose on the coffin before he comes back to his seat.

Malin and Tove look at each other, wondering what to do with this moment.

And then Tove sets off towards the coffin, and without trying to force out any tears she lays her rose on top of it.

Tove doesn't whisper anything, doesn't say anything, just comes back to her seat, and Malin looks towards her father, then Tove once more, and wishes she could read their minds, but instead she sees Janne approach the coffin with ritualistic movements, as if everything that happens on this spring day in the Chapel of the Resurrection is a piece of theatre that must be played out to its end.

Please, just let this be over, Tove thinks, and closes her eyes. She doesn't want to watch all the old people she doesn't know go up to the coffin one by one and whisper things that can't be heard.

'Adieu,' one of them says audibly, and Tove jerks, opens her eyes, and from the corner of her eye she can tell that Grandad is crying, she feels sorry for him, she's always liked him, but Grandma? She never knew Grandma, and if you never knew someone, you can't grieve when they're gone. Even Mum doesn't seem particularly upset, although Tove can tell she's trying.

Feigning emotions.

Everyone she knows seems to do that.

She thinks about the letter she's expecting. She hasn't told anyone, she daren't say anything to Mum. It was wrong and immoral of her to forge her signature on the form.

But it might work.

And then she'd be happy, wouldn't she?

No.

That wasn't certain. It was very far from certain.

Mum might well freak out totally.

And Tove can't help smiling when she thinks about the letter that might be on its way, but she can't smile here. Even if there isn't an absolute requirement that people should cry here, you definitely shouldn't smile.

A hymn fills the chapel. The sound of the organ tries to force the stale air aside, trying to imbue the daylight with the natural warmth it lacks.

The last time Malin was here was when a murder victim was being buried, a lonely fat man whom the world seemed to have abandoned from the start.

She walks behind her dad towards the exit, sees him nod to people lining the aisle.

Malin nods.

She imagines that must be what you're supposed to do.

Then the chapel door is opened and, suddenly backlit, her dad becomes a strange black outline, and around him seem to float two little girls with angels' wings.

Their faces are white and full of fear.

Their fear is so strong that Malin feels like rushing over, pulling the girls down out of the air and holding them close to her.

She blinks.

Now only her dad is there, once her eyes have adjusted to the light. Only Dad, and the smell of distilled fear.

3

Malin and Mum, over the years

When did I lose you, Mum?

That time you disappeared? Because you did go away when I was little, didn't you, and where were you then?

On planet Look-after-number-one. And I would go to you, and I was allowed to sit on your lap, but never for more than five minutes, then you would have to do something else, I was too heavy, too hot, too in the way. How can a mother think that her own daughter is in the way?

So I turned away.

I would run to Dad. He was the one who came to my athletics competitions, who gave me lifts to football matches, who made sure I got my hair cut. That was all true, wasn't it?

You turned me towards Dad, didn't you? You did, didn't you?

I remember sitting in my room out in Sturefors, waiting for you to come to me, Mum. Waiting for you to say something nice, rub my back with your hand.

But you never came.

Instead I would lie in bed and stare up at the white ceiling, unable to sleep.

One night when there was a storm I went to your bed and crept in beside you. I was five years old.

You turned on the lamp on the bedside table.

Dad was sleeping next to you.

You looked at me.

Lie down next to me, you said. Are you scared of the thunder?

Then you turned out the light and I could feel your warm body against mine under your nightgown, the way it carried me off to sleep as if your whole being were a vessel of bubbling warmth.

When I woke up the next morning you were already gone. I found you in the kitchen.

Sleepy, with bags under your eyes.

'I haven't slept a wink,' you said. 'And it's all your fault, Malin.'

I never felt the warmth of your body under your nightgown again.

You hardly ever got angry, Mum.

It was as if you didn't really exist, even though you were there in those rooms out in the villa. You decided how I should dress, or wanted to decide, at any rate, trying to make me more girly, because that's what girls were supposed to be like. I hated the skirts you tried to make me wear. The dresses.

And I tried to rein myself in. You tried to get me to feel small in the world, to know my place.

You're not that intelligent, Malin.

Make sure you find someone with money.

Maybe you should be a nursery teacher. That might suit you. But try your best.

Make sure you find someone with a good name.

Becoming part of my own failure, my inability to accept what I had, what I had created for myself.

You hated reality, Mum.

Did you hate me? Because I was a reminder of your own reality?

The words, said in your grudging voice when I came home with my school report.

Have you been flirting with the teachers?

And when Tove arrived. You cursed me for my clumsiness, how could I get pregnant, just like that? So young? You said that I, we, weren't welcome, that you'd die of embarrassment in front of all your acquaintances because I couldn't keep my legs together.

Tove.

You never looked at her. You never held her in your arms. You'd made up your mind that she was a disgrace, simply because she didn't suit your plans, or fit in with the image of the perfect life that you were trying to create.

But no one cared about that picture, Mum.

I cared about you.

I wanted your love. But because I didn't get it when I was little, maybe I didn't really want it once I was grown up, and you didn't want to give it to me either.

Was there ever any love?

What were you scared of, Mum? God knows, I could have done with your support when I was studying at Police Academy and was on my own with Tove.

Dad used to come to Stockholm sometimes.

But you refused.

Women shouldn't be police officers.

The distance grew over the years. The lack of love became greater than the love, eradicating it, and in the end I had to ignore you, Mum.

I miss the mum I never had, but I can't mourn the mother I did have.

Does that make me a bad person?

4

An acrid, burned smell in the air, presumably from the construction blast earlier, cutting through the air and seeming to trouble the spring sun.

Malin moves closer to her dad on the paved path outside the chapel, feels like putting her arm around him, can see he'd rather be somewhere else.

The wind is rustling the top of an oak tree whose green buds are still holding back on the showier part of their annual repertoire. I was right, Malin thinks, the branches that looked most dead are vibrant with life, the trees are bursting into leaf all over Linköping.

The priest smiles, takes Dad's hand, mutters something Malin can't hear. Then Malin takes Dad by the hand, and she soon feels Tove's soft, slender fingers take a firm grip of her other one. Janne has gone on ahead and is standing beside his latest car, an old silver Jaguar that he has restored himself, and it looks as if he'd like to light up a cigarette, even though Malin knows he's never smoked.

Her dad pulls free. Takes a few steps to the side, then the other mourners file past and shake his outstretched hand.

'Thanks for coming.'

'You're welcome to come back to Barnhemsgatan for coffee with us.'

'You will come, won't you?'

The mourners at Malin's mother's funeral aren't yet

marked by old age, but they're starting to get older, and are probably just glad it isn't one of them in the coffin.

As a swallow chases a gust of wind across the copper roof of the chapel, she allows herself to imagine them as her colleagues in the Crime Investigation Department of Linköping Police. A thickset woman with red hair becomes Sven Sjöman, her sixty-two-year-old boss, who over the past year has put on all the weight he had previously lost, and now puffs and pants at the slightest exertion, a sound that makes Malin think he could go the same way as her mother at any moment.

An elderly man with thinning hair turns into Johan Jakobsson, the tired but thoroughly decent young father who seems happy with suburban life. A suntanned gentleman becomes Börje Svärd, now without his drooping moustache since his wife, Anna, died of MS a year or so ago. Börje hasn't met anyone else yet, instead choosing to devote himself to his dogs, the firing range, and work.

The lunatic, Waldemar Ekenberg, the violent, heavy-handed police officer from the neighbouring district of Mjölby, is here represented by a little woman desiccated by decades of smoking, with a scratchy, firm voice.

'I'm sorry for your loss. I'm afraid I can't come back for coffee. She was a lovely person.'

Her closest colleague, Zeke, becomes an amiable old man with a sharp nose, and twinkling eyes, not entirely unlike the real Zeke, with his shaved head, steely gaze, and a penchant for sleeping with the beautiful forensics expert Karin Johannison, even though they're both married to other people.

And with that the parade of mourners is finished.

They head off towards their cars in the car park. None of them was like Karim Akbar, the Kurd in his early forties who is head of the Linköping Police. Karim has picked himself up again after his divorce, and has finished his book about integration issues, and has appeared in the papers and on television with his impeccable suits and well-groomed hair. He has met a new woman, a prosecutor whom Malin can hardly bear to look at. She's a weak prosecutor, a true careerist who won't even let them question suspected paedophiles.

Silly games, Malin thinks. Mum's dead. This is my own mother's funeral, and all I'm doing is playing silly games in my head.

Tove has gone over to Janne by the Jaguar.

They put up with each other, she and Janne, for Tove's sake.

Malin says nothing about anything whenever she meets Janne. It's best that way, best to hold the anger and bitterness and loneliness at bay by not putting it into words.

They talk about Tove. About things she needs, who's going to pay for what, how and where their daughter should spend her free time, her school holidays.

Is he seeing anyone else?

Malin hasn't noticed anything, hasn't seen anything, hasn't heard anything. She's usually good at picking up the signs, and Tove hasn't mentioned anything about there being a new woman out in the house in the forest on the way to Malmslätt.

Malin takes her dad under the arm and leads him off towards the car park, and asks: 'Are many of them coming back for coffee?'

'All apart from Dagny Björkqvist. She's got to go to another funeral out in Skärblacka.'

Skärblacka.

The site of the biggest waste incinerator on the Östgöta plain. Sometimes the smell from Skärblacka hangs over Linköping like a stinking cloud.

No Skärblacka cloud today, thank goodness.

Only the strange, faint smell of something burned, as if from an explosion or – and Malin doesn't even want to think the thought – burned flesh, fear.

Could that smell be coming from her mum?

They cremate bodies here, in a facility connected to the chapel by a tunnel: could they have been so quick that Mum is already burning, that her body is already surrounded by destructive flames, that it's the smell of Mum's burning flesh spreading invisibly through the air?

No.

They couldn't move that quickly from the end of the funeral to cremation.

The coffin is still there in the chapel, and Malin feels a sudden urge to run back in, open the coffin, put her warm hand on her mum's cheek and say goodbye, goodbye Mum, I forgive you, for whatever it was that meant things ended up the way they did.

But she doesn't move from her dad's side in the car park.

She watches the cars drive off, one by one, and pushes all thoughts of the coffin aside. Instead she switches on the large-screen mobile phone that she pestered Karim Akbar for, the only technological investment in the force that year, and fingers the keyboard nervously, and the moment the phone finds a signal it starts to ring.

Sven Sjöman's name on the screen.

Sven.

Now?

He knows I'm at the funeral, so something terrible must have happened, and Malin can feel the familiar tingling, the excitement she always feels when she senses, and almost starts to hope, that a new, big, important investigation is about to start. Then comes the shame, a double dose this time, that she should think of her work as a release, and in such a way.

Who's in trouble this time?

Some drunks who've managed to kill each other?

A violent robbery?

Children?

The girls, the angels just now.

Dear God, please not children. There's no defence against that sort of crime, evil aimed at children.

'Malin here.'

'Malin?'

Sven sounds upset, almost bewildered. Then he pulls himself together.

'I know this is a bad time to call, but something terrible has happened. Someone's set off a bomb in the main square. A big one. A lot of people seriously injured. Maybe even fatalities. It's total fucking chaos . . .'

She hears Sven's words, but what the hell is he saying, what's he actually saying, and she understands without understanding and her lips move: 'I'm on my way.'

Her dad looks at her, hears her words and knows she's on her way to something else, and he looks scared but nods calmly to her as he stands beside his old black Volvo, as if to say: 'I'll be all right'. But the look in his eyes contains something else as well, something intense, a different sort of relief that Malin can't quite grasp but knows is important.

'Drive straight to the square.'

'I'll be there in five minutes. Maybe ten.'

She clicks to end the call, adjusts her long black dress and rushes over to Janne and Tove.

Janne looks worried, his brow furrowed as he watches her running towards him, hampered by the long dress.

Must have seen her talking on her mobile, can see that her work persona has taken over.

If anyone from the emergency services is needed in the square right now, it's Janne.

Whatever must it look like there?

Like a war zone. Dismembered limbs and blood and screaming. Janne knows how to deal with that. Rwanda, Kigali, Bosnia, Sudan. There's no recent trouble spot where his need to demonstrate compassion hasn't found an outlet.

'We've got to go. The pair of us,' she says, tugging at his arm, and then she explains what's happened, and Tove says, her eyes clear in her open teenage face: 'Go, both of you, I'll look after Grandpa and the coffee, just go, that's more important.'

'Thanks,' Malin says, and turns away from Tove, and it feels as if she's done it a thousand times before, a thousand times too often.

Her dad has come over to them.

'Dad, that was work, something terrible's happened, I have to go.'

'Go,' he says without hesitation. 'We're not going to have much fun back at the flat anyway, I can promise you that.'

He doesn't ask what's happened, doesn't even seem curious.

A minute later Malin's sitting in the new white Golf she uses for work, with Janne beside her.

Dad and Tove can take the Jaguar.

The rays of spring sunshine have somehow made the car as hot as a desert bunker. In the rear-view mirror Malin can see her dad and Tove standing in the car park in front of the chapel. They're hugging each other, but Malin can't see if they're crying. She doesn't think they are, she'd prefer to believe that they were taking strength from each other in order to deal with the rest of the day, and all the future that lies beyond it.

Janne takes a deep breath and clears his throat before he says: 'I've seen what explosions can do to the human body, Malin. Be prepared for the worst.'

5

Two grey-white pigeons are pecking at something that Malin thinks looks like a piece of meat, it must be human flesh, mustn't it? Flesh from a body that's been blown apart, as if razor-sharp lizard's teeth have torn it to pieces.

The paving stones of the main square are littered with dust and debris. A dirty paper sign bearing the handwritten word 'Sale' in orange ink blows past her along with hundreds of pink tulip petals.

Is that really flesh in front of her?

Malin moves towards whatever it is on the ground some ten metres in front of the chemist's. She raises her arms to scare the pigeons away, they shouldn't be pecking at that.

At what it looks like.

No, it mustn't be that.

No, no, no.

Her black dress is lifted up by a gust of wind as she slowly walks towards what she doesn't want to see.

She and Janne had parked outside the Hamlet bar, and from the main street, there had been no sign of any destruction, nor any sign of any people. Instead there was just an all-consuming silence when they opened the car doors and set off at a run towards the square and the devastation they were expecting.

Maybe the phone call from Sven was just a bad dream? Maybe there hadn't been any explosion? Maybe it wasn't a bomb but a gas leak, but surely it had been years since they stopped using gas in Linköping?

Then they got closer to the square.

They slowed down, as if they wanted to calm their hearts, steel themselves, prepare themselves, adopt their professional roles.

The ground in front of the shoe shop and the newsagent's was covered with broken glass from the shattered windows. The smell of scorched flesh and hair was noticeable, but she couldn't hear any screaming.

They turned the corner at the end of the shopping centre and saw the square.

The scene of devastation almost made Malin collapse. She had to stop and catch her breath as Janne rushed on towards the ambulances and fire engines that had driven into the square down by Mörners Inn and the Central Hotel.

Firemen and paramedics were swarming around people lying on the ground with shimmering metallic blankets over their bodies and clumsily bandaged bleeding heads. Several of the injured were talking on mobiles.

Presumably to their families, and Malin herself felt a strange desire to call Tove even though they had only just seen each other.

There was glass and debris and dust everywhere. The little flowerstall had been blown over, tulips everywhere. A lost white greyhound was rushing to and fro with bleeding paws, and grey and white pigeons were circling the scene, flying low, back and forth, seeming to look at their reflections in the mass of broken glass. All of the hotel's fifty or so windows facing the square had been blown out, the glass scattered in a million fragments down below. On the ground floor, the hotel's restaurant and bar lay deserted and open to the elements, as if God had come down to earth and declared that the Day of Judgement had arrived.

Malin narrowed her eyes.

Noticed the smell of burned flesh and fabric once more.

Saw uniformed police officers setting up a cordon.

She tried to acclimatise herself to the scene, understand what she was looking at, tried to get her eyes to accept the knife-sharp spring light that was making all the as yet winter-pale people in the square look almost dead, lifeless, with a skintone that made the blood on the paving stones look even redder.

The hotdog-seller.

The parasol above his stall was a stripped metal skeleton.

The tubs of sausages had been tipped onto the pavement, and the canvas awnings over the terrace cafés had been blown off, as if a giant maw had leaned down from the sky and sucked up all the air, only to spit broken glass over all the locals who had been enjoying the spring sunshine in the city's largest square on this particular day.

Two marked police cars were parked over by the old courthouse. There was a smoking black hole where the SEB cashpoint had been. But there were no scraps of money on the square, every last note must have been consumed in what seemed to have been the core of the explosion.

Could it have been an attempt to blow open the cashpoint machine that had gone wrong?

No.

There hadn't been a single attempt to blow open a cashpoint anywhere in the country for years. Anyone who wanted to steal from a cashpoint did it through skimming or getting hold of codes and cards.

And the bomb was far too powerful, Malin thought. Maybe a robbery that went wrong?

Incredibly, the surveillance camera above the cashpoint

looked as if it was still intact. The windows had been blown out, and some of the bank's metal windowframes must have melted in the explosion.

Overturned bicycles. Shredded tyres.

Sven? Zeke? Börje? Johan? Waldemar?

Malin rubbed her eyes, unable to see any of her colleagues, but aware that they had to be somewhere in all this quiet chaos.

There was nothing but emptiness and silence from inside the bank, and a crowd of curious onlookers at the corner, by the café and the Passagen art gallery. There was another cashpoint machine in the neighbouring building, Handelsbanken, and that seemed to be intact.

Why? Because they couldn't be blamed for the financial crisis, unlike the SEB? Because they'd behaved better? Malin couldn't help thinking of the managing director of SEB, Annika Falkengren, who had earned twenty million kronor the year the crisis hit, and intended to increase her regular salary still more. The way her leadership had contributed to driving people into misery while she grabbed what she could without any inhibitions at all.

A heavily made-up vampire slurping champagne in a castle out in the smart Stockholm suburb of Djursholm.

Someone might well have wanted to blow her sky-high. Or everything she stood for.

Numerous times in recent years Malin has felt utterly nauseous at the greed of bank directors. And she isn't alone in that. The directors ought to be begging in the streets, the way other people have been forced to now.

So should those onlookers be there? So close to the bank?

What if this is a terrorist attack? What if there's another blast?

A pram on its side.

What would it take to knock me off balance? Malin thinks as she sees the pigeons pecking at that scrap of meat whose origins she absolutely does not want to think about.

Some firemen she doesn't recognise are lying yellow plastic sheets over other pieces of meat, other fragments of people. A foot. A small foot, an eye, a face, what the hell has actually happened here, what the hell is this? Pieces of two faces. No.

The greyhound barks.

It shakes its bloody, glass-splintered paws, spraying blood over the broken glass and pavement, then Malin sees the solid figure of Börje Svärd catch hold of the dog's lead, kneel down and pull it towards him, calming it with measured strokes.

Nauseous.

Thirsty.

When does the Hamlet open? A beer and a tequila would slip down very nicely right now, and those pigeons really shouldn't be pecking at that, they're back again.

A stretcher with a drip attached is being lifted into an ambulance by the hotel entrance, a doctor that Malin recognises at its side. His blue tunic is covered in blood.

The pigeons.

She moves towards them again.

Keep your head cool now, Malin, stay focused, pull yourself together, and she sees Janne, he's wearing a yellow Gore-Tex jacket over his new suit, and he is calmly and methodically taking care of two wounded students that no one has had time to look at before now. He is bandaging the small cuts on their arms, talking to them, Malin can see his mouth moving, and even though she can't hear what he's saying she knows he's professional to the core, a solid, warm tree of a man who can prevent shock from taking hold. Once again she feels like running away to the Hamlet.

But that won't do.

The pigeons.

They're pecking at the flesh, the skin, the hair, the child's hair. Malin is running now. Her arms outstretched to mimic a bird of prey.

Unseemly.

She rushes at them and the pigeons take off into the sky, joining the low-flying swallows.

She stops beside what the birds were pecking at.

Sinks to her knees.

Adjusts the black cloth of her dress.

Feels her stomach clench, but manages to hold back the urge to vomit.

A scorched cheek. A child's beautiful cheek, torn from the head and cheekbone with perfect destructive force.

Then the eye, still in place, just where it should be, just above the cheek, as though it can still see.

A small, brown eye, open and staring at Malin, wanting to tell her something, ask her for something.

She looks away.

Calls to the firemen with the yellow plastic sheeting.

'Over here. Come and cover this up.'

Is that me you're looking at, Malin Fors, or is it my twin sister?

I don't know, I can't bear to look, to see the remains of what used to be me, us, my sister and me.

We were six years old, Malin.

Six.

How short a life is that?

We want more.

Maybe you could give us more life, Malin. And Daddy, where's he? Why isn't he here, he ought to be here and we want him to be here, because Mummy's over there in the ambulance, not far from us, isn't she?

It's lonely and dark here, and the bleeding white dog dancing isn't nice. Get rid of the dog, Malin, get rid of the dog.

Now you're walking across the square, you couldn't bear to look at the cheek and eye. The glass is crunching under your smart black shoes and you're wondering how many people have been killed. Two children? Two girls, more?

We know all that now, Malin, the way you think, even though we're just six years old. We suddenly know everything, and we know the words, and with that knowledge and awareness comes the realisation that we don't know anything, and it's that realisation that scares us, that makes us so frightened that you can hear our fear streaking through the air like the sound of a dog-whistle: there, yet simultaneously not there.

Sven Sjöman and Zeke are standing beside a black car outside Mörners Inn. You're approaching them, Malin.

You're scared as well, now, aren't you? Scared of where this explosion might take you. Scared of the desire, the longing for clarity that our violent and abrupt deaths can set in motion within you.

Because that can make everything you know about evil dance inside you.

We're six years old, Malin.

Just six.

Then we were wiped out. And you know that we can wipe you out.

That's why you love us, isn't it? Because we can give you peace. The same peace you can give us.

Sven Sjöman is leaning against the car, and the black paint makes his profile and the deep furrows in his brow look even more prominent, lending his face a hard, unshakeable determination.

In spite of the outward appearance of calm, they're all feeling wound up.

Zeke has just acknowledged her arrival. Nodding to Malin in a way that she knows means, 'Hi, partner, let's get to work', and she had looked at him, thinking: What would I do without you, Zeke? Could I handle this job if anything happened to you?

Zeke seems to be absorbing the smells of the square, letting his hard green eyes work their way over the scene.

'Two dead. At least,' Malin says. 'Two young children.'

Zeke shakes his head, closes his eyes.

'One woman with serious injuries,' Sven says.

'And how many others wounded?' Malin asks.

'Maybe thirty,' Sven says. 'Not too serious. Cuts, mainly, most of them look worse than they really are.'

'That's bad enough,' Zeke says. 'Two kids, I mean. How old?'

'Don't know yet,' Malin says. 'But I saw enough over there to know that we're talking about at least two children. Karin and her team are just arriving, they'll have to look into it.'

From the corner of her eye Malin can see the smart figure of forensics expert Karin Johannison heading towards the yellow plastic sheet covering the ground where the child's cheek is lying.

'Is there any risk of a second explosion?' Malin goes on. 'That's often what happens with terrorist attacks, first one explosion, then another when everyone is running away in panic in one particular direction.'

'That's what happened in Kuta, on Bali,' Zeke says.

'We'll have to move the onlookers back,' Sven says. 'Increase the perimeter and get the dogs to check the area, and get the injured away from here. And we need to talk to anyone who might have seen anything.'

'I don't think there can be a second bomb,' Malin says. 'It would have gone off by now if there was.'

'Do we even know that it was a bomb?' Zeke asks. 'Could it have been anything else?'

'So what the fuck could it have been?' Sven asks, and it occurs to Malin that she hasn't heard him swear for at least ten years before today, if she has ever actually heard him, and she can see panic hovering in his eyes. After almost thirty-five years in the force you should have seen and heard pretty much everything, but now this: a powerful explosion, a bomb in broad daylight, in the biggest square in the city. Where to begin, where to stop? How to protect the city's inhabitants? How to protect yourself and your colleagues while you're all doing the work that has to be done? Could this be bigger than they can handle?

'A gas leak,' Zeke says calmly.

'Gas hasn't been used in Linköping for the past ten years.'

'Could it have been aimed at the cashpoint?' Zeke asks. 'An attempted robbery that went wrong?'

'The explosion was way too damn powerful to blow open a cashpoint machine,' Sven says. 'But of course there are plenty of idiots out there. I was in the bank just now, and there was no attempted raid before the explosion. But they were pretty shaken up, we'll have to organise proper interviews with the staff as soon as we can.'

'This is something different,' Malin says. 'All three of us know that.'

'Any threatening calls?'

'Not to us,' Sven says.

A black Mercedes has made its way through the cordon, let through by the uniforms, and stops down by the cinema on Ågatan.

Karim Akbar, head of the Linköping Police, steps out, dressed in a pinstriped black suit and a neatly ironed pink shirt.

Malin looks out across the square again and notices something she hadn't seen before: Daniel Högfeldt from the *Östgöta Correspondent*, and some other journalists milling about among the people with minor injuries who haven't been removed from the cordoned-off area yet.

Can't someone get rid of them?

She can hear the journalists' questions as background noise, the clicking of the photographers' cameras, she can see the little red lights flashing on top of the television cameras, then Karim's voice.

'This is going to be the biggest thing we've ever had to deal with. The media invasion has already started,' and she feels like punching him on the nose, screaming at him: 'Children have died today, blown into tiny pieces, and you're thinking about the media!'

'Karim,' Sven says calmly, 'in all likelihood, a bomb has gone off in the square today. In all likelihood, two young children are dead, and a woman is seriously injured. A lot of other people have been wounded. So that's probably our biggest problem, isn't it? Not the media?'

Karim frowns.

'I didn't mean it like that. Is there any risk of further explosions? This could be a terrorist attack on an international scale.'

'There's always that risk in situations like this,' Malin says.

'Get those people away from the square,' Karim goes on. 'Now.'

And with those words he leaves them, setting off towards a group of uniformed officers standing beside a police van that has just arrived.

'Listen up,' he yells to them.

'What do we think this is all about, then?' Sven says in a low voice as he pulls his stomach in. 'Malin, what do you think?'

Malin shakes her head.

'No idea.'

'Zeke?'

'This wasn't any ordinary robbery. And it wasn't a prank. That much is obvious. If the plan was to blow the cashpoint open, they'd have done it at night, not now, when there are so many people around. No, this is something else.'

They stand in silence.

Then Zeke says: 'I don't even want to think that thought. But could Karim be on the right lines when he talks about a terrorist attack with an international aspect? Could it be Islamic terrorists? But what the fuck would they be doing in Linköping of all places?'

They stand there in silence for a bit longer.

Yes, Malin thinks. Why would terrorists detonate a bomb in Linköping of all places? But, at the same time, why not? A flat in Skäggetorp, or Ryd, or Berga, could just as easily house a terrorist cell as a flat in Rosengård in Malmö, or Madrid, or the southern suburbs of Paris.

The uniformed officers that Karim has just been yelling at are now driving the journalists, photographers, and curious onlookers from the square, away from the devastation, and Malin sees the city's young police chief take charge of a situation that isn't in any instruction manual.

Could he, with his background as a Christian Kurd, imagine that there is some sort of Islamic connection? Apparently. What are most Kurds? Shiite Muslims, aren't they? Or are they Sunni Muslims?

The paramedics and firemen remove the remaining injured people as Börje Svärd leads the greyhound off towards Hospitalstorget.

Soon every approach to the square is cordoned off with blue and white tape.

'What the hell is this all about?' Sven says once more.

The three detectives can feel inertia spreading through their bodies like a paralysing poison, but none of them is capable of breaking free of it, as if all three of them had expected any manner of things from this day apart from this. As if the forces that had been let loose in the city felt alien to them in an almost supernatural way, as if the responsibility that the day had placed on their shoulders was unbearable even before they had realised it was there.

Then they look at each other. As if all three of them are wondering: Where the hell do we start?

'How was the funeral?' Sven asks eventually.

'Yes, how did it go, Malin?' Zeke asks.

Malin stares at the pair of them, looking from one colleague to the other, refusing to answer such a ridiculous question: how the hell can they imagine she has time to think of the funeral now?

'We'll have to call everyone in straight away,' Sven says. 'Anyone who's not on duty: Johan, Waldemar, absolutely everyone. We'll start over there. OK?'

Sven gestures towards the square, and the gaping windows of the hotel.

He looks tired, Malin thinks, properly old, for the first time.

'We'll stay here for a while, get as many statements as we can,' Sven goes on. 'Then I'll put Aronsson onto making sure that everyone who was actually in, or in the vicinity of the square, gets questioned. As I said, there was no attempted robbery before the blast. The bank's employees are gathered in a conference room. They were fairly calm when I was there a short while ago, no one seemed to be injured, so the force of the explosion must have been focused outwards. I had a quick word with the manager. He hadn't noticed anything unusual, just said there was a massive explosion, out of nowhere.'

Malin can hear a ringing sound in her ears.

A thin, high note, and she wonders what it could be.

'Can you hear that?' Malin asks. 'Could that be another bomb?'

The words fly from her mouth and the others stare at her anxiously.

They listen.

'I can't hear anything,' Zeke says.

Sven shakes his head.

Then the noise vanishes again, seemingly sucked up into the empty rooms of the Central Hotel.

The pigeons are back.

They're tugging at the yellow plastic sheets covering the parts of the girls' bodies, and the sun has found its way between two buildings and is making the shards of glass sparkle, and Malin thinks: What is it that's been let loose here, blossoming so darkly?

Some evil, full of potent force, deeply rooted in life?

Then there is another sound.

A high note, like a monotonous whistle, from a black bag that the explosion seems to have thrown against the veranda of the hotel, where several onlookers are still staring out at the square.

Fear in Zeke and Sven's eyes.

'Fuck,' Zeke yells. 'Fuck!'

Then he rushes off towards the bag, and Malin can see Janne heading towards it from the other side of the square.

6

Zeke picks up the black bag.

Malin shouts: 'NO! NO!'

His first thought was to throw himself on top of it, let his own body absorb the force of the coming explosion.

It's against all the rules, but who cares about rules when something's about to explode?

A bag that's been left behind should be shot at and destroyed in circumstances like these.

But Zeke picks it up anyway.

Has to throw it as far away from anyone as he can.

But the noise stops abruptly.

And he lowers the bag again and passes it to Janne, who opens the zip.

Rifles through it.

And Zeke can see the sweat on his brow, as he becomes aware of Malin approaching them.

Clothes.

Books.

An iPod.

And a mobile. Janne looks at the screen, then holds it up towards them, one missed call.

'Fucking weird ringtone,' he says, one corner of his mouth twitching in a crooked smile. Then he drops the bag, and a few seconds later a middle-aged man appears from inside the hotel and says, 'That's my bag. I was sitting outside Mörners. It must have been blown here by the explosion.'

Johan Jakobsson and Waldemar Ekenberg have arrived in the square, and together with Malin, Zeke, Börje Svärd, and Sven Sjöman they set about methodically taking statements from anyone with minor injuries who's still at the scene, those who are considered well enough to go home after being questioned without there being any risk of them falling into a state of shock. Then they interview all the onlookers who have come to the square, drawn by the commotion and devastation, by the rumours spreading through the city like the shockwaves from the explosion.

Everyone needs to be questioned.

Who knows which of them might know something? Who knows what direction this investigation is going to take?

Johan seemed shocked at first. Especially when he heard about the dead children, children the same age as his own. Börje has been strangely calm from the start. Waldemar is as unshakeable as ever. A cigarette hanging from the corner of his mouth, and with the friendly look in his eyes that he pulls out when he needs to. Malin knows his wife lost her job a few months ago, when the redundancies hit Rex Components. But her being unemployed doesn't seem to have had any noticeable effect on Waldemar.

Zeke is professional yet still upset, as if he wants retribution for what has happened in the square, and hasn't established any distance whatsoever from it, still gripped by the force field of the explosion. It makes him seem grand and diminished at the same time.

They ask thousands of questions.

But almost always get the same answer.

'Did you see anyone suspicious?'

'No.'

'What were the minutes leading up to the explosion like?'

'I was drinking coffee, everything was normal.'

'I don't know anything.'

'I didn't see anything.'

'I was curious so I came down.'

The fear in people's eyes, in their bodies, is shared. What's happened? Denial and realisation all mixed up in a way that takes in the form of a fear that still isn't quite strong enough to keep the curious away from the devastation. Like after 9/11, when hordes of curious onlookers streamed to the site where the towers had stood and thousands had died, and you could see on television that the curiosity in their eyes was greater than the fear.

Malin questions one person after the other.

A student with a plaster over a cut on her forehead, maybe just four years older than Tove, and she says: 'I was having a Coke at Mörners, wanted to get a bit of sun before I went off to the library to study. It seemed to me that the explosion came from up by the bank. At least that's what it felt like. What do you think happened? Who could have done something like this?'

'That's what we're going to find out,' Malin replies, and she can see that the girl in front of her doesn't have any great faith in the abilities of the police.

Then, after an hour or so, everyone in the square has been questioned. Along with the staff in the bank, including the branch manager. Several of the bank's employees have left the scene and gone home to their families.

A large number of uniformed police have helped take statements in the square. Hesitant, almost scared, they've gone out among the citizens of Linköping who have turned up, with their notebooks in their hands, and have received the same answers as Malin and her colleagues from the Criminal Investigation Department.

No one saw anything. No one knows anything.

Aronsson has made sure that any of the injured who have already been taken to hospital will be questioned, as well as anyone whose names they have been given as having been present in the square, but who had already left without being interviewed.

Malin moves through the debris, feeling the glass crunch beneath her feet, and sees Karin Johannison fine-combing the area around the bank, looking for anything that might mean something.

Loads of police officers here.

When something like this happens you don't notice the cutbacks that have been made in recent years as a result of the financial crisis. Budgets will have to be grappled with later. But they could do with many more police officers in the city. Mainly, perhaps, in the domestic crime unit. Plus they have a pathetically low prosecution rate for things like suspected paedophile crime. Only one report in every ten ever leads to criminal charges.

Hopeless. Surely we have to be able to protect children? Malin thinks. What's a society worth if it can't even protect its children?

The children. The child's cheek.

Who were you? Malin thinks, as she walks over towards Sven.

The panic and fear are gone from his eyes now.

All that is left is the calm determination of experience.

'Let's get back to the station,' he says. 'Put our heads together. Try to get some sort of overview of what's happened.'

At first Malin drove past her mum and dad's flat on Barnhemsgatan without stopping, thinking that she ought to get to the police station in the old barracks of the Garnisonen district as quickly as possible. But then she turned back towards the flat.

Have to go home, home to Tove and Dad, to the drinks after the funeral, and do my bit.

She parked down by the old bus station, where one of the city's increasing number of homeless was rooting through a rubbish bin, and a gang of teenage girls in short skirts and thin blouses was walking past with an older lad in a padded jacket.

Even here the smell was in the air, the faint smell of burning from the explosion, but also the smell of dogshit from down in the Horticultural Society Park, all the shit left by dogs whose owners hadn't bothered to pick it up in the cold of winter, the smell of which was now spreading in the spring air.

There was still grit on the roads. It was treacherously slippery, a reminder that the cold still wasn't that far away. In the car park, she had felt like running away in vain from the changing season, and now she is standing in her mum and dad's living room, by the window, where their long since dried-out plants once stood. Malin looks around, listening to the sound of her dad and Tove in the kitchen.

All the guests have gone.

She missed coffee, but the buttery, sickly smell of biscuits and sandwiches is still hanging in the air, making her feel hungry.

In the kitchen her dad is standing at the sink, giving the old porcelain a rudimentary scrub with the washing-up brush, as Tove dries it.

'There's food in the fridge if you're hungry.'

He smiles at Malin, looks almost relieved. Do you feel free now, Dad, is that what it is?

'I'm not hungry,' she replies.

'You should be,' Tove says. 'Eat something,' and Malin opens the fridge and picks a few prawns from a sandwich.

There's a bottle of mandarin liqueur in the fridge in front of her.

The urge wrenches at her stomach, heart, soul, and Malin says: 'You used to love these pre-packed prawns when you were little, Tove.'

'I can't believe that,' Tove says. 'Surely I had better taste than that? I wouldn't have eaten pre-packed prawns, would I?'

Then Dad laughs, but abruptly cuts his laughter off.

'The will's going to be read on Thursday,' he says. 'With Strandkvist, the solicitor. Two o'clock in his office, number 12, St Larsgatan. It has to be done.'

Of course it has to be done, Malin thinks. And against her will she thinks of what Mum has left behind, knows that Dad will get everything as things stand, but still feels greed grabbing at her, and thinks how nice it would be to get a share of the millions of kronor that her parents' flat in Tenerife must be worth.

I want it.

Give it to me.

It's mine.

Human greed is the best friend of evil. I don't give a damn about the inheritance.

'Reading the will is going to be fine,' Malin says once she's thrust such thoughts aside. 'It's just a formality.'

Dad nods, then goes on: 'It's not that, it's just that . . .'

'I realise it's difficult,' Malin says. 'But we'll be there together. It'll be fine.'

'Do I have to go as well?' Tove asks.

'You don't have to,' Dad says. 'We're done here, aren't we?'

Tove nods, and leaves the tea towel on the worktop.

'I have to get back to the station. This is going to take a lot of work.'

None of them has mentioned the explosion up to now.

As if what happened just five hundred metres away belongs to another world.

'We understand,' Tove says. 'We saw the local news on television. Is it true what they said about the children?'

Tove is not scared.

Not keen to hear gory details.

Just curious. All too aware of the crap the world can throw at anyone, far too good at dealing with crap for someone so young.

'I can't say.'

'What do you know so far, then? There must be something you can say?'

And Malin realises that they don't know anything, except that they mustn't let themselves panic, that the shock felt by the city and its inhabitants at what has happened can't be allowed to spread to the police. We have to keep our heads clear, she thinks. We have to, even if it's difficult. Who knows what Karim might get into his head?

Malin leaves them in the kitchen, framed by the bright green kitchen cupboards that must have been the height of fashion twenty years ago.

You two seem to enjoy each other's company, she thinks as she hurries down the stairs.

Åke Fors watches his daughter from the living-room window.

Sees how the spring seems to embrace her, how the yellow crocuses by the roadside seem to reach out to her, wanting her with them as protection against an uncertain future.

He runs his finger across one of the plant pots and

realises that he won't manage to say anything to her, it will all have to play out in their meeting with the solicitor. That everything must run its course and that everything will get sorted out, because surely it must now, mustn't it?

He sees Malin walk past Janne's Jaguar in a light that transforms her hair into a halo.

He sees her radiant figure, and he thinks: You have no idea of the bomb that's about to go off in your life. No idea, and I hope you'll be able to forgive me.

The whiteboard in the meeting room is already full of ideas when Malin walks into the room at a quarter past three, the last of all the officers in the case unit of the Crime Investigation Department.

She's still wearing her black dress.

Aware that it isn't at all suitable here. And it's covered in dust as well.

Her colleagues are back from the square.

They're all there.

Their clothes are all flecked here and there like Malin's dress, reminders of the noise and dirt and chaos down in the square.

But there's a remarkable calm in the room, in spite of everything.

A calm that is probably hiding its own chaos, a deep unease. What's happened? What sort of evil has emerged from its lair under the snow? Was a completely different world hiding under the snow, a world that has mutated in the cold? And is what we have taken to be the beauty of spring actually some new sort of evil, hidden behind layer upon layer of exquisite colours and smells?

Malin sits down opposite Zeke.

She wants to be able to look out at the playground of the nursery school outside the windows. The children are out there, playing in the sandpit, pushing toy cars, playing with skipping ropes, clambering up the new climbing frame that was installed just a month or so ago, the solid pastel colours of which remind Malin of what it was like to have a really bad hangover.

All the police officers are sitting in silence, waiting for Sven Sjöman – who has been appointed head of the preliminary investigation – to start the first meeting in the investigation into the presumed bombing outside the SEB bank in Linköping's main square on 10 May, an explosion in which two little girls, as yet unidentified, lost their lives, and five other people were seriously injured.

Sven stops writing on the board and turns around, and for a moment the officers hope for a miracle, that Sven has somehow solved the case at once, so that they can declare the emergency over and tell the city's citizens the truth.

But this spring is no age of miracles in Linköping.

'Well, the first thing I should say,' Sven Sjöman begins, 'is that the Security Police are on their way. We could well be dealing with a subversive act against national security. Obviously, we still have primary responsibility in formal terms, and we'll be expected to help the Security Police with their parallel investigation, but I doubt we can expect any help from them in return.'

'They're quick off the fucking mark,' Waldemar Ekenberg snarls.

'Take it easy, Waldemar,' Karim Akbar says. 'I've just spoken to Karin Johannison. She's done a quick analysis of the crater by the cashpoint machine: we are dealing with a bomb attack. So we need all the help we can get. It looks as if the bomb was placed outside the cash machine rather than inside it, and most of the force was directed away from it. From what we can tell so far, the charge was pretty large, equivalent to a kiloton or so. Previous attacks against cash machines used much smaller amounts, only about five per cent of that. So I think we can safely rule out any possibility that this was a straightforward attempted robbery.'

Sven points at the board.

All the officers seem to agree with him: this is no ordinary crime.

'I've written up some possible lines of inquiry for us to think about,' Sven goes on. 'About people who could be behind something like this.'

Something like this, Malin thinks.

The cheek. The eye staring at her.

Two young children are dead.

And Sven calls it 'something', but that's just his way of creating the necessary distance from the crime in order for the investigation to run as efficiently as possible.

'What do we know about the victims?' Malin says.

Her colleagues look at her, the looks in their eyes revealing that they have only just remembered what she was doing earlier that day, what is going on in her life at the moment.

Concern.

Sympathy.

She hates sympathy. But there's doubt as well: Is she going to buckle under the strain? Start drinking again?

'No need to worry about me,' Malin says, in an effort to pre-empt the thought. 'Besides, I'm needed here now, aren't I?'

Johan Jakobsson nods. Karim does too, before saying: 'We're grateful to you for putting the victims first.'

'So what do we know about them?'

'Nothing so far,' Sven says. 'One theory is that they were

the children of the woman who's in the University Hospital
at the moment with severe injuries. It looks as if she and
the children were closest to the bomb when it went off.
Karin has already been able to confirm that we're talking
about two young children. But they haven't yet been identified.'

Malin nods.

'Could the children have been the target?' she asks.

'In all likelihood they were innocent victims,' Sven says,
'who just happened to be there by some cruel twist of fate.'

Cruel twist of fate?

Malin can feel that she has taken the children's side.

If they care, wherever they are now.

We're here, Malin.

Close to you.

But simultaneously everywhere.

*We can't be bothered to listen to everything you say in your
meeting room, talking about various factions in society.*

*You go on and on like that, like adults, you want to under-
stand everything.*

*About the right-wing extremists who are growing in strength
in the city. Could they be behind the explosion? But they love
the banks, don't they? Capitalism? Anyway, behind their noisy,
sick ideas they're pretty harmless, they've never caused much
trouble in Linköping apart from a few demonstrations that
have got out of hand.*

The man called Karim is talking.

*Do we have to listen to him? We want to drift off, to Mummy,
and stroke her on the cheek.*

But we stay, listen.

He raises the idea of terrorists.

*The rest of you don't want to think this thought, but he
raises it, and maybe he knows something that you don't.*

He asks the question straight out: could Islamic extremists have been responsible? Could there have been a terrorist cell hidden away in Linköping? Could they have set off dark undercurrents among the city's Muslim population, making some of its young unemployed members focus their energy in the wrong direction?

But Sven protests, saying that none of the city's Muslims has ever reported that sort of extremism. That there are no greater social problems among that group than in any other group with high unemployment.

Karim persists: someone will have to talk to the local imam sooner or later. And perhaps the Security Police know something that you don't know. Even if it's a long shot, and even if it might look racist, we need to talk to him. Look at what happened in Örebro. That Guantanamo inmate used to go to the mosque there, then he went off to Pakistan and was accused of being a terrorist. But what did the imam in Örebro know? And what's to say that there isn't an active terrorist cell here in Linköping?

And we can hear what Karim's thinking, he's thinking: even though there are Swedish troops in Afghanistan, people still don't seem to realise that there's a war on. The Islamic extremists want to kill us. They want to kill our families, our wives, women, and children. It's us or them. It's as simple as that.

And he's thinking about his father, Malin. Who was forced to flee nationalist Muslims in Turkey, and then committed suicide in Sundsvall. Alone, unwanted, and desperately homesick.

You think so much. Trying to make evil simple, comprehensible.

We don't think that much. We feel. But is that any better?

You talk so much.

No, we can't be bothered to listen to you talking about how our bodies shattered, Malin, how we were blown up, how our blood stained the beautiful spring square and the plants outside the chemist's and made everything red and horrid. No, we'd rather watch the children playing in the nursery playground, pretend that we can still sing, go down the slide, run and jump, maybe just have some fruit as a snack.

That sort of thing's fun.

Proper fun.

And he's right, Sven, that is our mummy lying in hospital with tubes going in and out of her body, and breathing in a way that frightens us.

Now you're all babbling again, even if those two, Börje and Johan, are mostly silent. But you, Malin, occasionally you say something, and Zeke has his say, while Waldemar is mostly just sceptical and looks on sullenly, we think he could do with a cigarette to help him calm down. Our daddy did that sometimes. He was kind. But he's not here now.

You talk about activists in Linköping. Those on the left, the students who managed to shut down all the fur shops in the city, maybe they've started attacking the banks now. And maybe this was an attack aimed at the SEB bank, the avaricious heart of the capitalist swine.

It would be worth checking out what known activists have been up to, Sven says.

You're wrinkling your nose, Malin, don't you believe that? But then who would ever have believed that a bomb could go off in Linköping?

The children outside. They're climbing high, but we're drifting even higher.

We flying higher than everyone.

You talk of security cameras, getting hold of recordings and studying them, to see if there's any sign of a culprit, or if there's any sign of the bomb before it goes off.

Forensics are working on it, Sven says.

Gathering evidence, finding out more about the bomb, identifying the victims.

You need to find out if there had been any threats made against the bank.

There were no other bombs in the square, but might there be more against other banks? Here? Or elsewhere? You're all wondering the same thing, but it's Sven who voices the idea. Impossible to know, Karim says, but until someone claims responsibility for the bombing or makes threats about new attacks, we can hardly cordon off the whole of Linköping.

Don't you ever stop talking, Malin? This isn't fun at all.

Karim talks about his press conference, and outside the police station at least a hundred journalists have gathered, calmly waiting for someone to give them something new to report.

They're bored, the journalists, but they can turn in a moment and become a horde of bloodthirsty reptiles.

So many possibilities, you think, Malin, so many paths, where to begin?

Then Sven's phone rings.

The woman with the tubes in her stomach and neck and thighs, the woman who's our mummy, she regained consciousness briefly, and said her name. Her name's Hanna, Hanna Vigerö, and us, our names are Tuva and Mira, and only you can help us now, Malin, only you, and we're relying on you.

Sven Sjöman closes his mobile.

'We know who the woman in hospital is now. A Hanna Vigerö, forty years old. She had twin daughters, so in all likelihood the two fatalities are Tuva and Mira Vigerö, six years old, from Ekholmen.'

'Is she awake?' Waldemar Ekenberg asks. 'If she makes it, then the bastard or bastards who did this will have one less life on their consciences.'

'If they have a conscience,' Börje Svärd adds.

'They can't have,' Waldemar says.

'She only regained consciousness briefly,' Sven says. 'We need to check what family she has, and let them know.'

'I can do that,' Johan Jakobsson says in a calm voice. 'While I'm checking the animal rights activists and right-wing extremists.'

'Can we talk to her?' Malin asks.

'Not according to her doctors. She's got serious injuries, and is basically out of reach,' Sven says. 'She's going to be having a major operation later this afternoon. We'll have to wait and see about questioning her. Aronsson and a number of our colleagues are at the hospital interviewing the other people injured as we speak, evidently none of them was so badly hurt that they can't be questioned. Then they'll deal with anyone who managed to leave the square whose names we've still got. Malin, you and Zeke go and talk to the imam, even if you don't think there's any point focusing our attention in that direction at the moment.

'Waldemar, you and Börje talk to any bank employees who weren't there earlier today. OK? Ask about cameras. And try to find out about other cameras around the city. The council should have a register of permits, shouldn't they?'

Börje nods, and says: 'We'll get onto it at once.'

'I can smell blood,' Waldemar says with a grin.

'I'll take care of the hyenas,' Karim says. 'The media are going to have a field day. And we'll have to wait and see what happens when the Security Police show up.'

The whiteboard behind Sven has heavy underlining beneath the words 'Islamic extremists' and 'Activists'.

Malin looks at the board.

'Could this have been aimed at that family? Rather than at the bank, or society in general?' she says.

Her colleagues look at her, clearly none of them has considered that.

'It's not very likely, Malin,' Sven says. 'This is something bigger, something else. They just got in the way. Anyway, if someone was after them, there are far simpler ways of going about it than placing a bomb outside a bank, aren't there?'

Malin nods.

'I just wanted to raise the idea.'

'You'll all be offered debriefing and counselling, after what happened today,' Karim says. 'There'll be good people at your disposal. You just have to say the word.'

Subtext: Don't say the word. Ideally, never say the word. Don't be pathetic. Stay strong, do what's expected of you, carry on without blinking, don't give in to any weakness or vulnerability inside you. Now's a time for action, not soppy bloody therapy.

'Start with the imam,' Sven says. 'But be careful. We don't want the papers screaming that we're Islamophobic racists. Anyway, it's highly unlikely that we'll be able to make any connection as things stand.'

'Maybe we should hold back for a bit?' Malin suggests. 'Wait and see, as far as that's concerned?'

'Go and talk to the imam,' Karim says. 'That's an order. OK, we're going to get the bastards who did this. Those children had their whole lives ahead of them. Just like those children out there. If that means we have to tread on a few toes, then so be it. Understood?'

'Of course we have to talk to the imam,' Waldemar says, but she can see doubt in Zeke, Johan, and Börje's eyes: what's the point, so early in the investigation, when absolutely nothing points in that direction apart from a sort of general feeling among the public.

But that's the way prejudice works.

And it influences us. Particularly when there's an external threat that's hard to pin down.

Malin looks out through the window. In the nursery playground two children are crawling into a dark playhouse, and she thinks that it looks as if the children are disappearing, swallowed up by a different dimension.

7

We're messing about in a playhouse without walls, in a space that's so dark and cramped that we might never find a way out.

But are we the sad ones crying?

Or is that some other children?

Who are still alive? Whom evil is getting closer to?

We can see them now, Malin. It's a little girl, and an even younger boy, and they're locked in, and it's so dark and they're scared and they're screaming.

They're connected to us. How, Malin? How? We have to know.

Bad people outside, or one bad person. They're crying, they want to sleep. They're really sad.

But we're happy now.

Chasing each other through the white world that is ours, where endless cherry blossoms flower, showing off their beauty, their lust for life.

I chase her, she chases me, we chase each other.

We're the cuddly toys on our beds at home.

We leave the nursery playground, the playhouse, the games we can't join in with.

The lamps are shining in the ceiling, blinding us, but Mummy's eyes are closed, and we don't know if she's ever going to look at us again, stroke our backs with her warm hands as we lie in bed in our room, trying to go to sleep.

Mummy.

*The doctor's cutting you now, but we don't want to watch.
A green sheet covers you as he lowers the scalpel and we close
our eyes, and that's nice.*

Cover our eyes for us, Mummy.

Daddy. He should be here, shouldn't he, Mummy?

But he isn't here, at least not with us.

Mummy.

What about you?

Aren't you coming? Coming here to be with us?

*The drips falling from the operating-theatre lamp onto your
cheek are our tears.*

I want to be with you, children.

I can see you and hear you, but I can't be with you yet.
First these nice men and women are going to try to make
me better again. But I don't want to be better, I don't want
whatever love and happiness there might yet be in the
beauty of this month of May.

I want to be with you, with Daddy, I want us to be a
family again, and that means I can't be here.

Don't cry. Don't be scared. I can feel your tears. I'm
asleep, and it doesn't hurt when the nice man cuts me,
he's only trying to help.

Maybe I'll be coming soon.

But I can't promise anything.

You don't always get to choose. But you know that
already, don't you?

Life isn't a lamp that you get to decide when it goes
out.

The flashbulbs love me, Karim Akbar thinks, they love me
and they make the adrenalin pump, coursing through my
veins and making me feel full of life.

There must be a hundred journalists in this large,

panelled courtroom they've had to use for the press conference.

Karim is standing behind a long, pale wooden table. He raises his arms, tries to get the crowd to be quiet and stop the chorus of questions. Because it needs to be managed, directed, this crowd.

He holds his hands out, tries to calm them down, get them to sit, and it works.

He thinks that if he felt insecure and weak when his wife left him, then his new love has made him stronger than ever, now he knows he can deal with anything.

What does a short period of loneliness matter? There's always a new love for someone like me. I can afford to be a bit arrogant, can't I?

Soon the crowd is sitting down and listening to him, the flashes die out and he tells them what they know, about the bomb, that the victims can't be named until their family has been informed, but nothing more. Nothing about lines of inquiry, suspects, and when he stops the storm of questions breaks out again.

'Do you think it's terrorists?'

'Are the Security Police involved?'

'Could the attack have been aimed at the bank?'

'Is there a risk of further attacks?'

'Has anyone claimed responsibility?'

He skirts around all the questions, says that they're keeping an open mind at the moment, that no one has claimed responsibility.

'What about the victims, who were they? Is the woman going to survive?'

'Out of consideration to their family . . .'

Ten, twenty more questions, then he stands up and says: 'That's all for the moment,' and he leaves the room in triumph.

* * *

Daniel Högfeldt turns off his tape recorder and looks at the reinforced white door through which Karim Akbar has just vanished. The other journalists around him look unhappy, wondering how the hell they're going to make any sense of all this. He can see the doubt in their eyes: Has this really happened? Has a bomb really gone off in a godforsaken provincial backwater in Sweden? And there's anxiety as well: If this can happen, then anything is possible. No one is safe, ever, anywhere.

The police are closing ranks. The way they always do before they've made any progress.

Karim Akbar looks like a bloody politician, Daniel thinks. With a newfound self-confidence, the sort you hardly ever see, as if he's suddenly found something inside himself that's prepared him for a serious challenge.

Malin.

Bound to be at the centre of the investigation. Its informal leader.

A long, long time since they last saw each other. He's only met her once since she came out of rehab, but she had been irritable and hadn't seemed altogether there when they had slept together in his flat.

Once upon a time he had actually thought he was in love with her.

That was before he met the woman he's seeing at the moment. Malin would probably go mad if she knew about that.

But I don't give a damn what you think, Malin. You had your chance.

But he can't help wondering how she is. If anything has happened in her life. He has no idea, hasn't heard anything. But isn't that what's supposed to happen with failed love affairs?

And Karim Akbar.

What a stuck-up prick he's become. For a while I thought he'd actually changed. But no one ever changes.

'Are women allowed in here?'

It's just after five o'clock.

Malin and Zeke are standing in the declining afternoon light outside the factory building in Ekholmen that houses the mosque serving Linköping's Muslim population. The building is at the foot of a wooded slope, as though pressed up against silence and a meaningless darkness. Whitewashed brick walls, peeling paint, small windows under a roof of brown-stained metal sheets with rusty iron fixtures, and a metal door with even more rust on it. An altogether depressing building, Malin thinks, looking up at the slope, which is covered with wood anemones and cowslips. Nature seems to be bursting with desire right now, with the sweet smell of two people who've just made love. Slightly over-ripe, as though the best is already past. There are a number of misplaced chestnut trees around the mosque, and it occurs to Malin that the oversized candles of blossom look like mouldy, white, erect cocks.

She's felt a longing for another body this spring.

For a seriously hard fuck, no questions asked, either before or after.

She knows she has to relieve the pressure. But with whom?

Unless I actually need something else?

Love? As if that's likely to come my way now. And she feels her stomach clench, as a cold, black, metal hand grabs at her heart. The loneliness she feels is different to a mere lack of sex, she wants a warm embrace to curl up in, ears that listen to what she has to say, and a brain and a heart that respond, that wish her well, that like her for who she is. Malin thinks, I feel a serious longing, maybe for someone to love, but actually admitting that to myself isn't at all pleasant.

Focus, Malin thinks. On work, on their visit to the mosque.

'On a day like this surely any police officer can go in,' Zeke says. 'Even female ones.'

'Do you think he's here?'

Mohamed Al Kabari.

Familiar from the *Correspondent*. Familiar from local television. Usually depicted in the media as a bearded demagogue refusing to distance himself sufficiently from the 9/11 terror attacks in New York or the train bombs in Spain.

But he did condemn all forms of violence, Malin remembers that, and suddenly she feels uneasy about their visit. What are they doing here, so soon, without any evidence?

Zeke tries the door, but it's locked. There's an old-fashioned doorbell, black and white, below a small window.

Malin presses the button, no sound can be heard, but two minutes later the door opens and Mohamed Al Kabari's bearded face is smiling at them.

Around fifty years old. His sharp nose emphasises his intelligent brown eyes.

'I've been expecting you,' he says in perfect Swedish. 'Come in.'

Malin looks at him questioningly and he realises what she means.

'Women,' he says, 'are welcome here. Just as much as men. With or without a headscarf.'

Mohamed Al Kabari moves smoothly in his long white tunic.

The mosque consists of a large main room with white walls, a small lobby with coat racks, and another door that presumably leads to toilets and a washroom. On the floor there are oriental rugs, closely woven and pleasant under-foot.

'Take your shoes off,' Al Kabari tells them in a fatherly voice that leaves no room for protest.

The room is larger than you'd expect from outside, with a high ceiling, yet Malin still feels boxed in. Al Kabari sits down on a carpet in a corner where there's a patch of sun, and crosses his legs beneath the white fabric.

'Sit down.'

Malin and Zeke sit down, and Al Kabari looks at them, waiting for them to speak.

'We're here because of the explosion in the main square earlier today,' Malin says. 'I presume you've heard what happened.'

Al Kabari nods and spreads his arms.

'Terrible,' he says.

'Two little girls are dead,' Zeke says.

'I understand why you're here,' Al Kabari sighs, and Malin hears herself apologise, even though she never apologises during the course of an investigation, not for anything.

'Our boss wanted us to come and talk to you. You know, bombs and Muslims. For most people in society they go together. I apologise if you feel that you're under suspicion – either individually or as a group.'

Al Kabari looks at them sympathetically. He adjusts his tunic over his legs.

'Your boss is a Christian Kurd, isn't he?' he says.

'That's right,' Zeke says.

Al Kabari shakes his head.

'So much resistance,' he says. 'I work to promote under-standing and tolerance. For members of our community to feel they belong in this city. But it isn't easy. When I condemned the attacks in Madrid, it wasn't even reported in the *Correspondent*. I got the impression that it didn't fit their world view.'

Malin looks around, feels that she's being watched, under surveillance.

No flashing red light up in the ceiling. No camera recording this.

Of course there aren't any cameras.

Just my paranoia.

'Let me be blunt,' Zeke says. 'Have you noticed or heard anything in your community that might have something to do with this?'

Al Kabari shakes his head.

'Why would you need to ask that question?'

Then he pauses before going on: 'I can tell you that my community is calm. I promise you that there's no fanaticism of that sort. There are no madmen here, no desperate kids, no crazy Taliban hiding in some tiny flat. I can pretty much guarantee that. All we have here is a group of people trying to make a decent life for themselves.'

Malin can hear the honesty in the imam's voice. His sorrow at the state of things.

'We're going to have a meeting here this evening. A lot of people in the community are worried about what's happened. I know you have to catch the person who killed those girls,' he says. 'I don't know anything that can help you. But I hope that the perpetrator gets his just punishment.'

Malin hears her mobile ring as they are walking back to the car between the white blocks of flats in Ekholmen, thinks that it must be her dad or Tove. What are they doing now? I should be there with them.

She fishes her phone out and sees Sven's name on the screen.

She stops, clicks to take the call, and beside her Zeke's skull-like features emerge from the fading light.

'Sven here. How did you get on at the mosque? Did you get hold of him?'

'We've just come out. In all honesty, I really don't believe this has any connection to Linköping's Muslim community.'

'He didn't know anything?'

'No, and I think he was telling the truth.'

'You were careful about what you said, weren't you? Was he angry that you went to see him?'

'He wasn't angry, Sven, he was very understanding. Is there any news?'

'The uniforms have talked to everyone who was in the square now, the wounded in hospital, and the ones who were OK and didn't hang around. But no one saw anything unusual. Not a thing. Then there's the guy from the hotdog-stand. We must have missed him in all the confusion. He said he recognised Hanna Vigerö, she used to come to the square some mornings with the children.'

'Is that significant?'

'She works in a home for adults with learning difficulties. They have a rota that means they're sometimes off in the mornings, so there's nothing odd about that. And she's been off sick for a while, so she's had plenty of opportunities to be there.'

'What about Waldemar and Börje? They were going to the bank?'

'Yes, they've asked for the recordings from the bank's security cameras, we'll be getting them from Stockholm tomorrow, everything is stored centrally there. They got hold of the last of the staff as well. No one seems to have noticed anything odd, or seen anyone acting suspiciously. And I got hold of the SEB's head of security in Stockholm. According to him there haven't been any threats at all against the bank. Obviously he questioned the idea that the bomb was directed at them specifically, and seemed to be suggesting that it was just coincidence that the explosion happened there. But they've closed all their branches for the foreseeable future.'

'Did they speak to the branch manager again?'

'Yes. He said he hadn't noticed anything out of the ordinary either. He made a point of it.'

'What about Johan?'

'He's busy trying to get an overview of left- and right-wing extremists in the city at the moment, trying to piece together everything we know, identify a few key individuals for us to talk to, but it's not easy, they've been pretty quiet for the past few years.'

'Some new idiots might have moved here,' Malin says. 'From Umeå, Lund, or Uppsala.'

She hears Sven pondering this on the other end of the line.

'And we've found out a bit more about Hanna Vigerö,' he goes on. 'There's a good reason for why she's been on sick leave. Her husband, a Pontus Vigerö, the girls' father, died in a car accident six weeks ago. Ice. Evidently he was on his way to work and went off the road, straight into an old oak tree. You remember, that cold snap at the end of March, when the roads were like glass and we got all that late snow. He worked for Tidlund Lifts out in Kisa.'

'Anything odd about the accident?'

'No, the investigation concluded that it was just an ordinary accident as a result of ice.'

'Poor woman,' Malin says. 'First her husband, and now the children. That's terrible.'

'To put it mildly,' Sven says.

'Any other family?'

'None that we've been able to trace. No grandparents on either side, they died years ago.'

'Friends?'

'No. They seem to have been pretty self-contained.'

Beside Malin, Zeke is tapping his foot restlessly on the grass, staring up at the small balconies where the white moons of satellite dishes point out at the world.

'How about the girls? Have they been formally identified yet?'

'No. Karin and her team in the National Forensics Laboratory are working as hard as they can on the DNA analysis, comparing them against samples from Hanna Vigerö. Karin hasn't got anything else for us yet either.'

There's a moment's silence on the phone and Malin breathes in the smells of the area. Fried meat and toasted cumin, perhaps a hint of cinnamon, and Malin feels hungry again and wishes people had the decency to cook with their windows and balcony doors closed. Then she detects the verdant, slightly bitter smell of spring grass, and it reminds her of when she used to race across the lawn in their garden out in Sturefors as a child, and how the smell carried with it a promise of movement, physical activity, and how she always loved that feeling, the feeling of unlimited freedom.

'Are you still out in Ekholmen?' Sven goes on.

'Yes.'

'You might as well take a look at the Vigerö family flat while you're there.'

'So this is where they live, then?'

'I said so at the meeting.'

'I missed that. Zeke too.'

'There's a lot going on. It's hard to take it all in,' Sven says.

My brain's not working at its best, Malin thinks, there's

too much happening, too quickly, it's as if my whole world is one big explosion.

'What do you want us to do in the flat? Is it OK to break in just like that? I mean, they are the victims.'

'Break in,' Sven says. 'It's important. Get a sense of who they are, or were. You know, Malin. Listen to the voices of the investigation.'

The voices, Malin thinks. I'll listen to them.

But will there be any to hear in the flat?

'Number 32A, Ekholmsvägen. Head over there now. See what you can find.'

Malin hears a buzzing sound.

'I'd better go,' Sven says. 'Someone's waiting to come into the office.'

8

Sven Sjöman leans back in his office chair and the men opposite him sip coffee from grubby 7-Eleven mugs.

They've introduced themselves, but only by their surnames.

Brantevik, a man in his fifties, wearing a worn brown corduroy suit and blessed with a rugged red face that's been wrecked by smoking.

Stigman. A man of Malin's age with short blond hair and a sharply chiselled chin and similarly sharp eyes. Elegantly but casually dressed in a pale-blue jacket and black jeans.

The Security Police.

It's not even six o'clock and they're here already.

'Have you got anywhere?' Brantevik asks in a hoarse voice.

Sven briefs them on their lines of inquiry, carefully and thoroughly.

The two Security Police officers nod. No follow-up questions.

'How about you?' Sven asks, looking out of the window, towards the orange panelled façade of the University Hospital and the hundreds of cars in the car park.

'What can you give us? For instance, is there any sort of international connection that we ought to know about? Anything to do with religion? Politics?'

Stigman takes a deep breath and starts talking in a tone

that lets on that he really likes the sound of his own voice.

'At the current time any information of that sort is confidential, but between us I can say that we have no such indications. We didn't receive any prior warning.'

Sven nods.

'We're booked into the Central Hotel.'

'Are they open?'

'Yes, the rooms at the back of the building.'

'Bloody hell.'

'Apparently they'll be serving breakfast in one of the conference rooms, and the reception area made it through the explosion without too much damage.'

'And there are just the two of you?'

'For the time being,' Brantevik says. 'There'll be more coming tomorrow. I'm in charge of our investigation. Keep us informed about your work.'

'And you'll doubtless be keeping us informed about yours?'

The men on the other side of Sven's desk smile.

Stigman seems to want to say: 'Sure, Charlie, sure,' but stays silent.

When the Security Police officers have left the room, Sven leans over the desk and looks down towards the hospital again.

Hanna Vigerö.

She's in there somewhere, fighting for her life.

Another ten or so of those injured are being kept in for treatment, some of them probably for several weeks. Those with minor injuries can go home, and those in shock have had treatment, but the shock permeating the city will last a long time, perhaps it will never fade completely.

What on earth have they been hit by?

He thinks about his detectives.

Reflects that Waldemar Ekenberg's relentless determination will definitely be needed now. That Johan Jakobsson's talent for digging things out with his computer – God knows how he does it – will come in handy. Similarly Börje Svärd's maturity, and Zeke's steely core. But most of all they're probably going to need Malin's intuition. Who knows, it might lead them in the right direction.

And Karim Akbar.

He seems to have reached a watershed moment in his life, and instead of becoming more tolerant he's choosing to see things in black and white, us against them, and who can really blame him when something like this happens?

Malin.

He knows he ought to talk to her, but there's no time for that. He knows she's likely to throw herself at the case, and that perhaps she ought to be doing the exact opposite right now, look after her nearest and dearest, not least Tove. But the general public, Linköping's taxpayers, need her now.

I need her now, Sven thinks.

So I'm going to let her follow her instincts.

The stairwell on Ekholmsvägen smells of sweat and smoke and wet animal fur. It's strangely damp here, a sense of something steaming, as if they had been instantaneously transported to a thick jungle. A faulty fluorescent light is flickering in the ceiling, making the yellow-painted concrete walls look pale, and the speckled grey stone floor look as if it's covered with crawling worms.

Malin rings on the door that says Vigerö.

'Out of politeness,' she says.

She and Zeke wait.

Malin rings again.

'Let's go in,' she says.

'Not sure about that.'

'It's OK in a situation like this,' and she pulls out her keyring, finds the lock-pick, and a minute later the door of the flat is open.

What does normal look like?

Floral wallpaper in the hall. A coat-rack from Ikea, and below it a shoe-rack, neat rows of children's and adults' shoes.

A clean kitchen with yellow units. Two stools at a round kitchen table, two ladder-back chairs that look new. A living room with a green-checked corner sofa, a flatscreen television. On the walls, black-and-white photographs of coastal scenes, probably from Ikea as well.

They go into a bedroom. The blinds are closed and faint light seeps through the gaps. White duvets on two beds.

Malin reaches for the light switch. Turns it on.

The room is bathed in a gentle light and Malin sees framed photographs above the beds, images from the girls' lives, playing in a sandpit when they're little more than a year old, riding a pony, playing on a beach, getting bigger, the last day at nursery, going down a blue slide in a playground, standing outside Gröna Lund funfair in Stockholm.

Colourful plastic toys in a wooden box. Games in neat piles. Two identical dolls.

Close-ups of the two girls.

The prettiest kids you could imagine.

Beautiful big eyes.

One picture in which their mother is stroking their cheeks.

Malin can hear Zeke breathing heavily behind her. His grandchild is two and a half years old now. A little boy. He's only seen him twice, Malin knows that, it's difficult arranging regular contact when your son is a star ice-hockey player in the NHL.

'Fuck,' Zeke says. 'Fuck.'

Malin sits down on one of the beds. Lays her hands on the neat white duvet.

Sisters. They probably stuck together. Best friends. Us against the world. The way sisters sometimes are. The way brothers are.

Then the lamp in the ceiling flickers, and there's a clicking sound, and the room goes dark again, and Malin thinks she can hear the whistling sound again, the one she heard in the square.

She sees the eye from the square in the room's darkness, and the cheek, the torn-off scrap from a human face, a child's face. She can see it clearly in her mind's eye, and she knows now that the eye, the cheek, belonged to one of the girls, which one doesn't matter, it might as well be the cheek of both twin girls.

Let them be at peace, Malin prays, and the sound vanishes, and she fumbles through the darkness of the room, the world black in front of her blinded eyes.

Malin, Malin.

We see you and Zeke making your way through our rooms, hear you swear when you see our lovely beds.

Aren't they lovely?

You don't find anything odd, you don't find anything. Just perfectly ordinary things, ordinary records and images from a life where everything was ordinary. Wasn't it?

A twin existence. Twice as much love, twice as much good. Mummy's asleep now.

Do you think she'll live here again?

We won't.

Because now feelings are our home.

All feelings. Everything a person can feel, even the things far, far beyond what can be expressed in words.

It's dark and cold here. Like a long spring night, and we want Mummy and Daddy to come and give us a hug.

But where's Daddy, Malin?

Where is he?

Where are they?

Now you're closing the door of what used to be our home.

You look around the stairwell, Malin, wondering what those shapes are that you can make out in the darkness.

You hear the whistling again. Is it the birds singing?

It's only us, Malin, our drifting bodies trying to find peace by making the most of physical space.

But it doesn't work, Malin, we can't find any peace.

9

Karim Akbar is sitting in his office, feeling as if he's chained to the chair. The leather behind him is warm against his back, and he is longing for his new girlfriend's body, longing for all that she is.

He wants to hear her voice, and the intelligence contained within it. He wants to feel her breath as she whispers in his ear, feel how she desires everything about him, the same way that nature desires life itself in the spring.

His former wife, who took off for Malmö with a counsellor and their son Bayran, she can go to hell.

The arrogance that comes with being the object of someone's infatuation.

I can indulge myself a bit, Karim thinks.

Vivianne's a prosecutor, transferred from Norrköping a year ago. Five years younger than me. She offers a bit of resistance, and she's smart, and it's as if she awakens the beast in me with her ambition, she's made me really keen to make a career for myself again. And she herself is probably going to end up as Attorney General.

The Justice Minister has just called.

She wanted to find out what the situation was, hear about the investigation, and Karim wasn't surprised to hear from her – their bomb is leading all the news broadcasts.

He has the television on.

The main evening news. And now he can see pictures of Linköping, of himself, and outside the window the police station car park is empty, and the street lamps are casting a peculiar yellow glow over the spring evening, and he knows it's chilly out there.

Then the Justice Minister's face appears on the screen. Wrinkled from smoking, soothing.

'At this moment in time there's nothing to indicate any connection to international terrorism . . . I have full confidence in the local police . . .'

Karim turns off the television.

He looks over towards the offices on the top floor of the district court building.

There's a light on in one of the rooms. Her office. He can see her silhouette, sitting in front of the computer on her desk.

Then his mobile buzzes.

He reads the message.

'I can see you. I'm touching myself as I watch your shadow. Come over.'

Malin is walking home from the station, feeling the perfumed smell of all the flowers in the Horticultural Society Park, sensing how the pistils of the flowers seem to be sending coded signals to her body: break free, do something stupid, give in to your weaknesses, who cares what happens?

But she has to stay focused.

She knows that.

It's past ten o'clock in the evening, and it feels as if one of the longest days of her life is drawing to an end. It's gloomy now, the cones of light beneath the street lamps free of insects, yet still somehow vibrating with life.

The cordon around the main square has been lifted now.

People have started lighting memorial candles on the ground in front of the hole in the wall where the cashpoint machine had been. Maybe a hundred candles there already, flowers, little notes written to the children who the media have said were killed, but who still haven't been officially identified.

Some girls the same age as Tove are standing in the middle of the square, hugging each other, crying, whispering to one another.

Candles everywhere.

Maybe five hundred in total, spread out across the square. The flames light up this everyday space like anxious little beacons, and Malin thinks that it looks as if goodness itself is seeping from the paving slabs, rising up against the violence that has hit them all.

The flames are flickering muteness, their holders little cocoons of hope that everything might turn out to be a mistake, a misunderstanding, and that what happened didn't really happen. The light spreads across the world, trying to find a foothold, trying to take over. Will it succeed?

On the *Correspondent*'s website Malin has just read that all the churches in the city are open. That anyone can go along to talk, meet people, grieve for their anxious souls. A service is underway in the cathedral, and at least a thousand people have made their way to the great stone chamber, and it must be very safe and beautiful in there, but Malin still doesn't want to go, she wants to go home now, has no need of collective fear and sorrow and denial.

Her body is aching with exhaustion and confusion, and there is still a hint of the smell of dust and burned fabric and flesh in the air. At the Central Hotel, glaziers are busy putting new windows in, and outside Mörners some waiters are mopping down the wooden decking of the terrace.

Mörners is open, insanely enough. It's completely empty.

A beer?

That would be wonderful.

Just one, Malin thinks as she walks past the bar on the way down towards Ågatan.

But no.

No, no.

However much her body might want it, no matter what the scent of the flowers whispers.

Her dad and Tove are at home in the flat. She's just spoken to them, they're expecting her, watching television, and Malin hopes they're tired and don't want to talk about anything. It feels as if today has already used up all its words.

She sees Tove before her, one, two, three, four, five, six years old. She sees Tove doing all the things the girls were doing in the photographs in the bedroom. Sees Tove doing everything she's done since she was that age. All the good things she has experienced, in spite of everything, and will doubtless go on to experience.

Then she feels a pang of conscience. Thinks that she neglects Tove too much.

It's got a lot better since I stopped drinking, but I still work too much, Malin thinks, I still can't quite get a grip on her world.

That's just the way it is.

I can't try to deceive myself about any of this, and she curses her weakness, wants to be part of Tove's world, her dreams, her life.

But is that what Tove wants?

She's sixteen now. More independent with each passing day. Strong and uncomplicated in a way that I never have been.

A scent of summer in the spring evening.

A scent of summer and a stench of evil that's been hidden under snow. Two little girls' tattered, burned bodies.

10

Malin hesitates at the front door of the building on Ågatan. She listens to the hubbub from the Pull & Bear pub on the ground floor. It's as if she can hear the beer fizzing as it gets piped out of the barrels and into the waiting misted glasses.

The sound is an illusion, she knows that, and it doesn't scare her, she knows she can control any feelings that it awakens.

She digs her fingernails deep into her arm. Pain helps. She's spent more time than ever exercising since she dried out. Endorphins and physical pain keep the urge in check, even if they can't banish it. Running back and forth along the banks of the Stångå, swimming ten kilometres in the Tinnerbäck pool, fifty-metre lengths without taking a breath, feeling her body about to burst from the inside, feeling the urge for alcohol crumbling.

Hours in the gym of the police station last winter. The bar of the bench press dangerously close to her throat, carrying more than a hundred kilos. Push it up, otherwise you're dead, there's no one to help you down here in the basement, no one to hear your mute cries for help if you lose your grip and crush your larynx.

The longing for alcohol is cured by danger and pain that get the body's reward centres going once they've been overcome. The longing fades with physical exhaustion.

But it can reappear at any moment. Show its leering

face and whisper gently: 'Do what you like, Malin, I'm always here, I'll always be here, and I'm in charge.'

She tries to brush aside the noise from the pub.

Springtime in the city.

Blinding sunlight during the day, lighting up all the dirt that's been hidden by the snow.

Scantily clad girls for the men to dream about after a winter spent in frigid abstinence. Nature reawakened, only to die again in a few months' time in an endless cycle. Carnivores waking hungry from hibernation and setting out to hunt. Stalking and killing other animals' young to feed their own and help them survive.

Lightly clad men. Her own lust unshackled, everyone's innocent search reduced to a dance of hormones.

Slack bodies.

Hard bodies.

She stands still outside the building.

Presses her nails harder into her arm, but not hard enough to break the skin.

I'm going in circles, Malin thinks. Is disappointment etched in my face? Bitterness. I'm almost thirty-seven years old. Time is passing me by. There has to be something more to all this apart from this fruitless hunt for something.

Something needs to happen.

Secrets.

The search for something that can make my feet carry on moving me forwards. Faith in myself, other people. Something that can cure my fucking restlessness. An ordinary spring can't do that.

Can a bomb? Two innocent, dead girls.

Maria Murvall? The rape victim from an unsolved case that I've become obsessed with. Can you help me move on, Maria, you, still sitting in your room in Vadstena

Hospital and refusing to come out of yourself, or what was once yourself?

You feel longing, don't you, Maria? A longing for non-existence, in the same way that the two Vigerö girls are probably longing, screaming, and crying for more life.

She lets go of her arm.

Her black dress is grubby and crumpled.

The funeral that morning.

It feels like a thousand years ago. Can't be bothered to think about it. Better to look forward, surely?

Malin opens the door, and a minute later she's standing in the hallway watching Tove pull on her beige trenchcoat, a Burberry copy from H&M. Malin thinks the coat makes Tove look older, more self-aware, better than this grubby rented flat, better than she herself has ever been.

'Are you heading back to your dad's? You're welcome to stay here.'

'I know. But it's been a long day, and I've got books there that I need for school tomorrow.'

Sure, Tove.

You're running away, aren't you? Just like your dad has always done.

'Can't you stay?'

'Mum, please.'

OK, Malin thinks. OK. But I've been sober now for almost eighteen fucking months, can't you stay here a bit more often?

'For Grandad's sake?'

'I've spent all evening talking to Grandad. He said it was OK.'

The television is on. Some gameshow, and Malin can hear her dad's heavy breathing in the living room, but he isn't asleep, he's waiting for her, his daughter, for them to see out the day together, the day on which he buried his wife, and she her mother.

Malin looks at Tove. Then she gives an involuntary shake of the head.

'What is it?'

'Nothing. I'm just tired. Off you go, so you don't miss the bus. Be careful. Anything could happen out there. Would you rather take a taxi?'

'No.'

'OK. Get the bus.'

Malin lets the word bus hang in the air like a weary curse.

'You're not upset, are you, Mum?'

'Tove. I buried my mother this morning. Of course I'm upset.'

Tove looks at her.

The look in her eyes reveals that she can hear how false what Malin has just said sounds. So Tove smiles, takes two steps forward and gives Malin a hug, and mother and daughter stand in the hall, in the dull light of the weak bulb, and Malin can smell Tove's cheap perfume, how it makes her smell sweet and soft, the most familiar scent on the planet.

But at the same time Tove smells different, like something new, an unfamiliar being that Malin will never learn anything about, will never understand.

She hugs Tove tighter.

Tove responds.

And Malin has to hold back tears, force her wretched tears back down into her throat.

The door closes behind Tove with a dull thud, as Malin sinks onto the sofa beside her dad.

He switches off the television with the remote and they sit next to each other in silence, watching the verdigris tower of St Lars Church loom outside the window, as high clouds cover the vibrant evening sky.

Her dad's profile is sharp, and she thinks how handsome he must have been once, that he's still an attractive man, and that she hopes he'll meet someone else, someone nice, because she doesn't think he'll be able to cope with being alone.

'How are you?' she asks.

'Fine,' her dad replies.

'Sure?'

Her dad nods, and Malin has a feeling that he wants to tell her something, that he's finally going to tell her what she knows he has to tell her.

She gets up. Goes over to the window and looks out for a while before turning around again.

The look in her dad's eyes is clear, but weary.

'Isn't it time to tell me?' Malin asks.

'Tell you what?'

And her dad looks lonely and scared, scared of loneliness itself, and Malin realises that there's no point in pushing him, that if he has anything to say that might jeopardise anything, he's not going to say it now, not tonight.

'I'm tired,' Malin says. 'It's been a long day.'

'Do you want to go to bed?'

She nods.

'I should probably go home.'

'Why did you both come back here? You could just as easily have stayed at yours.'

Her dad looks at her pointedly.

'Did Tove want to come back here?'

'No, she didn't say so.'

'So you wanted to. Why?'

I'm interrogating him, Malin thinks. I'm interrogating him.

'Why did you want to come back here? Did you want us to talk about Mum? But there can't be much to say about her, not really? You know damn well we never really got on.'

Her dad gets up.

Stands beside the living-room table with his hands in the pockets of his grey cord trousers, and his face looks oddly round in the light of the orange floor-lamp.

'Please, Malin. She's only just been laid to rest.'

'And not a moment too soon, if you ask me.'

And she feels how a sudden burst of anger throws the words from her, as impossible to stop as the old impulse to drink herself senseless, wonderfully and hopelessly drunk.

Why am I saying this? Malin thinks. Mum was an ice-cold person, but she never did me any physical harm. Or did she? Did she used to hit me, even though I don't remember? Have I suppressed the memory?

'I'm going now,' her dad says. 'If I don't see you before, I'll see you for the reading of the will at the solicitor's.'

But he doesn't go.

'Malin,' he says. 'It wasn't my fault she was the way she was. I tried to talk to her about it. Get her to care more about you, about Tove.'

'And now it's too late.'

'Don't judge her too harshly, Malin. Because then you'll be judging everyone.'

'What do you mean?'

'I mean that you can only throw the first stone if you're free from guilt.'

'So now it's my fault that Mum was an emotionless fucking bitch?'

Her dad closes his eyes, it looks as if he's suppressing anger and wants to say something, but instead he just breathes out in a long sigh.

'You need to get some sleep,' he says. 'The square must have been a terrible sight. Those girls.'

The girls.

The eye.

The face.

And Malin feels her anger drain away, and she nods to her dad, she nods several times.

'Sorry,' she says. 'It was wrong of me to speak ill of Mum today.'

'It's OK,' her dad says. 'We need to talk some more another day. Forgive me if I'm acting oddly.'

Oddly?

You don't seem very upset, you're not desperate with grief, you're not in pieces because you're a widower now. So how do you seem, Dad? Secretive, empty, bewildered?

'I'm going now, time to get some sleep,' her dad says.

Then he goes out into the hall, and Malin hears him put his coat on before calling: 'Goodnight, sleep well!' into the living room, and Malin calls back: 'Bye, Dad, goodnight.'

Tove sees the letter on top of the chest in the hall of the house out in Malmslätt. Dad must have put it there when he got home from work.

She sees the logo in the corner, and can hear Dad doing something in the living room. Is he hoovering? She has a feeling that someone's just left the house, that someone else, a stranger, has just been there.

Dad.

There he is, and she gives him a hug, and he's more solid than Mum, more reliable and simpler, but also more boring, she can't help thinking it, feeling it.

'You've got a letter,' he says when they break the hug. 'I couldn't work out where it's from.'

'It's just an advert from some school,' she replies, hoping that he can't see through her lie. 'Has someone been here?'

Her dad looks at her in surprise.

'Here? Who'd be here on an ordinary weeknight except you?'

'I suppose so,' Tove says, and now it's her turn to sense a lie in the air, and she takes the letter and starts to go upstairs to her room.

'I'm tired,' she says. 'I'm going to go to bed.'

Her dad looks at her. Nods, before asking: 'How's your mum?' and his voice has a dutiful tone that instinctively annoys Tove.

'Fine,' she says curtly.

'And Grandad?'

'He's fine as well.'

The letter in one hand.

She feels her hands shaking as she tries to open the envelope without damaging the contents.

The school's logo on the outside.

The dream.

Something better that the damn Folkunga School. Far away from all her problems.

From Mum.

God, she feels ashamed of thinking like that.

She drops the envelope. Picks it up again and manages to open it neatly.

A single sheet of paper.

Extra thick. That can only mean one thing, can't it? She takes the letter over to the bed, turns the lamp on, and unfolds it. Then she reads, and smiles, and feels like jumping up and leaping in the air and shouting, but then she feels her stomach clench, Mum, Mum, how am I going to tell Mum about this?

Malin has undressed and got into bed, under the cheap duvet cover.

She feels the soft, familiar, lonely mattress under her body.

Tries to summon an image of her mum from inside, but it doesn't work, her mum's face won't assume real features, only an outline.

Why can't I see you, Mum? Why don't I feel any grief? Have I suppressed it?

I don't think I have. You abandoned me once, didn't you, and the sorrow I ought to be feeling now hit me then, is that it? Maybe that's the sorrow I've felt throughout my life?

Is there ever a valid reason for letting your child down? Abandoning it? Abusing the only unquestionable loving relationship? Turning against it with cruelty? Exploiting it?

No.

If you do that, you deserve to die. That makes you guilty of betrayal.

The secret is Dad's now, but I know that something's going to snap.

Malin rolls onto her side.

Tries to get to sleep, worries that sleep might be a long time coming, but it comes to her at once.

In her dreams she sees Maria Murvall.

She sees a little boy lying in a bed in another hospital room, and the boy has no face, but he has a gaping black mouth, and out of the mouth come words in a language Malin can't understand, and she doesn't even know if it's a human language.

Then the girls from the square are with her in the dream.

They're drifting, white and beautiful, above their mother's sickbed.

A life-support machine bleeping in the dream.

Bleeping that there's still life, there's still hope. The girls drift onwards, upwards, out across the forest, and on towards a quiet, dark stretch of coast.

Then the girls scream. They turn their faces to Malin and scream straight out in terror. Other children's voices join in, and soon Malin's sleep is one single scream.

'Let us out,' the scream goes.

'Let us out. Let us out!'

II

Sven Sjöman couldn't sleep, the bedroom was too warm, so he got up and made his way down through the dark house, over the creaking stained floorboards, down to the kitchen, where he made himself a cheese sandwich with his wife's homemade bread.

Then he did what he's done thousands of times before.

He went down to the cellar of the villa, to his carpentry room, whose walls had been insulated with old eggboxes. He ate the sandwich standing at the lathe, unable to bring himself to start the machine, let alone pick up any of the pieces of wood he was currently working on.

Now he's sitting down on the stool looking at his lathe, his tools, and feeling the loneliness of this room, and thinking about all the bowls he's made, sold to new owners in the handicrafts shop in Trädgårdsgatan.

A bomb has exploded in his city.

Who would ever have dreamed that something like that could happen, but now it has. Two girls are dead, and while everyone else is rushing about, while the general public is suffering from collective panic, he stands there like an ancient pine tree, unbreakable by any storm.

Malin.

He's not sure what's going on with her yet. She seems to be able to keep the drink at bay, and she seems to be getting on well with Tove again. But Janne?

I don't regret forcing her into rehab, but somehow I get

the feeling that she'll never completely trust me again, as if she used to take it for granted that I'd listen to whatever she wanted, no matter what happened.

She was guilty of drink-driving.

She was drunk on duty.

It could have turned out really badly, and someone else could have got hurt. And I couldn't let either of those things happen.

And now her mother. I remember when my mother died. It was as if all my security was pulled away, as if I finally grew up, liberated by the reality of her death from the fear that she might disappear.

I grieved, but I also grew as well. She had lived her life, she was old, and I can still feel her love to this day. But if she had lived her life without showing me love, maybe I'd feel differently. Maybe I'd feel that there was a hole in me that could never be filled now.

She's balancing on a very fine line, Malin. Anything could tip her into the darkness. But Malin's a human being, and that's what we all have to deal with, being human.

Vulnerable little people.

I'd kill anyone who attacked them.

Kill them.

Johan Jakobsson watches his children sleep in their beds in the room they share on the ground floor of their terraced house. Lets his feelings run free, refusing to let guilt tarnish them.

His children are almost the same age as the girls who died in the square. The whole thing seems unreal. Yet still horribly real.

And Malin.

She buried her mother that morning. The explosion seemed in some paradoxical way to hold her together. As if it made her more focused, made things clearer, helping her cope with the very fact of being human.

He closes the door to the children's room.

Stops in the darkness of the hall.

Whoever it was who carried out the bombing, we're going to catch him, or her, or them.

There's a dividing line there, he thinks. Anyone who is guilty of violence against children, the abuse of children, breaks our shared human contract, and that contract can never be restored. Those people have forfeited their right to be part of society.

Why does anyone join the police? Why did I join the police?

God knows, I'm not a macho-man like Waldemar. Or Börje, come to that.

But I like the intricacy of the work. Mapping out people and events. Digging into people's pasts. Seeing the patterns that have led them to a particular point in their lives.

And the clarity. In cases like this. Because behind the smokescreen, the conflict is straightforward. Me against the people who harm children. Black and white. It's as easy as that.

Börje Svärd is asleep.

Waldemar Ekenberg is asleep.

They're asleep in their respective unassuming Östergötland villas, united by their untroubled breathing.

Börje's Alsatians are lying on his bed. They're allowed on there now, it makes the nights feel less lonely, and he's noticed that it makes them feel more secure.

That he himself feels more secure because of the dogs' watchful, protective presence.

As if they are capable of holding evil at bay.

Börje had been in the cathedral, at the service, together

with another two and a half thousand of the city's inhabitants. He was standing right at the back of the church, looking out over the rows of people in the pews, seeing the soft yet powerful light shining on the crucifix on the altar, and the lamps on the walls made the stone sing, demanding something from the congregation, demanding that their fear and anxiety be brought under control, and that was also the bishop's message: 'In times like this we must stick together. Not point the finger, but show tolerance and not let fear rule our lives and our choices. By having faith in the good within us, we can defeat evil.'

And Börje had been scornful. How had faith helped Anna? Had it overcome her evil, evil illness?

No, hardly.

But until close to the end she'd had a good life. Difficult and painful, but every day he had seen the unshakeable power within her, the desire to live, and possibly also faith in human goodness.

He had thought about Malin in the cathedral.

The way she actually seemed to be carrying the same torment as Anna. How she tried to reach out for goodness even though a powerful dark force was constantly threatening to take over. But, he thought, it's probably only when life becomes so black and white that existence becomes truly clear to us, when we might feel able to understand that its inherent contradictions are the whole point.

But here, in this cathedral, he had thought, we try to convince ourselves, jointly, that those contradictions don't exist, no matter what the bishop says. In times of need we seek solace, otherwise we don't give a damn.

He had left the cathedral before the end of the service.

He had felt the oxygen in the air running out, as the flames of the candles reached out to him. He had walked home through the mild spring evening. Longing to be at home with his dogs' simple, easily comprehensible love.

Waldemar Ekenberg has his arm around his wife. She's awake, and is looking at him, admiring his solidity, his ability never to give in. She doesn't mind about his tendency towards racism and over-simplification. He probably has good reasons. He looks after her, always has done. They can manage on his wage alone, if they have to. She never liked the job at Rex Components, sitting in front of a screen and typing in data all day long. But at the same time, it was nice to feel needed. But Waldemar seems happy about her not working, because then everything at home works perfectly, and he gets properly cooked meals on the table every evening.

Waldemar cares about the people closest to him.

His colleagues.

Börje, Johan, Sven. And Malin. He said he was worried about her at the dinner table this evening. Worried she was going to start drinking again now that her mother was gone. But she seems to have a grip on things, doesn't she, he says, as if I'd know. I do know one thing, though: however much you might want to help someone, he or she will eventually have to overcome their demons themselves.

And who knows what nightmares are really haunting that Malin?

Zeke is sitting in front of his computer in the kitchen of his villa. He's just woken up and couldn't get back to sleep.

He's opened a picture of his grandson in Canada. His name's Per, but he's called Pelle, and Zeke has seen far too little of him.

Inside the bedroom his wife is snoring, and the soft,

rumbling sound of her breathing makes Zeke feel calm, at the same time as making him feel wide awake.

Bloody awful, those girls in the square.

What would he do if anything like that happened to Pelle?

He'd smoke the bastards who did it out of their holes.

But he knows that unfocused aggression is pointless in a situation like this. Now was the time for them to be methodical, not let themselves be blinded by hate or anger.

He looks at the picture of his grandson.

Taking some of his very first steps in his son Martin's lush garden.

Bloody awful.

He knows he can let rip if need be.

Go to hell, Zeke thinks, and in his mind's eye he sees a monster in human disguise.

12

Tuesday, 11 May

What does a journalist want?

To capture the truth. To let it loose.

Become a parasite on it, profit from it. Give their own view, share it with those who choose to listen. If they actually want anything, journalists.

It's only a quarter to seven when Malin parks outside the police station, but in spite of the early hour there's a minor horde of journalists outside the entrance.

There are vehicles from Swedish Television and TV4. With a case like this, in such an extreme situation as this one, it's even more important than usual to hold the media at a distance, not let the vultures set anything in motion that might affect the general public and foster fear in society.

But perhaps Linköping's inhabitants ought to be afraid now? Who knows when the next bomb might go off? Or what has already been set in motion?

Malin breathes in the morning air. Detects the smell of newly woken chlorophyll, life waiting to be lived, the way the whole of nature seems to want to make love to itself in a boisterous orgy.

Is Daniel Högfeldt there? In the horde?

She can't see him, and as she approaches the entrance the journalists shout at her: 'Malin? Have you got anything for us? What are your main lines of inquiry? Activists, Islamic extremists . . . Has anyone claimed responsibility?'

She shakes her head, puts one hand in front of her face, and wishes she had put her sunglasses on, but is still glad she's wearing her nice blue dress if she has to have her picture taken. The holster containing her SIG Sauer is concealed beneath a white cotton jacket. White plimsolls, French sailor style. She felt properly chic when she looked at herself in the mirror in her bedroom, and that cheered her up, the way her appearance has recovered and improved since she stopped drinking.

Properly attractive.

Vivacious skin that sits tightly on her high cheekbones, glossy hair. Alert blue eyes.

Not bad at all.

So why am I still so alone? she had wondered.

'No comment,' she says as the crowd parts, possibly out of respect for her, a number of them have covered other cases she's been involved in, and they know what sort of person she is.

Then the automatic doors open and she goes in, hears the sucking sound as they close behind her, then her mobile rings. She looks in her bag, gets hold of it, sees Daniel's number and doesn't feel like taking the call, but does so anyway.

'It's me, Malin.'

And she can hear from the efficient tone of his voice that this is strictly a work call.

He doesn't want to meet up for a fuck.

'Listen,' he says. 'I wanted to call you first considering the current situation. I've received an email in the newsroom from a group calling themselves the Economic Liberation Front. They say they're at war with all banks, which they call outposts of greed, and they're claiming responsibility for yesterday's explosion. And they say they're going to strike again.'

Malin stops in front of the reception desk, and Ebba, the receptionist, who's just arrived, nods in her direction.

'What did you say?'

'You heard. The Economic Liberation Front. Ever heard of them?'

'No. Never.'

Malin starts walking towards her desk in the open-plan office, the first detective on the team to arrive, but there's a countless number of uniforms and civilian staff wandering to and fro with cups of coffee and bundles of documents in their hands.

'I've never heard of the Economic Liberation Front,' she says.

'But they seem to be genuine,' Daniel says. 'They sent a link to a website, and it's not a pretty sight.'

In front of her computer now.

'The address, Daniel. The address.'

'As it sounds. Dot S E.'

'Hold on, I'm opening it now. And the email address?'

'The mail came from an anonymous server.'

Her fingers race over the keyboard.

Wrong.

Damn. Then she gets the right address in the browser.

Heavy blue text on a pale green background. A graphic consisting of the burning logos of SEB, Nordea, Handelsbanken, and Swedbank.

She reads:

The country's banks and the indescribable greed expressed by them and their owners, management and staff, are threatening the whole climate of society. Their behaviour is creating a predatory cage for our children to live in.

The Economic Liberation Front is therefore declaring war on Sweden's banks. They and their greed will be wiped out.

Pictures from the main square following the explosion.
Malin scrolls down.

Pictures of bank branches in other cities. The caption beneath every picture is the same.

The next target?
The next target?

Then, at the bottom of the page, another short text:

Civilian casualties cannot be ruled out in our struggle to save public decency, selfless compassion for others and love between people.

'Have you looked?'

Daniel's voice is full of fear and distaste, but also expectation, as if he's waiting for a pat on the back.

'Yes.'

No other pages, nothing more about the organisation than what it says on the home page.

'Bloody dodgy,' Malin says. 'Have you put this up on your own site?'

'No. I came to you first.'

'Can you hold back for a bit? Until we can check this out. Bloody hell.'

'I can't wait, Malin, you know that.'

'You could start a panic, Daniel.'

'People have the right to know, Malin. And what's to say they haven't sent this to loads of people in the media? If you check, you'll probably find the link on other sites.

Hasn't anyone else contacted you? You didn't get the email?'

Did we get the email? I don't know. Has anyone else received it? Or just Daniel? If so, why just him?

She shuts her eyes. Sees the photographs of the girls on the bedroom wall in her mind's eye, and she knows that Daniel's right.

People have to know.

'OK,' she says. 'Do what you have to do. You haven't got any idea why you specifically were sent this email?'

'No. But I'm the lead reporter in the city's pre-eminent news organisation, so it's hardly that surprising, is it? If they've got local connections.'

'But shouldn't they have gone to the national media?'

'Maybe they have, who knows? It'll only take two seconds, then it'll be everywhere else anyway. Maybe they wanted to maintain the local angle. How the hell should I know? They must have known it would spread, whatever they chose to do.'

'OK. Thanks again. We'll be in touch. Not least Forensics, when they get to tracing the email. Can you forward it to me?'

'Of course.'

'Good.'

Then silence on the line.

'How are things otherwise?' Daniel asks after something like ten seconds, which feel like a year. 'I heard about your mum . . .'

'Sorry. I haven't got time to talk about that now. I need to get going with this.'

She hangs up.

Civilian casualties cannot be ruled out . . .

The photographs of the scene seem to have been lifted from various newspapers. Sharp and edited, the way that professional news photographers' pictures always are.

The yellow plastic sheeting clearly visible in the pictures of the square yesterday.

Doesn't want to think about what's under it.

. . . war on Sweden's banks. They and their greed will be wiped out.

Can this be true? Malin wonders. Is the demon of money behind this? The bizarre greed of the banks and financiers, biting itself in the tail?

Half an hour later the entire investigative team is standing in Sven Sjöman's office.

Waldemar Ekenberg, Börje Svärd, Johan Jakobsson, Zeke, Malin, and Karim Akbar. They're staring at the computer, trying to grasp something that they imagine is there.

'That's it, then,' Waldemar says. 'We just have to get hold of the nutters behind the Economic Liberation Front, then case solved.'

'Doesn't that site look a bit thin?' Johan says. 'And I haven't come across any Liberation Front in my search of extremists in the city up to now. The ones around here seem mainly interested in animal rights.'

'New groups do pop up,' Börje says. 'Who knows what a financial crisis and insane levels of injustice can drive people to, how desperate they might get?'

'We'll get the technical guys to try to trace the email and the server the site's hosted on,' Sven says. 'We haven't heard anything from any of the other media, and the *Correspondent* put the details up on its site five minutes ago, so the chances are that the email was only sent to Daniel Högfeldt.'

'Which suggests a local connection,' Börje says.

'Well, it might do,' Malin says, 'but at the same time they might be using the *Correspondent* to get us to think that they have a local connection.'

'If they're any good at technology,' Johan says, 'they could already be a hundred steps ahead of us. It might be impossible to track them down this way.'

'How many of them can there be?' Zeke wonders.

'It's impossible to say,' Sven replies, updating the site on his computer.

The page has changed.

At the top there is now a videoclip linked to YouTube.

Sven clicks to start the film.

A man wearing a grey hooded jacket and black jeans, with a black mask over his face, is standing in what looks like a warehouse with a sheet of paper in his hand. The hand holding it appears to belong to a white-skinned person.

'This looks like an Al-Qaeda video,' Karim says. 'One of the ones where they cut the head off some westerner they've captured.'

'Shit,' Zeke says, and Waldemar exclaims: 'We're going to get that bastard.'

Malin thinks it takes an age before the man starts reading from the sheet of paper into the camera.

A sharp but slightly hoarse voice. No accent, and evidently distorted to make it hard to recognise.

'People of Sweden,' the man says. 'Stay away from the banks. You never know when the next greeting from the Economic Liberation Front will come. The banks and finance companies and venture capitalists must be punished, wiped out. Quake, oh ye capitalists, and let a new age be born, with new ethics and compassion between people, free from avarice.'

Then the clip ends.

The detectives stand in silence around Sven's computer.

Malin thinks that something like this was bound to come sooner or later, however this all fits together.

She looks out of the window.

Towards the hospital. Where nurses and carers slave for long hours for a fraction of what the fat-cats in Stockholm earn, and have always earned, for pressing buttons, for lunatic business deals that have driven the country into the financial abyss. The hospital where patients are given substandard food. Where the unemployed and lonely and anyone surplus to requirements nowadays fill the psychiatric wards with their despair and angst.

Greedy vampires.

Obviously someone was bound to react in the end.

A cloud drifts in front of the sun and darkens both the day and the room.

'Bloody hell,' Waldemar says. 'I'd happily take him out with a shot to the back of the neck. Looks like he's a Swede.'

'For God's sake,' Sven says. 'None of that talk. Pull yourself together, Ekenberg. But you're right, he seems to be Swedish. We need to keep our heads clear and take this one step at a time, and work through the investigation methodically. OK, this might be the right line, but as far as we know it could also be a red herring, a few idiots playing a prank and trying to exploit the situation.'

'Do you believe that?' Waldemar says. 'Does he look like he's joking? I say, let's burn the nutters out of their holes.'

'We need to get someone from the technical division to analyse the video. See what we can get from that,' Sven says, then there's a knock at the door, and a moment later a freckled female constable pops her head in.

'A courier's just delivered the surveillance recordings from the camera outside the entrance to the bank. The others will be here as soon as they've identified them,' she says, holding out what looks like an ancient videocassette in her hand. 'The bank's head of security has written some notes. He says we ought to look at the video as soon as possible.'

13

Are we about to see the face of the murderer?

Malin feels adrenalin clutch at her heart, making it race.

The entire investigative team has moved into their usual meeting room, where someone has wheeled in a television and video player.

The nursery playground is empty and the beautiful spring weather makes the swings and climbing frames look as if they're crying out for children.

Still no results from Forensics, even though Malin knows that Karin Johannison and her team have worked through the night. What was it that exploded? What sort of substances was the bomb made of? How was it detonated? Remote control? A timer? And exactly how powerful was it?

None of us has had time to reflect properly, Malin suddenly realises.

The bomb exploded yesterday.

Then we ran off in every direction we could think of, and now the Economic Liberation Front, and this video that we're about to watch.

Things have been happening, one after the other, and she gets the feeling that they're all in a kind of vacuum. It's as if none of the officers in the investigating team has yet realised that a bomb actually went off in the largest square in the city.

We're rushing in all directions, never stopping for breath,

Malin thinks. We're haring after ideas the moment they pop into our overcrowded heads. No time to stop, no time to think. A growing but unspoken sense of panic, wrapped up inside the question that we can probably all hear being whispered within us: is this more than we can cope with?

Can Linköping deal with this? Fifteen thousand people visited the city's churches yesterday. Trying to find comfort where they imagined it might be found. And there are more candles in the main square, more flowers the whole time, people have evidently started ordering flowers to be delivered to the square from Stockholm, Gothenburg and Malmö, and God knows how many other towns.

This can't be happening. Hasn't happened.

But it has happened. And then what do you do? When you can no longer deny it, and are left alone with your fear? Then you send a flower, seek comfort in our collective fate. And maybe it's even some sort of a relief that there's actually a real, tangible crisis, not just the slow, abstract assault of the financial mess?

What about me? Malin thinks.

I buried Mum yesterday.

Where do I want to go? What do I want?

If I slow down, I might be forced to answer that question.

Better to watch the video.

Then Karim Akbar presses play, and the police officers lean back in their uncomfortable chairs and watch the recording, shot with an extremely wide angle. At the edge of the screen a man in a black hooded jacket leaves a bicycle beside the cashpoint and then walks away slowly, heading off towards Hospitalstorget.

Soundless black-and-white pictures.

Silent police officers.

The posters in the bank's windows are clearly visible in the video. Kurtzon Funds.

Kurtzon.

Malin recognises the name, but can't put it into any real context. Some sort of new investment company? But that isn't interesting, watch the video instead.

A black rucksack is fastened to the bicycle's parcel rack.

The bastard, Malin thinks. But who is he? The same person in the video on YouTube?

Then, as if in a circle in the middle of the screen, they see the two girls wearing pink jackets and jeans running towards the cashpoint, as a blurry man with bare arms leaves the bank.

Impossible to see who the man is.

An ordinary customer.

But doesn't she recognise him?

No. I'm just imagining things, and none of the others reacts.

But dear God. I recognise the girls.

They walk close to the cashpoint, then disappear again.

Then, maybe five minutes later and after two more customers, they're back again, the children, and you can just make out their mother behind them.

Their hair dark grey on the black-and-white video, and, in spite of the poor quality of the recording, it's possible to see that their eyes are shining, that they're enjoying their morning in the square, conquering the world with each moment.

Malin closes her eyes.

Zeke has seen the same thing as her. No doubt any more, it's the Vigerö twins, the shattered, dead children.

The force of the bomb in the rucksack must have been directed towards the cashpoint and out towards the square. Not impossible for an expert to arrange.

The cycle was utterly destroyed. They didn't find any twisted remnants outside the bank. Karin would have noted it if there had been any. It must have melted, and then been turned into atoms? In the dynamics of an explosion most things are possible.

Then the girls look at the cycle, at the rucksack, as if it's making a noise, then everything turns black and silent.

Malin.

We see ourselves in our last tremulous seconds, but we can't feel any pain.

It didn't have time to hurt.

We're happy about that now.

Malin, what are you going to do?

Are you worrying? You saw the man who left the bike outside the bank. It was him. He was the one who blew us up, who made us dead, because that's what we are, we're dead.

Everything went dark, Malin.

Then light and clear and cold. As if we can't be free from ourselves until everyone is free.

You no longer understand what we mean, do you? All the lonely people, full of life, longing.

Malin.

What do you see when you see us get blown up? See us become dead?

The other children are alive, the captives, and we're jealous of them for that.

But we don't want to be where they are. It's disgusting and horrid there, and the boy is crying and his big sister tries to comfort him, but it doesn't work, Malin, it doesn't work, because they're so alone and scared of everything that's beyond the darkness, scared of all the fury.

See us, Malin, see us as we were.

* * *

Soundless pictures, but Malin still thinks she can hear the murmuring of the two little girls. But she can't work out what they're saying.

So she shuts out the murmuring and listens to Sven Sjöman.

'Consider this an official investigative meeting,' he says. 'We need to structure our work. We've been too unfocused so far. To start with: what are we looking at here?'

'That could be the same man as in the video on the Economic Liberation Front website,' Johan Jakobsson says. 'Or someone else. The style of clothes is the same, though. And the build is similar.'

Then Johan falls silent, but the others realise that he wants to say something else.

'That fucking bastard,' he snarls. 'I hope he burns in hell.'

All the other police officers look at him, ashamed that they're thinking the same thing, surprised at Johan's outburst, which is anything but characteristic of him, and Waldemar Ekenberg says: 'He'll burn.'

And then Malin sees Börje Svärd take a deep breath.

'For God's sake, guys, you need to tone this down a bit. We're all upset at what's happened, but this really isn't helping.'

Then Sven speaks again.

'So now we know that the bomber arrived by bike from the north, and heads off to the east. That gives us the chance to try to pinpoint other security cameras very precisely.

'The process of tracking down recordings is already underway,' he goes on. 'And I want the pictures from those cameras inside the bank. And we need to get hold of the other people in the video if we haven't already done so. We'll have to put out a request for information from the public as well. Did anyone see a man in a black hooded top in the area? Notice him, recognise his face, maybe the way he looked? And obviously the technical team will have to analyse the video as well.'

Sven falls silent, suddenly seems tired of his own voice. 'Any thoughts?' he asks eventually.

'It looks like he was alone,' Zeke says. 'But we don't know if he had any accomplices nearby, or somewhere else. But presumably we can assume that the bomb was in the rucksack.'

'We can,' Sven says. 'Karin's going to confirm that. Let's start with the Economic Liberation Front. There were pictures of banks in various towns on their website. I'll make sure the police in those towns know, and can take the necessary precautions. I'm sure the Security Police will be doing the same, and I'll get the computer guys in Forensics onto it. From now on they're going to have to put all their resources into tracing the email to Daniel Högfeldt, the video, and the website.'

'Are they going to contact YouTube to find out who uploaded the clip? And which IP address it came from?' Johan asks.

'I assume so. As you all understand, this new group is our primary line of inquiry. We need to dig them out, at all costs. In all likelihood the man outside the bank is a member of the group. Johan, have you got any ideas about known activists who could be behind something like this? Or the pattern at least, first the attack, then a website and threats?'

The other officers in the group turn expectantly to Johan, and Malin can see he looks worried.

'Well, this is definitely not the work of right-wing extremists. It goes against their whole ideology. But I did come across a Sofia Karlsson during my search yesterday, a left-wing radical,' he says. 'A diehard vegan, and she's done time for burning down a mink farm in Kisa. Twenty-five years old now. Back then, she and her accomplices used a similar method. They called themselves the Animal Guardians. I remember her from her interviews. She seemed pretty furious about almost everything, but simultaneously capable and intelligent. And evidently she lives in Linköping. We could always have a word with her as a first step.'

'Good, Johan,' Sven says. 'Malin, Zeke, get onto that as soon as we're finished here.

'Anything else, Johan?' Sven goes on, and Malin thinks how good it is that he's in command, bringing all his experience and authority to bear.

'From what I was able to find yesterday, she was really the only interesting one. But I'm happy to carry on looking.'

'OK, carry on with that,' Sven says.

'What about the Security Police?' Zeke says. 'They ought to know something, what can we expect from them?'

'Nothing,' Karim says. 'Absolutely nothing.'

'They called earlier,' Sven says. 'I gave them what we had, but they had nothing for us. Or so they said.'

And before her Malin can see a dozen men dressed in suits. The nightmare image of the Security Police, sweeping in and ruining everything in their path with suspicions and wrong-headed, clumsy assumptions.

'It's nice not to have too much to do with them,' Malin says, thinking: the bastards from the Security Police presumably think they're better than a group of ordinary detectives in a provincial backwater.

She realises how foolish her thoughts are. Stop feeling inferior, Fors. You aren't.

'National Crime?' Börje asks.

'No, for fuck's sake!' Waldemar exclaims.

'Not at the moment,' Karim says. 'Too many cooks.'

'Let's get on with analysing the video and the clip on YouTube.'

Then he falls silent. Stares out into the room as if he's waiting for someone else to suggest something, but the other detectives remain silent.

'Any other ideas of how to crack the mystery of the Economic Liberation Front?'

'We could check the experts on domestic security in Swedish universities?' Zeke says. 'See if they know anything about the Economic Liberation Front?'

'Good idea,' Karim says. 'I'll get onto that.'

'Anything else?' Sven says. 'We'll just have to hope we get something once the public have seen the recording and the clip.'

Malin holds her breath.

Listens to the others breathing.

Knows they're up against it now, that their chances are best during the first seventy-two hours of an investigation.

'OK,' Sven says. 'That's what we'll do with the Economic Liberation Front. It could be a group, a single individual, or something else entirely. Well, are we all in agreement? We'll just have to see what turns up. OK, now on to the general state of the investigation.'

Sven gives them a summary, as if he were telling them about a holiday or a conference in a luxurious country house.

None of the interviews with people at the scene, or those with minor injuries came up with anything of interest. But the number of people questioned could be expanded to cover anyone who saw anything unusual anywhere in the city centre. Neither the staff in the bank nor the branch manager seemed to have noticed anything particular. Some of the staff were still in shock, but they had all been questioned now.

And the Islamic line of inquiry.

Nothing had cropped up there. And the interview with the imam hadn't led to anything. Maybe it had been a clumsy and over-hasty response. From now on caution and respect were the order of the day there, absolute caution.

'I don't want to have any accusations of racism in the media,' Karim says when Sven stops talking.

'He seemed very reasonable,' Malin says. 'And the mosque was full last night. They're just as worried as everyone else.'

'Good,' Karim says. 'But I'd like to point out that I still think it was right to talk to Al Kabari. He, if anyone, ought to know what the mood is among Linköping's Muslim community.'

'We'll keep that line of inquiry open anyway,' Sven says. 'We can't afford to drop anything as things stand.'

'I agree. We can't drop the Islamic angle. But even so, we know who did it now,' Waldemar protests. 'It has to be that bastard Liberation Front. Why would any innocent group claim responsibility for something where two girls were murdered?'

'For the fun of it,' Malin says, crossing her legs under the table.

'That's horribly cynical,' Johan exclaims. 'For the fun of it?'

'Or to take the opportunity to focus attention on issues they think are important.'

'Bollocks,' Waldemar says. 'We'll have them soon enough.'

'Any other lines of inquiry?' Zeke wonders. 'Biker gangs? Cashpoint raiders?'

'We can drop the cashpoint idea,' Sven says. 'There's nothing to suggest that was what it was. And the way things look at the moment, we've got no connection to any biker gangs.'

'OK,' Zeke says.

'What about the explosives? Where could they have got hold of them? What sort was it, and what reagent did they use?' Börje asks.

'Karin is going to let us know. Soon. You and Waldemar can take a look into how they might have got hold of it,' Sven says. 'Have there been any thefts from munitions stores recently? Or construction companies that stock explosives? Can you buy anything online in Sweden? You seem to know a fair bit about that, Börje.'

'I'm just an interested amateur,' Börje says, putting his hands out. '*The Anarchist Cookbook* is bizarre, but it's an entertaining read. It'll be easier to track things down once Karin's worked out what was involved.'

Outside the windows the doors of the nursery have opened.

Brightly coloured youngsters pour out.

They throw themselves at the various apparatus, giddy at their bodies' capacity for movement.

Malin thinks of Tove, who must be in school at the moment, the way her movements are so completely different from these children's, so languid, almost lethargic, yet still conscious and measured, unbelievably sexy to any boy of her own age. Then she thinks of her dad, probably clearing away the last remnants of the previous day's gathering after the funeral.

And she thinks of her mum, who in all likelihood is ash now, and it occurs to her that they haven't discussed what to do with the ashes. Are they going to scatter them some-where? They didn't do it immediately after the funeral, so Dad probably has the urn at home. Are they going to be scattered on the golf course in Tenerife? Or is she going to end up in the memorial grove where Malin sometimes goes when the sense of loss for something she's not quite sure of gets too much for her.

Have I been suppressing something? she wonders again. And if so, what? But she has no time to linger on that thought before she is roused from her reverie by Sven's voice, summarising what they know about the girls, and their mother, whose operation the previous day was a success, though she still isn't out of danger.

'We can't talk to her yet, according to the doctor I spoke to,' Sven says. 'Tomorrow at the earliest. Possibly even later than that.'

'You saw the video,' Malin says. 'The bomb could have been aimed at them. It was detonated, if they used remote control, when the girls had returned to the cashpoint.'

'Hardly,' Waldemar says. 'That's too much of a long shot.'

'Malin, Waldemar's right,' Sven says. 'We can assume that the family were innocent victims.'

'Should we put a guard on Hanna Vigerö in the University Hospital?'

'You heard what I said.'

Malin nods.

Thinks that the girls were probably just that: innocent victims. They were certainly innocent, no matter what the circumstances.

Then Waldemar says: 'Those bastards could have spared the kids. If they wanted to. That's obvious enough. But they wanted to prove they meant business.'

14

Time spares nothing and no one.

The clock on the dashboard says it's eleven o'clock, and the radio news comes on as Zeke and Malin turn into Rydsvägen and glide slowly past the northern end of the old cemetery. The trees inside the cemetery wall seem eager to catch Malin's attention. Their crowns are covered with little pink flowers that sway in the wind, and it seems to Malin that the flowers want to stay, hold on to the branches at all costs, even though it's a hopeless battle.

You can't fight against what you are.

Just ask someone who knows.

One thing that's changed since she stopped drinking is that her intuition, what some people might call her visions, has become stronger. Especially in her dreams. As if the absence of alcohol makes her consciousness clearer, more receptive to things that are hard to explain.

It doesn't scare her.

But she knows it scares a lot of people.

Instead she tries to open herself up to her perceptions, accept the gift of being able to see more, intuit more than other people do.

But what does it mean?

There's no point trying to make any sense of it.

She sees it like this: a wind blows through a leafy treetop. You hear a voice whispering. Or else you don't hear it. Nothing more to it than that, really.

Anxious shadows on the grey, moss-covered stones of the cemetery wall.

The flowers, vibrant with both life and death, an ending but also a beginning. Pink is the colour of everything newborn, isn't it?

The memorial grove.

Malin can't see it through the flowering trees. Is that were Mum's going to be laid to rest?

'How's your dad doing?' Zeke asks.

'He seems to be dealing with it OK.'

'How about you?'

'Me?'

'How are you dealing with it?'

'Don't worry about me.'

'You know I do that automatically.'

'What for?'

Zeke laughs.

'Because you've got previous as a major fuck-up. That's why.'

Malin grins back. They drive on in without talking.

She concentrates on the news.

The bombing is the lead story.

The newsreader says nothing they don't already know, then he goes on to talk about deserted banks, and that there are reports from various parts of the country that people daren't even walk past banks.

Nordea's head of PR says they're raising the level of security in all their premises, and that, like all the other banks, they're keeping their branches closed until further notice, but that it looked as if it would be entirely safe to carry out your business with the banks within a day or two.

'Naturally, we're taking this extremely seriously.'

'Like fuck,' Zeke snarls, and outside the car it's the sort

of spring day you dream about, when the mercury climbs unexpectedly high and there are just a few confused clouds in an ice-blue sky.

'Nice that those bastard banks are going to be closed for a while,' Zeke goes on. 'Like a physical sign of the shame they ought to feel after all the trouble they've caused in the past few years.'

'I'd be happy to see them stay open if it meant we could have avoided this,' Malin says.

'Obviously, Malin, that wasn't what I meant.'

'I know.'

They drive past Gamla Linköping.

People are wearing less with each passing day. As if they dare to trust the spring and the warmth, in spite of what's happened.

Some of the blocks of flats they pass could do with painting, but the council has had to postpone the work, they don't have the money now that the number of unemployed in the city is going up. There's also been talk of shutting the Tinnerbäck pool one day a week, and withdrawing funding for the city's playgrounds.

Fucking banks.

Don't those bastard bank directors and venture capitalists realise that their greed is directly connected to the country's children being worse off? That they run the risk of hurting themselves on broken climbing frames?

Responsibility, Malin thinks, has little meaning these days, except for the responsibility for your own bank account.

The radio is droning on about some Komodo dragons being born in Kolmården Zoo, the first time that's ever happened in captivity.

What do baby lizards eat? Malin wonders. Then she sees a mental image of ten baby lizards ripping a mouse apart.

Who's ripping Linköping apart?

Sofia Karlsson?

The activist.

Who spent two months in Skänninge Prison for the attack on Kindstrand's now defunct mink farm in Kisa. She only got two months because it was impossible to prove that it was her, or the group she belonged to, that set fire to the farm. She was found guilty of making threats against the owner.

Animal rights activist.

Proud of ruining decent businesses, proud of her claim that animals were as equal in value as people.

Malin closes her eyes.

Hears the car engine do its job. Thinks: Just let me manage to do mine.

The stairwell of the yellow-brick, two-storey block of student flats smells of a mixture of pizza and piss.

It's a hundred metres from here to the university, and the students are among the more fortunate residents of Ryd.

The people living in the ordinary council blocks are generally regarded as the dregs of the city: unemployed labourers, immigrants, single mothers with young kids, alcoholics, people with mental illnesses.

No one chooses to live in Ryd of their own accord, except for the students who have managed to get hold of a student flat.

And that's what Sofia Karlsson has done.

According to Johan Jakobsson she's studying biology, which makes Malin think of worms eating their way through a wooden coffin as she stands in the stairwell and rings the doorbell beside the graffiti-covered door of the flat.

Zeke standing beside her.

Leaning forward slightly.

Ready.

Ready to draw his pistol if anything happens. Ready for the violence, the force needed if they think they're getting close to something.

The door opens and a thin, petite young woman in her mid-twenties pokes her head out and looks at them.

Sparkling nose-rings, several in each nostril, and her hair, twisted into tight dreadlocks, shines greasily in the light falling through the windows of the stairwell.

Cops.

That's what she seems to be thinking. Then she makes an attempt to close the door, but Zeke puts his foot in the way.

'Not a chance.'

And Sofia Karlsson gives up, opens the door, lets them in, and the single room of the flat is tidier than Malin was expecting. Neat and organised, with small china animals on a crocheted cloth on top of a metre-high bookcase. There's a computer on a table, and a sofa bed covered by a rasta-coloured blanket. A faint smell of hash.

The only indication of Sofia Karlsson's activism is a poster for Animal Guardians.

A polecat eating a woman in a fur.

Blood pouring from wounds in the woman's legs.

Sofia Karlsson says nothing, just sits down on the bed and looks at them.

Malin and Zeke stand in front of her and show their badges.

'Can we assume you know what's happened?' Malin says.

'No, what?'

'The bomb in the main square. The Economic Liberation Front. Do you know anything about them?'

'No. Why would I know anything about them? Apart from what I've heard on the radio this morning and seen on the Net.'

'Have you looked at their website?' Zeke asks.

Sofia Karlsson nods.

'Do you know anything about them?' Malin asks again. 'Their pattern of behaviour, action followed by a media campaign, is very similar to what you did with the mink farm.'

'So you think I'm involved in some fucking explosion?'

Zeke takes a step forward and leans down towards Sofia Karlsson: 'Two children are dead,' he whispers. 'If you know anything, you'd better tell us.'

Zeke backs away, then sweeps his hand over the bookcase, knocking off the small glass animals, which shatter on the yellow linoleum floor.

At first Malin wants to stop him, then changes her mind. At a time like this they need Waldemar Ekenberg's type of anger.

Sofia Karlsson stands up and yells: 'You're mad, you fucking pigs. Completely mad.'

'Sit down,' Malin says, and Sofia Karlsson sinks onto the bed again, shaking her head.

'I had a lecture when the bomb went off yesterday. You can easily check that.'

'What, you think we suspect you?' Zeke says, in a exaggeratedly friendly tone of voice.

'Why else would you be here?'

'We're fishing,' Malin says. 'Trying to find a bomber, a child-killer. Do you happen to know anyone like that?'

'You can leave now if you're only here to bully me.'

'What do you think about what they've done?' Zeke says. 'About what this Liberation Front claim to have done?'

Malin looks at the computer.

Can we seize it?

No. We've got nothing on Sofia Karlsson. Just a link in a line of inquiry, if it can even be called a link.

Sofia Karlsson looks up at them from her bed.

Runs her hands over the bedspread.

A pained, anxious expression in her eyes is replaced by a cool, delighted, almost manic look.

'I think it's great,' she says. 'The banks needed to be taught a lesson. Greed has to be wiped out. And that might mean sacrifices have to be made.'

Malin stifles an urge to punch her in the face, to beat some sense into the girl in front of her.

'But I don't know anything about it,' Sofia Karlsson goes on. 'Not a thing.'

'Do you smoke dope?' Zeke asks. 'It smells like it.'

Sofia Karlsson doesn't answer. Just stares past Malin and Zeke.

As they leave the house in Ryd a black Volvo pulls up outside the door and two men in jeans and almost identical blue jackets get out.

They must be the Stigman and Brantevik that Sven mentioned.

Malin and Zeke nod to them.

'All yours,' Zeke says as they meet on the pavement. 'All yours,' and the two Security Police officers can't help smiling, as if this is all a game to them.

Security Police pigs, Malin thinks. You think you're pretty special. But tell me, what good have you done at all in the past twenty years?

She opens the car door with a jerk.

Once they're out on the main road, four motorbikes drive past them.

Hang on.

Hang on a moment.

The man in the video, by the cashpoint, the one coming out of the bank.

'Get back to the station. I want to watch the video of the cashpoint again.'

'There. There!' Malin says, pausing the recording.

The meeting room is stiflingly warm from the spring sunshine, her stomach feels swollen with the flatbread wrap she ate at Snodda's kiosk on the way back to the station.

Zeke is sitting beside her, and they both lean closer to the screen, and Malin points at the fuzzy outline of the bare-armed man leaving the bank just before the explosion.

'Do you see him? Do you see who that looks like?'

'No. I can just see a general outline.'

'Can we zoom in with this?'

'Malin, this is a twenty-year-old VHS, so I'm pretty sure we can't.'

Malin adjusts one of the video's controls and the film from the surveillance camera moves on, one frame at a time.

'There.'

She pauses the picture. The man's face is suddenly clear.

'I bet you that's Dick Stensson,' Malin says.

Zeke screws up his eyes.

'Bloody hell, you might be right.'

Dick Stensson.

Leader of the local biker gang, the Dickheads, loosely associated with the Hells Angels. They've never been able to get him for anything on the long list of his suspected crimes: extortion, drugs, fraud, weapons offences, assault, murder . . .

'If it is him,' Malin says, 'what was he doing in the bank just a couple of minutes before the explosion?'

'You mean he could have been the target?' Zeke says.

'Los Rebels in Rimforsa are flexing their muscles, we know that. And they're associated with the Bandidos.'

'No one in the bank mentioned Stensson when they were questioned after the bomb.'

'Maybe he's just another ordinary customer to them,' Malin says. 'He's not well-known to the general public. Is he?'

'No,' Zeke says. 'And the people in the bank could have been more shaken-up than they seemed.'

'It still seems odd that he was in the bank just before the explosion,' Malin says.

A hint.

A spark.

And the investigation is wrenched in another different direction. The moments of clarity and focus she felt after their last team meeting have dissolved into a new chaos, like the minutes following an explosion, when debris and dust sinks to the ground like sooty stars.

Or am I at the centre of an explosion? Malin wonders.

And I just don't realise it?

'It's still a bit odd,' Malin goes on.

'Stensson's got as much right as anyone else to have a bank account,' Zeke says. 'Maybe we should take a trip out to Jägarvallen, the Dickheads' hangout, and ask Stensson what he was doing at the bank?' he adds.

'I think we should ask the branch manager first,' Malin says.

'I've got a better idea,' Zeke says. 'We let Waldemar and Börje talk to the bank manager. See if they can get him to tell them if Stensson was at the bank yesterday.'

Malin nods.

Waldemar Ekenberg isn't worried about ramming his pistol deep into someone's throat if he wants to make them talk.

The SEB branch manager might not have any idea of who Dick Stensson really is.

But letting Waldemar loose on him won't do any harm. Why should we show any compassion to a banker? There mustn't be any more explosions. And they don't deserve gentle treatment, those idiots in the banks.

'What about us? What are we going to do?' Zeke asks.

'Let's see what Forensics have come up with. You'll get to see Karin, Zeke.'

'Be careful, Malin,' Zeke says. 'Just watch it.'

Malin sees his eyes flash in the light of the frozen television screen.

You're still fucking her, Malin thinks.

God, I wish I had someone to make love to.

15

What must it look like when Zeke has sex with Karin Johannison?

They've been having a secret affair for almost two years now.

But they hide it well, Malin thinks.

Karin Johannison is sitting behind her desk in the National Forensic Laboratory. She is slowly stirring a cup of hot tea. Her straight blonde hair is hanging down over her aristocratic cheekbones.

She's wearing a thin white blouse that emphasises her breasts, and the walls of her windowless office are covered with shelves holding bundles of papers, files, and books in a fairly bohemian muddle. On the floor is a pink and red oriental carpet, and that overblown leather-clad office chair that she must have paid for herself. Malin recognises the design but can't place it, and it annoys her, and then she gets annoyed at the fact that she gets annoyed by such insignificant things.

They're each sitting on a leather stool opposite Karin.

How is she looking at Zeke?

I want you. Now.

That's how she's looking at him.

And in her mind's eye Malin once more sees the pair of them tightly intertwined on a bed in one of Linköping's cheaper hotels, perhaps the Stångå down by the railway station.

'We know what sort of bomb it was now,' Karin says. 'What explosives were used, and how it was detonated.'

'Shoot,' Zeke says, and Karin smiles.

'The bomb was detonated remotely. We found the remains of a detonator cap that's usually used for remote explosives, as well as parts of a transmitter. You can pretty much stand as far away from that sort of detonator as you like. We're talking about an IED here, an improvised explosive device. A bomb that someone put together themselves from various parts and substances. The basis for the bomb was acetone peroxide, or TATP as its known in the trade. The army keeps stocks of acetone peroxide, and it's also commonly used on construction sites in Sweden. It's probably the most widespread type of explosive.'

'So where exactly would someone get hold of some of this TATP?' Malin asks, leaning forward to show her interest, feeling the buttons of her dress strain, and wondering if she shows any skin when she does that. She thinks: He could have spared the girls, if he or they could see the bank from wherever they detonated the bomb. Does that mean anything? Apart from the fact that they wanted to show they meant business?

'You can buy it from a wholesaler if you've got a licence. Most construction companies are licensed. And if you're an officer in the military you can probably get hold of it. And of course there's a whole lot of illegal material circulating out there. Things that have been stolen from military stores and building sites. And you can get hold of that if you've got contacts in the underworld. You can probably buy it online as well, from other countries. But TATP has a short shelf-life, so there's a constant flow of it out on the market. Supplies need to be replenished, so whoever's behind this bomb must have got hold of it fairly recently.'

Zeke nods, and Malin sucks in her lips, thinking that

Börje Svärd and Waldemar Ekenberg can focus their search more precisely now that they know what was used, although that probably only makes it harder. Standard-issue explosives. Probably impossible to trace.

'Is TATP common in other countries?' Zeke asks.

'It's available in every country in Europe. It's produced in several countries, but not here in Sweden. If you wanted to get hold of some, you could. You could even make it yourself. A lot of the bombs in Iraq and Afghanistan are made of TATP, in case you're interested. And it's been used in several terrorist attacks, most recently in the attacks on public transport in London. But that doesn't necessarily mean anything, seeing as it's probably what anyone wanting to make a bomb would use.

'In Iraq and Afghanistan the perpetrators also use ammonium nitrate, which has a similar chemical structure, but that's too bulky for our case. You'd need at least a ton to produce the explosive effect we saw in the square.'

Karin can see how disappointed Malin is. And she realises how difficult it will be for the detectives to do anything useful with this new information.

'Sorry, Malin. I wish I could give you something more specific. But I can tell you that whoever put this bomb together knew what they were doing. This was no amateur job, but a stable device cased in some sort of metal construction. TATP is extremely sensitive, a lot of amateurs manage to blow themselves up, so this person knew what they were doing. And using a remote is pretty advanced.'

'So we're talking about a professional?' Zeke says, and Karin nods.

'And it looks like he was able to direct the force of the blast towards the square on purpose. But that's impossible to say for certain. The charge ought to have weighed between three and five kilos. That much TATP would be enough for a bomb like ours.'

'And the detonator?' Malin asks.

'I only found one small fragment. I'm afraid it isn't possible to say anything about it.'

The man in the black hoodie.

The man who left the bomb outside the bank, on the bike.

He must have left the square, Malin thinks, then stood somewhere and detonated the bomb. Could he see the square from there? The girls? Maybe he'd gone further, out of sight, because if he saw the girls getting closer and still detonated it, what sort of evil are we dealing with then? The demiurge itself, fashioning the world out of chaos, the skinless, bloody monster waking up in its pit in the spring after its winter sleep and setting out to hunt for human souls. A beast that kills for the sake of killing.

A finger pressing a button.

Possibly a solitary perpetrator. The head of the Economic Liberation Front? Or someone else? A biker trying to get Stensson? But the bomb missed Stensson by a considerable margin, and why would that happen if it was detonated remotely? But surely there are often problems with bombs? That seems to be the rule rather than the exception, judging by known cases, so we can't rule out the possibility that Stensson was the target.

It could also be a religious group, showing their strength by demonstrating that they can strike anywhere, at anytime, but there's nothing to support that theory.

Al Kabari probably keeps a close eye on his flock, Malin thinks. And I got a strong feeling that he was telling the truth, that he really does want to help create an integrated society.

'What about the detonator caps. Can they be traced?' Malin goes on.

'The same thing there, all I've been able to conclude is
that they were the most common sort. Maybe he or they
knew that the detonator caps would be practically impossible to trace.'

The three of them sit there not saying anything for a
while.

Karin takes a deep breath.

'And finally, I can confirm that the dead girls were the
Vigerö twins. Tuva and Mira. They saw a dentist when
they were five, and he took X-rays because they had unusual
teeth, some of them had grown together in pairs. We've
compared the records with what we found in the square,
and there's no doubt at all.'

'So now we know for certain what we already knew,'
Malin says.

Where there used to be panes of glass in the SEB bank in
the main square there are now large sheets of plywood, as
if someone has covered the windows in advance of a
powerful hurricane.

Waldemar Ekenberg and Börje Svärd knock on the
already replaced door. Behind them the memorial candles
have gone out and the flowers are already beginning to
wilt. But new people are arriving all the time, with new
candles, new tulips in the same fiery colours as the core
of the explosion, bringing with them new fear, a new,
strange sorrow that their sense of security has been pricked.

A young woman in a grey dress opens the door of the
bank a minute or so later.

They go in. In the absence of daylight the whole building
is like some dark chamber.

Some scared-looking cashiers are trying to appear busy
behind an oak-veneered counter, their jobs must be secure
in spite of the crisis. The only people who seem to be

earning more money than ever are the banks and their employees, despite their huge credit losses, Waldemar concludes.

It's stupid to be scared, he thinks as he approaches the counter, followed closely by Börje. If there's one bank that it's safe to visit, it must be this one, and he can feel his irritation rising.

Bastard bankers. His body is twitching for a chance to express its displeasure.

Fine, beige stone dust covers the internal ceiling. Some newly woken flies have wandered to and fro through the dust, leaving little trails that together form an unsettling, incomprehensible pattern.

Like a sketch of the whole investigation, Waldemar thinks as he pulls out his wallet from the back pocket of his brown wool trousers and shows his police ID to one of the cashiers.

'We're looking for your boss,' Waldemar says, trying to sound as intimidating as possible. 'I believe his name's Jeremy Lundin.'

He sniffs the air.

Only a day since the explosion, but it feels like much longer ago than that. The bank is almost completely undamaged, the bomb must have been planted by an expert, all the force directed outwards, towards the square, the people. But shouldn't it have been the other way around, Waldemar thinks, if the bank was the primary target? Shouldn't the force of the blast have been aimed towards the branch? But the bomber might have been nervous, and could have parked the bike with the rucksack the wrong way around.

For the first time he entertains doubts about the Economic Liberation Front. To start with he didn't even want to hear about this business with Stensson on the video, still less follow it up with an interview. But now he's starting to wonder if there might be something in it.

And why would the Economic Liberation Front appear out of nowhere like this? Mind you, that's what happened with Baader–Meinhof in the seventies. Out of nowhere.

Almost.

'He's in his office,' the young red-haired woman says.

'We want to talk to him.'

And the woman makes a call. Talks, nods, and when she hangs up Waldemar asks: 'Do you know if Dick Stensson was in the bank yesterday? He is a customer, isn't he?'

'I wasn't working yesterday, thank goodness,' the woman says. 'And I can't divulge anything about the bank's customers. You'll have to talk to Jeremy.'

'You know who Dick Stensson is?'

The woman shakes her head.

None of the bastards employed here mentioned Stensson yesterday when they were questioned. They didn't mention any customers by name, perhaps because they've had it drummed into them: our customers' identities must be kept confidential. Yet they still get milked for as much money as possible.

Or did the explosion just leave them confused?

It feels as if the whole world is turning too quickly.

Waldemar puts both hands on the counter in front of the woman.

'These are exceptional circumstances,' Börje says.

Waldemar's eyes narrow to thin strips. Almost without moving his lips he says: 'Two young girls were blown into tiny pieces. They were six years old, but a little bitch like you doesn't feel able to divulge anything. We're going to get the recordings from your cameras in here soon enough, and there's a good chance he's on there. You know who he is.'

The woman looks up at them.

Without fear.

More with a sense of clarity in her eyes.

Then she nods, says: 'He's one of the bank's customers, yes, but I don't know if he was here yesterday. You'll have to talk to Jeremy about that.'

'Thank you,' Waldemar says.

'You can go through to Jeremy now. The last door in the corridor over there.'

'Is Dick Stensson one of your customers, and was he here before the explosion?' Waldemar says, leaning across the desk towards Jeremy Lundin.

The branch manager, in his mid-thirties, overweight and dressed in a shiny blue suit, with his long blond hair slicked back over his head, looks horrified as he sits there in his chair. It looks as if he wants to pull back, away from Waldemar's nicotine- and caffeine-tainted breath, but also from his anger.

Jeremy Lundin pants, filling his pudgy cheeks with air, as his watery grey eyes try to understand what's going on.

'Calm down,' Börje says, taking on the role of good cop.

But Waldemar doesn't back down, and says: 'Listen, you little shit, Dick Stensson was in this bank just before the bomb went off yesterday, wasn't he?'

Jeremy Lundin drums his fingers on the pale desktop, looking past them at an empty wall.

'Stensson was here, yes. He's a customer here.'

'And you know who he is?' Börje asks.

Jeremy Lundin nods.

'And you, you little shit,' Waldemar says, 'didn't realise that this was extremely important information for us when you were questioned yesterday? You must know perfectly well who he is. And it's not entirely unknown for rival biker gangs to try to blow each other to pieces.'

'Why didn't you say anything?' Börje says, sitting down in one of Jeremy Lundin's visitors' chairs.

Waldemar remains standing, rocking back and forth towards Jeremy Lundin.

'I didn't think it was important. But now I can see that it might well be. I was thinking of calling you. But we're very careful with our customers' confidentiality. And he's a good customer. He has several successful businesses, all with accounts at this branch.'

'What was Stensson doing here yesterday?' Börje asks calmly.

'And you're going to tell us the truth,' Waldemar hisses, sitting down on Jeremy Lundin's desk, close to his computer.

'He was here to pay some money in.'

'I presume he brought cash? Does he do that often?' Waldemar asks.

'Every Monday morning, same time each week. At the counter out there. I took the cash in person yesterday. But don't get any funny ideas. He always has receipts to prove where the money has come from.'

'Same time every week?' Börje asks.

'Yes,' Jeremy Lundin says. 'There's nothing odd about that. I know about his reputation, but he's never been convicted of anything, and his companies are all legitimate. For us he's just another customer, like all the rest.'

Is he lying? Waldemar wonders. Probably not. For him Stensson's just an ordinary customer. Whose anonymity needs to be protected at all costs, no matter what the circumstances. And that way the bank and its profits are protected.

'At some point we'll be requesting all the details of Stensson's transactions here at the bank. You can be sure of that,' Waldemar says.

Jeremy Lundin smiles.

'Go ahead,' he says.

'One more thing: what do you know about the Economic Liberation Front?'

'Not a thing,' Jeremy Lundin says, as a greasy lock of hair falls across his brow.

16

It's almost four o'clock when Malin and Zeke park outside the industrial building that the Dickheads biker gang calls home.

Low clouds have drifted in from the south, and the clear May sky is smeared with grey, seeming to press the bikers' fortress into the ground.

Jägarvallen.

A sleepy little industrial estate a few kilometres from Ryd. Closed-up workshops, a popular dog kennels in front of a hesitant patch of woodland, and the biker gang's walled collection of buildings, with security cameras above the two rusty metal gates in the wall.

A doorbell and speakerphone.

They ring the bell, Malin's never been inside but has a mental image of an open gravel clearing with motorbikes, a few workshops and a run-down office building.

Drugs.

Extortion.

Cowboy builders. Protection rackets, fraud, counterfeit money. There are plenty of rumours about what the Dickheads are involved in.

Contract killings.

They got one of the leaders of the Hells Angels in Gothenburg for murder last year. But in Linköping they haven't got anywhere with their associates, the Dickheads, nor with their rivals in Los Rebels.

A hoarse, tired, almost hungover voice: 'Who are you and what do you want?'

Malin looks at the gates and feels that she's standing outside an impregnable fortress based on pure evil.

You mustn't let the shit get a foothold.

Because then it takes over.

The world becomes a dark place.

Zeke holds his ID up to the camera.

'Police. We'd like to talk to Dick Stensson. Is he here?'

A long silence. Then there's a crackle over the speaker and the gates open with a grinding sound, and Malin can see how well her mental image matched the reality. Big, long-framed motorbikes lined up in front of two grey-painted workshops.

What's in here? Where are the bodies hidden? What's locked away?

A shabby office building, then a bearded ape in a leather tunic and checked shirt striding towards them with threatening, heavy steps, holding out his hand and saying in a mild, friendly voice: 'Welcome to the Dickheads.'

A firm but not unpleasant handshake.

Zeke shakes his head gently as they follow the man towards the office building.

'Dick will see you at once,' the man says, and a minute later he leaves them alone in a waiting room outside a solid oak door, and if the building looks shabby on the outside, it's in perfect condition inside. The walls shine with white paint, and the ceiling is smooth, with inset halogen lights, and the leather armchairs beside Malin and Zeke are plump and modern. The black leather looks soft and malleable, and Malin knows it must have cost a great deal, and she has the impression that she's in the home of a successful entrepreneur with very good taste.

Then the oak door opens and a deep voice, slightly bored

but businesslike, calls from inside the room: 'You can come in now,' and a moment later Malin sees Dick Stensson sitting behind his desk in a grey hooded top, beside a large, flat computer screen. Then, as if he were a financial advisor in a bank or insurance company, he asks: 'And how can I help you?'

An amused smile on his thin, strong face, and Malin feels the whole of her weight as she sinks into one of the two office chairs positioned in the middle of the room.

'You were in the bank yesterday, just before the explosion. Is that correct?' Zeke asks.

Dick Stensson nods.

'That's correct,' he says. 'I was seriously lucky not to get caught up in those lunatics' evil act. I'd got as far as the castle when it went off. It sounded extremely loud, even up there.'

'What were you doing in the bank?' Malin asks.

'I was paying in money. The weekly takings from our various businesses, and a bit of private money. Nothing funny. I checked my shares. I've got a few Kurtzon global shares. Highly recommended.'

'The director, Lundin, said that you usually visit the bank at the same time each week.'

'He's a branch manager, not a director. I'm the sort of man who likes things to be regular,' Dick Stensson replies, leaning back, his eyes twinkling.

He's good-looking, Malin thinks. Almost attractive, with all his self-confident authority.

Is attractive.

Focus, now.

'You're not scared of too much regularity?' Malin asks, and Dick Stensson grins at her, then adopts a look of surprise.

'What would I be scared of?'

'Regularity might make you easy to get at.'

Dick Stensson nods.

'But it also proves that I don't care, doesn't it? That I'm the one in charge.'

Malin nods, thinking that the man in front of her is intoxicated with himself, he thinks he's invincible, and there's something in that which she reluctantly has to admit arouses her physical interest.

'So you don't think someone who was after you could have left the bomb outside the bank?' Zeke asks.

'I think that would be unlikely,' Dick Stensson says, as his fingers dance over the keyboard in front of the screen, as if he's answering an important email that can't wait.

'Why would it be unlikely?' Malin asks. 'You don't have any enemies?'

'No enemies,' Dick Stensson replies with a shake of his head.

'Have you noticed any increase in threats against you recently?'

'Why would there be any threats against me?' Dick Stensson says. 'I'm just an ordinary entrepreneur.'

'We've received reports of an increase in violence between you and—'

'Like I said. I'm just an ordinary honest businessman.'

'Lay off that crap,' Malin says. 'All three of us know perfectly bloody well who you are and what you do. Two young girls are dead. We're trying to find out what happened. If you've got even the tiniest idea that could help us, you'd better tell us, otherwise I'll be on your arse like a soldering-iron until you're in your grave.'

Dick Stensson smiles.

'So the little lady has a temper,' he says in an amused voice, and Malin feels like flying across the desk and wrenching the biker bastard's nose, but she holds back.

'Easy now,' Zeke says. 'Nice and fucking easy. So you

haven't got anything to tell us?' he asks in his steely voice, as if to demand respect from Stensson and calm Malin down.

'No.'

'You can be sure we're going to be taking a good look at your affairs pretty soon,' Zeke says. 'Don't be in any doubt about that. Every single scrap of paper.'

'Do the police have time for that?'

Dick Stensson is smiling again.

'And I don't know anything about that Liberation Front.'

'You've heard of it?' Zeke asks.

'It's the lead story on *Aftonbladet*'s website.'

'Did you see anything unusual in the square yesterday, anything at all?' Malin asks.

'I saw the girls. I saw them eating hotdogs and I thought they were pretty. I'm fond of children and I remember thinking that they were too beautiful to exist on our cruel planet. I remember thinking that, Malin.'

Dick Stensson fixes his gaze on hers. The look in his eyes is hard and cold and factual, and she tries to see some sort of warmth there, but there's nothing remotely like it.

'You ought to concentrate on catching those activists. In the Liberation Front. After all, they've confessed.'

'We're working on it,' Zeke says, and Malin can tell he's annoyed with himself for responding to Stensson, that he's somehow gone on the defensive, justifying himself, us, the police, to this bastard.

'Thank you. That's all,' Malin says, getting up.

We can hear engines, Malin.

Inside the workshop.

We hear them running, like nasty, hungry animals, hear them grunting out their song into the afternoon.

There are lots of closed doors there. Do they have to be opened?

Our names are on the Internet now. On the newspapers'

websites. Everyone knows who we were.

The Vigerö girls.

Mummy.

She's breathing. She's fighting. We're trying to persuade her to come to us, calling to her, but she's resisting, wants to stay where she is, but she'll probably come to us soon anyway.

She's got a temperature. She's dreaming dark dreams full of our faces and men who aren't human.

Men who consist of just a few limited characteristics.

We call for Daddy.

We can see the man in the hood, the man with the rucksack on the bike.

Who is he, Malin? Is he our fear? Is he our desire for more life? More and more and more.

We weren't ready, Malin. Aren't ready. We want more life. Can you give it to us?

We want you to help us, Malin, to become the girls we were, become the girls we were supposed to be.

Now the other children are calling again, Malin. They're calling for you.

'Come, come,' they call, and they call for their daddy, but he doesn't know where they are, and their mummy can't come because she's dead like us.

Actually, Malin, we don't want to help them. Because why should they get to live when we can't? But we're supposed to help each other, be nice, everyone's supposed to, so help them, Malin, save them.

They're waiting for you to come and save them. Do it, and you might be able to save yourself.

If you listen carefully, you'll be able to hear them too.

Grown-ups are supposed to come when you call.

But you can't hear them.

You can't hear them.

* * *

Zeke drops Malin off outside the sand-coloured apartment block on Ågatan.

There are lights on up in the flat.

Maybe Tove's there? Hope so.

Malin's longing to curl up next to Tove on the sofa. For Tove to feel that she's the sort of mum who cares. Who doesn't put her job, or drink, first. Who doesn't have to call from some bloody rehab centre and say she feels better.

I'm longing for a friend as well, Malin thinks. A proper friend to have a serious talk with. To dare to be silly with. Maybe Helen Aneman, the radio presenter, could be that sort of friend? Possibly. Helen is smart and funny and sympathetic. But somehow they never manage to meet up. And Malin isn't good at getting in touch out of the blue. Mostly she's only heard Helen's voice on the radio over the past year.

In the car on the way back from Jägarvallen she and Zeke talked about Stensson.

Let their thoughts roam free.

Could someone have wanted to get at him, then set up the Liberation Front website to mislead the police and focus suspicion elsewhere?

Maybe.

There's no limit to the lengths organised crime will go to. And those fucking crooks can live handsomely from their crimes, better than any ordinary wage-slave can dream of, living in the sort of luxury that would make an unemployed labourer pass out.

Honesty doesn't pay very well.

Or did a few activists simply take the opportunity to promote their message when the chance of getting a bit of attention came along?

As they were approaching the city centre, Malin called Sven Sjöman. Forensics hadn't made any progress with their digital inquiries during the day. The IP address of the Liberation Front was hidden behind some advanced technical trickery. The question was whether they would ever be able to get at it, or even persuade the IP provider to surrender the information. They were also trying to find out where the email to the *Correspondent* had been sent from, and had sent a request to YouTube for information about the video, but any answer from there was likely to take a while.

The source of the material used in the bomb would also be hard, if not impossible, to trace.

During the afternoon, Johan Jakobsson, Börje Svärd, and Waldemar Ekenberg had questioned more known activists, but that hadn't given them anything. No one knew anything about the Economic Liberation Front. It had appeared like a cloud of smoke after the explosion, and maybe it would vanish just as quickly, without trace. No other media apart from the *Correspondent* had received the email, and they'd spoken to a professor in Stockholm who had never heard of any financially motivated activism from the left in Sweden, let alone the Economic Liberation Front itself. Certainly, the communists had once protested outside the Enskilda Bank, but that was back in the seventies. And the professor thought it unlikely that they were dealing with right-wing extremists. However, he did think it possible that a new type of revolutionary movement might have arisen because of the financial crisis and the growing inequality in society. It was just a question of when those who felt they had been sidelined would react, not if.

Forensics were carrying on with their analysis of the surveillance video covering the cashpoint machine. The recordings inside the bank had provided little of interest, but they did show Stensson on his way towards Jeremy Lundin's office with a briefcase in his hand.

There had been no new activity reported from the bank branches identified on the website. All the country's banks were still closed until further notice. The Security Police had remained silent, nothing about any Islamic extremists, and Karim had spent most of the day trying to hold the media at arm's length. One of them would be bound to find out about the connection to the biker gang and Stensson, and then the papers would go into overdrive. There would be someone working in the bank, possibly even Jeremy Lundin himself, who wouldn't be able to resist the temptation to get their hands on some of *Aftonbladet*'s reward for a tip-off. They had decided not to dig any deeper into Dick Stensson's affairs for the time being, in all likelihood that was beyond the remit of this investigation, and they needed to maintain their focus, even if that was pretty much impossible in a situation that seemed to change by the minute.

'We'll carry on with this tomorrow, Malin,' Zeke says now, just before she closes the car door.

The sky has grown even darker.

There's rain in the air, maybe the spring is turning back into winter now. Maybe it'll be like up in Norrland, Malin thinks. Where nature leapfrogs spring and goes straight to summer, letting everything skip childhood. Maybe to avoid the torments and vulnerability of youth?

'Hope the rain holds off,' Malin says.

'Good work today, partner,' Zeke says, and Malin nods, wants to be able to accept praise, let it sink in.

'See you tomorrow.'

And she shuts the door.

Looks up at the flat.

My daughter.

Are you there?

She thinks about Tove.

About the little six-year-old girl she once was.

17

The Ikea clock in the kitchen is ticking.

It says quarter past eight, and Tove is calmly and methodically chopping a carrot, wants to cook even though Malin is too tired and thought they could splash out and get a takeaway from the Ming Palace.

Tove is wearing a short cotton skirt. A pink blouse, far too thin, black leggings, and when Malin first saw her outfit she felt like saying something, pointing out that she was hardly dressed, but stopped herself, thinking that this is probably what a teenage girl is supposed to look like in spring this year.

'Haven't you got any food in the flat?'

'I've got the ingredients for spaghetti bolognese, if you'd like that.'

'We could make a big batch and freeze some,' Tove said.

'OK,' and now the onion and garlic are sizzling in the large frying pan, and the water is bubbling in the saucepan.

'Shouldn't we call Grandad?' Tove says. 'He might be hungry.'

'Don't you think he'd be too tired?'

'With his Spanish habits? He told me he and Grandma used to eat dinner at ten o'clock.'

'Maybe he'd like to be left alone,' Malin says.

'I doubt it,' Tove says. 'I think you're the one who'd like to be left alone.'

Foiled, Malin thinks.

The truth-sayer.

The precocious girl.

Where's life going to take you, Tove?

'I'll call him,' Malin says, and an hour later the three of them are sitting in Malin's kitchen shovelling down spaghetti bolognese and cheap, freshly grated parmesan, not the expensive matured sort, and it feels good to be sitting there together, talking about nothing. When her dad asks about the case, and whether they're getting anywhere with the bomb attack against the bank, she tells them about their various ideas, and explains that they can't rule anything out at this stage of the investigation, or ignore any possibilities just because a new organisation has popped up in the media and claimed responsibility.

'People are talking,' her dad says, and Tove agrees.

'Everyone's frightened,' she says. 'Scared there's going to be another blast. Like they said on YouTube. Everyone's seen the film. Do you think there's going to be another bomb?'

Malin puts her cutlery down.

Thinks how wonderful it would be to have a glass of bog-standard red wine with the pasta, but instead they're drinking soda water, made in Malin's recently bought Sodastream, and the bubbles in the water remind her of the enticing bubbles in an almost ice-cold lager, but in a good way, nothing unpleasant.

'I don't know if there's going to be another explosion,' Malin says. 'But you can try to avoid it by not going near any banks.'

'Not so easy in Linköping,' her dad says. 'There's one on every square.'

'And there doesn't seem to be any end in sight for the financial misery,' Malin says. 'DT Trucks! I thought that was the most stable company in the world!'

More redundancies were announced today. Just when everyone had started to hope that things might be properly looking up, that it wasn't just the stock exchange rising, but the real economy as well. Three hundred and twenty people were going to be laid off from DT Trucks in Mjölby, a place that's already been hit hard.

'You can't take it for granted that anything's going to last forever,' her dad says laconically.

'And another service in the cathedral today,' Malin says. 'They were expecting a lot of people again. And apparently there's going to be a memorial service at lunchtime tomorrow in the square, and a minute's silence covering the whole district at four o'clock in the afternoon.'

'I think all the churches are open,' her dad says. Tove, who has been silent up to then, opens her mouth.

'Typical. As soon as something bad happens, they all run for the churches. God, how transparent.'

'That's a bit harsh, isn't it, Tove?' Malin wonders.

'Maybe. But surely not even God wants to provide comfort the whole time? She'd probably like a bit of attention when things are normal, don't you think?'

After dinner they sit on the sofa and watch an episode of an American series about a terrorist cell in the US. About how mild-mannered men turn out to be Muslim fanatics out for revenge for injustices against them and their families.

'This can't be the way it works in real life,' Malin's dad says, and Malin doesn't know how to respond, and says: 'They're probably a bit more obscure in real life. I guess. What do you think, Tove?'

Malin turns towards her daughter and sees that she's fallen asleep, sitting there with her mouth open and her eyes closed, on her way into deep, peaceful teenage sleep.

'I'll carry her,' her dad says, and Malin wants to protest,

wants to carry her teenage daughter through to her childhood bed herself, but stops herself. Let Dad do it.

'Great. She's too heavy for me. Your back'll be OK, won't it?'

'Nothing wrong with my back.'

'I'll go through to the bedroom first and pull the covers back.'

Malin's dad lays Tove down carefully on the bed. They leave her jeans and top on, and stand beside each other in the darkness, watching as Tove pulls the covers over her in her sleep, rolls onto her back and stretches her arms over her head.

'When children sleep like that, it means they feel safe,' her dad says.

'She's not a child any more.'

'You never slept that way, Malin,' he goes on. 'You used to curl up into a little ball. I used to think it looked as if you thought the whole world was after you. Wanted to hurt you.'

'Did you try to reassure me while I was asleep?'

Her dad nods.

'Every night. I used to go into your room every night, stroke your cheek, trying to persuade your dreams to stay gentle. But it didn't help. You always curled up, as if you were trying to protect yourself.'

'Against what, Dad? Come on, tell me now.'

Dad walks out of the bedroom.

'Children understand and feel much more than we think,' he says out loud as Malin hears him running some water in the kitchen.

They think I'm asleep, Tove thinks.

It's nice, lying here and listening to them talk, listening

to Grandad talk about Mum when she was little. I've never heard them talk like that before, and Mum doesn't even seem annoyed or irritated, I wonder what it is that she wants him to tell her?

Now Mum leaves the room as well.

Leaving me alone in here.

Tove stretches, and it strikes her that it never even crossed her mind to tell her mum about the letter, she'll have to do that another day, there's no immediate rush, and her mum would never be able to say no anyway.

Or would she?

She'll be cross.

Tove feels her stomach tighten, and realises that she has to tell her soon.

Because Mum will ask when she got the letter, and if too many days have passed she'll get suspicious, feel like she's being criticised and sidelined, and then she'll get angry, and then anything could happen.

Absolutely anything.

She mustn't start drinking again. She mustn't.

So how to tell her?

It's already turned into a secret now. Something that needs to be revealed. And she forged their signatures on the application.

Tove feels her thoughts wander off, and she daydreams her way into sleep, into high-ceilinged schoolrooms and benches full of people far more interesting than the bumpkins that make up most of her class at the Folkunga School.

People with style.

Like characters in a contemporary Jane Austen novel, Tove thinks, then the daydream vanishes into itself and soon she's sleeping without any awareness that she actually exists.

* * *

They're sitting at the kitchen table.

Sipping cups of herbal tea, and Malin can feel calmness spread through her body.

Her dad opposite her.

His familiar features look oddly different, his dark eyes full of feelings she can't place.

He wants to talk, I can see that, Malin thinks, then he says: 'Malin, do you want to hear something awful? Can I tell you something terrible?'

Malin feels a black, ice-cold fist hit her in the stomach, then the hand twists her gut and she feels frightened, doesn't want to hear what's about to come, is this the secret about to be revealed, is there even a secret? And she nods, can't manage to make a sound, and her throat feels dry, and all she can hear is the ticking of the clock.

'I don't miss your mum,' he says. 'I feel relieved, and I'm ashamed of feeling that.'

Malin feels the pressure in her guts ease.

So this is today's confession.

'I don't miss her either,' she says. 'And I don't feel guilty about it.'

'Don't you, Malin? I can't really believe that. I feel horribly guilty, but at the same time I still feel the way I feel.'

'Don't be too hard on yourself, Dad,' she says. 'That doesn't make anything better.'

'I'm not going back to live in Tenerife again. I'm going to stay here.'

'I thought you loved the heat?'

'I do. But she was the one who wanted to move there. Not me.'

'Are you going to sell the flat?'

'She could be difficult, actually pretty awful, we both know that.'

Malin smiles.

Understatement of the year.

'I just feel lonely sometimes. That's all.'

'You lived together for a long time. Maybe you're just suppressing your grief? That happens to a lot of people.'

'I think I've been grieving for a long time. For all the things that never happened,' her dad says, then they sit in silence opposite each other, drinking the soothing tea.

'Feelings are never wrong,' Malin says.

Her dad looks at her for a while, then says: 'No, maybe not. What about lies, then? Aren't lies wrong?'

'Which lies do you mean, Dad? There are different sorts of lies, aren't there?'

Her dad rubs his eyes.

Malin wants to ask him about her mum's ashes. He must have got the urn by now. Where's he going to scatter the ashes? But she can't summon up the energy to ask.

'I'm looking forward to getting to know Tove properly,' her dad says. 'I don't think it's too late.'

'It isn't,' Malin says. 'It's what she's been wanting. But those lies, Dad, which ones are they?'

'I'm going now,' her dad says, and he gets up, and she feels that this is the thousandth time he's running from something which is unavoidable, and she feels like shaking him, forcing him to tell her, the same way they sometimes have to force the truth out of a suspect.

But she doesn't move.

Hears him disappear out into the Linköping night.

What are my lovers doing?

Malin is lying naked in her bed, with her hand between her legs, but she feels tired and brittle.

Have I even got any lovers?

It's been months since I had Daniel Högfeldt. And it's

all over with Janne, for good, and that was more than eighteen months ago, and I haven't had anyone else since them.

She pulls her hand up, puts both hands on the covers and listens to the darkness.

Are you there, girls? she wonders. Are you the girl I once was? Am I the two of you?

She gets out of bed.

Goes over to the window and pulls the blind up and sees that the clouds have gone and that the night outside is clear and full of stars, with a pale light that seems to caress the whole planet and wish its inhabitants well.

She shuts her eyes.

Opens them again, and then she sees two girls drifting like wingless white angels outside her window.

She sees them talking, whispering, arguing, chasing each other in their own domain without noticing her.

She smiles and laughs at them, knows who they are, but doesn't want to disturb them.

Is everyone there? Are you there, Mum, and do you want to show yourself to me? Do you want to say sorry?

Then the girls stop and turn towards Malin, and suddenly the calm is gone from their faces, their flesh somehow torn into bleeding wounds, their eyes covered in layer upon layer of soot.

Their arms are stumps.

Their legs wriggle, torn off, and the girls scream, but no sound comes out of their mouths.

They're screaming.

I don't want to hear your screams, Malin thinks, and shuts her eyes again, hoping the girls will be gone when she opens them again.

Eyelids open.

And there is nothing but a lonely, star-covered sky.

Malin can hear the sound of her own breathing.

A solitary person's solitary breathing, and it's nothing, yet simultaneously everything.

18

Wednesday, 12 May

Malin picks the newspaper up from the hall floor, the whole of the front page is devoted to their case, to the bomb that has shaken the city to its foundations.

There's a picture of the lizard that's been born at Kolmården in the top corner.

Malin puts the paper on the kitchen table, reading it as she puts coffee on and feels her brain waking up as she goes about her various chores.

Every last little fucker wants to have their say.

The district governor; an overweight former agriculture minister; an old right-wing hag – they all say that people have to feel safe, and want to see more police on the streets. Karim Akbar says: 'No comment.' Mohamed Al Kabari talks about racism, and says it's tragic that just because a bomb has gone off, everyone is pointing at the city's Muslim community. But Kabari is also sympathetic: considering all the things that have been done in the name of his religion, it's understandable, but very sad. There's a statement from the Security Police, a Superintendent Frick, about the fact that they're conducting a parallel investigation alongside the Linköping Police, and that the collaboration is working well, in an almost exemplary fashion. The only one who hasn't spoken up is Dick Stensson, but Daniel Högfeldt has already found out about his visit to the bank, and is openly speculating about whether the bomb was aimed at Stensson.

Nor is there any new statement from the Economic Liberation Front, just their announcement, or manifesto. Screenshots in the paper, and the fact that no one has managed to find out anything about the organisation, that it was previously unknown, and that the police are treating the Liberation Front as their main line of inquiry, but that they can't assume that they were the people behind the blast. Karim Akbar: 'Previous international experience has shown that people and organisations often come forward to claim responsibility for similar acts, even though they had nothing to do with them.'

Pictures of the girls.

Tuva and Mira.

Vigerö.

Tuva and Mira Vigerö, six years old.

Their identity officially confirmed.

No other family found, apart from their mother. And she's still unconscious in hospital.

Then the surveillance tape. The man with the hood like a shadow in the pictures, it's impossible to see who he is.

Evidently the film has been shown on all the television news broadcasts. Maybe they've received some tip-offs about who their bomber might be?

The *Correspondent* has screenshots of the man in the paper. They've interviewed several Linköping residents, letting them have their say about the man in the video, and even if their hatred has been toned down for the newspaper, it's unmistakeable.

'No punishment would be enough for someone like that.'

'Shoot him.'

'Maybe he's the devil himself?'

It's as if the citizens needed something on which to focus

their anger, their hate, their fear, and now they've got it with the man in the video. He has become the evil demon to be hunted down and banished.

But he's still a person, Malin thinks. What he's done is terrible, and we're going to catch him.

The *Correspondent* knows as much as we do, Malin thinks, taking a bite of a sandwich. We haven't got a damn thing, really, apart from a load of suspicions and guesses. But plenty of successful police investigations have started out that way, with quiet voices whispering into tired police officers' ears.

Then Malin is jolted out of her thoughts by Tove, standing in the doorway in her dressing gown. She rubs her eyes, says: 'Good morning', and it occurs to Malin that Tove must have got up and taken her clothes off during the night.

'Up early,' Malin says.

'Is there any coffee?' Tove asks.

'Coffee? Since when do you drink coffee?'

'There's a lot you don't know about me, Mum.'

'Since when?'

Tove shakes her head, goes over to the coffee machine and pours herself a cup of the black, oily liquid.

Malin looks out of the window.

The sky is shimmering blue in a cold light with a hard core of warmth, and the trees outside the window, all their buds, seem ready to explode, burst into life, and Malin looks at Tove. Her breasts are obvious, almost impertinent, beneath the worn yellow towelling of the dressing gown.

Nothing came of the threatened cold rain from the night before. Nothing can hold back the power of spring.

At nine o'clock precisely the meeting of the investigating team begins.

Tired, hollow-eyed detectives sitting quietly around a table, playing at being detectives, playing the game, dancing the dance as they wearily run through the state of the investigation that the world demands should make progress, give the people the truth, deliver justice for the victims of violence.

Nothing has come of the video being screened on television yesterday. Nor did anyone seem to know who the man in the Economic Liberation Front's clip on YouTube was.

They work through all the other lines of inquiry.

And then silence.

An awareness of how little their ideas have actually led to, the feeling that they're already starting to get bogged down, even though it's only two days since the bomb went off.

And Malin looks at Zeke, who's sitting with his back to the children playing outside the nursery. The bags under his eyes are sagging and she can't help wondering if he went to see Karin Johannison last night after dropping her off. If he fucked her on a stainless steel bench down in the National Forensics Laboratory, beside a ventilator cabinet smelling of chemicals, and an oscillator for shaking test tubes.

Zeke's wife Gunilla has no idea he's having an affair. No one knows apart from me. But I'd never judge you, Zeke. You do what you have to do. We always do what we have to do. Don't we?

Waldemar Ekenberg breaks the silence: 'Are we going to take them alive?' he asks the room in general, and Johan Jakobsson and Börje Svärd say at the same time: 'For fuck's sake, Waldemar.'

'We've got some more information about the Vigerö family,' Sven Sjöman says, ignoring Waldemar's comment.

'Their finances look perfectly ordinary. Before his death the father was a mechanic at the lift factory in Kisa. It looks like Hanna Vigerö worked with people with learning difficulties, but only part-time since the children were born.

'Then there's her husband's car crash. Nothing odd about that either.'

'What's the latest on her condition?' Börje asks.

'More stable, apparently,' Sven says. 'But we still can't talk to her.'

Maybe you'll make it after all, Malin thinks. Maybe there's a slim chance, but how on earth could you move on from this?

Your husband's dead.

And now both your children.

Could I go on living if anything happened to Tove?

I almost drank myself to death the time I came close to losing her, and I almost drank my relationship with her into the ground as well.

Almost managed to do what the killer didn't.

What have I not put Tove through, really?

Malin feels the urge to go down to the gym in the basement, wants to feel a far-too heavy dumbbell drive the desire for alcohol out of her body, make it disappear for good.

And as soon as she thinks about alcohol, the urge is there again, and she digs the nails of one hand into the palm of the other, pressing until she feels a reassuring pain.

It works.

As usual.

'There was nothing unusual in their home. Nothing to suggest anyone had made any threats against them,' Malin says. 'Maybe we should check with the people she worked with? See if they know anything else about the family?'

'We can't waste resources on that,' Karim Akbar says.

'These are just ordinary people. Who happened to get in the way of a terrorist attack. Now we move up a gear in the hunt for the Liberation Front. Who are they? We need to look under every stone, interview anyone we can find with any activist connection, left- or right-wing, and keep on at Forensics, they must be able to come up with something.'

I'll look into Hanna Vigerö's background myself, Malin thinks, but knows it will have to wait, now she has to show her loyalty to the investigation as a whole, any division at this point could mean they lose what little momentum they have.

'That will have to be our main priority for the time being,' Sven says. 'Johan, Waldemar and Börje, you carry on with that. We'll put in a request for Stensson's records from the bank and get the Financial Division to take a look. There might be something there.'

Malin nods without quite knowing why. She shuts her eyes, hoping her brain can make sense of all this, but she can't find any structure in it, maybe they're looking in the right direction, but she's far from certain.

Then Sven's phone rings and she hears him muttering, saying yes, no, yes, yes, then he hangs up.

'That was Andersson from Forensics. They've worked out where the email to the *Correspondent* was sent from. It was a computer in the Sidewalk Café in the City Terminal, up at the Central Station in Stockholm.'

'I know where that is,' Malin says. 'There's bound to be a security camera there. We might be in luck.'

'We need to get hold of any recordings from there at once,' Sven says. 'It ought to be easy enough to find out who owns the building, and who provides the security.'

'Nothing definite about the email server?' Johan asks.

'Nothing,' Sven says. 'They haven't managed to get past

the anonymous sender of the initial mail from the Liberation Front.'

'OK. Does everyone know what they're doing now?' Karim asks in conclusion.

The officers around the table nod.

It seems to Malin that their various lines of inquiry are circling the case like the various parts of an atom circling its core. Particles like lost moons.

Islamic extremists, biker gangs, and the hottest lead, in all probability the key to the mystery: the Economic Liberation Front. The video on YouTube, like something from Islamic extremists, and the man in the security footage of the cashpoint.

The same man? No. That much was clear, but who knows how many people there might be in the Liberation Front?

'Just give me a vegan so I can ram a bit of meat up their arse,' Waldemar suddenly says, and the others fall silent and stare at him.

'Sorry,' he says. 'I just feel we have to make some real progress now. This is pointing in so many directions, it's like the spines on a hedgehog.'

'Malin, Zeke,' Sven says, 'come back to my office with me and we'll put our heads together and try to work out who sent that email to the *Correspondent*. OK?'

'OK,' Malin says. 'Let's go.'

19

Sven Sjöman is sitting behind his desk, his cracked, ivory-coloured phone held to one ear, and the whole of his office seems to glow with concentration. Malin and Zeke are leaning forward in their chairs.

After three short calls Sven has got through to the right person, the man at Securitas who's in charge of the surveillance cameras in the City Terminal in Stockholm.

Malin has just been watching Sven work, and once again she is surprised by his authority and experience, the way all his tiredness seems to vanish when he can focus on something that means something to him.

'Hello, yes, my name is Sven Sjöman, from the Linköping Police, head of the preliminary investigation into the bombing in the main square. Yes, well, of course you know about that . . .'

Sven falls silent.

Malin can see him clench his jaw as he listens to what the person at the other end of the line says.

Then silence.

'So you're saying that the Security Police contacted you yesterday to ask for the recordings from the time in question? And you let them have them?'

Another silence, then Sven's voice, commanding and pleading at the same time.

'What about copies? I presume you store everything digitally, so surely you could send us a copy? By email?'

Then Sven's face contorts into a grimace.

'So you mean you only had one copy? An old VHS tape, and you gave that to the Security Police?'

Sven looks at them and raises his eyebrows, and Malin realises that this is going to be a problem, there isn't a hope in hell that the Security Police will give them a copy of the tape, not now they're a couple of moves ahead.

'Well, we'll have to take it up with the Security Police. Thanks anyway, thanks for your help.'

Sven hangs up.

Slumps down in his chair.

'The Security Police got there first,' he says. 'You can guess the rest.'

'We need that damn video,' Zeke says, and Malin grins.

'So what do we do?' Malin asks.

'You two go and see the Security Police at the Central Hotel. See if they're prepared to give us what we want. Put whatever pressure you can on them.'

The main square is a hive of activity in the spring sunshine. Millions of floating grains of pollen reflect the sun's rays and cast microscopic shadows on the freshly washed pavements.

Carpenters are fixing new canopies over the terrace in front of Mörners Inn, stretching new canvas over the Central Hotel's repaired loungers. Glaziers are fitting new windows in the hotel's veranda, workmen are installing a new cashpoint machine outside the closed SEB bank, as even more glaziers replace the large sheets of plywood temporarily nailed up over the windows with sparkling new glass. Down by the newsagent, some council workers are tipping the last of the debris and dust from the explosion into big yellow skips.

But the burned-out candles are still there. And the

flowers. Even if most of them are wilting, and no new ones have been laid.

Considerably fewer people in the churches yesterday evening.

A bomb, Malin thinks.

Opportunities for work.

Temporary work is sorely needed by the citizens of Linköping. Some of them, anyway. For some of the many who have lost their jobs and can't find anything else, the ones with no education, or those who are simply too old, the ones the world has chewed up and spat out, finished with.

Black swifts are flying low, sweeping over the muted colours of the shining rooftops.

They're not singing, Malin thinks as she and Zeke head towards the hotel entrance. Do swifts ever sing?

Pigeons coo, I know that much, and she realises that thinking about birds is a way to stop herself thinking about the girls, about the shredded cheek and the single, scared eye that she sees staring up at her again if she so much as thinks about it. They were beautiful girls, was that what he said, Stensson? Running about, eating in that wonderful, greedy way that only young children do, with an absolute focus on their hunger and how to ease it, as if there was no tomorrow.

'Don't think about them, Malin, not like that,' Zeke says beside her, and she nods. Then they're inside the lobby of the Central Hotel, walking up to the young, blonde, attractive, heavily made-up girl behind the mirrored reception desk in which Malin can see the reflection of her blue skirt and her white trainers. She holds up her ID and says: 'The Security Police. Where are they based?'

And the girl seems surprised to see Malin, perhaps she recognises her from the *Correspondent*.

'The Folke Filbyter room on the third floor. They've set up a temporary office there.'

Malin and Zeke wait by the lifts, have already pressed the button when the girl calls out to them: 'There's no rush. I have to call and check if they can see you.'

'No need,' Malin says. 'They know we're coming,' and the lift doors close, and the lift glides slowly upwards.

The walls of the compact little cell are covered in yet more mirrors, and she and Zeke see themselves reflected in a thousand different distorted versions. The smell of salesman and businessman sweat is overwhelming, then – *ping*! – they're there, and right in front of them is the door to the Folke Filbyter room, slightly ajar, and from within they can hear voices, over-confident Stockholm voices, proof of people who think they know everything, can do everything.

Malin steps through the door.

His name is Stigman, he's about thirty years old, and he's wearing a snazzy suit, and Malin recognises him from outside Sofia Karlsson's flat. He's sitting with an older, worn-out-looking man called Brantevik behind a conference table where two iPhones have been nonchalantly tossed on a thin bundle of papers.

Malin and Zeke are standing opposite them, both of them annoyed, irritated, and frustrated in the way you get when you realise you're in a situation beyond your control.

Stigman, the little idiot, has just told them that there are now six Security Police officers on site in Linköping, but that many more are working on the case, and that their work has now reached a very sensitive stage in which all information must remain entirely within the Security Police's own ranks. So he's sorry, but they can't see the recording from the security camera from the Sidewalk

Café. Nor does he have any other information he can share with them.

'I have to say, it was very clever of you to find your way to that information so quickly. I wasn't expecting that.'

And Malin feels like telling the little idiot to go to hell, shout at him that that was quite enough cloak and dagger crap, that another bomb might go off at any moment, and that they might be able to stop it if they are given a copy of that fucking video.

Zeke sighs loudly, rubs his shaved head, then turns and walks out of the room.

Malin is left alone with the Security Police officers. They're looking at her as if they are looking at a prostitute in a window in Amsterdam's red-light district.

'Surely I can see the video? Here and now?'

Stigman shakes his head.

'Sorry, it's in Stockholm, I don't have a copy here, and even if I did, you wouldn't be allowed to see it.'

'You little bastard,' Malin says, unable to hold back any longer. 'You're obstructing my investigation. Do you fancy reading about that in *Aftonbladet* tomorrow? Or see it on the news? How the Security Police are impeding our investigation?'

'Do what you like,' Stigman says. 'But I think you're smarter than that. It doesn't look very good to leak stories about divisions within the force to the media. But perhaps you don't care about your career?'

Threats and counter-threats.

A pointless circular game.

'I know who you are,' Malin says, 'and one day I'll do the same thing to you.'

Stigman grins at her again.

'Don't shoot the messenger,' he says, and Malin realises he's right. Stigman didn't take the decision about the video, someone else did, someone who believes themselves to be omniscient.

As Malin leaves the room, Brantevik calls after her: 'Listen, girl. Let the big boys take care of this. Go and have a coffee, it's nice weather outside.'

And that's what they do.

They go down to Gyllentorget, and sit down at the Gyllenfiket café there, and each drink a double espresso. The strong coffee tastes good, and there are hardly any other people moving about today, and they're the only people sitting on the outside terrace.

No mums with prams. No unemployed. No students. And the absence of people makes the empty shop windows around the square even more obvious, and the gaping holes of small shops that surely all hide private financial tragedies become a story of our times, of all the dashed hopes and broken dreams, which for many, so many people, are the consequences of the financial crisis.

The few people who do walk past look at them.

Suspicious glances.

Hurried movements, as if they want to get away from the open space as quickly as possible. An elderly man sits by the entrance to the new shopping centre, begging. Slavic appearance. 'Hungry', his sign says. Presumably he's got some connection with the gangs of beggars from the Balkans. Unless he really is desperate? He's not actually allowed to be there, but we have other things to worry about, Malin thinks.

'What a day!' Zeke says. 'It's a shame people don't dare to come out.'

'That's not so strange.'

'Not as strange as you.'

'Shut up, you randy old goat.'

'Randy old goat. What do you mean by that?'

'You know perfectly bloody well what I mean.'

Zeke grunts. Sips his coffee.

After a while a waitress removes their cups.

'Not many people about,' Zeke says.

'No one dares to come into the city centre,' the girl says. 'Everyone's terrified. The only thing anyone seems to talk about is when the next bomb is going to go off.'

'What about you?' Malin asks. 'Aren't you scared?'

'No, to be honest I'm not. I don't think there's any danger. But I'd happily wring the neck of that bloke on the video, the one who left the bomb outside the bank.'

Malin starts at her choice of words. Wring the neck of . . .

She's only a year or two older than Tove, and quite pretty, but she's got an ugly scar on her chin. She seems pretty tough, knows what she wants.

Then the waitress stops by their table with her tray in her hands.

'Anyway, even if I was scared, I can't let any stupid terrorists rule my life, because then they've won, haven't they?'

The coffee makes her body twitch with a thin veil of energy as they walk back towards the car, parked up by the Hamlet bar.

When was it they were going to be having the memorial ceremony in the main square? Lunchtime? Malin wonders. If so, it's almost time, maybe we ought to go, see who shows up, how much of a crowd there is.

Her thoughts are interrupted by Zeke.

'That espresso did the trick,' he says, and Malin nods, then feels her mobile vibrating in her jacket pocket.

'Sven, that was absolutely hopeless,' she says when she

answers. 'They're refusing to let us have the video.'

'I've done it the formal way as well,' Sven says. 'I sent a request to the head of the Security Police himself. That might get us the video.'

'Was there anything else?'

'Yes,' Sven says. 'I've just had a call from the University Hospital. Hanna Vigerö's doctor. He says she's awake, that we can have a very quick chat with her, as long as it's very short and very careful.'

Without thinking about it Malin starts to run, eager to move towards what she imagines is the truth, and Zeke follows, close on her heels.

'We'll be there in five, maximum ten minutes,' Malin says.

'Ask for Peter Hamse,' Sven says.

An idiot doctor, Malin thinks. Lots of idiots today.

She can feel the adrenalin mixing with the caffeine in her blood, making her feel high, a bit like the only time she ever tried cocaine, at a party that got out of hand, while she was up at Police Academy in Stockholm.

20

She's on her way now, Mummy, to talk to you.

And in the main square, where the bomb went off, loads of people are gathering.

Really loads.

They're holding each others' hands, feeling the spring sunshine on their cheeks, the pure, clear air in their lungs, and lots of them are crying. Mummy, say they're crying for us, they are, aren't they, unless they're also crying for their own sakes?

You've got something to tell Malin, Mummy, but the question is whether you can find the words, if you can understand what it is that she needs to hear.

We hope so, but most of all we want to have you here with us, and maybe we will soon, don't you think?

The evil is moving like lizards with no legs.

Their black tongues licking the air.

The real horror is on the move, and it's getting closer to you, Mummy, but you can't run.

And we don't want to save you, because we want to have you here with us, and then perhaps Daddy will come too.

But, still, Mummy . . .

Tell her what you know, what you can. Try to get it to work, glue and tape and stick all the images, memories and thoughts together, and move your tongue, move it, let it say the words that will make us a family again.

You're breathing on your own now. The tubes in your nose are gone and the light is quivering in your hospital room, but not the beautiful spring light that's everywhere out here, but a rotten light.

Keep them away, Mummy, keep them at a distance.

Come to us instead.

Come to us who love you, then we'll rescue the other children together.

I am someone who breathes.

I know that.

The air fills my lungs and I can see something metal under a ceiling. But my body doesn't exist, where's my body, and is that you I can see, children, are you there, girls? And what was it that happened, what was that powerful white light that came and wiped out the sunlight?

I must have eyes.

But have I got arms, legs? And does it really matter? Because what do I want with arms and legs, hands, when I can no longer touch, caress, chase, play with you, girls? Because I know you're gone, even though you're here, and I know I don't want to live without you.

I hear you calling in this dream, which I know isn't a dream. I want to be with you, but I can't.

I'm in a hospital, aren't I? This is a hospital room, and I'm sick. But how am I sick? There's no physical pain. I should be happy about that.

Tell her, you say. Lead her onwards. But what should I tell her?

I try to say something. But my tongue doesn't want to move.

Unless . . . yes, it's moving. But it's not saying the words that need saying, is it?

★　★　★

The doctor.

He's standing in front of Malin.

But what's he saying?

He's extremely good-looking.

Zeke is standing beside her in the hospital corridor outside Hanna Vigerö's private room.

Her doctor, Peter, Peter Hamse, is wearing a white coat, and he's whispering to them, but Malin can't concentrate on what he's saying.

You have to, Fors. Pull yourself together.

Is he the one I want?

He's the same age as her, has no ring on his finger, and they noticed each other over in the office just now, Malin saw that, and she's still having trouble concentrating on what he's saying, looking instead at the little dimple in his chin, his sharp nose, his almost perfectly shaped cheekbones.

What's this spring doing to me?

Have to listen to what he's saying.

But instead she feels that she wants to drag this Dr Peter Hamse into the nearest toilet, the nearest nurses' office, the nearest shower room, and just let things happen.

Then she tears her eyes from Peter Hamse and looks along the corridor, and the yellow linoleum floor seems to melt like a layer of piss-stained snow, and the two girls' faces appear in the window at the far end.

She shuts her eyes.

Suppresses the tingling in her body.

Fends off her lust.

The girls.

What do you want here? You want your mum with you, don't you?

Then she looks at Zeke, and then at Peter Hamse, who is staring at her now, with interest and warmth, and Zeke grins, shakes his head, then Peter Hamse says: 'Five minutes.

And nice and gentle. Call if there's any deterioration in her condition.'

Then he turns and walks down the corridor, across the bubbling floor towards the waiting faces of the blown-up girls.

A machine with a flashing green light, bleeping every ten seconds.

A strangely pale yet still intense light, a woman's heavy breathing, and an aggressive smell of chemicals.

Malin absorbs Hanna Vigerö's room.

There are tubes attached to her body, the bed is flat, yellow hospital blankets are covering her battered legs, legs she will probably never be able to move again.

Are you here, girls?

You're here, aren't you?

Malin can feel them, doesn't have to see them, isn't scared of them, wants their help.

Zeke goes around the bed and stops so that he's shading Hanna Vigerö's face from the light, and her bruised features are clear, she looks nice, warm and good, what you'd call a decent person, whose life has been shattered into pieces, and who is now lying alone in a hospital room with her head swathed in bandages and a body that would probably really want to stop working.

Malin strokes her cheek, says her name, who they are, tells her what happened without mentioning the girls, and Hanna Vigerö opens her eyes, stares into space with a look of anxiety.

Don't be scared, Mummy.
  She wants to be nice to you.
  Don't be scared of what's happened.
  Soon you'll be with us.
  Pretend it's our little hands stroking your cheek.

Pretend it's our warm skin you can feel.
Try to tell her.
You know, you do know.

What are you saying?

Is there someone there? Who's there? What did you just say? I know what happened to my girls, why you're here, and I'm trying to tell you something, it's like I know what I'm supposed to say, but I can't gather the thoughts, the words, into any sort of order.

The hand, the warmth against my cheek is nice.

Don't stop, please. Whoever you are. Or is there more than one hand? Yes, it's your hands, girls, so maybe you do exist outside my dream?

What I saw?

I saw the girls, and the light.

But that's not what I say.

If I know anything significant? If anyone could have been trying to hurt me, us?

I saw the girls running towards the cashpoint, then I saw a brighter light than I've ever seen before. Now I see a face I don't recognise, and it's the face of a young woman, not a girl's face, and she's looking at me, a friendly, kind look. Her hair is cut in a bob and her mouth is moving and I wish I could hear what she's saying but I can't hear anything, and I know my tongue is moving but I don't know what I'm saying, or what unconscious thoughts precede the words.

It doesn't make sense.

I don't make sense.

And I want to come to you, girls, to your daddy.

But I don't know how to do that.

Tell me, how do you go about dying?

★ ★ ★

Hanna Vigerö stares, blinks, stares again, and there's no calm, just fear, almost panic in her eyes, and no matter what Malin asks, her answer is the same.

'The money, the money, the girls' money.'

'Were you going to withdraw money from the cashpoint?'

They've got the details from the bank.

The family didn't have much money, but the girls each had a savings account with a few thousand kronor.

'Were you going to withdraw the girls' money?'

'The money, the girls' money,' she whispers again.

Zeke looks at Malin.

Shakes his head, gives her a look that says: we ought to stop now, she's rambling, she's stuck in the worst moment of the horror and we shouldn't keep her there, let's stop this now, and Malin falls silent, strokes her cheek, sees Hanna Vigerö close her eyes and start to breathe calmly as the words stop flowing from her mouth.

The girls, Malin thinks, then she strokes Hanna Vigerö's cheek several more times before she stands up.

They leave the hospital room. Out in the corridor Malin takes some deep breaths. Out here the air is different, clearer.

There was a smell of death in there, she thinks.

'Did you feel it?' she asks Zeke.

He nods.

Zeke has gone to the toilet, and she is standing on her own with Peter Hamse by the lifts that lead down to the main entrance of the main hospital building.

He's absurdly handsome, Malin thinks as she hears herself tell him about their conversation with Hanna Vigerö, how she seemed scared and confused, and that she didn't say anything very significant, just seemed to get caught in the unbearable memory of a terrible moment.

Peter Hamse looks at her with genuine warmth when

she says the words 'terrible moment', then he says: 'There's no need for her to be anxious. I'll see that she gets a decent shot of tranquillisers. There's no need for her to be in any pain either.'

'Will she make it?' Malin asks.

'I think so.'

'But she'll have lasting injuries?'

Peter Hamse nods.

'In all likelihood, yes.'

Then they stand there in silence looking at each other, and Malin moves unconsciously closer to him, and he takes a step forward, and Malin notices that she's swaying, drawn to that dimple in his chin, and then they smile at each other and Peter Hamse throws his arms out and says something about bad timing, and then Malin says: 'It must be spring.'

'It must. And the sap is rising,' Zeke's voice says, and a minute later they're standing in the lift, Zeke grinning beside her, and Peter Hamse's words are ringing inside Malin: 'I'll get in touch if anything happens.'

Something has happened, Malin thinks, then feels ashamed of what she can sense going on within her body.

Ashamed because of the girls, and Hanna Vigerö, and Dad and Mum and Tove and Janne, and even Daniel Högfeldt.

'Go for it, Malin,' Zeke says. 'It's perfectly OK. You might as well let your own sap rise.'

And she tries to laugh at Zeke's joke, but it doesn't work, she feels like running down to the Hamlet instead, settling down on a bar stool, and drinking all these damn emotions away, obliterating herself until there are only tiny pieces left.

21

Evening has taken over Linköping, and the dusk is coloured mauve outside the living-room window, and Malin is sitting on the sofa beside Tove, waiting for the soap opera they're watching to end and the news to start. She's drinking a glass of cranberry juice.

Malin was sitting at her desk in the police station when the minute's silence for the Vigerö girls took place at four o'clock, and a remarkable thing happened. Suddenly all activity stopped, people stopped moving, sound somehow ceased to exist, and with it the world as she knows it.

The silence and respect almost tangible in the station.

But the girls weren't there.

Malin could sense that they were somewhere else.

Then the minute came to an end, and the usual hubbub of the station started up once more.

Malin stretches her legs.

Maybe, just maybe, the main television news will have something about the case that we don't know, she thinks.

Tove has been quiet and withdrawn all evening, but she wants to stay the night in the flat on Ågatan, she's got a big maths test tomorrow and wants to relax as long as possible before setting off for school.

Or is she just keeping an eye on me?

I think she trusts me more and more, but maybe that's just what I'm hoping, could that be it?

An explosion.

She thinks about the doctor she met today.

Peter Hamse.

She's never felt instinctively drawn to anyone like that, and she's sure he felt it as well. She can hardly breathe when she thinks about his face, his body under that white coat, and she wants to give in to those feelings, sneak out to the bathroom and free herself from the almost medieval lust that seems to have taken over her body, piece by piece.

An explosion.

That's what it feels like, as if she's at the centre of an explosion in which everything is being thrown at her all at once, where everything happens in a short, condensed moment, where matter becomes compressed and concentrated and nothing has time to stick, nothing has time to take hold, nothing has time to mean anything, and she is forced to go along with the emotion of each moment.

Mum's dead.

My mother died three weeks ago, and tomorrow the will is going to be read. Dad will be there, he's in charge of everything now, must have realised that I have to focus on work, even if he hasn't said anything. Unless there's some other reason?

Something's approaching in the explosion and I ought to be grieving, I ought to feel much, much more, but I can only see Dad, walking to and fro in the apartment on Barnhemsgatan and finally feeling liberated, apparently enjoying his newfound freedom.

Mum.

Your face like an empty mask, your life seen through a sort of forced perspective, like a stage set, a lie, lies within lies within lies, and in the end they become true, and then one sunny day you go and have a heart attack on a golf course.

It's odd, but I don't feel any grief, I don't feel anything, just relief and possibly fear that the core of a secret is about to burst, like some bastard red rosebud, and that I'm about to find out why I am the way that I am. But not even that feeling sticks, no, instead it's as if the explosion takes over, tossing me this way and that, and everything just happens and happens and happens. I can see it, but I can't get a grip on it, still less control it or do anything about anything.

An explosion of faces. That's what the investigation is like. Words and contexts that don't fit together, or at least they don't to me.

Mohamed Al Kabari on his rugs in his mosque.

Racism. But is it so odd that we should look there?

Or could the girls have been the target? But what evidence is there for that?

Dick Stensson. Repulsively attractive. His arrogant smile, his money. His stinking money.

And then the man in the hoodie in the video. The man who actually planted the bomb outside the bank. The man the whole city seems to hate.

Is he the Economic Liberation Front? Does Sofia Karlsson have anything to do with it? Are there others, and who's the person in the video from the City Terminal in Stockholm? The one those bastards in the Security Police are refusing to hand over.

Malin closes her eyes.

She lets her brain explode into thoughts, and when Tove asks her what she's thinking, she replies: 'I'm thinking about absolutely nothing, I'm just trying to clear out my brain. There's so much madness going on right now, Tove, I don't feel I can keep up with it.'

Peter Hamse.

Same age as me. No ring on his finger. I have to contact him.

And then she sees the girls again. The fragment of a face, the eye.

Their mum, Hanna's staring eyes in the hospital.

Children shouldn't die.

Children shouldn't be murdered, blown into tiny pieces. Mum's death is OK, she was almost seventy, after all.

What's Dad doing now? What's Janne doing? Daniel Högfeldt? I ought to talk to Tove, find out what's happening in her teenage life, what her dreams are, but I'm scared she'll tell me something new, something else I don't want to hear, and I know that only the bottle, tequila, and beer, can save me if everything gets too much, and they'll destroy me if I can't handle everything.

It's two days since I stood in front of Mum's coffin.

What did I say to her?

What did I whisper?

What did I want to say?

Peter Hamse.

His face, his body, the way he looked at me, his explosion into awareness.

Take me in your arms. Save me from my longing.

'I'm just going to the loo,' Malin says, getting up.

Peter Hamse has finished his shift at the hospital, he's just looked up Malin's number on the Internet and now he's sitting in front of his computer in the bedroom of his flat on Konsistoriegatan wondering whether or not he should call her, if he'd look too keen if he called straight away, yet at the same time he knows that he might not ring at all if he doesn't do it at once.

God, she was so attractive!

Sexy, taut, and athletic, with intelligent eyes and a blonde bob, exactly the sort he usually goes for.

But she had something more.

Something else.

A sort of messiness and vulnerability combined with a primitive strength that made her unbelievably fucking sexy.

He types her name into Google.

Malin Fors.

More than five thousand hits, and he reads the online articles about various murder cases she's been involved in, and he thinks that she's seen pretty much everything, coped with pretty much everything, she must be pretty damn tough.

Almost scary.

Maybe best to retreat.

But she's definitely not gay. There was a ridiculous tension between them. Like teenage infatuation on hormone overdrive.

He gets up.

Thinks: I'll call her.

Tomorrow. Maybe. Or we'll just bump into each other again, in connection with Hanna Vigerö. Best to approach this with caution.

'You look more relaxed now, Mum,' Tove says when she comes out of the bathroom, and Malin thinks: Is it that obvious? What do I say to that? She feels her cheeks go red, and hopes Tove doesn't notice.

'I'm just tired, Tove, it probably shows.'

'No, it's something else,' Tove says, and Malin thinks that she can read me like an open book, but she probably doesn't have a clue about what I was doing in the bathroom, because it isn't in a child's nature to see its parents as sexual beings.

What do I know about Tove's sex life? Nothing, she never talks about what she does with her boyfriends, the ones she's seeing. But she can't still be a virgin. Can she?

The soap opera finally comes to an end.

The news starts, and Tove gets up, saying: 'I can't bear to watch this, I'm going to have a last look at my maths,' and Malin nods, concentrating on the television.

One of the usual newsreaders appears on the screen, a young woman. Says: 'Just half an hour ago our reporters were shown a video by the Security Police. It shows a man who is presumed to have a connection to the bombing in Linköping in which two young girls lost their lives. The video you're about to see shows the man sending an email from the Sidewalk Café in the City Terminal in Stockholm at five-thirty on Tuesday morning. Anyone who has any information about this man is asked to contact the Security Police as soon as possible on 010 568 70 00.'

The video starts to play.

A man in a black hooded jacket is typing at a computer in one of the waiting rooms. His hood is down. He is sitting alone at a row of five computers and his face is visible.

Black-and-white images.

But clearer than anything else in the investigation so far.

Bastard Security Police.

Happy to give the recording to the television news.

But not us.

What's the explanation for that?

It's always impossible to explain their actions. Secrecy for secrecy's sake. An explosion of fucking secrets.

The recording plays again.

The same man as outside the bank?

Maybe, unless this one is slightly smaller, thinner? How old? Twenty-six, maybe, twenty-seven, sitting there writing his email to the *Correspondent*.

The pictures aren't very clear.

The features of his face seem elusive, almost a mask. Am I looking at the murderer, the bomber, the child killer, and what's he doing in Stockholm? His features look typically Swedish, sharp and smooth, innocent, and she catches her breath, if anyone in the country recognises this young man then they'll have a name by tomorrow morning at the latest, or rather, the Security Police will have a name. But in all likelihood someone will probably call them as well.

Do I recognise him?

No, never seen him before.

Then the man stands up and disappears from the screen, leaving just the row of computers in the deserted waiting room.

Then the newsreader's face again, repeating what she said before the video was played, as the phone number appears at the bottom of the screen. She adds that the video is available on their website, and that it will be played again before the end of the bulletin.

Malin gets up.

The video is playing in her mind, and she thinks that this is the breakthrough in the case, it's about to crack.

Then the phone rings.

Sven Sjöman.

His voice sounds thick, tired, irritated, hopeful, all at the same time.

'What do you think?'

'Looks like the Security Police want to play this their way.'

'But things are going to start happening now,' Sven says. 'Why the hell couldn't they let us have the video?'

'Prestige,' Malin says. 'You know how it is.'

'Two six-year-old girls have been killed. In principle every single bank in the country has been threatened with bombing. Plenty of people are too terrified to go out. And they're thinking about prestige.'

'That's how it is,' Malin says.

'Hang on, I've got another call, hold on.'

A minute later Sven's voice comes back on the line.

'The man's been identified.'

Sven says a name.

'He's registered in Linköping,' he goes on. 'See you at the station as soon as you can get there. I'll call Zeke in as well.'

No journalists outside the police station.

Just an empty car park where the cones of light from the street lamps are trying to shut out an unwelcome darkness.

The time is twenty-five to ten.

Almost pitchblack now.

Malin had rushed in to see Tove, sat down on the edge of her bed and spoken to the back of her head as she sat at her desk.

'Something's happened. I've got to go into work.'

Without turning around or looking up from her maths books Tove had replied: 'Go ahead. I've got plenty to do here. You know I can look after myself.'

'Sure?'

'Go.'

Malin had almost felt that Tove wanted to get rid of her, but realised that that was a way of rationalising what she felt about leaving her daughter alone yet again, and yet again putting work first. And Malin had felt ashamed as she left the flat, but now she's here anyway with Zeke and Sven Sjöman in the lobby of the police station, listening as Sven says: 'It was his mum who called. From Gränna. She's sure it was her son she saw in those pictures.'

'Why did she call us?' Zeke asks, and he looks tired, as if he'd already gone to bed when Sven called him in.

'She didn't seem to have thought about it, or else she just didn't manage to write down the Security Police number.'

'And who is he?'

Malin hears how impatient she sounds, how the words are launched clumsily into the air.

'If this is right, his name's Jonathan Ludvigsson. According to his mum, they haven't had any contact for the past five, six years, because she thought his opinions were getting too extreme, about everything from food to the economy and the environment. But particularly about the social effects of the economy. His dad was evidently laid off from a factory that ran into problems when a firm of venture capitalists loaded it with too much debt.'

'A vegan,' Zeke says, unable to conceal his distaste, 'frustrated about the economy.'

Sven nods.

'So where is he now? Did she know?'

'She thinks he lives up in Umeå.'

The wrinkles around Sven's eyes seem to deepen, and he lets out a deep breath, making his big stomach even bigger, and Malin knows there's something he's not saying.

This Ludvigsson was supposed to be registered in Linköping, after all.

'Out with it,' she says.

'We've done a quick check,' Sven says. 'And you know what, he lived in Umeå until six months ago, then he moved down here to Linköping.'

'And?'

'What else?' Zeke says.

'He's registered at the flat of a certain Sofia Karlsson. And of course we all know who she is.'

'Bloody hell,' Malin says.

'No shit,' Zeke exclaims.

'Let's get over there before the Security Police march in.'

'If they aren't already there,' Sven says.

'Are we going in mob-handed?' Zeke asks.

'We'll take back-up,' Sven says. 'But we'll go in nice and calmly, don't you think?'

'Yes. If we go in too heavy, anything could happen,' Zeke says.

'Boom,' Malin says quietly to herself.

The stairwell in Ryd stinks of piss.

Worse this time than before.

And there's a smell of spilled wine.

Malin feels the urge, tries to suppress it, but it chimes within her like a never-ending note.

Sven Sjöman, Zeke, and Malin are wearing bulletproof vests. Malin's holster is tight under her white jacket, she's left her jacket undone and is ready to draw her pistol in a second if she has to.

Two police vans are parked just out of sight of the flat, ten uniformed officers in protective gear positioned around the building and nearby, in this late spring evening that doesn't seem able to decide whether to be warm or cold.

Malin is breathing heavily, and she can hear Zeke's light footsteps behind her on the stairs, then Sven's strained panting, and she prays that his heart can cope with this, that he doesn't collapse onto the cold concrete.

No Security Police.

Maybe no one called them.

Maybe they're all snoring peacefully in their comfortable rooms in the Central Hotel.

Bastards.

Is he, Jonathan Ludvigsson, in there, behind the door that looms in front of Malin for the second time in two days? She managed to maintain her façade last time, Sofia Karlsson, but Malin can more or less remember what she said: 'The banks need to burn. And then there'll be casualties.'

Are these youngsters – because that's how she wants to see them – really cold-hearted terrorists, a sort of new Swedish Baader–Meinhof gang? And if they are, how could Jonathan Ludvigsson be so careless that he didn't think about the security camera up in the City Terminal? But maybe he didn't think his email could be traced?

The Economic Liberation Front.

Is the flat booby-trapped? Should they be more careful? Call for reinforcements? There were lights in the flat, the flicker of a television, and maybe, if Jonathan Ludvigsson saw himself on the news, they're in there panicking.

They breathe out, catch their breath. The door has no security peephole, and Sven and Zeke draw their pistols and stand behind Malin. She rings the bell, and the sound it makes becomes a slowly burning fuse, and she hears steps approach the door, slow, tired, alone.

The door opens.

The rings in her nose.

The dreadlocks.

Tiredness in her eyes, fog, and Malin can smell hash, strong and unmistakeable.

'You?' Sofia Karlsson says. 'What are you doing here?'

'I think you know.'

'What?'

She looks genuinely surprised, Malin thinks, then she pushes Sofia Karlsson aside and steps into the hash-haze of the flat.

She doesn't even seem bothered that we're here, even though she must have smoked a whole damn cake of hash in here.

Sven and Zeke glide past Sofia Karlsson, pistols drawn, she doesn't even seem to notice them, then she hears them call: 'Clear.'

'Clear.'

'The whole flat's clear.'

'Take it easy, hey? Just take it easy,' Sofia Karlsson says.

Sofia Karlsson is sitting on her bed, on the rasta-coloured throw, trying to keep her eyes open, evidently making an effort to absorb what they're telling her about Jonathan Ludvigsson, her lodger. She clearly hasn't seen the item on the news.

They tell her everything, and she frowns exaggeratedly, but she's so high that she's hardly in a fit state to lie, Malin thinks.

'Is Jonathan supposed to have something to do with the bomb? Mind you, I can just about believe that, but I don't know anything about it, no word of a lie. But good for Jonathan. Cool.'

Cool?

Are you mad?

Two six-year-old girls died.

Malin clenches her fists, sees Zeke do the same, but Sven raises his hand in warning to calm them down, then gestures towards himself as if to say: 'I'll deal with this.'

'We don't think you had anything to do with this,' Sven says. 'But you'll have to come down to the station with us and sleep off the drugs, and we'll have to take your computer.'

'He hasn't touched my computer.'

'Does he still live here?'

'What?'

'Does he live here?'

'He's just registered here. His post gets delivered here.'

'You're sure about that?'

'You mean was I fucking him?'

Sofia Karlsson looks up at the ceiling and puts her hand over her crotch.

'I'd never do anything like that with him. I only like black men.'

Push her now, Sven, keep going, Malin thinks.

'So he's never actually lived here?'

'No. I'm pretty sure he lives in a caravan out on the plain, somewhere outside Vadstena. I've never been there, but he lives there with a few other people.'

'Outside Vadstena?'

'No, Klockrike, I mean. Near the old Pentecostal church. I've been there.'

'So you have been there?'

Sofia Karlsson puts her hands over her mouth, then makes a gesture to indicate smoking a joint.

'I see,' Sven says. 'Do you know if they have any weapons out there?'

The bluntness of his question makes Sofia Karlsson jerk, open her eyes wide, and for a second her eyes clear and Malin thinks she's about to protest, switch back to her activist persona, but then the hash-haze descends again and she becomes amenable, telling them what they need to know.

'Of course they've got weapons. Pistols. A few hand grenades. And that fucking AK4 that Jonathan bought.'

'As many as that?' Sven says, without sounding particularly surprised or upset.

Sofia Karlsson nods, then her eyelids sink and she says: 'You're going to have to go now, I need to sleep.'

Then Malin goes over and gives Sofia Karlsson two hard slaps on the cheek.

'Like fuck you do. You're going to show us the way to Klockrike.'

23

'Down there. Behind that big house. The one that looks like it's got black eyes.'

Sofia Karlsson points from where she is sitting between Malin and Zeke in the back of the police car.

She's less high now, the veils have lifted from her brain, and now just the tiredness and thirst are left, and she hasn't had the energy to cause them any trouble, and has led them in the right direction. And Malin feels like asking why, why betray your friends, but something must have happened between them, Jonathan Ludvigsson can't be an easy man to deal with.

'Have they got explosives?'

Sven's final question in the flat, and Sofia Karlsson replied that she didn't know, then she had asked Malin for another joint, without seeming the least bit concerned about being slapped.

The big, dark building – presumably the church meeting house – lies there dimly lit up in the moonlight on a side-street in Klockrike, a small village cast out in the middle of the Östgöta plain, painfully exposed to wind and cold and summer heat.

Beyond the back of beyond. Maybe three hundred inhabitants, who probably like their simple life in the countryside. But the church looks abandoned, now that idiotic television programmes, online games, and surfing for porn have taken over people's souls.

Inside the houses, most of them in darkness, people probably still play Bingolotto whenever they get the chance.

The meeting house that the caravans are supposed to lie behind sits in splendid isolation on a small hill on the edge of a forest, and seems to keep watch over the little community, saying to the inhabitants: We're watching you.

'How many of them might there be?' Malin had asked when they were halfway to Ljungsbro on the motorway.

'Maybe just him. Four at most,' Sofia Karlsson had replied.

Karim Akbar, who had come with them, grunted from the passenger seat beside Sven, then said: 'We'll let the uniforms take care of this.'

Malin had wanted to protest, then she thought about Tove at home in bed. She stayed quiet. Instead Zeke spoke up.

'Malin and I are going in. That's obvious. We've got vests on.'

'Out of the question,' Karim said, in a voice that didn't allow for any discussion, and the subject had been dropped in the darkness of the car as its headlights eagerly swallowed up metre after metre of the road that was going to lead them to the people who might be responsible for one of the worst crimes in the city's history.

Sven isn't using the radio. Doesn't want to risk being overheard. He uses his mobile, with the speaker on, as he gives orders to the officers from the police van that followed them there. An officer by the name of Sundblom, who has a Finnish–Swedish accent and is new to Linköping, is in charge of the group of ten uniformed officers in full gear, reporting over his headset as they approach the meeting house.

'No sign of any caravans yet.'

Malin can just make out the police officers up by the

building. They're maybe five metres apart as they move at a crouch around the end of the building, dividing into pairs, then they get swallowed up by the darkness.

'We have visual on the caravans. There are lights on.'

'Execute,' Sven says, and there is a muffled crash, probably a door flying open, Malin thinks, then shouting but no shots, then more shouting, voices yelling: 'Calm down, get on the floor, lie still, we've got you now you bastards,' and now Malin can see a dark figure rushing past the end of the building, and just has time to think, That can't be a police officer, before she sees the figure disappear down towards the street and off across a dark field that seems to roll like a calm sea under the light of the moon.

'Shit,' she says, then she's out of the car.

She runs down the street, out into the field, rushing after the figure, which is moving like a shadow up ahead of her.

Whoever it is, they're trying to escape capture.

Her heart is pounding in her chest.

Don't draw your pistol. Get closer, then pounce, let all those hours in the gym in the basement of the station over this past sober year do their work, the countless kilometres on the treadmill, all the physical pain she has imposed upon herself to help her forget the urge to drink, to conquer the body's greedy explosions. Her heart is pounding but her body can cope, she can feel it, and the figure ahead of her has slowed down, maybe running out of energy, is it Jonathan Ludvigsson?

Impossible to tell in the darkness.

And the passport photograph they got hold of was ten years old.

Can he hear me?

He's walking now.

Another hundred steps or so and I've got him.

And she runs towards her prey, runs towards the moon, and two wingless girls with white faces and white hair drift in the light, encouraging her onwards.

Run, Malin, run.
Whatever that is ahead of you in the field in the darkness, it's something you need to chase, isn't it?
Bring it down.
Is it an animal?
It's exciting, Malin, watching you chase him, but it isn't the nastiest thing that might happen tonight.
The captive children are sleeping. They belong with us. The nasty lizards are gnawing at the cages, they can hear the lizards and the men in their dreams.
Do you feel the wind, Malin?
The cold wind sweeping over the city and across the plain?
Deep inside that wind death is whispering, Malin. And maybe, just maybe, death is whispering for you.
We don't know.

What are you saying?
What do you want with me? I haven't got time for you now, and Malin can feel the lactic acid surging through the muscles of her legs, finding its way up through her stomach to her lungs, before it takes hold of her heart like a dark, glowing pair of glass-blower's tongs.
But I can't give up now.
Then the black figure ahead of her in the field stops.
Turns around.
Seems to be searching through a pocket. Is he pulling out a gun?
And if he pulls out a gun he might be faster than me. Am I going to die now? Is that what's about to happen?
And she digs deep for the last of her energy, zigzagging

the last twenty metres towards the person in front of her.

There's a flash.

From the barrel of a gun before the sound of the shot that kills me.

But no sound? Has he got a silencer?

She throws herself forward. Feels a warm blow to her cheek.

Zeke walks up to the caravan, a KABE, it must be twelve metres long.

Dim light from the caravan's windows.

Outside the caravan, among a great mass of clutter, there are three large oil drums, and he sees six beefy police officers leaning over what look like three young men dressed in those shabby, dirty clothes that itinerants, or the unemployed, or homeless New Age travellers usually slum about in.

'Which one's Ludvigsson?' he asks.

'None of them,' Sundblom says from the door of the caravan. 'Apparently he was outside having a piss.'

'In that case he's the one Malin set off after,' Zeke says. 'He took off across the field.'

'Did she get him?'

'Don't know. I rushed over here. Karim and Sven ran after her, we left Sofia Karlsson handcuffed in the back of the car.'

Sundblom nods.

'These are Konrad Ekdahl, Jan Thörnkvist and Stefan Törnvall, I've managed to get that much out of them.'

'What have you got in there?'

'I've found computers so far, but there's a hell of a lot of cubbyholes in a caravan this size. They seem to be pretty well connected, though.'

Cables are draped through the trees around the caravan, leading to an aerial on the roof.

'Anything about the Liberation Front in there?'

'The website was open on one of the computers. I haven't touched anything else.'

'Good,' Zeke says. 'Johannison's already on her way.'

Karin.

Trying to give the impression of distance, saying Johannison. Never using her first name.

Ridiculous.

We're having sex with each other. That's all. It's not a question of love.

He can see Karin's absurdly aristocratic face in his mind's eye, how it can switch in an instant and become bestial when she picks up his scent.

'Forensics can carry out the search,' Zeke says.

From the three captured men on the ground come groans and whimpering, met by 'Shut up, you fuckers,' and all sound seems to disappear into the darkness, muffled by the weak light of the moon.

'Where's Malin?'

Why's it taking so long? Zeke wonders.

It wasn't a gun.

He had stopped to light a cigarette and wait for whatever fate had in store for him, had heard her behind him and realised he wasn't going to get away, that the game was up.

She had knocked him to the ground.

Burned herself slightly on the cheek with the end of the cigarette.

She pressed his face down, hard, down into the sucking mud of the field, not bothered whether he could breathe.

'Are you Jonathan Ludvigsson? Did you kill two little girls? Well, did you? If you did, you don't have to worry, I'll make sure you breathe your last in this fucking field.'

She paused for breath. Went on pushing his face into the damp ground as she tugged at his long, matted dreadlocks.

'Can you breathe? Well? Can you? Those girls aren't breathing any more, you know that, don't you?'

Then she felt a blow to her side and she lost her grip of his head and fell, taking a bit of dreadlock with her, and the man on the ground tried to get some air, but didn't make a sound.

'For God's sake, Malin! Are you trying to kill him?'

Sven doesn't sound upset, it's merely a statement of fact.

And now Malin is on her knees beside the man.

Panting, looking up at Karim's agitated face, sees Sven put handcuffs on the man and pull him up.

'I was just holding him until you arrived.'

'Like fuck you were.'

The man.

He can't be more than twenty-five years old.

Bearded.

Pure Swedish features, angry blue eyes, long, filthy dreadlocks.

She recognises him from the video.

'That's Jonathan Ludvigsson,' as she gets to her feet and starts heading back across the field, towards their cars and the caravan.

24

Thursday, 13 May

Jonathan Ludvigsson is sitting in interview room number one, on the other side of the big black table, in the light of a halogen lamp.

Malin is watching him through the glass of the observation room, through what looks like a mirror inside the interview room. Karim Akbar and Sven Sjöman are standing beside her. Sven was very clear: 'You're not taking the interview. You thought he tried to kill you out in the field and that's not a good starting point. Zeke can take it, with Johan Jakobsson, he's just got in and is fresh and alert.' She had protested, but to no avail.

Now, through the glass, Malin can see the defiance in Jonathan Ludvigsson's eyes: 'I'm not going to say a fucking thing.' And he's declined the offer of a lawyer, saying: 'They're part of this rotten financial system, the whole lot of them. Every last one of them, and I don't want anything to do with any of them.'

The clock on the wall says twenty-five to one.

Ludvigsson is staring down at the tabletop, and Malin can only see his dreadlocks.

They didn't find any of the weapons Sofia Karlsson mentioned in the caravan. No pistols, no hand grenades, nothing. No explosives, but Karin Johannison is there now, searching the caravan and the vicinity with a toothcomb in the hunt for evidence. And there don't seem to have been any leaks; there haven't been any journalists in Klockrike yet.

Malin's body is screaming for sleep, her eyes are itching, and her muscles ache in a plaintive grumble, and she presumes Zeke inside the room must be just as tired, and the same goes for Jonathan Ludvigsson. She looks at his hair, the way his dreadlocks resemble dirty earthworms in the glow of the lamp.

Johan looks alert. Maybe the children fell asleep early and he along with them, so that he's already had a few hours' kip?

The tape recorder in the room starts to turn. The other three they picked up in Klockrike are sitting in the cells. Börje Svärd and Waldemar Ekenberg have just got in and are about to interview them, while they're still confused and sleepy.

'So,' Zeke says, and his voice sounds gentle through the loudspeaker in the ceiling, just above where Malin is standing. 'What were you really doing in Stockholm the morning of the day before yesterday?'

'I wasn't in Stockholm,' Jonathan Ludvigsson says without looking up. 'And I'm not going to say anything else.'

'Look at us when you're talking,' Johan says. 'Got that? We know you were in Stockholm, and we know you sent the email about the Economic Liberation Front to the *Correspondent*. We know you're behind the website, and it's only a matter of time before we know you carried out the bombing in the main square in which two little girls died.'

Jonathan Ludvigsson carries on staring down at the table.

Silence in the room.

'You're in the shit. Do you realise that?' Zeke says, and all the gentleness in his voice has vanished, and he looks over at the mirror, as if to say to Malin: OK, this fucker's going to talk. 'You might as well start by telling us about the Economic Liberation Front. Who are you exactly?'

Malin drums her fingers on the ledge under the window of the observation room, looks at Zeke, at his skull-like face in the dim light, senses Karim and Sven's presence, their heavy, tense, expectant breathing.

A pistol. That turned out to be a cigarette. Her rage from the field gone now, but she is aware that it could flare up at any moment. There is a slight bruise on Ludvigsson's cheek after their tussle.

'It would be best to tell us,' Johan says softly. 'For your own sake.'

'And for the girls' sake,' Zeke says. 'The ones you killed. They were only six years old. How does it feel to have killed two little girls?'

Jonathan Ludvigsson goes on staring down at the table.

Doesn't even shake his head.

Sighs and takes a deep breath before he looks up at Johan and Zeke with empty eyes, as if he's just found a different part of himself, a neutral part.

He looks over at the mirror. Smiles at the people he must know are behind it.

'You're a child murderer,' Johan says. 'The worst sort of murderer. In two hundred years your name will live on as a child murderer.'

Jonathan Ludvigsson blinks.

Runs his forefinger and thumb over his mouth.

Zip.

'We're about to talk to your comrades,' Zeke says. 'One of them's bound to talk. They looked like they were about to crap themselves.'

'Like frightened little rabbits,' Johan says, and looks at Ludvigsson.

A bomber? Malin thinks.

Maybe. The Olympic bomber in Stockholm was precisely the same sort of wayward political fanatic who'd gone off the rails. But he actually succeeded. The Olympic Games didn't come to Sweden in the end, which was probably just as well.

She looks at Ludvigsson through the glass, as he swings between fear and arrogance.

'Tell us about the Economic Liberation Front,' Johan says. 'There'll be a lot of people who agree with you in principle. Everyone hates the banks, that much is obvious. And there'll be plenty of people who think the banks deserve everything they've got coming.'

Ludvigsson smiles at him, a conspiratorial smile.

'So if you talk, if you confess, your ideas will get massive exposure in the media. You might even end up as a martyr, but that will only happen if you talk to us.'

'So, your dad,' Zeke says. 'He got laid off?'

'Yes. And now he'll probably never get another job. And all because the banks lent so much fucking money to a bastard venture capitalist. It's people like that Falkengren who are ruining my dad's life, and there are plenty of people like my dad in this country. But the banks and their stooges are grabbing whatever they can get, Falkengren earned twenty million last year, while Dad got laid off because the bank had over-extended the finance of the company he worked for. It's sick. Completely sick. It has to be stopped.'

With that last word Ludvigsson raises his eyebrows, then he shuts his eyes and looks as if he's pretending to be asleep.

'OK, time to start talking, you child-murdering little shit. Got that?'

Zeke stands up.

Takes two steps forward, grabs a handful of dreadlocks, and drags Jonathan Ludvigsson from his chair. Malin sees it happen, feels violence taking hold of her: Get him! Get the child-killer! The same uncontrollable urge she had out in the field. Karim and Sven are calm beside her, focused.

'You're going to talk, you bastard. Tell us all about the Liberation Front, what you were doing in Stockholm, how you and your friends rigged the bomb.'

'You sent the email and someone else detonated the bomb,' Johan shouts, and his fury sounds hollow, as if he doesn't have the right sort of anger in him. 'Who was he, the man with the bike?'

'What is this?' Jonathan Ludvigsson yells, standing on tiptoe in the face of Zeke's assault, grimacing with pain. 'Fucking Guantanamo?'

But Johan doesn't answer. Ignores the question. No more Mr Nice Guy, he seems to be thinking. He carries on: 'Who was the man on the bike, the one who left the bomb outside the bank?' and Zeke lifts his arm, and Jonathan Ludvigsson's feet leave the floor.

'CIA, fucking hell, you're CIA, I don't know anything about any man with any fucking bike.'

Zeke lets Ludvigsson fall back onto his chair.

'You don't know?' Johan says. There's real harshness in his voice now, as if it were his children who'd been killed by the bomb.

So he does have it in him after all.

Violence against children always reveals a person's true character.

It's unforgivable, Malin thinks. It should be unforgivable.

'And you expect us to believe that?' he roars.

Jonathan Ludvigsson flinches.

'Even if I did know, I wouldn't tell you, would I?'

Then he repeats the gesture with his finger and thumb

over his mouth, and Zeke moves forward again, and
Ludvigsson ducks, then Karim makes a move beside Malin
and opens the door to the interview room. His dark face
in profile is even darker in the dim light as he says author-
itatively: 'That's enough. Enough now. You two go home
and get some sleep. You too, Malin.'

Karin Johannison has dusted the caravan for fingerprints,
has searched through all the cupboards for evidence. She's
been over every inch with a fine-tooth comb, looking for
traces of the explosives, the TATP, and anything else needed
to make a bomb.

Hours have passed.

And now she's standing alone in the confined space.

Brushes her blonde hair from her face, feeling tired, but
she still wishes Zeke were there with her.

What had started as a bit of innocent extramarital sex
has become something more for her, but not for him, and
that wasn't what she'd been planning, and she realises now
that she had expected it to be the other way around, that
she could toy with him, making the rather uncouth, rough
policeman dance to her tune.

He helps himself to me.

Whenever he wants.

Not the other way around. And I no longer have any sex
life with Kalle, I can't bear him any more, and he doesn't
seem to mind. Do we even have fun together these days?

Am I in love with Zeke? I can't bear to think about it.
Instead, she swears out loud to drown out her own thoughts,
and thinks about the three computers they've seized, and
the one laptop, and the way the caravan was like a little
IT lab. She stops, breathing in the stale smell, the smell of
cheap camping holidays and poverty and cigarette butts
and empty bottles and dirty pots caked with dried-on lentils,

and she swears again: 'Fuck,' then thinks: We're missing something, and she falls to her knees and starts searching along the edge of the caravan's cork floor, pulling at the lintels of the benches, but they're stuck tight, don't seem to have been touched since the caravan was built. She carries on towards the toilet and kitchen, crawling on all fours, until she works her way around to where she started.

She gets up again.

The top cupboards are fixed to the roof.

But doesn't the roof seem lower than it should be?

Karin stands on one of the caravan's built-in benches, opens the top cupboard again, pulls out the stuff she's just put back in, then shoves the fingers of one hand up at the top of the cupboard and pushes.

The ceiling of the cupboard suddenly comes loose, seeming to fall from the roof of the caravan as if under some great weight, and she feels cold metal against her hand.

Rummages about.

Pulls out her finds.

An UZI. A SIG Sauer. Three hand grenades, and she delves into the space between the caravan's outer shell and internal roof, and suddenly feels something doughy between her fingers.

Should I be more careful?

What if he's armed it?

And she can't help herself, and pulls the package out, and sees what looks like three large parcels of explosives, white crystals under pale plastic, enough to blow an entire block of Linköping into the air.

Careful now, Karin.

'I need help here!' she shouts from the caravan to the uniforms she hopes are waiting outside. 'NOW!' and she hears an angry bleeping sound, a sound that echoes through her flesh and blood and into whatever unknown substance lies beyond her marrow.

'We don't know anything.'

The sessions with the three other activists haven't produced anything.

'So he had the website open when we got there, but pretty much everyone in Sweden is looking at that right now, aren't they?'

Waldemar Ekenberg had resorted to violence.

He split Konrad Ekdahl's lip, but they still didn't manage to get anything out of them.

Sven Sjöman is sitting slumped in the leather chair in his office.

It's half past two in the morning, but it hasn't started to get light yet, and he wonders how Karin's getting on out at the caravan.

Has she found anything?

The other detectives in the team are at home now, in their beds, and he's thinking of snatching a few hours' sleep here at the station, in the staffroom, the sofa in there will have to do.

He kept switching between the interviews.

The three bewildered young men appeared to be telling the truth. They claimed they had gone to the caravan to have a few drinks, that they didn't have a clue that Jonathan Ludvigsson was involved in or was behind anything called the Economic Liberation Front. Sofia Karlsson, who had sobered up completely by now, also seemed to be telling the truth, and she didn't know anything either.

Frustrating.

But Jonathan Ludvigsson could have had plenty more comrades.

Or just been working with one other person.

He thinks of his wife at home in bed in their villa. What wouldn't he give to be able to feel the warmth of her body right now?

Sven shuts his eyes.

Maybe he could sleep here, in his armchair?

No. It would cripple his back.

He gets up.

And then the phone rings. He thinks: It's bound to be Karin, now that she's finished out at the caravan.

25

What happens at night when everything's dark?

We see you sleep, Malin.

You came home, looked at Tove in her bed for a while, then you fell asleep, didn't even bother to take off your clothes.

But we understand that you're tired. Because what happened to us is a drain on your mind, your heart, your soul.

Who could it have been who harmed us?

Jonathan? Al Kabari's fellow believers? Those men who like motorbikes? Someone else? And what's happened out at the caravan?

Who would detonate a bomb in Linköping on a sunny spring day?

What is the point of being mean? Are they planning to harm the captive boy and girl? The children you must hurry to save.

And everything else, Malin.

Your body is screaming for something strong to drink.

Your mum. Your dad and Tove. With their secrets. We like secrets, but not that secret. That's horrid.

Lizards' teeth, Malin.

The hungry beasts are waking from hibernation tonight.

Who's that heading towards the hospital? Towards Mummy who's struggling without knowing what she's struggling against in her bed in the lonely hospital room.

Something dark is moving towards her.

Wake up, Mummy, wake up.

No, don't wake up.
Come to us instead. Don't wake up, never wake up again.

Malin is sleeping with her arms stretched out above her head, but it isn't the secure sleep of a child.

Her dream is a dream of faces.

Her mum is standing in a darkened corner and shouting in annoyance, but no comprehensible words are coming out of her mouth, just a sludgy mess of sound that cuts through Malin's body. The Vigerö girls are playing in another corner of the room with two other children. They're pushing little Lego cars back and forth in a pattern that seems to lead back into history, back to the very first time a human being ever wanted anything.

Dad is standing with his hand stretched out, he wants to give her a doll, a little boy doll that seems to be reaching its plastic hands out to her, a gesture that says: Help me, Malin, help me – and Tove is staring at her from somewhere in the middle of the room, her eyes filled by an endless unfamiliar landscape where pink clouds are falling apart far off above a burning horizon.

Faces come and go. Sven Sjöman's, Zeke's, Karin Johannison's, Mohamed Al Kabari's, Jonathan Ludvigsson's, Dick Stensson's. They're all laughing at her, yelling: 'How can you be so fucking stupid?'

Then the dream contracts to a dense black point of matter where everyone's bad deeds and contradictory desires seem to accumulate, and then her eardrums burst and the skin melts away from her bones, and bleeding arms, fingers, eyes, and brains spread through the air like burning rain. A bear eats a bearcub in a cave on an isolated, forgotten, lost island, eating its own young.

Allahu Akbar, Allahu Akbar, Allahu Akbar.

The chorus is overwhelming in the black banks of dust that make up the last eddies of her dream.

Allahu Akbar.

The words become a whistling sound, and the girls drift inside Malin's eyelids. They're scared and calm at the same time, and in her dream she knows everything that has happened and is still to happen.

Then everything becomes peaceful and quiet.

Like after a sudden explosion.

She is having trouble breathing, taking deep breaths, but the air doesn't seem to want to fill her lungs, she is bursting from a lack of oxygen, but finally she manages to roll over. She was lying face down on the pillow.

Then she takes a deep breath and disappears into black, death-like, empty sleep.

Jonathan Ludvigsson is lying on the bunk in his cell.

Can't sleep.

A guard looks in through the hatch in the door, probably checking I haven't committed suicide, he thinks.

Presumably the cops have found everything out in the caravan by now.

So what happens next?

I don't care.

Just stay quiet. Like before. The others can't say anything about stuff they don't know.

Some things are bigger than me, and can there be anything more unreal than an explosion? It happens, but it doesn't happen. And if there's one thing I've learned, it's that if you don't make your voice heard, you don't exist.

There's a battle underway on this planet right now. Between us and nature, between us and our own nature, and in that battle all means are justified.

But maybe I, we, went too far this time.

The custody cell is cold, and the orange blanket doesn't make much difference, his joints are aching, and the hatch in the door opens again and he sees a black eye.

Bang.

The eye's gone, but it's still there in the door, and it's a different eye now, it looks like a girl's eye, and it seems to want to strangle him with its rage. He sits up on the edge of the bunk and wants to get rid of the eye, and why can't I breathe?

I've got to get out, got to get rid of the eye.

Jonathan Ludvigsson leaps up from the bunk and over to the door, and starts yelling: 'Let me out, let me out!'

He bangs on the hatch, at the girl's eye that seems to be radiating rays that can stop his heart.

'Easy, easy.'

The guard's voice from the other side of the door, then it opens.

Light from the corridor.

'What is it?'

The guard's eyes.

'I want to talk,' Jonathan Ludvigsson says.

'Talk about what?'

'What I've done.'

Karin Johannison is delving through the weapons and grenades in the caravan, carefully, so that nothing happens.

She scared herself badly before, when the alarm clock that was hidden under some cushions on a chair at the front of the caravan went off and started to bleep. She thought the caravan and weapons store were booby-trapped, and that she was about to be blasted into atoms, like those girls very nearly were.

But it was only a bloody alarm clock.

And during those short seconds while the clock was ringing she saw her life flash past.

Kalle, Mum, Dad, all the lovers she's had. Zeke. How she wanted to hold onto him in those moments, take him with her to wherever she thought she was going.

Then everything had gone silent. Peaceful and lonely, and she realised what was missing in her life.

She knew already, she knew she should have felt the longing, but it had never happened. And unborn children had drifted before her eyes, and she had felt a longing she had never felt before, never knew she had within her, a longing that was bigger than the longing itself, a greed for more life just as life was about to end.

As if everything became clear only when she herself was about to be struck by a terrible calamity.

And life changes. Gently and imperceptibly, then suddenly and clearly.

But it wasn't a bomb.

It was an alarm clock.

Sven Sjöman is sleeping, curled up on the sofa in the darkness of the staffroom. He got Karin's call about the weapons and explosives and the other things they found out in the caravan. But couldn't even summon up the energy to think of questioning Ludvigsson again. It's time for Sven to sleep, so that he can wake up and see everything with fresh eyes, get a fresh grip on one of the messiest, most slippery investigations he's ever been involved in. It makes him feel he's at the centre of a torrent of events that are governed by their own internal mechanisms, and over which he, they, have absolutely no influence.

There's a knocking sound in his dream.

'Sven. Sven.'

But he doesn't want to wake up.

An old body, a tired but sharp mind, both wanting sleep, file the day's thoughts into shiny neat boxes that can be arranged in clearer, more comprehensible ways.

But someone doesn't want that.

Someone is shaking him.

'Sven. Sven, you have to wake up.'

He sits himself up.

Rubs his eyes. Looks at who it is who's standing beside him: Constable Antonstjärna, an intelligent young man, only twenty-five or so, far too young to be a police officer.

'He wants to talk,' Antonstjärna says.

'Who wants to talk?'

'Ludvigsson wants to talk about what's happened, what he's done.'

Sven gets up and stretches his back.

'What time is it?'

'Twenty-five past four. It'll soon be light.'

We have power, we can convey messages, can't we?

We aren't as small and helpless as you all think, we can help you, Malin, we really can.

But you have to believe that we exist, because if you don't we'll vanish and won't exist at all.

We're with Mummy now.

Sitting on her bed and whispering nice things in her ear, and now someone is approaching her along the corridor; slowly, slowly, the person is getting closer, the person who has made their way unnoticed through the hospital's subterranean passageways and up the stairs to the ninth floor, and who is now approaching her room like the invisible man.

We want to help him, because we want you here with us, Mummy.

We don't want to exist without you, and we know you're in pain, so much pain, and you'll always be in pain. Yet that doctor still seems to think that you're a bit better, and maybe we could help you now, Mummy, but we're not going to.

The door of your dark room slips open.

A person in a black hood steps in.

And we disappear from here, whispering in your ear, Mummy: See you soon.

Hanna Vigerö can feel the air running out. It's disappearing slowly, yet still suddenly, the feeling is like cotton wool, and she tries to breathe but it doesn't work.

I was aware that you were here just now, girls.

I know what you want.

And I want the same thing.

That's why I'm not even trying to struggle, not the tiniest little bit, even if I were physically capable of it.

But I'm not struggling mentally either. I want this to happen, and I can even control my most basic instinct.

No.

I can't.

I want to breathe, breathe, but I can't.

Is someone whispering an apology? Forgive me?

I want the person pressing the pillow over my face to succeed in asphyxiating me. But still I try to breathe.

The person pressing is pushing down hard now.

The air is gone, everything goes black, and white, and black, and I leave the hibernation of the hospital room, see my room disappear into a black dot, only to explode into white light, burning hot magnesium and white phosphor, and then I am somewhere else.

I can feel that you're here, girls.

Mummy's here now.

I call your names.

Mira! Tuva!

Over and over again, I call your names.

You're here, but you can't hear or see me.
But you're here.
I know that.
And I promise I'm never going to stop looking for you.

PART 2

Out of the black, into the white

In the chamber of darkness

Daddy!

Help!

Little brother's really scared, Daddy, and so am I, more scared than when Mummy went up to heaven.

Come on, Daddy! Now!

The men are nasty. Angry. And dark, it's too dark here, and I try to hug little brother, but I'm too little and it's horrid here, and he doesn't like how horrid it is, and I don't either. I'm scared, Daddy, and I try to think about birthdays instead, about Christmas and other nice things, about my friends, even though they aren't here.

We want you to rescue us now, why don't you come, why did you let us go on the aeroplane with the men?

I'm scared of the lizards.

They showed them to us. Said they'd eat us up if we weren't good.

They were chewing at the bars with their teeth. Banging their bodies against them.

They wanted to eat us, I could see that. And they had narrow, glowing, mean eyes.

You should be here, Daddy. We're not supposed to be alone.

And little brother, I hug him, and he plays, and I play with him. We draw with the crayons in the darkness, even though we can't see what we're drawing.

We're hungry, Daddy. We don't want to be dead. We don't want to be locked up any more.

We want to get back to the other side of the bridge.

Mummy's in heaven. She must be. You said so, Daddy,

but we don't want to be with her yet. We want you to come, and get rid of the nasty men and then give us a big, long hug, and then we want to play, and go swimming, and play, and forget about all the horrid things.

But everything's horrid here. It smells of death here.

I want to get away from here, Daddy. Right away.

Only you can take us away.

Unless someone else could?

I'm screaming again now, I can't do anything else, and he screams too, and then we scream together, Daddy, listen to us yell.

Are you there, girls?

Every day I wonder what's happened to you, lying here in my dark, stinking room and wondering if I did the right thing.

Now I know what's happened to you. You were blown up into little pieces.

I'll never be able to forgive myself.

But I was forced to keep you away from the monsters at all costs, I was forced to save you, that's the foremost duty of every parent, to protect their children. And I did what I could, but it wasn't enough, and all I want now is to be allowed to come to you. But why should you welcome me, I who have let you down most of all?

The flame of the wax candle lights up my damp walls, the dirt runs slowly down to the black floor, making it cold and sticky, impossible to lean on.

I can hear the trains above and below me, feel how they make the rock shake.

I want you here, but the thought of you, and of what I am and what I've done, always gets too much for me.

I prepare the syringe.

Then I find a little vein between two of my fingers, I

feel the prick, wait a few seconds, blow out the light, and soon my darkness becomes a different darkness, a white, smooth darkness, the darkness of lies, I know, but sooner that than the darkness of reality, of the truth.

26

Sven Sjöman called.

He sounded as though he'd just woken up, and it was still night, or possibly early morning.

His words: 'We've found guns and explosives in the caravan. Ludvigsson wants to talk. I want you to take the interview now, it was you who caught him, and you'd be best at reading his voice, getting him to tell us everything, the whole truth.'

'I need to sleep, Sven. OK? I thought I was about to get shot out there. And I used excessive force, so why would he confess to me? Can't someone else take it?'

Sven falls silent, evidently thinking.

'I need you here, Malin. He might be scared of you, and fear can be good in this sort of situation. You've had time to calm down. You can do this, Malin. You can sleep later. During the day. In the staffroom. I've just had a nap in there. It works.'

Maybe this isn't the time to sleep after all, Malin thought. Maybe another bomb's ticking somewhere else, and she got in the shower, letting the cold water shake some life into her body, got dressed, wrote a note for Tove, then headed straight to the station.

And now, at a quarter past six, Malin is sitting in interview room one opposite a wide-awake Jonathan Ludvigsson, with a cup of pitch-black coffee in her hand, and she's just switched on the tape recorder and is trying to sort out her thoughts so she can best get to what she wants, what they want.

She looks at Jonathan Ludvigsson.

Innocent blue eyes. Not the eyes of someone who would resort to violence. In that case, why the weapons? Why the Economic Liberation Front? It could have been you caught by the surveillance camera with your bike in front of the bank, but I don't think that's very likely.

Forensics are busy analysing both videos, comparing your walk with that of the man at the bank, they're getting an expert in movement to examine them.

And the explosives that were found in the caravan.

Forensics are trying to work out if they were the same sort as the explosives used in the main square.

Malin's thoughts are interrupted by Jonathan Ludvigsson's voice: 'Are you tired? You look tired, but I wanted to talk now, straight away, something really weird happened down in that cell.'

'What do you want to talk about?'

Malin leans across the table. Looks him in the eyes.

'I promise you can talk in confidence to me. I'll be reasonable with you.'

Ludvigsson blinks slowly, then takes a deep breath.

'The others haven't said anything, have they?'

'Not beyond the fact that didn't have a clue that you're the person behind the Economic Liberation Front.'

'That's true. They didn't know anything. The whole thing was my idea.'

'I wouldn't call a bomb in the main square that kills two little girls a thing. Take it from the start, the whole story, nice and slow. Who put the bomb together? Did you do it yourself?'

Malin hears her voice.

She sounds soft, but manages to summon up a vague

sense of threat, and knows she wants to flatter him, wants him to feel important, clever, and get him to reveal the truth that way. Because even if he says he wants to talk, there's no guarantee that he's thinking of letting the truth pass his lips.

'You certainly managed to get a lot of attention for what you did. I heard the *New York Times* had a piece on it.'

Jonathan Ludvigsson nods.

'That was the point,' he says. 'Attention. I wanted to take the opportunity to focus people's attention on the banks' exploitation of ordinary people, like my dad, and the way they're ruining the whole of society with their arrogance and greed and lack of any sense of history, I wanted to use the bombing to do that, and find a quick way to spread the anti-capitalist message. So I came up with the Liberation Front as a way of spreading the word.'

Her brain.

Still tired. But if I understand him right, Malin thinks, he's saying he didn't have anything to do with the bomb. Maybe this whole Liberation Front is just a clumsy way of trying to make up for what happened to his dad.

'So you're saying you came up with the Economic Liberation Front after the explosion, to spread your anti-capitalist message and somehow do right by your father?'

'Exactly,' Jonathan Ludvigsson says, twisting two of his dreadlocks in one hand. 'I put the website together in a few hours on my laptop when I was up in Stockholm seeing a friend, I downloaded the pictures of the banks, filmed the video myself against a white wall in his flat, then put it on YouTube.'

'I'm having trouble believing this,' Malin says. 'You're just trying to find a way of wriggling out of it, aren't you? You killed two little children, and now you're trying to wriggle out of it.'

'I can show you how I put the code together for the website, and the firewalls around my IP address and server. You haven't managed to get around it or crack it yet, have you? I can show you how I did it, and where the page is hosted. That ought to be enough to convince you.'

'Convince us of what? That you're not behind the bomb?'

Jonathan Ludvigsson looks at Malin, and seems to realise just how unrealistic what he's just said is.

'I know all about decrypting,' he says. 'I studied it at university in Umeå, among other things.'

'We found explosives in your caravan. Was it the same substance you used in the bomb in the main square?'

'I'm not responsible for the bomb in the main square. I didn't kill any young girls.'

Desperate now.

A hint.

'Two little girls,' Malin says. 'And you've got a history of militant activism. If I'm going to believe you, you need to give me better evidence to prove that you're not responsible for the bomb. Can you do that?'

'Yes.'

'How?'

'My friend, in Stockholm. I was with him, in his flat in Hornstull when the bomb went off, so it couldn't have been me. Could it?'

But you could have been working with other people and still be behind the bomb, Malin thinks. You could have constructed it and planned it, but been in Stockholm when it went off.

'What's your friend's name?' Malin asks. 'Where does he live? What's his phone number?'

'His name's Johan Sjö. He lives on Hornstulls strand.'

And Ludvigsson gives a telephone number.

Malin knows they will have heard the number on the

other side of the mirror. That Sven will instigate a check immediately.

'I sent the email the next morning,' Jonathan Ludvigsson goes on. 'From the bus terminal in Stockholm, before I caught the coach down to Linköping.'

'So you weren't bothered by the security cameras there? How am I supposed to believe that, when you seem to have thought of everything else?'

'I'm good at encryption and online anonymity. I've even helped PirateBay. But not surveillance. I made a mistake with the camera. But I want to stress that I came up with the Economic Liberation Front entirely on my own, none of the others out in the caravan had anything to do with it, nor did Sofia Karlsson. And I didn't have anything to do with any bombs. I swear on my life.'

'What about the explosives, the weapons we found in the caravan?' Malin persists. 'Did you make them up as well? Those will get you several years in prison on their own.'

'This is the biggest mistake I've ever made. I didn't kill those girls. I'm not responsible for any bombs.'

You don't want to talk about the explosives.

Why? Malin wonders, before going on: 'Even if you were in Stockholm at your friend's, the Economic Liberation Front could still be behind the bombing. There could be a lot of you. We've no way of knowing one way or the other.'

'You won't find anyone else, because there isn't anyone else. I'll help with all the technical stuff. Show you everything, then you'll believe me.'

'You didn't want to talk yesterday. Why now?'

Jonathan Ludvigsson stares at Malin.

Fear and anxiety in his eyes. He takes a deep breath before replying.

'I saw one of the girls' eyes. I know it sounds completely mad. But it was there, sort of on the hatch in the cell, and it was staring at me like it wanted to kill me, and I realised it had all gone too far.'

You're fucking right there, Malin thinks, looking at Jonathan Ludvigsson and trying to work out if he's lying or telling the truth, and she believes him, his wide blue eyes are honest, and he seems to be smart enough and naïve enough to be both sophisticated and pretty crazy at the same time.

And scared of the eye.

'What about the guns? The explosives? How do you explain them?'

Malin stands up.

'This is the third time I've asked about them, so you'd better tell me now.'

Jonathan Ludvigsson looks at her with a different sort of fear in his eyes.

'I got the chance to buy them,' he says. 'So I did. I thought they might come in useful.'

'Useful?'

'There's a war going on,' Jonathan Ludvigsson says. 'Between the forces of good and evil. I hate greed and capitalism and meat-eaters. I'm on the side of good, and at some point the guns and explosives might have come in handy, if things got desperate, but they haven't, not this time anyway.'

'For the last time: where did you get hold of the weapons?'

Jonathan Ludvigsson hesitates, then shuts his eyes.

'I bought them from the Dickheads. I got in touch with their leader, Dick Stensson, and asked if he could arrange something. He threatened to beat me up, then one of his colleagues called a month later.'

Stensson.

This case is going in circles, Malin thinks, the different lines of inquiry are biting each other's tails. So what does this mean? Does this all fit together? She closes her eyes, and hears Jonathan Ludvigsson say: 'Check with Stensson. I'm probably signing my death warrant here, but check with him.'

'What about the money? Stuff like that costs a fair amount.'

Malin looks at Jonathan Ludvigsson again.

'Vegan Power, the animal rights group that I run, sometimes gets large donations. From anonymous individuals. I got the money from there. It all happened at the beginning of March. You can check the withdrawals from our bank account at Swedbank.'

Malin gets up.

'We've got a few things to follow up,' she says. 'You can be damn sure I'm going to want to talk to you again.'

27

Where do all the secrets come from?

Tove leans her head against the window of the bus, watching the pavement of Vasagatan bow under the morning light. The trunks of the birch trees are almost grey after the winter, and the buds on the branches seem to belong to another world.

There was a terrible smell at the bus stop. From a litter bin. Something must have rotted inside it, and she had to hold her nose, then she slipped on the last of the winter grit as she was about to get on the bus.

But she didn't fall.

She never falls.

She wonders why she can't tell her mum about the letter she received? Even though what it said made me so happy?

I was relieved she was so tired yesterday, and that she'd gone back to work again by the time I woke up.

I know why I daren't say anything.

I'm scared she'll cross the line again, start drinking, start behaving like a different person, not the one I know she can be, the one she wants to be.

I'm not really sure I can leave her, but I have to. I have to, and I want to go for my own sake. I can't be her mother, her guardian. I've carried that responsibility for far too long. I'm not going to do it any more. It's completely wrong.

Tove looks out of the bus window again.

The Abisko roundabout.

There's a tattoo parlour by the square. It's supposed to be the best in Linköping, and she'd like to get a tattoo on her shoulder. A dragon with wolf's jaws. To represent her, the way she's managed to move on after what happened that summer when she was kidnapped by a killer and almost murdered.

That was when Mum lost control. That was when she flung open the door to the darkness, to a room so full of horrors and loneliness that in the end it would only have had room for death itself.

Mum's note on the hall floor that morning.

Have to get to work early. Something's come up.

Something always comes up, and will go on coming up. That's just the way it is, isn't it, Mum? But that doesn't really matter now, I'm heading out into the world, I'm going to make it mine, I'm not going to stick around in this shitty dump, not like you.

I think I can see what you're doing more clearly than you can, Mum. You slave away at your work to get away from yourself. You fight, Mum, you really do, but you should probably stop for a bit, don't you think?

It's a shame I have to leave soon, now that Grandad's come home.

I like being with him, he's not as odd as other grown-ups, he seems to like spending time with me and hearing what I've got to say. But at the same time it's obvious he's scared of something when he's with you, Mum, as if he's hiding a secret, a truth, that could ruin everything.

Her cheek gets cold against the glass.

Tove sits up straight in her seat.

The bus is approaching her stop.

★　★　★

The clock on the screen of Malin's computer says sixteen minutes past eight.

The pictures and words on the screen are blurring together. She has to make a real effort to see, to read. Has to get some more sleep soon.

The *Correspondent*'s website already has the news that Jonathan Ludvigsson has been arrested in connection with the investigation.

They've found out about the caravan as well. The pictures of it look as if they were taken at dawn.

Pictures of the man planting the bomb on the bicycle. Question of the day: 'What punishment should he get?'

'Shoot him,' says a baker from Ljungsbro.

'Lock him up and throw away the key,' says a nursing assistant from Linghem.

'We've got confirmation.'

Sven Sjöman comes over to her and Zeke's desk in the open-plan office. His eyes look steady, his voice tired but firm.

'We've managed to get hold of Jonathan Ludvigsson's friend in Stockholm. He confirms he was with Ludvigsson in his flat at the time of the explosion. Apparently there's another person who can back that up. He says he doesn't know anything about any Liberation Front. Stockholm are pulling him in for a more detailed interview.'

'Doesn't really surprise me,' Malin says as she closes her browser.

'And we've just had the results from Forensics' expert in video analysis and body language,' Sven goes on. 'In his opinion, the man at the computer in the City Terminal can't be the same man who left the bomb outside the bank.'

Malin grits her teeth.

In her mind's eye she can see the different hooded men, their motivations, their intentions.

'It could still be him, or them,' Zeke says. 'Jonathan Ludvigsson may be saying he set up the Liberation Front on his own, and he may have a reasonable explanation of how he got hold of the weapons. But we've still only got his word for it. Could he really have set up this whole charade himself?'

Sven nods, then looks at Zeke and Malin, and Malin shakes her head.

'Forensics are checking his computers, and the laptop. We'll have to see what they come up with. Ludvigsson can show them around his encryptions. And we need to do another round of interviews with the men we picked up last night.'

'We can hold them on suspected firearms offences,' Malin says.

'We can bring in other people with connections to Ludvigsson,' Zeke says. 'Put some pressure on them. If we can find any.'

'What do you think?' Sven says. 'Could the whole Economic Liberation Front be an invention, like he says. Just to get a bit of attention?'

'Wouldn't surprise me,' Malin says. 'Has Karin had time to compare the explosives?'

'Yes,' Sven says. 'What we found in the caravan isn't the same sort that was used in the bomb in the square. And we've received information from Swedbank confirming that a large sum was withdrawn from the Vegan Power account at the time Ludvigsson claimed. The branch manager was extremely helpful.'

What a surprise, Malin thinks.

'Which leads us to the next subject,' Zeke says. 'Jonathan Ludvigsson said he bought the guns from the Dickheads, from Stensson. We ought to question Stensson about that. As soon as possible.'

'We'll get started on that,' Sven says.

'Let's take it slowly,' Malin says. 'If Stensson's heard we've arrested Jonathan Ludvigsson, then he knows we might be onto him, in which case anything could happen. Right now we're not actually after him, but the people who really did this. The chances that he was behind the bombing are pretty slim. He'd hardly have tried to blow himself up. And arms dealing would be a separate investigation, wouldn't it? Unless he just happens to have supplied the people responsible for the bomb. I think we should call Stensson, basically. Ask what he has to say about Ludvigsson's claims.'

'That makes sense,' Zeke says. 'Maybe we'll finally be able to get him for something after all.'

'OK, that's what we do. Get onto it after the morning meeting.'

'Anything from the Security Police?' Zeke asks.

'Not, not a peep,' Sven says. 'But they'll probably want to talk to Ludvigsson at some point today.'

Sven leaves them.

Malin leans back, then goes back into the *Correspondent*'s website. The homepage now has Jonathan Ludvigsson's passport photograph alongside the pictures of the caravan.

There's a basic article about the arrest, and his attempt to get away, saying that's he suspected of being the man who planted the bomb outside the bank, as well as the man on the video from Stockholm.

We're ahead of them, Malin thinks. Just for once, and if she goes over to the window she'd see the journalists who have gathered outside the station, standing there in the early spring light letting the sun's rays hit their cheeks as they suck on cigarettes and drink coffee bought at the Statoil petrol station down by the roundabout.

Nothing new with the Islamic extremists, she thinks.

Can we write off that line of inquiry? No, not entirely, not yet.

Then the phone on Malin's desk rings.

She picks up the receiver and answers.

Ebba, the receptionist: 'There's a doctor who wants to talk to you. A Peter Hamse.'

And when Malin hears his name it's as if she loses control of her own body, and she suddenly has a quivering sensation all over, but focused mainly on her crotch, and she finds it hard to breathe. She hopes there's no outward sign of what's happening to her, that Zeke can't tell that she's been left feeling exposed and weak and red-cheeked at the mere mention of a name.

Deep breath.

Then out, slowly.

And she says: 'Put him through.'

And then she hears his voice, slow but firm, as if he's going to tell her a secret that he's been keeping to himself.

'Is this Malin Fors?'

'That's me.'

I haven't spared him a thought since the business with the caravan kicked off, Malin thinks. She's had to concentrate on the tangible problems facing them.

'Good to hear your voice,' she says.

And she says it without thinking and can hear how stupid and wrong it sounds, yet still somehow right, and she feels embarrassed but still feels that something important has been said. Then she looks at Zeke, sees him raise his eyebrows in surprise, then Peter Hamse says: 'Good to hear your voice too, Malin, but that's not why I'm calling. I'm phoning to let you know that Hanna Vigerö passed away during the night. I thought she was getting over the worst of it, but for some reason her injuries got the better of her. As far as we can tell, she simply stopped breathing.'

Hanna Vigerö.

The third victim of the bomb, the man with the bike, and Malin feels excited, randy, and angry, and sad all at the same time.

Good to hear your voice too.

Stopped breathing.

'I seem to remember you saying she was going to make it.'

'In difficult cases like this you can never know, but yes, I thought she was going to make it.'

'What was the time of death?'

'She passed away at a quarter past five.'

Malin looks at the clock on the screen. Almost eight. Should they have called at once? Should he have called at once?

No.

She passed away as a result of her injuries.

'You didn't notice anything odd? There was nothing unusual about the way she died?'

'No. The alarm on her monitor went off, and the night staff went to her room at once and found that she'd stopped breathing. They tried to resuscitate her, but in vain. Obviously there'll be a post-mortem by the coroner.'

Malin nods, and says: 'Thanks. OK, now we know.'

Then silence, and the phone feels damp in her hand, and she can hear him breathing, would like to feel his breath in her ear, this strange yet somehow familiar man. Can she say something now, does she dare? It feels as though he's thinking something, hesitates, then he says: 'It would be good to meet up sometime. I mean, if you'd like to, and get a chance? Off duty.'

'We've got our hands full with the case,' she says. 'I've got to go.'

She shuts her eyes. Breathes.

Then she clicks to end the call.

Why?

Why this wall around me? All I wanted was to shout out how much I wanted to see him.

Then she looks at Zeke. He's waiting intently to hear about the call.

'That was Hanna Vigerö's doctor,' she says. 'She passed away early this morning. Couldn't survive with those injuries. There doesn't seem to be anything unusual about it, just that her body couldn't carry on, or didn't want to.'

28

At nine o'clock the officers from the Crime Investigation Department gather in their usual meeting room.

They've acquired a third victim overnight, and picked up a prime suspect who has confessed to crimes other than the one they're investigating.

Sven Sjöman.

Karim Akbar.

Waldemar Ekenberg.

Johan Jakobsson.

Börje Svärd.

Zeke.

And Malin.

No one has said anything about counselling since the first meeting. It would be shameful to ask for that sort of thing right now. That's their tacit understanding.

The detectives are sitting around the table, twisting and turning the facts, evaluating the likely truth of people's words and stories, feeling the truth evading them, trying to slip through their fingers and vanish into the dark hole that an unsolved case always becomes.

In any place, at any time, outside any bank, another bomb could go off.

People are frightened, and fear can't be allowed to take hold in a civilised society.

Fear needs to be vanquished.

Otherwise society as we know it will collapse. That is

the collective belief of the detectives, the nameless feeling
that takes hold of them as they work through the lines of
inquiry.

Like scalding debris from a blazing star, that's what lines
of inquiry in this case are like, Malin thinks. In her mind's
eye she can see Peter Hamse, then Tove, and her dad and
mum, and everything that seems to be going on now, as
if all the elements of her life are coming together into a
single event.

Wasn't something supposed to be happening today?
What have I forgotten?

The shouts and cries from the children in the nursery
playground can't be heard in the room, but in the detectives' ears two floating little girls are whispering words
about fear, and wondering where their mummy is, shouldn't
she be here now? Daddy, Daddy, where are you?

But the detectives can't hear the girls, they're listening
to Sven instead.

There have been reports from Gothenburg about
increased tension between the Hells Angels and the
Bandidos – there's supposed to have been a big fight in a
club on the Avenue. So something's going on with the biker
gangs, Malin thinks. Could the bomb itself be part of an
escalating bikers' war? Could the three members of the
Vigerö family be innocent victims of blunt, unfocused
gang-related violence? What about all the activists down
in the cells? What do they want?

Dozens of possibilities.

Malin can feel her brain getting tired. She thinks about
the girls, about the eye above the cheek, thinks: I'm doing
this for you. That's why I'm sitting in this room in the
middle of what feels like an ongoing explosion.

Sven seems to see how tired she is, knows how cruel it
was of him to call her in to question Ludvigsson.

'Malin,' he says. 'After the meeting you're to go and get some sleep in the staffroom. You look shattered.'

'That's an order,' Karim agrees.

She doesn't actually want to sleep. But her body is screaming for rest, every muscle aches.

But an order's an order, isn't it? And a weary brain can't do any good.

Malin is sitting at her desk. Rubs her eyes. Hears Zeke talking to Dick Stensson on the phone as she gets ready to head into the darkness of the staffroom. She closes her eyes. Listens to Zeke's conversation, but can't keep her focus. Instead she thinks about the city preening itself in the spring light out there, a light that's far too sharp for her eyes.

Events are coming one after the other, she thinks. No time to stop, think, reflect. And that makes us bad detectives.

Like children playing football, twenty little bodies all chasing the ball.

Memorial ceremonies. Church services. A minute's silence.

That's all dying out now. People have to find their own solace, their own peace, faith.

Malin can feel a dull pain at the base of her spine and feels like drifting off to sleep here at the desk, but she can't let herself do that.

She opens her eyes.

'That was pointless. Stensson just laughed at us. Said Jonathan Ludvigsson's talking crap and that he's never met him. Stensson said we were welcome to check his phone calls and emails,' Zeke says after he hangs up.

Malin rubs her eyes again.

'Maybe Ludvigsson's making it all up. He seems prone to exaggerating his own importance. As far as we know, he could have bought the guns somewhere else entirely.'

'Maybe,' Zeke says. 'We won't make any more progress there.'

'I'm going to get some rest,' Malin says, getting up.

Without looking up from his keyboard Zeke says:'I'll get our paperwork sorted. I'll wake you if anything happens.'

The windowless room is illuminated by a small, white tablelamp. Sven was resting in the room not long ago, Malin can still detect a faint scent of him, and it makes her feel calm.

She switches on the 'engaged' sign.

Lies down on the fairly comfortable sofa, leaving the light on and letting her thoughts roam free.

Janne. I hardly ever think of him any more. He isn't inside me the same way, but he's there as someone to lean on.

When I saw him in the square after the bomb I was impressed. We need people like that among us, solid trees of people who grow in the very worst of times, who step forward, and whose calmness and composure show the way forward.

Is he likely to meet anyone new?

How will I take that?

Don't even think about it, I'll go mad, I know I will, I haven't got that far yet, I'm not ready to accept something like that.

Janne, as though made to take care of the wreckage after an explosion.

But what if the whole world explodes?

If a proper war breaks out? But war is conducted in miniature, every day, and she feels as if she's missing out on something.

My days pass, she thinks. And I breathe and I breathe and I breathe. But do I feel anything? Do I participate in anything?

Peter Hamse.

I could feel something for him.

I want him inside me, it's as simple as that, isn't it?

Keep calm, Fors, the last thing anyone needs right now is for you to lose your focus.

Tove. My love for her is a given. It is worth everything, and therefore nothing.

How the hell can I even think that? What's wrong with me?

War. A heavy bomber in the sky, then people sitting in badly lit rooms in cramped flats where no one actually wants to live, making bombs that will tear small children to pieces.

How did we get there?

She shuts her eyes. Feels the thirst.

But the desire for amber-coloured sweet tequila finds no foothold. There's a different anxiety in her body instead. Wasn't there something I was supposed to do today?

Something was going to happen. Something important. But what? Can't remember.

She thinks about Zeke instead. The deep humanity in his voice, full of testosterone and power, but also balance. Somehow Zeke always manages to hold his life together no matter what happens.

Infidelity.

The son who has become a famous ice-hockey player and moved to Canada.

A grandchild he never gets to see.

A wife who is just that, a wife, one he's had for a long time, and whom he plans to keep hold of out of habit.

But Zeke stands there, stable and free in his life, apparently happy with his decisions, with no real doubts.

Doesn't he want more? Isn't there anything that arouses greed in him? Yes. Sex with Karin. He wants more of that. But apart from that?

There's something I'm forgetting.

What time is it?

She looks at her mobile.

Almost ten.

She turns out the lamp. Leaves her mobile on. Feels the darkness embrace her like a pair of warm, longed-for arms.

Two o'clock. Something was going to happen today at two o'clock, wasn't it?

But what?

Åke Fors is pouring a cup of coffee in his flat on Barnhemsgatan. He's just spoken to the estate agent in Tenerife, they've received an unexpectedly quick offer on the flat. Maybe not quite as much money as he'd been hoping for, but these days any offer is a good offer. We, or I, he corrects himself, have friends who haven't received a single offer on their flats in several years, and who've been forced to stay on the island even though they wanted to move home to Sweden.

Dare I do it? he thinks.

Sell up.

Who knows what's going to happen once the will is read out today. Is Malin going to go mad, is she going to push me away, is she going to forbid me to see Tove? He knows she's been longing to know the truth, that she's felt that there's been a secret in her life, and she's asked him, several times, straight out, to tell her what it is.

But that wasn't my responsibility, Åke Fors thinks, sipping the hot coffee as the wind moves the treetops outside the window and the yellow-green buds seem to wave at him, telling him that today is the start of something new.

I've missed Malin. Tove. But I don't miss you, Margaretha, he thinks.

For all these years you got me to do what you wanted.

I went along with you, denying Malin the chance to be whole, and she's going to hate me for it, isn't she?

Am I going to be forced to run away to a lonely life in the sun on Tenerife? Do I even have the right to demand to be part of their lives?

I wonder if she's remembered the meeting with the solicitor today, I ought to call her, and Åke Fors goes out to the phone on the wall in the hallway, dials his daughter's number and waits.

One ring.

And even though Malin never lived there when she was little, he can see her as a six-year-old running across the floor, the beautiful little girl with her hair flying around her head, and she's crying and bubbling and howling with laughter as she runs through the rooms.

Then she stops in the hall. Right in front of him. Looks at him, wants to ask him something, but can't seem to find the words, and then she runs off again, and he sees her looking for something in the living room, intently, lifting the rug, the cushions on the sofa, saying: 'Where is she? Where is he? Where is he?'

And Åke Fors wants to run over to his six-year-old daughter and help her, and now she's saying: 'Where's Mummy? Where's Mummy?'

And he wants to answer, but he knows that none of what he can see really exists except as electrical impulses, created by memories and dreams inside the meandering pathways of his own brain.

The phone rings several more times.

No answer.

Åke Fors hangs up.

Hopes that everything isn't already too late.

★　★　★

She hadn't had time to fall asleep. And she sees her dad's name on the screen but doesn't feel like answering.

But it makes her remember the meeting with the solicitor.

The will.

Today.

She'd completely suppressed it, but she has time to get a bit of sleep and still get there in time.

Try to sleep now, Malin. You need to rest. Even if you don't want to.

Concentrating on the present moment, that's the only way to survive.

Malin.

You're asleep in your staffroom now, with your phone switched on, but no one seems to want to disturb you. You're lying there, Malin, and you're missing your mummy, even if you don't realise it, even if you don't feel it.

Our mummy isn't here. Even though she ought to be, and you, you still don't know what happened to her, and maybe you're never going to find out.

Maybe the old man who's just been cutting into her broken, dead body in a room in the hospital won't find anything odd about the way she died.

Be careful with it all, Malin.

Tove likes you, your daddy likes you.

Don't be scared of what's about to happen, try, try not to get angry, not to judge people for not being able to control, or understand, their feelings.

Deep down, you know better than that, Malin.

As for us, we're afraid, because it's lonely here, and dark and cold and it's like we're in one of those nightmares you used to have when you were little. You used to dream you were all alone in the world, that there was no love for you.

When your mummy left you she was sad.
Because she was leaving you.
Just like our mummy left us.
We know that now.
And she ought to be here. With us, but she isn't here and nor is Daddy, and we want to be together again. Sleep next to each other in a big bed with white sheets, snuggling under white sheets that can shut out anything nasty, anything cruel.

The other children's mummy keeps to herself, maybe she's trying to be there for them, like we are for you, Malin? And if she is, then she'll hear them breathing now, see them banging on the door, scared of the anger, scared of getting out, scared they're never going to get out.

The boy is crying. The girl hugs him, says: 'Don't be sad, don't be sad.'

The monotonous whistling.

It's started again.

Stop that fucking noise. I want to sleep. I want to stay in my lonely darkness.

Sleep comes to an abrupt end and she opens her eyes, feeling with her hand over the sofa for her mobile.

There it is.

And by mistake she dismisses the call, but hardly has time to switch on the tablelamp before it starts ringing again.

She doesn't recognise the number.

What the hell is the time? How long have I been asleep? Fuck.

She sits up, answers.

'Malin Fors.'

'Ah, hello. My name is Johan Strandkvist, I'm a solicitor. We're waiting for you here at my office. It's ten past two, and we had a meeting that was supposed to start at two, so I just wanted to see if you . . .'

'I'm on my way,' Malin says, and ends the call.

Got to get the meeting out of the way. It can't take more than half an hour.

Then it will all be done, she thinks.

I don't have the time, or the energy, for any more worries.

29

She's driving too fast.

Not long awake, yet her head feels strangely clear.

Malin accelerates.

Djurgårdsgatan is shut for roadworks.

The car sweeps past the edge of the old cemetery, where small leaves are starting to blur with the buds on the trees, and on one grave a solitary woman is laying a large bouquet of what look like red and white roses.

She thinks about the case.

She's sure Jonathan Ludvigsson is telling the truth. He is, and will remain, an activist who went too far, but he's no murderer. The Economic Liberation Front is an invention. He's the sort who would travel the length and breadth of Europe to protest outside meetings, and demand the nationalisation of the banks, and the firing-squad for their greedy directors.

But the guns? The explosives in the caravan?

Romantic revolutionary dreams.

Like the Italian anarchists in the USA in the early years of the last century.

But she's convinced Jonathan Ludvigsson hasn't used any weapons. That they caught him in time. So who's the man with the bicycle? Where does he come from? What are his motives?

Malin stops at a red light beside the old fire station. A car pulls up alongside her.

A young family, dad driving, mum and two children in the backseat.

Green.

Malin puts her foot down again, then she hears an earth-shattering bang and feels like crouching down behind the steering wheel, feels her stomach clench, and she thinks that it's happened again, but she can't see any smoke, can't hear any real silence.

How far away?

Where has something just been blown up? Who? Are there going to be body parts raining from the sky?

She stops again. The car with the family has braked beside her, the children are screaming in the backseat, and the woman is comforting them.

Then the father points ahead and starts to laugh, pointing and laughing and pointing.

At the bus stop fifty metres away, beside the shiny multi-storey car park, stands a bus, its bulk leaning to one side like a badly listing ship.

The bus driver is inspecting one of the front tyres, the one with no air in it, the one that just a few seconds before must have exploded.

Malin pulls open the door of Johan Strandkvist the solicitor's office after knocking, but without waiting for a 'come in'.

Sleepy, out of kilter again now.

The solicitor, about forty years old, greasy curls reaching his collar, dressed in a blue blazer and a bright red shirt. His drink-swollen face is lined with deep wrinkles, and Malin thinks he must have done some serious drinking the night before, this is just a routine meeting for him, a meeting he needs to get over and done with, and that's how I see it as well, don't I? This needs to be done so we can all move on. In purely legal terms there's nothing to discuss, Dad's going to get everything, and then I'll inherit everything from him when the time comes.

The deep wrinkles aren't the only thing that makes her feel uneasy. There's also a tension in the solicitor's face, and he looks as if he'd prefer just to run away. Maybe this isn't merely a routine meeting after all, and she looks at her dad, sitting in an armchair by a wall covered in bookcases full of legal volumes.

Dad isn't looking at me.

His back is straight, and he's looking the other way, like Mum used to.

He's looking at the solicitor. Or is he looking out of the window, at the cloudless blue afternoon sky? Is he thinking about Mum's ashes, wondering where to scatter them?

Malin knows what he's looking at.

She realises now, from her instantaneous scan of the room, yet she somehow, within a fraction of a second, managed to suppress the sight, because she doesn't even want to try to understand this scenario. Because who's this woman in her sixties, sitting in another armchair and looking at me, smiling a friendly but strangely businesslike smile?

Malin takes a step into the room, holds out her hand to the woman in the armchair, as if they both require politeness and respect, and says: 'Malin Fors. And you are?'

'Take a seat,' the solicitor says. 'Welcome.'

'Yes, sit down,' her dad says, she doesn't remotely feel like sitting down, damn it, no one tells her what to do, then the woman nods, gives her a look that seems to want to say: 'It'll all be fine, but you should probably sit down', and Malin recognises that look, it's the sort of look she adopts when she has to pass on news of a death, or give people some other really bad news.

She sits down.

Allows her buttocks to be abused by the hard wooden chair positioned between the two armchairs, and she looks at her dad, but he refuses to meet her gaze. His shoulders are slumped now, as if weighted down by shame and a secret that has unjustly remained a secret for far too long.

The solicitor.

He's steeling himself, and Malin can see how hungover he is now, recognises it, knows how much effort he is having to make to take command, become the master of the moment and do what is expected of him.

A tequila, she thinks.

What I wouldn't give for a tequila now, and she digs the nail of her forefinger hard into her thumb, and then he is there as an image inside her, the faceless boy she has been dreaming about for so long, so many times over so many years, the boy she has perhaps been looking for without understanding what it was she was looking for. Is this my real mum, sitting there in the armchair, was that why you were never there for me, Mum, why you turned away from me, and why I had to search for your love?

No. That's not it.

Mum. I've seen pictures of you with a big stomach when you were carrying me. Pushing my pram. So who is this woman? What's she doing here?

'Who are you?'

And Malin realises that she sounds aggressive, doesn't want to sound aggressive – but I feel threatened now, something's attacking me, attacking what might be my very core, and if darkness is the only thing you have, you cling onto it.

Don't you?

That's what you do.

'This is Britta Ekholm from Norrgården Care Home in the village of Sjöplogen in Hälsingland.'

The woman nods.

Malin nods back, and then she looks at her dad, and asks: 'What's she doing here? Who is she?'

Tove is sitting in the garden of Janne's house, hoping to get a bit of a tan in time for the end of the school year.

Mum.

I love you, Mum, no matter what nonsense you get up to. But I think what you need most of all is someone to cuddle up to, someone who likes you for who you are.

Sometimes I get the impression that you're not going to manage, that you're going to let the darkness take over, and start drinking again, that you're just waiting for an excuse to start knocking back the tequila again.

I've seen it in some of the boys at school.

They drink the way you sometimes did.

Like there's no tomorrow, like it's in their genes to destroy themselves.

I love you, Mum, you need to know that, I'll never give up on you.

Even if I move away, go somewhere else.

Janne can see Tove sitting with her head turned towards the sun. Her body slumped on the plastic chair.

He's standing on a rickety ladder down in the garden's small orchard, working his way through the branches of an apple tree with a pair of secateurs. He knows he ought to employ a gardener to get the most out of his fruit trees, but who can afford to get a professional in to do the pruning?

Tove.

It's as if she got the best of both of us.

Malin's intelligence and determination.

My calm, but not my restlessness. Nor has she inherited

my inability to cope with responsibility, the way I feel like turning and running the moment things get tricky in any relationship.

She's going to forge her own way through life. She's meant for greater things than the two of us. That much is obvious. Malin and I aren't the sort of people who have grand visions. We might be good at what we do, very good, even, but that's as far as it goes.

A few seriously large branches fall to the ground.

The grass beneath them is pale green after the sunshine of recent days, but without any real life-giving warmth or moisture.

We won't leave any trace.

Your mum didn't either, Malin, but she couldn't even manage to show her own child any love, didn't even take that responsibility, and we've always managed that, even if I know you sometimes think that we didn't, that we didn't show our love to Tove, that we somehow managed to let her down with our own indecisiveness, our own inability to sort out our own love.

But she's fine.

She's stronger than we have ever been, or ever will be.

Janne drops the secateurs.

Shit, he thinks.

Climbs down from the ladder.

Kneels down beside his tools. Sees her, the other woman's face, in his mind's eye, and he daren't even imagine how Malin is going to react if things go far enough for it to become official. Tove doesn't know anything, he doesn't think she even suspects anything, she's so preoccupied with her own life, blind to certain things in that way only teenagers can be.

The secateurs in his hand.

Maybe she ought to become official.

Malin.

Maybe that's the only way we can cut our ties to each other, the grown-up ties of love that we still carry.

They need to be cut. After all, we'll always be connected through Tove anyway.

She is us, she is the best of us, she is the person we have made.

30

We see you, Malin, in the solicitor's office. You're about to find out something, you're upset and scared and you feel like you're about to explode, that all the feelings in the room where you've gathered are going to make you burst.

The solicitor has introduced the woman.

She's asked him to let her explain who she is. Stay calm, Malin, she isn't your mother.

Calm down.

She's about to start talking, and even if you feel the world quake, you should know that she's bringing an opportunity, a present, the most beautiful present of all.

Malin's nostrils flare, and she feels them develop a nervous twitch, and looks at the painting – or is it a photograph? – behind the solicitor's head.

She recognises the picture. Can't quite place it. It's a photograph of people in a hammock, but they're just silhouettes, as if they've abandoned their lives. Didn't it used to hang in Skogså Castle? The castle where they found the IT millionaire murdered in the moat?

Malin feels like sinking into the picture, but the present wants her here.

Dad.

He hasn't said a word and it's as if Mum's spirit is floating in the room and once more turning him into the wimp he so often was in her presence.

But now she recognises what it is. He isn't in control here, and this drama, written and directed by another force, is to be played out to its end.

The woman, this Britta Ekholm, is facing Malin, looking her in the eye, as she starts to talk.

'As Mr Strandkvist has just said, my name's Britta Ekholm. For more than thirty years I've worked at Norrgården Care Home in Hälsingland, the last fifteen years as manager. Norrgården isn't a home for the elderly, we're mainly a home for children whose parents can't quite manage to look after them, children who were either born with a severe handicap, or developed one early in life. Some of them have been with us for a very long time, and Norrgården has become their home.'

Fuck.

She has an idea of where this is going, doesn't want to hear any more, or does she? The woman's voice, a gentle narrator's voice.

'For over thirty years I've been Stefan Malmå's legal guardian.'

Malmå.

She wants to turn to her dad, but can't, wants to yell at him and ask what the hell is this? What have you done? What did you do? But she stays silent, lets Britta Ekholm carry on.

Malmå.

Mum's maiden name, and the rest of the stories told by the woman and the solicitor are like a long exhalation, as if someone's been holding Malin's breath for her throughout her life, and now she's free and can breathe again.

What next?

Then an indescribable anger wells up. A sense of having been betrayed. Robbed of something important. Something that has made her feel like half a person all her life.

Then the desire for revenge.

★ ★ ★

'So, Stefan Malmå lives in our care home. He's thirty-one years old, and he's severely handicapped, both physically and mentally. He's spent his whole life with us, since he was just a few weeks old. I'm here to represent his interests when his mother's will is read.'

The solicitor clears his throat, stretches his neck and looks less hungover now, but his attempt to look authoritative fails, and he just ends up looking rather foolish.

Britta Ekholm falls silent as Johan Strandkvist goes on: 'While I was working on the will, a second child appeared in the records. It turns out, Malin, that your mother had a son for whom she surrendered responsibility shortly after birth, and who is now entitled to a share of the inheritance. This will not be applicable until after your father's death, but in purely legal terms this needs to be taken into account, and the rights of a child of a different union protected. I should point out that this came as a surprise to me, and that I was the person who found the information.'

Dad.

You must have known.

Malin shuts her eyes, is taking short, shallow breaths, then she says: 'So this Stefan Malmå is my brother?'

'He's your brother,' Britta Ekholm says.

A face, a faceless face, a mask turning into a person's face.

'Your half-brother,' Britta Ekholm clarifies.

'So I've got a little brother?'

Dad. Malin can't see the look in his eyes, is it apologetic? Is he sad? Ashamed? He's slumped deeper into the armchair, his shoulders look weighed down by some invisible force.

'In all these years your mother didn't want any form of contact with us. I called her several times, but she got angry and upset each time, and told us to leave her family alone.'

Mum?

Dad? What about you?

It's as if you're not really here in the room. That both the solicitor and the woman from the care home have decided to despise you.

A brother? A half-brother? So, Dad, you're not his father? And me, why was I never told of his existence? Surely that ought to have been my fucking choice, and she gets up, looks at her dad, then turns to the woman and yells: 'Why the hell didn't you contact me? If he's been there in the home all my life, surely you could have contacted me? I might have wanted to meet my brother.'

She knows her anger ought to be directed at her dad instead, but she can't bring herself to force him up against the wall and demand an explanation.

'We were under the impression that the whole family wanted to be left alone. Your mother stressed that point, time and time again. Our duty was to look after Stefan as well as we could.'

Official records, Malin thinks, sitting down on her chair again. If only I'd ever looked up our family in the records, just once, I'd have found out about this long ago.

Clarity.

And unreality, and she sees a skinny little boy lying alone under a yellow health-service blanket on a hospital bed pushed into the corner of a dark, featureless sickroom, marked out by the fact that none of his own flesh and blood care about him at all.

A room without love.

She gets up and shouts: 'So you, you're not his father?'

The woman said half-brother.

Her dad is staring down at the floor.

And the solicitor says, in a voice that sounds as if he is summarising a boardroom decision: 'Your father isn't the boy's father. His father was a travelling salesman dealing in office supplies, she met him while she was working at Saab.'

Dad nods slowly, as if to confirm the story.

'She spent one night with this man at the Central Hotel. He, Stefan Malmå's father, died just a few months later in a car accident. When your mother realised she was pregnant it was too late for an abortion. She refused to acknowledge her condition for a long time. Then she left you and your father to conceal her pregnancy from everyone.

'She gave birth to the child in Hälsingland and was planning to have it adopted. As I understand it, she didn't want to cause a scandal or disturb her marriage with an illegitimate child. But when the child turned out to be severely handicapped, that was no longer even an option. Social Services stepped in and arranged a place in the care home, with Britta Ekholm here as his legal guardian.'

'And the years passed,' Britta Ekholm says.

She holds back what she was about to go on to say, breathing calmly and looking at Malin, as if to calm her as well.

Malin's thoughts are spinning. Was it you, Dad, who refused to accept the child? Or was it her? It must have been Mum, so worried about protecting her precious fucking reputation at all costs.

'I can tell you that Stefan is a very special young man. You should meet him. He'd probably love to meet you,' and there isn't an ounce of criticism in the woman's voice, no reproach, just hope for something new, perhaps an end to loneliness, and Malin feels her eyes filling up, then she takes two steps towards her dad and starts slapping him hard about the head and face, over and over again, but she doesn't shout, she just goes on hitting him, and he makes no attempt to defend himself and just accepts her blows.

Then Malin feels arms around her, the solicitor and the woman from the care home, and she realises that this is all true and she has no idea what to do next, how to get out of this situation, and she thinks that she has to visit him, now, now, now.

I have to see my brother, I have to hold him, let him know I exist before it's too late, because who knows what this wretched world might come up with, what it wants with us?

She spins towards the door.

Wriggles out of their snake-like grip.

Wants to strike out again.

But her body has no more blows in it, not at the moment.

'Bastard,' she says to her dad.

His head bowed.

'You fucking bastard. You knew all along, didn't you? You hid the truth from me, you're nothing but a fucking coward and I hate you. Did you refuse to accept him? Maybe it was you who forced Mum to give him up? Who are you? Don't you ever come near us again!' she yells. 'If you so much as phone me or Tove or anyone else who has any damn thing to do with us, I'll kill you. Got that?'

'Malin, I—'

'Shut up!'

'Malin—'

'Shut up!'

And she opens the door, wants the woman to tell her to stay, that there's so much she doesn't know yet, needs to know.

'You bastard!' she shouts at her dad. 'You didn't even say a word about this to the solicitor? Did you? Did you think it was just going to disappear?'

She wants to go to Hälsingland now.

To the care home. Can't the woman ask her to go with

her? To the darkest of forests, to a room waiting for some light.

But no one asks her anything. The three people in the solicitor's office sit in silence, have nothing more to add, and Malin can see that the woman is embarrassed, can see her looking with derision at Malin's dad, who is sitting there without saying anything, as if shame has sewn his lips together.

She slams the door shut.

A short, pointless bang.

Breathes.

Wondering: What the fuck happens now?

31

Malin, Malin.

You're rushing across Trädgårdstorget. You need something to cling onto, don't you?

Where are you going, Malin? Where do you want to go? Do you think you can escape?

Concentrate on us instead, Malin, us, the blown-up girls who are like you in so many more ways than you can imagine. So are the other children, locked up as they are in a room without love, with no chance of escape.

Malin stops in the middle of the square.

Leans forward.

Puts her hands on her thighs and fights an urge to throw up, as she feels her heartbeat thundering beneath her ribs.

She inhales her own anger and feels the chill in the spring air, then she stretches.

The terrace cafés on the square are half full of people drinking coffee and beer in the spring sunshine, maybe the fear of another bomb is starting to subside. But I wouldn't be so sure, she thinks.

That bloody solicitor.

And the woman. What was her name again? Have to talk more with her. She tries to ignore the image of her dad with his head bowed.

Tove.

Mum's got a little brother.

You've got an uncle.

Shall we go and see him? Shall we go together, into the heart of the forest, and meet him?

We won't be seeing Grandad again. He doesn't exist.

No.

I say no.

I do not accept this, and she feels that she has to put everything, absolutely everything, to one side and focus on not going mad, but how the hell is she supposed to do that?

They'll be expecting me back at the station soon, but how can I bear to go back there? Hamlet's open, the bar is probably empty at this time of day, I could sit there and drink myself far away from everything, I could drink for a long, long time, and never come back to this.

I need something.

Daniel Högfeldt.

Maybe he's at home now? His flat's only a three-minute walk from here, and I could go there, I'm going there now, I need something, and she starts to walk across the square, and there are people, industrious Linköping citizens, all around her, black shapes with glittering stars for eyes, and it seems to her that the beams from their eyes are hitting her, making her unsteady somehow, in a way she has never been unsteady before.

The boy. Or the man, the one who's my little brother. In his bed. Handicapped. Abandoned, can he talk? He has no face, can he even learn my name, can he even understand that I exist? Does he know that I exist?

Malin stumbles across Drottninggatan and tries to find her bearings in the afternoon light.

The clock above McDonald's says a quarter past three.

She heads towards Linnégatan.

Daniel lives at number 2, and she still remembers the code for the door, taps it in and the door unlocks.

He lives on the third floor of four, and she is out of breath by the time she rings the bell after running up the three flights of stairs. She can tell from the smell of disinfectant that someone's just mopped the entire stairwell, as if to make it nice and clean for her arrival.

She can hear something behind the door.

Voices.

Daniel's voice.

She feels all her desire, all her hunger for clarity gathering in her crotch and in a longing to rest in his arms, and she rings again, wants him to open the door so she can drag him into his bedroom, and that's the security chain, she can hear it being undone, then he opens up.

Naked. He has a blue shirt in his hand that he's holding in front of his crotch.

'Malin,' he says. 'What are you doing here?'

'I was just passing,' she says. 'It's been a while.'

Then she hears a voice, a female voice, and it sounds familiar, she recognises the voice, hears it regularly, and the person sounds recently fucked, happy and irritable and self-assured all at the same time.

'Daniel, who the hell is it? Shut the door and get back here.'

And she knows whose voice it is.

The radio presenter. Her friend.

Helen Aneman. Are they fucking? How the hell could she? I'll kill her.

Easy now, calm down.

Daniel smiles at Malin.

And she gathers all the saliva in her mouth and spits it at him, and it hits him right in the eye and he looks surprised and innocent, as if he really is? As if the cunt he's got in there is innocent?

'What the hell are you doing, Malin? Have you gone totally fucking mad?'

And she spits again and he yells: 'You never gave a damn about me, and I can't even remember how fucking long it's been since you last showed up to use me as your flesh-and-blood dildo, so you can fuck right off!'

Helen appears behind Daniel.

Her blonde hair is tousled. She looks at Malin as if it's the first time she's ever seen another person.

'Just fuck off, Malin,' Daniel says, and Helen takes his arm, but doesn't try to calm him down.

And the words hit Malin like powerful gusts of wind, driving her down the stairs, away from there and out into the street again.

The sun has disappeared behind the trees of the Horticultural Society Park, and she rushes over there and finds a bench under a Japanese cherry tree in full bloom, thinking that the stupid little pink flowers are mocking her, then she calls directory enquiries.

'Can I have the number of a Peter Hamse in Linköping, please.'

'I've got a mobile number here, would you like me to connect you or send you a text?'

'Both,' and Malin holds the mobile in front of her, watching the call to him get connected, the embodiment of her physical desires, and her life raft.

Then she feels terrified.

Terrified of everyone.

She never wants to have to talk to another person again, and she clicks to cancel the call. She puts the mobile in her jacket pocket and heads off towards her car, parked at the old bus station.

Just as she is opening the gate to leave the park, her mobile rings.

Must be him. He saw I called, and she wants to take the call, presses answer without checking the caller's identity.

'Malin.'

'This is Britta Ekholm. We met a little while ago.'

No.

No energy. But I have a thousand questions.

'I was thinking that you might want to know a bit more about your brother? I can quite understand you getting upset.'

She goes through the black metal gate, heading towards the heavy traffic on Drottninggatan, can just make out her car in the furthest row in the car park.

'Do I want to know?' she asks.

'He's seriously handicapped,' Britta Ekholm says. 'He's almost completely blind, and he has learning difficulties. But it's possible to have a conversation with him, he has his own language, and he's very loving.'

Her rational brain clicks in, in the same instinctive way that she just lashed out at her father.

'Can he walk?'

'No, his motor functions were severely damaged at birth. But you'll like him, I'm sure of that.'

Britta Ekholm goes on to tell her about Sjöplogen, the village where the care home is, and in her mind's eye Malin can see a large white castle, with lunatics sticking their heads out of the windows and shouting happy hellos to everyone walking past. Not scary lunatics, just happy crazy people.

'I want to apologise,' Britta Ekholm says. 'For never getting in touch with you. I was relying on what your mother said, that none of you wanted any form of contact with Stefan.'

'You probably did the right thing. Your duty was to his welfare, and why would you insist on him seeing people who said they didn't want anything to do with him?'

'Yes, but I saw you in the paper once,' Britta Ekholm says. 'I thought about calling you then, because I got the impression that you were the sort of person who could deal with this sort of responsibility.'

'What sort of responsibility?'

'The responsibility to love,' Britta Ekholm says.

Malin puts the key in the ignition and pulls out of the car park. She drives out of the city and soon the car is crossing the fertile fields of the Östgöta plain, and on the cloudy horizon dark trees are swaying towards a half hidden sun. She lets her hands relax on the wheel, and she is on her way towards Hälsingland and the village of Sjöplogen.

So much loneliness.

So little time.

So many miles to cover, and then a light spring rain starts to fall on the windscreen, and she looks off to the side, sees the plain open up to the raindrops, accept the moisture like an invaluable gift, a possibility.

The drops of rain like diamonds.

She shuts her eyes for a moment, not looking at the cars coming towards her, and hopes nothing happens, and there's a voice there, she recognises it but doesn't want to listen to it, feels like telling it that she has to deal with her own concerns now, that she doesn't have time to rescue anyone else, so try to understand that, leave me alone, let me do what I have to do, now, now, now.

She opens her eyes.

Carries on.

* * *

Malin, listen to us now.

This isn't just about us, in a way there's no hope for us now.

You're the one who can give us back our parents. We're too little for this loneliness, too little to be abandoned by Mummy and Daddy. Just like the boy and girl are too little, but it isn't too late for them yet.

So listen now, Malin.

Stop the car.

Turn around.

You have to get to the captive children. We're jealous of them, more than anything we want what they've got, and we can never have that.

But no one should be as scared as they are. No one in the world.

The lizards in the long white buildings want to gnaw the flesh from their bones.

You can't leave now, Malin.

Not where you're heading. Your brother needs you. But the captive children need you more. He's alone, but they're alone and scared. And at least he isn't scared, Malin.

32

Something was whispering in the car, she thought she heard someone say: Don't go, don't go now. That must wait. First the girls' killer has to be found.

She turned back after a hundred kilometres, and now, as she pulls up outside the police station, it's early evening, and some thin, high veils of cloud have drifted in from the north, bringing with them a new type of cold in the air.

The warmth of spring is unreliable. Treacherous. Like the whole season, this event in the city's history.

She breathes.

Prepares herself.

Forces aside all thoughts of what happened today. Instead she needs to focus all of her attention on this damn investigation, on the work she is employed to do, she will use work as a fucking huge glass of tequila, downing it time after time, and not let anything else touch her.

No thinking about Dad or Mum or her little brother. Pretend that woman in the solicitor's office, and everything she said, doesn't exist. It might work for a while, and you, Mum, proved that denial is possible.

There is a cluster of media outside the entrance, and she feels an instinctive urge to make her way in through the county court premises, through the underground tunnels leading to the police station, thinking: We ought to set up a tent for them, get someone in to sell them coffee, because they might be here for ages if we don't get some-where with this soon.

She closes the car door.

Moves towards the crowd, and they catch sight of her but ignore her, focusing their attention instead on the lobby of the station.

She forces her way past them.

No Daniel Högfeldt here, of course. He's at home, in bed with Helen Aneman.

Bastard.

But why did I get so angry? He can do whatever he likes. I never let him into my life, and I have no right to demand anything from him. And Helen. We haven't seen each other properly for several years. She can't even have known that Daniel and I had an affair.

The doors to the station slide open.

Three young men in dreadlocks and rough, pilled, hooded jackets are standing with their backs to her at the reception desk, flanked by three uniformed officers. The dreadlocked men are signing forms, and she sees the door to the open-plan office open, and Sven Sjöman comes towards her with a look of weary resignation.

'Good that you're back,' he says, and now the dreadlocks are heading towards the exit, and she knows who they are, Jonathan Ludvigsson's colleagues, or friends, from the caravan outside Klockrike.

They're grinning at me. Aren't they? Unless I'm imag-ining it?

'It's been a hell of a day,' Malin says.

'But now you're back,' Sven says, and goes on, 'we've had to release them all apart from Ludvigsson. The prosecutor couldn't see any reason to hold them. We have no evidence whatsoever that any of them was in any way involved in either the bombing or any of Ludvigsson's other activities.'

'I daresay the prosecutor's right,' Malin says. 'But I'm far from convinced that they're entirely innocent.'

Outside the entrance the flashbulbs are clattering around the young men, as the reporters shout their questions all at the same time.

'And we've got a preliminary report from the experts about their examination of Ludvigsson's computer. There's nothing to suggest he had any contact with anyone else, not about the Economic Liberation Front, and not about the bombing.

'They've also found the coding for the website, and the original video file that was posted on YouTube. It certainly does look like Ludvigsson created the Liberation Front on his own, as a way of drawing attention to an issue he thought was ideologically important.'

'Idiot.'

'But nowhere close to as much of an idiot as plenty of other people,' Sven says. 'These days people seem prepared to do pretty much anything for what they believe in.'

'Does this mean that we don't think there's any threat to the country's banks?'

'The level of threat is certainly considerably less acute, don't you think? They could probably open up again, if only as a way of easing people's anxieties,' Sven says.

Detonating a bomb, Malin thinks.

In a little square in a nondescript city.

Blowing the life out of two little girls.

What sort of conviction could drive someone to that?

Nothing's shown up from Linköping's assortment of religious minorities. No sign that militant Islamists were involved.

'What about the connection between Dick Stensson and Jonathan Ludvigsson, this supposed weapons deal, has that produced anything?' Malin asks.

'Not a thing. We haven't found anything that can be linked to our case.'

'Can we seize the Dickheads' computers?'

'Not as things stand. We haven't got a shred of evidence that there was anything untoward going on.'

'Here's what I think,' Malin says. 'Dick Stensson and the Dickheads and Los Rebels may not be the nicest people on the planet, and they wouldn't hesitate to kill their rivals, but are they really child-killers? Terrorists who don't have any qualms about planting a bomb in the middle of a perfectly ordinary city, among perfectly ordinary people? I'd be extremely surprised.'

'In principle we can probably drop that line of inquiry for the time being,' Sven says. 'I agree with you.'

'What about thefts of explosives from military stores? Wholesalers? Construction companies?' Malin asks.

'So far we haven't found anything there. And there haven't been any suspicious purchases from any of the firms that supply TATP.'

Ebba nods in greeting at Malin from behind the reception desk.

Malin nods back.

'So we're back where we started, aren't we?' Malin says. 'We don't know who the man with the bike outside the bank on the video is. We haven't got a fucking clue, if we're being honest about it.'

Outside the station the chaos has died down.

The sun has moved lower, and the journalists and the released young activists seem to dissolve in the shadows. Malin looks at them through the window. Thinks that any one of them could be the man in the video, then realises that none of them is, but that they're still all actors in the tragic drama currently playing out, a drama that needs to reach a conclusion if any real calm, any passable illusion of security, is to return to the city, to the citizens who have chosen to make it their home.

But that won't bring me any calm.

Not a chance, Malin thinks as she forces it all away, and Sven goes on: 'You're right, Malin. We're treading water. But deep down in my detective's soul I have a feeling that something's going to happen, something's going to crop up that throws a new light on everything.'

'You think so?'

'It's time to listen to the voices,' Sven says. 'The investigation's voices. Hear what they're telling us.'

Sven's mantra, through all the cases they've worked on.

The investigation's voices.

Listen to them.

She has made the mantra her own, but now, in the drab lobby of the police station, the words sound hollow and meaningless. Of course she can hear the voices, she knows they're there, they're everywhere, and only those inaudible words can help them solve the mystery.

But how are you supposed to find the energy to care about the solution to the mystery when your very self is exploding, turning into the charred pieces of a jigsaw for no reason? How to find the energy for anything when you're being torn apart like this?

But maybe it has to be this way. First something inside you has to die, so that something new can take its place.

'I've got no idea where this is going to take us,' Malin says. 'What about the Security Police, have we heard anything from them?'

'Not a damn thing. I'm pretending they don't exist.'

'I still can't understand why they went straight to the media with the video from the City Terminal.'

'They wanted to show who's in charge,' Sven says. Then he asks: 'How did the reading of the will go?'

'Don't ask, Sven, just don't ask,' and then she leaves him, heading towards her desk in the office without really knowing what she's going to do there.

Zeke went home just after nine o'clock in the evening, once the day's paperwork had been dealt with.

Waldemar Ekenberg, Johan Jakobsson, and Börje Svärd have gone as well, and Malin has spent a while sitting at her computer, surfing manically around the news websites, reading about their case, about the day's ideas, about any imaginable and unimaginable line of inquiry. On one of the main newspapers' websites she found an absurd conspiracy theory, suggesting that the bombing had been carried out by an al-Qaeda commando who had been sent here from Afghanistan. Some mad professor at a Scottish university supported the theory, but it was just wild speculation, the story didn't seem to have any foundation in reality at all.

No.

In all likelihood, Islamic militants had absolutely nothing to do with their bomb. The likeliest explanation was that a different sort of primitive evil had blossomed this spring, and that the reason for the girls' death was to be found in something that was more clearly visible in our own society.

She shuts her browser.

The screensaver with the picture of Tove in a bathing costume on a beach at sunset clicks in.

I have to tell her, Malin thinks as she looks at the picture of Tove, I have to tell her, I have to take her with me to the care home in Hälsingland, I can't let her down again and keep her new uncle away from her. And then she sees the room with the boy again, her image of her brother, but behind it hovers the black hole of her hatred for her dad.

And possibly also for her mum.

How the hell could you, either of you, both of you? and she swallows hard and the sense of unreality takes over again, and that feeling becomes her best friend and she looks at Tove, this perfect incarnation of love and goodness, and she thinks that they will never abandon each other, that they will follow each other through life until she dies of old age in a comfortable armchair on a balcony with a view of the sea.

Outside the window, night is starting to mark its progress, and she wants to go home, go to bed and try to sleep, but how the hell is sleep going to come now?

You can't sleep in the middle of an explosion. You can't even shut your eyes when the world is tearing you apart.

But you can drink.

And the Hamlet is open.

She gets up, goes out to the car park and sits in the car. Turns the key and the engine throbs happily, and then she hears someone knock on her windscreen and she feels like ignoring it, because there can't actually be anyone out there, can there?

An eye.

A torn cheek. A solitary little girl's eye staring at her, begging her for something important. Is that eye my only salvation?

Hungry.

And she thinks of the hotdog-seller in the square. What had he said when her colleagues spoke to him? That Hanna and the twins were often there?

The knocking continues, breaking her train of thought, and the feeling of hunger.

Malin turns her head.

Sees Karin Johannison on the other side of the glass. A serious look on her beautiful face.

What the hell has happened now? Has Zeke dumped her? Or vice versa?

'Open up, Malin. Open up.'

And a minute later Karin is sitting in the passenger seat beside Malin, and Malin can smell the sweet, fruity scent of her perfume, and thinks that the scent smells as expensive as Karin's white and black dress looks. She imagines Zeke pulling that dress up, and the image doesn't fill her with distaste, but with a peculiar feeling of desire.

Karin looks at her.

An efficient look, somehow focused on the future, and Malin realises that her apparition here is to do with work.

'I wanted to tell you first,' Karin says.

'Tell me what?'

'We've just finished the post-mortem on Hanna Vigerö.'

'And?'

'The oxygen levels in her blood don't make sense, Malin. And some of the blood vessels in her nose were broken. A lot of them. And the capillaries in her lungs are unnaturally distended.'

'What do you mean?'

Malin looks at Karin. Senses that she is finding out something that she actually already knows, and she sees a small spider crawl across the windscreen, and it looks as if it's climbing across the sky, as if it were capable of finding a foothold where no other living creature could.

And she looks back at Karin. Sees the loneliness in her eyes, the confusion that has woken up there. The longing.

The family, Malin thinks. Someone was after the family. That's where we need to look.

'Hanna Vigerö was murdered,' Karin goes on. 'Suffocated. Most likely by someone holding a pillow over her face.'

PART 3
The Children

In the chamber of darkness

The sound of the lizards' teeth is horrible. Say they can't come and eat us. Say it now.

Take them away, take them away, and take away the men's fingers, scratching at the door.

Daddy, where have you got to? Can't Mummy come back from heaven and save us?

Come, just come.

My voice, ours, belong to other girls.

Little brother's scared, Daddy. More scared than ever. We want you to be here and we hug each other and there's a really, really big lizard creeping through the forest outside our room, there really is, and I dream about its sharp yellow teeth, dream about it grabbing us by our legs and biting until our feet aren't there any more, and then, once it's destroyed us, it creeps away through the forest, in amongst the leaves.

The men.

They're there, outside. They do something, and the ticking stops, then the ticking starts again.

Are they going to kill us now, Daddy? They're so angry.

Little brother's calmer now, quiet, like he's too tired to do anything.

In the end, he did jump into the pool. From the edge, when no one was looking, and his armbands helped him float. His whole head went under the water, but he wasn't scared, because he'd decided he was going to dare.

He did it! I cried.

He dared!

He has to dare again now.

I hug him, and he smells better than all the horrid things.

It smells so bad here, and we're the ones who smell, Daddy, you have to come now, or send someone to get us, because otherwise we'll end up dead and we'll go to heaven and God and Jesus.

It's getting worse, Daddy. We've done wees and poos, and no one's cleaned it up.

I see their feet under the crack of the door.

The light goes dark when they come closer.

They shout at each other.

They sound scared.

As if a cruel beast has caught them in the forest and is going to eat them, just like that, Daddy.

We cry. I cry and he cries but I don't shout any more because no matter how much I shout the scared bit of my stomach won't go away.

I'm so scared, Daddy, and so is he, and that will only get better if you come and get us. They hit us when we tried to run away, when they opened the door. So now we stay in the corner, Daddy, a long way from them, and maybe they'll forget about us, so we can sneak out, run into the forest and disappear.

But the lizards are out there. When the men showed them to us, when we got here after the plane, I realised that you weren't waiting for us, like they told us.

Spiders.

And snakes in their lairs.

They're going to want to bite us, snap at us with their warm teeth, make us poisonous so that no one will want to hug us again, so we'll never again feel warm skin against our own.

Tap your finger against a vein and it will come to life.

Become powerful and blue, and there are still plenty of

places to aim at on the map of my elbows and lower arms.

It's nice underground.

Here I'm left alone, at least most of the time, here I can let the syringe dip into a volcano and then have its contents trickle like magma into my body, making me forget everything that's happened, and think that I have a future.

The pain when the needle breaks my skin is wonderful, because it means that the great pain is almost over. I lie down on the damp stone, hear the underground trains rattling along the tracks above my head, and then I sink into a warm bed, feel warm water surround me, nothing but love caressing me until once again I feel all the love vanish and become impossible.

The years have passed.

I have disappeared from my family, changed my name, run away from everyone who hates me and wishes me harm. I live underground, stealing whatever I can get. I live alone, but sometimes they come, the men, and I don't know what they do with me, and then it happens, even though it's not supposed to, it shouldn't happen to a body as ravaged as mine.

I was separated from you the day you came out of me.

I left the hospital, made my way back underground. I turned my back on you, on love, so that you wouldn't fall into their brutal hands, because they are the sum of all evil in this world, they're a black beacon blocking the sun and firing pus-stained rays of blood into people's lives, predetermining what will happen and how things will be.

In the underground I can escape their rays of blood.

Is that someone coming?

Another needle-prick. Who are you? Are you coming back? I don't want to see Father again. He's worse than the others.

I disappear from myself and wake up with the worst monster of them all in front of me.

I don't know how I ended up back here again.

I'm sitting in the oval room with wood panelling, holding my dying father's hand. He holds my hand tightly, but I know he doesn't want to ask for forgiveness, that word doesn't exist in his vocabulary, regret isn't a feeling he's capable of dealing with.

But I'm here.

The others aren't. Neither of the monsters that are my brothers.

I'm holding my father's hand and I'm helping him to die, even though I hate him.

As for me, I'm already dead. I died when you died, girls, a long time ago. You're here now, aren't you, girls?

We don't know why we're here.

Why are we watching you kneeling by a sickbed in the innermost room of a large apartment?

The curtains are drawn. Outside it's dark and the light of the stars slips across water where motorboats mingle with small passenger boats and people are walking along a quayside where old wooden boats smell of tar.

You know who we are, don't you?

Mummy, she ought to be here with us. And Daddy. But instead we were drawn to you. Why? What is it we don't know, we who ought to know everything?

Mummy.

The man with the pillow in your room, who is he? How could he do that? Perhaps he had to do that to you, to us, to protect, save others from the same fate?

Perhaps everyone is innocent except the greedy.

They won't end up where we are.

They will end up among glowing worms, among burning

*lizards that eat human flesh until they burst, and thousands
of new, hungry lizards flood out of their bleeding entrails.*

*The other children are locked up in the anteroom of that
place.*

There can be no rest in that place.

Only screaming.

33

'What the hell do we do now?'

Sven Sjöman is leaning back in the sofa of his living room, and treats Malin's question more as a statement than a question.

Malin is sipping the tea that Sven's wife has just brought her, washing down the sharp taste left in her mouth from the Västerbotten cheese in the sandwich she's been given.

Darkness in Sven's garden.

She drove around to tell him the news about Hanna Vigerö.

Wanted to talk to Sven in person rather than sound the alarm, calmly discuss what it means for the investigation, the fact that Hanna Vigerö was murdered in her hospital bed. Let the others sleep, because they all need their sleep now, need to calm down, not rush off madly in all directions, as if they were all running away from a timebomb that only had seconds left before it exploded.

'Yes, what do we do now?'

Malin takes another bite of the sandwich. Thinks about how isolated the Vigerö family seemed, no friends, no extended family, no visitors to see Hanna Vigerö in hospital. And what the man with the hotdog-stand said, that they were often there in the morning.

The cheese prickles her palate.

She called Tove on her way to see Sven, didn't mention the reading of the will, wanted to say it would be better if she stayed at Janne's tonight, but Tove had insisted on sleeping at hers, and Malin got the impression that there was something important she wanted to say.

Maybe she's got a new boyfriend?

Malin's first reaction was that the last thing she wanted this evening was another piece of news. There'd been more than enough for one day, and all she wanted was to shut her brain down the way you switch off a computer, and let all conscious activity stop. And she didn't want to talk to Tove about the care home, didn't feel ready for that.

'OK, see you there,' she had said. 'We can watch some telly and eat pizza.'

Malin finishes her mouthful and takes another sip of tea.

'Maybe the people behind the bomb wanted to get rid of her. They might have thought she was a witness,' Sven says. 'Maybe they were just making sure.'

'Which means it could have been terrorists, activists, the Economic Liberation Front, a biker gang, or someone else entirely,' Malin says. 'It strikes me that the more we dig into any of those lines of inquiry, or dismiss them, the further we seem to get from the truth.'

'Or else it's there,' Sven says, 'and we just can't see it, just haven't managed to find the right thread.'

'There's something I'd like to ask you,' Malin says, looking Sven right in the eyes.

'Should I be worried?' Sven jokes. 'Out with it.'

'I think we should include a different, separate, line of inquiry from now on,' Malin says.

I know what I want to do now, Malin thinks. And you're going to let me do it, aren't you, Sven? She takes a deep breath and leans towards him to emphasise how serious she is.

'Well?'

'I'd like to work on the hypothetical assumption that the Vigerö family were the target of the bomb. That this isn't some big plot, some sort of conspiracy, or anything to do with politics at all. That could explain both the bombing and the fact that Hanna Vigerö was murdered in hospital.'

'That's what your intuition is telling you?'

'I don't know, Sven. But that hotdog-seller, didn't he say that he often saw the family in the square? Maybe someone had worked out their movements? And why would anyone take the risk of going into the hospital to murder Hanna Vigerö? How much could she really have seen? None of the witnesses in the square had anything very useful to say, so why would she? She must have known something else, something important for different reasons. Don't you think? And that's making me want to focus on the family. Feeling and logic, Sven. The way it should be with good police work.'

She takes another sip of tea before going on: 'Everything's gone so bloody fast with this. It's hardly four days since the bomb went off. It feels like we haven't had time to catch our breath, and that's no good foundation for any sort of intuition, that needs time, space. But I do think it might be a possible way forward for the investigation.'

Sven appears to consider what she's said.

'This is what we'll do,' he says, thirty seconds or so later, without a trace of hesitation in his voice. 'You and Zeke concentrate on that angle. The others will carry on with the rest of the case and the murder of Hanna Vigerö using the lines of inquiry we've already identified. Let me know if you need help bringing anyone in for interview.'

'We ought to talk to one of Hanna's workmates, someone at the nursery. Maybe Börje and Waldemar could help with that?'

Sven nods.

'You only have to ask.'

'Do you think it's possible?' Malin says after a pause. 'Do you think I could be right?'

Sven nods again, then says: 'Her husband was killed in a car accident, no other vehicle involved. That always makes me suspicious. What's to say he wasn't targeted as well? We'll have to take a closer look at that accident.'

'And see if there are any security cameras at the hospital that might have caught the perpetrator on film.'

'And talk to the staff on duty the night Hanna Vigerö died.'

Sven looks at her.

'Are you up to this, Malin? Taking this off in that direction?'

'I'm up for whatever it takes. Child-killers can't be allowed to get away with it.'

Sven nods, and she knows that their conversation about the case is over, and that Sven will steer the others in the direction demanded by their duty as police officers.

Keep all options open until we know for sure.

Don't shut anything off, don't get sidetracked. Keep an open mind. And Sven looks at her – right into me, Malin thinks, and then he leans forward and asks, for the second time that day: 'What about your meeting? The reading of the will. How did it go?'

And Malin can hear how serious Sven is, there's no quick follow-up question about hidden millions, just a long silence until she replies: 'I've got a brother, Sven. It turns out I've got a younger brother,' and she can feel her stomach clench, her eyes fill up, but she swallows, imagines she's downing a whole glass of tequila, and holds back the tears.

She clears her throat. Takes a gulp of her tea. Then she starts to talk, and Sven listens, and when she falls silent again he looks at her for a long time before saying: 'See it as an unexpected gift, Malin. Try to forgive. Otherwise it'll drive you mad.'

He takes a deep breath.

'And stay strong. There's no solution to this in the bottle. But you already know that, don't you?'

When Malin leaves him, Sven slumps onto the sofa in the living room, gazing out at his peaceful, safe home.

He hasn't got many years left before retirement. A year or so back he felt very tired, but that feeling has eased. Instead he's worried about stopping work, realises how empty life would be without all the low-key but unquestionable drama his job presents each day.

No calm drama in Malin's life.

Boom, boom, boom.

Events like a series of detonations from bombs dropped from a low-flying plane.

Bombs exploding in clouds of smoke.

And the world vanishes.

Is that how it feels, Malin? I can see you. Fighting to hold everything together.

Maybe you'll manage it. The only way I can help you is by giving you support at work, trying to keep you on the right track, pull you up if things get out of hand.

Rehab did you good. And you don't seem to resent the fact that I forced you to go.

If there's one thing you should know, Malin Fors, it's that I'll look out for you as long as I'm able.

Malin breathes in the air inside the car, with its smell of spilled coffee and sweat, of hours spent hunting and searching, of cherished work that's leaving its mark in the form of wrinkles that are growing ever deeper with the years.

Linköping, relaxing in the spring.

Coming to its senses.

This evening there is no extra service in the cathedral.

There are lights on in the flats built on the site of the old military barracks, people like dark aquarium fish behind the glass.

Tove must be back home in the flat now.

What am I going to tell her? Nothing. No energy, and inside her she sees the figure of her brother in a hospital bed, and she wants to go to him, they've already lost so much time, but is it really him she can see? Or is it Maria Murvall? Are the two of them the same person, is there yet another secret behind the secret?

But I have to tell Tove this evening.

Anything else would be out of the question.

Because she'll find out, and she'll know I didn't tell her straight away, and she'll hold it against me, lose her faith in me, a faith she's only just found, if it exists at all.

Shame like a black fist in her stomach. As ashamed as anyone can feel.

The dull rumble of the car.

The engine doing its job.

The lights of Linköping twinkle on the night sky in front of her.

Soon she'll be home.

She wonders about calling Peter Hamse again, maybe she could talk to him about the new information that's emerged about Hanna Vigerö, but it's late and he's probably busy doing something else. And it's not essential to the investigation and I'd just seem desperate. She feels the motion of the car in her body, and she becomes a shudder of contentment.

She stops at a red light at the junction of Drottninggatan and St Larsgatan.

Through the windscreen she can see people out for the night, dressed up and looking forward to an evening in a bar.

Hang on a moment.

That man there, in the blue suit, with the pretty young blonde on his arm, much younger, much prettier. I recognise him, but he's not supposed to be here like this, and what the hell is this? What the fuck's he doing here? She feels like jumping out of the car and running over to him, to Janne as he crosses the road in his funeral suit, chatting to the pretty young woman without looking in Malin's direction. She's finding it hard to breathe, feels the world as she knows it get torn apart.

But she stays in the car.

Unable to move.

The lights change.

And Janne and the young woman disappear among the buildings.

She sees them get smaller and smaller, can't hear the horns blaring behind her, the angry motorists who want her to move, off into the unknown world of the spring.

34

Keep it together, Malin.

Keep it together, Malin Fors, don't go mad, don't do anything stupid, leave the bottle alone, go up to your flat, tell Tove what you have to tell her, then go to bed and try to sleep, so you're not too tired tomorrow.

But how the hell could he? How dare he? And how old was she? She was pretty damn attractive, and Malin feels like running out to look for them. Where the hell have they gone? Aphrodite, the Greek restaurant, all yellow walls and candles, she'd put money on them being there, staring into each other's eyes.

She's pulled up in the car park next to St Lars Church, in front of her flat, and right under the inscription above the sidedoor.

She's read it a million times now, but reads it again.

Blessed are the pure in heart, for they shall see God.

My arse.

Janne. You fucking bastard.

She slams the car door shut and feels melancholy take hold of her stomach. She stands still in the spring evening and realises that what she has just seen marks the start of something new. That Janne is moving inexorably and conclusively away from her, and that what they had is fading away for good, and she can't help wondering just how melancholic the world can get?

Confused.

Obviously very confused. I've never felt more confused.

Malin looks over at the pub, the Pull & Bear. Bound to be full of people now, and she hears Sven's words: 'Alcohol can't solve your problems,' is that what he said? And her body is screaming that Sven is wrong, she wants nothing more than to settle down at the bar and drink her way into another dimension full of cotton wool and free of memories and future.

But there are lights on up in the flat.

Daniel Högfeldt.

You bastard. All men are fucking bastards who ought to have their dicks cut off. They're completely in thrall to their fucking cocks, and she steps through the door and thinks that she really doesn't have any right to demand anything from them, yet their behaviour still drives her utterly mad.

Jealousy.

She hates the word.

But knows that's what she's feeling.

I shouldn't feel like this.

Tove. What do you know about that girl Janne's seeing? Have you known about her but not told me? In that case, then . . . then what? No confrontations tonight. Don't say anything, don't do anything.

Tove can go and gets pizzas.

What do I want on my pizza? Ham, prawns, and salami. Maybe some artichoke hearts. Pizza with artichokes on is seriously good.

Tove's sitting at the kitchen table, in the cone of light from the ceiling lamp that Malin bought from Rusta a month or so ago, after the old lamp from Biltema broke.

She's got her head buried in a book, but looks up when Malin comes into the kitchen and says: 'You're home late.'

'You'd never guess what sort of day I've had.'

Then Malin realises that she can't help herself, and yells at Tove with a voice so full of fury that it takes even her by surprise: 'So, why haven't you said a word about your dad's new lover, then? Well? Did you think I wouldn't find out sooner or later?'

Tove stares at her.

Surprised. Roused from her literary dreams by sudden danger, and Malin watches as Tove pulls herself together, stands up and yells back at Malin: 'Stop shouting! What did you say? Has Dad met someone?'

Malin stops, wants to say something, but her tongue feels paralysed.

Instead Tove goes on in a calm voice, as if what her mum's just said has sunk in.

'I don't know anything about any lover. He isn't seeing anyone, is he?'

And Malin goes over to Tove and hugs her, feeling her thin, wiry, edgy teenage body against her, hugs her tightly and whispers in her ear: 'Sorry.' Then they sit down at the table, opposite each other, and Malin tells her what she just saw, and Tove listens, slightly distracted, and seems to think a thousand thoughts before she asks: 'What did she look like?'

Is that what you're wondering? What she looked like? And Malin feels like throwing the question back at Tove, but resists and says instead: 'Blonde, pretty.'

'How old was she?'

'Maybe twenty-five. No more.'

'But Mum, there's no need for you to be angry. It's not as if you're together, you and Dad. It's good if he meets someone, isn't it, so he doesn't have to be alone? You should try to find someone, so you don't have to be alone.'

Alone, Malin feels like asking, what do you mean, alone?

'He's hardly alone, is he?' she says. 'He's got you in the house. And I've got you, we aren't alone, either of us. I just don't want him to rush. I suppose I just don't want anything to happen.'

Tove smiles.

Seems to be weighing something up.

Then she seems to make her mind up, and Malin can see a nervous twinkle in her daughter's eyes.

'You're right, Mum. You're not alone. But you're soon going to have to get used to the idea of me not being around all the time.'

Then Malin sees Tove pull an envelope out of her book and put it in front of Malin, with a proud smile and eyes sparkling with anticipation and a look that shows she's being brave, doing something that has to be done.

'I haven't told Dad,' she says. 'I wanted you to be the first to know.'

Malin puts her hand on the envelope.

Not something else, she thinks, not something else, and tries to force a smile. I can't deal with anything else, and Tove says: 'Read it, Mum, read it!'

Malin doesn't look at the logo on the back of the already crumpled and opened envelope. She just opens it.

She unfolds the paper, then she sees an old-fashioned logo, and reads the words 'Lundsberg Private School', then:

*It gives us great pleasure to inform you that Tove Fors
has been awarded a full scholarship for the school
year 2010–11 from the Grevestål Memorial
Foundation for students with artistic talent from less
privileged backgrounds.*

The essay that Miss Fors enclosed with her application,
'Love in Jane Austen', was deemed by the scholarship
committee to be a mature and accomplished piece of
work, suggesting that we could be dealing with an
author of the future.

Words.

More words.

Then a request for Tove's guardian to contact the school's headmaster, an Ingvar Åkerström, to arrange the details of the scholarship, free accommodation, and everything else, all the formal arrangements that are required for a sixteen-year-old minor, even if the signature on the application was formal confirmation of parental consent.

Malin lets the letter slip from her hands.

Where the fuck is Lundsberg?

In Värmland.

She knows what sort of establishment it is.

It must be six hundred kilometres from here?

Formal confirmation? Signature?

She looks at Tove, who looks as if she's about to burst with pride, and it feels as if two fists are wrenching Malin's guts and heart out, and she stands up, throws her arms out, looks at Tove and says: 'So this isn't good enough for you? Well? Is that what you want? To go to some stuck-up school with a load of stuck-up toffs? Do you really think they're going to see you as one of them? Do you?'

She hears her words, how cruel and hurt they sound, their unvarnished, unforgivable self-absorption, but she still can't stop herself, and raises her voice before going on: 'For God's sake, surely you could have said something? Did you imagine I'd be happy just because you got a scholarship to some stuck-up school? Did you think I'd be happy about you going so far away? Bloody hell, I love you, Tove, and I want you here with me, surely you can see that? I've never seen anything so selfish. And what's this about signatures? Did you forge my signature?'

Tove looks past Malin, picks the letter up from the table, folds it carefully, and puts it back in the envelope, then tucks it inside her book, before standing up.

'I thought you'd be happy for me,' Tove says firmly, without sounding the least bit sad. 'You should be. Do you know what it means to get in there? Do you know what it costs? The contacts it gives you? And yes, I faked your signature on the application, because I was expecting you to be angry even if I hoped you might have changed your bloody behaviour.'

'That's against the law, Tove! Did you know that? Does your dad know about this?'

'You're mad, Mum, you know that, don't you? No, he doesn't know anything. I only needed one signature, and I didn't want to ask him either, because he'd have insisted on talking to you. And I wanted to tell you first.'

Malin breathes.

Snorts.

Shuts her eyes.

Rubs her temples, feels like screaming, screaming out loud, roaring meaningless sounds there in the kitchen, bellowing like a cornered animal, and only when her scream has died away does she open her eyes, look at Tove. Before her stands her daughter, smiling.

'I'm not going to listen to what you say, Mum,' Tove whispers. 'I know things must be hard for you right now, with everything that's going on, with Grandma.'

Calm, Malin calm. Pull yourself together.

And she manages, even though she can feel the tears running down her cheeks.

For the second time in just a few minutes Malin hugs her daughter, and whispers in her ear.

'Sorry. Sorry. I want you to be able to trust me. Let's go out for pizza, and I'll tell you something really weird,' she says.

'*Sturm und Drang*,' Tove says, and Malin tries to work out what she means, but fails.

Ham.

Prawns and ham.

But no artichoke.

They're sitting at a table for two in the Shalom Pizzeria on Trädgårdsgatan, in a brightly lit room with yellowing wallpaper, and Tove is eating greedily, only interrupting herself to take gulps of Cuba Cola.

They walked past the main square on their way here. A dozen candles were burning in the darkness, casting flickering, anxious shadows across the dark pavement. Most of the bars and restaurants already had new windows fitted.

They didn't talk about the bomb on the way to the pizzeria, discussing everything else that had happened instead.

The fact that Janne seemed to have met someone new really didn't seem to bother Tove, she didn't seem to feel any jealousy or desire for them to become a normal family unit again.

They talked about Lundsberg, and Malin told her about the boy in the care home, and now Tove says: 'We have to go and see him. I want to meet him. We can go tomorrow. He's my uncle.'

'We will visit him,' Malin says.

Tove had fallen silent when Malin told her about the reading of the will, and about her brother. Every time Malin repeated the story to someone else it became more real to her, as if it had somehow all been a dream, and now, when Tove says the words 'my uncle', for the first time Malin feels that there's someone else out there apart from Tove who is almost her.

She shakes her head.

'But I can't go tomorrow. I have to work.'

'Maybe this is more important,' Tove says.

'It's much more important,' Malin says, and her cheeks feel greasy from the pizza, and it occurs to her that Janne and his new girl might be sitting just a few blocks away.

Never mind that now.

Think about Peter Hamse instead.

Her little brother.

Tove.

Try to live in the moment.

'So, do what feels most important,' Tove says. 'Anyway, what's his name?'

'His name's Stefan.'

'Do they call him Steffe?'

Malin shakes her head, says: 'I don't know what sort of nicknames he's got. I know we ought to see him, but this case I'm working on right now . . . I get the feeling something's going on, something big and small at the same time, it feels like it's a matter of life or death, and that it's urgent, but I don't know how.'

'How do you mean? That there's someone you have to rescue?'

'Maybe,' Malin says. 'But I don't know who.'

'Maybe it's you, Mum,' Tove smiles. 'Maybe you have to rescue yourself. You're worried about seeing him, aren't you?'

'Yes, I suppose I am worried.'

'What about doing it for my sake, Mum? Can't we go right away for my sake?'

'We will go, Tove. Just not yet.'

'Then you'll be letting him down as well.'

As well. And Malin feels her shame flare up, at the way her drinking and long hours almost made her ignore Tove altogether. Am I doing the same thing again? No.

Shame is pointless, she knows that.

'Tove. I'm only human.'

'Really?' Tove says with a smile.

Then she takes a piece of pizza, pops it in her mouth, chews and swallows, evidently thinking, carefully weighing her words before she says: 'What are you going to do about Grandad? I can understand you being angry with him.'

'I don't know, Tove. What do you think?'

'There's only one thing you can do, Mum. You have to forgive him. You only get one dad.'

Mother and daughter walk hand in hand through the late spring evening.

They don't know it, but they're nudging up against one of the watersheds that make up the core of human life, balancing along the fragile line of their story.

Tove asks her mum: 'You're not going to report me for forging your signature, are you?'

'What do you take me for? Of course I'm not.'

'You are happy for me, aren't you? This is what I've always dreamed of.'

Malin lets go of her daughter's hand and wraps her arm around her instead, pulling her close, and they weave their way up the illuminated street.

'Of course I'm happy for you,' Malin says. 'I'm just scared of losing you.'

35

Can't sleep.

Have to sleep. Have I slept? Yes, I fell asleep to begin with, slept for a few hours, then woke up again, and now there's nothing I can do with my body, or my mind. I want to get away from it, into sleep and dreams, but there's no point trying.

Malin sits up.

Beyond the venetian blind she can just make out the still of night, and she knows Tove is lying in the next room, and Malin hopes she's sleeping.

Lundsberg.

Don't think about it. Let it happen. It's what Tove wants, and that's the most important thing. It was smart of her to forge my signature on the application, but why didn't she just ask us about it?

What must you think of us, Tove?

And Malin closes her eyes again, sees her mother's face in her mind's eye, chasing her through the house, going on at her to tidy up after herself, shouting at her not to talk so much, to be quiet when there are adults present, that nice girls do this or that, and you never give me a moment's peace, and Mum, you're dead now, gone, you don't exist, but you're going to be with me for as long as I live. You've done that to me, how can I move on from that?

You have to forgive.

Forgive the one who's still here. Make the most of the time we have.

I know what I have to do, she thinks, and gets up. She pulls on a pair of jeans, doesn't bother with a bra, just pulls a pink cotton top over her head.

Her tiredness is gone.

Her body had got a second wind.

She goes in to Tove.

Shakes her daughter awake. Tove sits up bewildered, looking around the room in the dim lighting from the hall.

'I'm going to see Dad,' Malin says.

'Don't,' Tove says. 'He'll be with that girl.'

'I mean Grandad.'

Tove gives her a hug, and whispers in her ear: 'I'll be fine on my own. Be gentle with him.'

And fifteen minutes later, tired and cold after a chilly walk, at a quarter past three in the morning, Malin is standing outside the building on Barnhemsgatan, and she hesitates, doesn't want to tap in the code, but her fingers move by themselves, as if the whole of her being knows that it has to hear her father tell the story of her little brother, Stefan.

The stairwell smells of mould and disinfectant, and Malin walks slowly up the stairs, feeling annoyed at having to be here, at this moment.

Thinks: I'm going to put you on the spot. I'm going to make you tell the truth, Dad.

Her dad is sitting in the large armchair in the living room of the flat, or the sitting room, as her mum used to call it. The green fabric of the armchair envelops his increasingly slender frame, and her dad's thin face, which usually radiates self-confidence and forcefulness, is now radiating a peculiar mixture of weariness and fear, a new sort of hesitancy that Malin is inclined to put down to loneliness.

She rang the doorbell.

He opened the door after the tenth angry ring, not annoyed at being woken – he actually seemed pleased to see her. As for her, she really didn't feel anything when she saw him.

They sat down opposite each other in the living room. Malin in the red chair where she's sitting now, feeling the rough fibres of the cheap oriental carpet under her feet. She's looking at her father, who knows what is expected of him, and he starts to talk, beginning with an apology, or at least an attempt to explain himself.

'I should have told you a long, long time ago. You had a right to know. But you know how it is, the way things can turn out.'

The way things can turn out? Malin thinks, and feels like interrupting, him but stops herself and lets him go on.

'The years pass and in the end the secret somehow grows bigger than it really is, we never spoke about it between ourselves, and we'd never agreed how we were going to tell you when you got older. Even when your mum died, I couldn't bring myself to say anything to you, even though I knew perfectly well that the truth was bound to catch up with us now. I was simply very weak, and I'd like to think I did it for your mum's sake, she wouldn't have been able to handle what had turned into the biggest lie of her life.'

You're not even referring to him by his name, Malin thinks. You're talking about him as a secret. A thing.

Her dad leans forward.

And Malin feels her anger take hold of her, and she feels like shouting at him again, but manages to suppress the outburst by digging the fingers of one hand deep into the stuffing of the armrest.

For Mum's sake? Or your own?

Don't you see, haven't you seen, the way I've been feeling? The way I've spent the whole of my fucking life feeling? And you've been aware that I needed to know, that I've been searching for something I felt was missing. My mother's love, or the brother I never even knew I had.

Malin sits in silence.

Her dad's voice is like an empty sarcophagus, an echo from someone who accepts their mistakes and shortcomings, and carries on living with them, without placing any specific demands on themselves as far as improvements and the truth are concerned.

A note of resignation.

A note that has more to do with death than life.

How the hell could you let me down like that? Let him down?

'You mum had an affair with an unmarried office supplies salesman. She met him at Saab, and then one night she was out at a dance with one of her girlfriends. One night at the Freemasons' Hotel where he was staying. You were three, almost four years old at the time, and she got pregnant, and the man was killed in a car crash a few months into the pregnancy. There was never any talk of a divorce. It was all going to be managed. And I forgave her, and then she moved out during the pregnancy, when it started to show . . .'

I know all that, Malin feels like screaming.

Tell me something I don't know!

How could you just hide my own brother away from me? Why couldn't you adopt him, seeing as his father was dead?

She listens to her dad. The words come flying at her like shards of glass, razor-sharp, red-hot.

'Adoption wasn't an option, no one wanted him, he

wasn't mine, and he was handicapped, I couldn't have stood it, it was better to pretend he didn't exist, never say anything . . .

'Then, after so many years, it was as if that had become the truth,' her dad says, and goes on, 'that the secret didn't exist. That it was just us, you and me and Mum, and she got obsessed with social status, her own life, her choices, with the fact that everything had to be so damn perfect and lovely when it was really just ordinary and built on shaky foundations. And I went along with it.'

Her dad falls silent, and Malin looks out of the window, at the slowly breaking dawn, thinking that her dad sounds strangely calculating, almost deceitful.

'Say something, Malin.'

'How could you just leave him there, alone, even if he wasn't yours, didn't you feel any responsibility?'

Her dad looks at her, tries to catch her eye, and Malin realises he wants her to say she understands, but she doesn't.

'Didn't you think I had any right at all to know about my own brother? You know how much I missed having a brother or sister, how the hell could you deny me that right?'

'He's severely handicapped, Malin.'

She gets to her feet and shouts: 'Like that's got anything to do with anything! For fuck's sake, couldn't you have said you were his father? Or didn't Mum want that? Or were you the one who forced her to abandon him? Gave her an ultimatum and tried to make her look like the cold, heartless villain, when you're actually no better yourself? You didn't want him either, did you? Maybe Mum did want him, and you just said no? It wasn't that fucking easy in those days to just leave your husband, was it?'

Her dad sinks lower into his armchair, holds out his hands, then quickly withdraws them, and it looks as though he's thinking, then he says, without a trace of denial in his voice:'I don't know what to say.'

'Don't say anything,' Malin yells. 'You've been silent for thirty years, so you might as well keep quiet for a bit longer.'

'I understand why you're angry. But times have changed, as you pointed out.'

She looks at him.

Times have changed? she thinks. You forced Mum to give him up, didn't you? And maybe she didn't want to? And that's why she ended up so cold?

A thin layer of snow melting. Still hiding the truth. Then the next layer melts, and a completely different reality is revealed. Then what? Layer upon layer of ice, of denial and life.

Malin sinks onto the sofa.

Catches her breath.

'I'm not angry, Dad. Well, yes, I am. But most of all I'm just fucking sad. I'm sad for my own sake. For his, my brother's sake. I'm sad for Tove's sake. For Janne's sake, and yours too, and Mum's, because this has affected us so much more than you can possibly imagine. You and Mum, together and individually, have trampled all over my life, and that makes me sad.'

Her father stands up, and the insecurity and fear have been replaced by a grown man's look, and she's seen it before, that look, in criminals confessing their crimes and prepared to take the consequences, but who still think, deep down in the bottom of their souls, that it was right to commit them.

He turns towards her.

'What am I supposed to do, Malin? What do you want? What's done is done, and it can't be undone. Obviously, I hope you can forgive me.'

You're crazy, Malin thinks. Completely fucking mad,

and she stands up again and leaves her father alone in his living room without another word. She leaves him alone in the flat, surrounded by silence, by the memories of choices made, hours and days lived in the milky, thin air of the lie, and she realises that his loneliness is aggressive, malignant, like cancer, and that she can leave him trapped in it without a second thought.

'I want to see Tove,' he calls after her. 'Let me see Tove.'

She doesn't want to see you, Malin thinks.

Lundsberg School like a fortress inside her.

Tove doesn't want to see anyone. She's on her way away from us.

And me, I know where I'm on my way to.

The first morning light breaks on the empty, scrubbed hospital room. Blue-and-white crime-scene tape is already stretched across the doorframe, and Sven must have called Karin Johannison after their meeting, and got one of her colleagues to go through the room. But they can't have found anything, today hospital rooms are disinfected the moment the dead and cured alike have made way for another patient.

The nurses on night duty were reluctant to let her into the room, even though she showed her ID.

She couldn't help herself, and asked after Peter Hamse, even though she knew he was hardly likely to be there at half past four in the morning, and the nurses seemed to have a fair idea of why she was really asking.

She looks around the room.

A man comes in there, she thinks, or a woman, and carefully pulls the pillow out from under Hanna Vigerö's head, gently putting his or her hand behind her neck and letting her head fall softly to the mattress, before pressing the pillow down over her nose and mouth.

Hanna Vigerö can't put up any resistance, and maybe

she doesn't want to either, maybe she wants to be with her girls, and in her mind's eye Malin can see the man – or is it a woman? – pressing the pillow over Hanna Vigerö's face, and how she gives in, her tensed fingers relaxing, then the straight line on the monitor showing her heartbeat.

Who were you?

What were you doing here? Was there more than one of you?

Did you enjoy the violence? Or did you really not want to do it, but were forced to? If so, by whom? Did you think a coroner or forensics expert wouldn't notice that she'd been suffocated?

Does any of this have any meaning at all? And then: Are you a ghost?

How else could you get in here at night without being seen or heard? Do you work here at the hospital?

Malin stares into space and tries to open herself up to any remnants of motives or feelings lingering in the air.

You know exactly what you're doing, she thinks.

But you didn't really want to do it? Is that it? Malin shuts her eyes, and inside her she sees the man in the hood turn to face the woman on the bed. He's asking for forgiveness, because you are a man, aren't you? And you're asking for forgiveness.

I can't see your face, Malin thinks. But who are you? You can't be Jonathan Ludvigsson, because we had him in the cells when you were here.

So who are you? And why, tell me why you were here?

Malin tries to make sense of the thoughts and feelings darting around the dark room. What evil is there in this hospital room?

Evil can come to you in any form.

It often takes you by surprise, but not always. You can devote your whole life to protecting your children, then you open the door to a man who ought to come with love, and when you turn your back he attacks your children, raping them without you even noticing.

Can you protect yourself from evil like that? Is your inattention an evil in and of itself?

The plank with the rusty spike in it under the snow. You notice it when the snow melts, but it's only a plank, you think, and then the spike goes through your shoe and into your foot.

The infection spreads through your body, your blood heading back towards your heart.

What do you do?

Can you protect yourself against the evil hidden beneath layer upon layer of goodness in those closest to you of all?

In the poisonous plants in the garden?

So what do you do?

Faith. Turn to faith.

Pure evil.

It does exist, Malin can sense it, and we have to keep it shut away. Not accept it, nor deny its existence. Instead we have to try to eradicate it.

A child wants goodness, but can be harmed. Because a child has no knowledge of the world.

You wished your girls well, Hanna, didn't you? You wished nothing but good for them. And what sort of evil, in whatever form, was it that found its way to you here and suffocated you?

Malin takes a deep breath.

She stands still in the drowsy morning, in the gloomy hospital room.

Then she feels a cold draught in the room, followed by a short burst of warm air against her neck, dancing against her throat before it moves up towards her ear and turns into a whisper.

There's someone here.
Someone's here with me.
I'll listen, she thinks. I'm not frightened. It's nothing odd.
Talk, and I'll listen, I promise.

36

We're here, Malin.

We're here to remind you about the captive children.

You have to hear them.

They need you, and in order to know who they are, you need to find out who we are, that's the only way.

We see you standing in the hospital room.

We're pressing up against you, our little fingers tickling your neck like peacock feathers, and you know we're here in the room where Mummy died, don't you?

That's why you came here, even though you ought to be sleeping.

It's dark here, but the day is waking up and in the earth there are millions of shoots moving, not sure if they dare to peep out.

The darkness of this room is nothing to the darkness you need to step down into, Malin. There's a darkness waiting for you that might never end. But don't be scared, because then you might not dare to go down into it, and then the darkness will only get bigger.

You're breathing.

Your eyelids are closed, and the room smells of disinfectant and death.

Can you hear us, Malin?

Can you hear us?

Malin opens her eyes.

The voices, the ones she'd been hoping to hear, aren't

there, weren't there, yet there's still something encouraging her to press on, making her screw up her eyes until her darkness becomes a flaming, steaming, pulsating hell, and making her realise that wherever the solution to the Linköping bombing is to be found, it will be in just such a hell.

A crow flies past outside the window. The bird has a worm in its beak, and in the darkness the worm becomes a little snake slithering across the cloudless dawn sky.

'You have to help them,' a faint voice says behind her back, making her jump, and she turns around, expecting to see one of the night-shift nurses who'd entered the room without her noticing. But there's no one there, just the dusty stillness of the hospital room, and the smell of a life that has reached its end.

'You have to help them,' the voice says again, and Malin feels her fear fade, and says: 'Is that you, Hanna? Are you here?'

She waits for an answer.

'Is it your girls I have to help? I'm trying to get justice for them.'

The room is silent and still, and Malin wants to hear the friendly, calm voice again, and then it returns: 'I can't see my girls here.'

'They aren't with you?'

The voice doesn't answer.

Malin senses it slipping away. Vanishing through the window, and she turns around and looks out at the sky. Wants answers to her many questions.

'Come back, Hanna,' Malin says. 'Come back, and tell me what I have to do to help them.'

'She's not coming back. She's dead.'

The female voice comes from behind her, from the door. Malin turns around once more, sees a sturdy body clad in white coming into the room, a coarse-featured face beneath cropped hair.

'Are you talking to the dead, Inspector?'

No trace of irony. No fear, no surprise, just mild bemusement.

'I don't know what got into me,' Malin says. 'Maybe I should call in at the psychiatric department?'

'Best to stay well away from there,' the nurse says, holding out her hand. 'Siv Stark, I work the night shift.'

'Were you on duty the night Hanna died?'

Siv Stark shakes her head.

'I'm afraid not.'

'We'll need to question everyone who works here.'

'Something's obviously happened, I can tell that much from the fact that forensics officers were here cordoning off the room and conducting some sort of search. What is it? Was there something funny about the way Hanna Vigerö died?'

'I can't say anything else at the moment, but if you could let the others know that they'll have to be questioned, I'd be grateful.'

Peter Hamse.

She simultaneously wants and doesn't want to talk to him.

Siv Stark nods, then smiles, and in the dawn light her mouth looks twice as big, yet without being frightening or grotesque.

'Was she here?' Siv Stark asks. 'Or her girls, perhaps?'

'I don't know. Maybe. I'm trying to listen to them. Believe in them.'

Siv Stark searches through one of the pockets of her white coat. Then she takes out a small tub of chewing tobacco and inserts a dose under her top lip, and the smell of the tobacco makes Malin feel sick, and she wants to get out, back home to her flat, to Tove, to the soft, clean smell of her daughter, a smell that will stay with her for the rest of her life.

The two women leave the room together.

They can't hear the desperate cries behind them.

Two girls crying for their mother.

A mother crying for her girls.

It's a quarter to six when Malin curls up in bed beside Tove.

She doesn't wake up, just makes room instinctively before cuddling up to Malin in her sleep and wrapping her arms around her. Malin starts to sweat, and thinks that she'll never get to sleep like this, yet this is still where she wants to be, just like this, finding some way of expressing all the love in the world, pressing against Tove until there's nothing between them. Soon she'll be gone, and that scares me, makes me scared of being lonely, and I want to keep her here.

Everyone lets me down.

Tove, who wants to go to Lundsberg.

Dad.

Janne, Daniel. Everyone abandons me, and Malin feels like crying, sinking into self-pity, but she knows that won't do, it just leads straight to hell, and instead she tries to enjoy Tove's warmth, and slowly her brain stops spinning at top speed, the images overlap each other more slowly, with less logic, and she is carried out into a flower meadow where she can breathe, and she's a little girl hurtling over the meadow, not looking at her feet, a little girl whose goal is the horizon.

Then a dog barks.

And the girl stops and looks at the ground and she screams, jumps, and tries to run away, but she's stuck in mud where little blood-stained baby lizards are trying to dig their teeth into her ankles, and spiders with long hairy legs crawl up into the girl's hair, trying to get into her eyes, mouth, and ears. The creatures want to make her mute, blind, and deaf, want to free her from all desires, from all greed, and Malin wants to escape from her dream, but forces herself to stay, and then the meadow is replaced by a hospital room, and she sees her brother lying there in bed under white sheets, asleep. He's grown up, and yet he's a little baby dressed in a pale blue rompersuit that she recognises from so many dreams dreamt.

His face is thin, and his chin is slight, and his body small and slender, and his sleep seems dreamless and free from worry. In her dream Malin thinks: I'm not the one who's been abandoned, you are, and if human life is a contest to see who has been most abandoned, maybe you'd win?

I've let you down. Haven't I? But why am I so scared of going to visit you? After all, I want to give you my love. Am I scared of the way you are, and what that's going to make me feel?

She feels like going up to her brother.

To stroke his cheek, but before she has the chance to move, the backdrop of the dream changes, into a stinking pit running with damp, surrounded by water on all sides, where two tiny creatures are whimpering in a corner, and she wants to get them out of there, but she can't, because they have no faces, no names, she doesn't know who they are.

You have to save us.

You have to.

And she stays in the room, freezing the image of the dirty, frightened children, letting Tove's body merge with the children's, the stuff that dreams are made of, the sense of proximity that only leaves Malin Fors when she wakes up.

* * *

Åke Fors has got up early.

He's sitting at his kitchen table with a cup of coffee in one hand and the *Correspondent* in front of him.

But he doesn't feel like reading the news, can't even be bothered to find out the latest about the bomb, because he's got enough to deal with from his own latest explosion.

From where he's sitting he can almost feel the grass in the park outside bubbling with life. He can feel the vibrations of the worms, of everything eager to grow, yet somehow hesitating.

Åke Fors hasn't got the energy to get up and look out at the park, and see the beautiful, almost perfect spring day that's coming into being.

Malin.

He takes a sip of coffee.

How will you ever forgive me? Do you even want to?

But we have to get closer to each other. We can't just give up.

I'm going to stay here. Not leave. Stay, with my regret and guilt.

If you'd drunk yourself to death, it would have been my fault.

Margaretha.

How the hell did you get me to do what you wanted? That was how it was. It was. Wasn't it?

Birdsong. A bumblebee buzzing.

I suppose it was easiest that way. However it came about.

37

Tove and Malin have opened the window facing St Lars Church, letting the warmth of the sun caress their faces.

Tove is drinking coffee.

They're both eating sandwiches, and Malin has just told her what happened at her dad's, at Grandad's, last night, and Tove repeats: 'You have to forgive him. Try. One way or another, there are just the three of us now, aren't there?'

Malin doesn't answer.

She just looks down at the recently smartened up St Lars Park, where a group of youngsters is busy setting up some market stalls.

'What do you think they're selling?' Malin asks.

'Secrets often end up like that,' Tove says. 'They get bigger and bigger the longer you hold onto them, and in the end you just can't talk about them.'

'We'll see. So, am I supposed to contact Lundsberg?'

'Ideally. But I could do it myself. Are you going to talk to Dad about it?'

Janne.

The blonde woman by his side last night.

'No need. I'll email the headmaster. It's a good thing, isn't it? Tell your dad it's OK with me. Pretty much every company director in the country went there, didn't they?'

'Almost,' Tove says.

'So you can end up as a director and look after me when I get old.'

'I'm not going to end up as some wretched director,' Tove says, and Malin looks at her, knows she's going to make a success of things among the posh kids, feels the word 'wretched' rolling around her head, she'd have gone for 'fucking' herself, but wretched is perfectly good for a smart girl in a situation like this.

Malin takes a deep breath.

The rays of the spring sun are warm, almost enough to burn, at least that's what it feels like, inside the open window of the flat.

Where are my sunglasses? Haven't bothered to dig them out yet, but it's almost time.

The clock on the church tower says half past eight, and even though Malin only got a few hours' sleep last night, she no longer feels tired, just ready and full of anticipation for the day's work.

She'll have to shelve all the other crap.

Lock it away in some distant little room in her consciousness. Take it out again when the time comes.

Börje Svärd is walking quickly through Tornhagen. Wants to get to the station in time for the morning meeting. He walks past the unassuming little houses and the yellow-brick blocks of flats.

His second walk of the day.

He was out with the dogs at six o'clock.

But he needs to keep moving, not to suppress Anna's memory, or any thoughts about the case they're working on, but because he wants to hold onto her memory.

He breathes in the spring air.

Remember Anna as a young woman, before her MS slowly sucked the life from her. But the illness never managed to steal her happiness. Just as little as the bomb in the square would manage to steal the city's happiness now.

The past few days' hard work on the case have taken their toll on both body and soul.

He heard on the radio that all the country's banks would be opening once again, but with rigorous security measures in place, and extra guards.

Börje reaches the Valla road, waits at the pedestrian crossing, and looks at the old buildings of Gamla Linköping.

Then he hears a car horn and turns to see Waldemar's green car pulling up at the crossing, and his weather-beaten face sticking out of the open window.

'Do you want a lift, partner?'

Partner?

Well, that's probably what they are.

'Sure.'

'Let's stop for coffee at the 7-Eleven,' Waldemar says once they're on their way. 'I need some decent coffee.'

'Why not?' Börje says. 'I don't know why, but I get the feeling this case is moving into a different phase now. Don't you think?'

Waldemar nods and lights a cigarette without asking if Börje minds.

Unusually few people in the police station.

Just a few uniforms meandering about trying to look busy.

But then Sven has probably arranged the interviews up at the hospital by now.

Where are Börje Svärd and Waldemar Ekenberg? She wants to ask them to go and talk to the staff at the children's pre-school again, the North Wind school in Ekholmen, and then someone at the day centre in Vidingsjö where Hanna Vigerö worked.

Malin's sitting at her computer, and thinks that that's where she wants to start.

Wants to get an idea of who Hanna Vigerö was, who the girls were. Properly. Strangely enough, no one has done that up to now. But everything has happened so quickly.

Zeke.

Where is he?

She ought to have called him, but she hopes Sven has explained the angle that he and Malin will be working on from now on.

Zeke will follow her lead. She knows that. And she knows she's going to need the energy and drive that he can contribute. Never backing down, getting on with the job.

He'll have the energy to switch to looking into the Vigerö family. To try to see every aspect of the investigation into the bombing in the main square in a new light.

He has to have the energy.

Six-year-old girls shouldn't get blown up.

Their mum shouldn't be asphyxiated during the night in hospital.

We should never accept that.

'Malin.'

She hears Zeke's voice behind her.

It makes her feel safe, finally anchoring her in the present. I've been falling through the air since the bomb went off, she thinks.

'Let's get to work,' Zeke says. 'Sven's told me about Hanna Vigerö, and what he wants the two of us to do.'

Malin nods.

'I thought we could start with population records.'

Zeke pulls his chair around the desk they share and sits down next to Malin as she starts typing on the computer, logging in with her police authorisation, and soon Hanna Vigerö's details are up on the screen in front of them.

Born in Linköping in 1969, parents Johan and Karin Karlsson.

Married Pontus Vigerö in 1994.

And twin girls.

Born 2004, January.

Nothing odd, nothing remarkable.

'The girls,' Zeke says. 'Check the girls, go into their records.'

'Haven't we already checked their birth certificates?'

'Not as far as I know. They were identified by their dental records. And we haven't had any reason to look into their files more closely.'

A black pupil, an angelic child's eye above a torn cheek.

I still don't know which of you the eye belonged to, which one of you was staring at me, Malin thinks, but does it really matter?

You were twins, so perhaps you thought of yourselves as one and the same person, the way twins often do?

They bring up Tuva Vigerö's record on screen.

'Hang on,' Zeke says. 'Are you seeing what I'm seeing?'

And Malin holds her breath.

Then reads: 'Born Stockholm, Karolinska Hospital, 2004. Adopted at birth by Pontus and Hanna Vigerö.'

'Is it possible to find out who their real parents were?'

'I don't know,' Malin says, clicking around the screen, but the information isn't there. Malin knows it must exist somewhere, just not available to them through the online population records.

'Bloody hell,' Malin says.

'Adoptions between Swedish parents are pretty unusual,' Zeke says.

'But they do still happen,' Malin says. 'But you have to be pretty damn lucky to be one of them, from what I've heard. There are only something like ten to twenty adoptions like that each year. I read about it somewhere, Social Services prefer foster placements.'

And Malin thinks about her little brother. No one wanted him. No one wanted damaged goods. Not even his mother.

They scroll down.

Bring up Tuva's twin sister Mira's records.

The same adoption details, of course.

They click through the rows of neutral words, the formal phrases that Malin knows hide a truth that hides further truths.

There's no further information about the adoption online.

Malin lets go of the mouse.

Turns to Zeke.

'Do you know where we can get hold of more information? Which organisations would have the records?'

'No idea.'

Malin calls Johan on his internal number, even though he's only at his desk at the far end of the open-plan office.

'District courts have to approve adoptions, in purely legal terms. I suppose there'd be something in their records,' he says. 'But you'll need to go to the actual archive itself, that sort of information isn't stored digitally yet. Because of data protection legislation.'

'Thanks, Johan.'

Then Malin sees Börje and Waldemar arrive at the station, deep in a new, jovial sort of conversation, and they look like old friends who have only just met after years apart.

She calls them over.

Tells them what she wants them to do, and fills them in on the latest developments.

And, against expectations, neither of them frowns or gets annoyed, they seem to accept her authority, saying: 'We're on it,' before heading back out the way they just arrived.

'I'll tell Sven that we can skip the morning meeting,' she calls after them.

★ ★ ★

The face in the mirror of the cramped, airless toilet seems to evade Malin, even though she knows she's looking at her own reflection.

But who is it really?

Do I actually have any idea?

And she wonders if her brother looks like her.

What do you look like? she whispers to herself, and she thinks about the girls, pretty, beautiful, their eyes so full of life in the pictures in the flat out in Ekholmen. Not so very different in appearance to Hanna Vigerö.

Adopted.

There was someone who didn't want you, but who wouldn't want a couple of girls like you?

Who abandoned you?

And no one, no one wanted you, my brother.

I would have wanted you, but I didn't even know you existed.

Malin splashes water over her face.

Shakes her head.

Are there any sensible officials working in the district court archive? If the children were adopted in Linköping, then surely the documents ought to be there?

Well, we'll just have to try to find one if we're going to make any progress. And we'll have to see what Börje and Waldemar come up with.

The wheelchairs seem to be streaming out of the community ambulances, their paint gleaming in the spring light. A strongly perfumed scent is spreading from the beds of tulips framing the single-storey brick building housing the Vidingsjö day centre.

Vegetables, Waldemar Ekenberg thinks, as he sees Börje Svärd's face contort, and realises that he must see Anna in the adults with learning difficulties and cerebral palsy who are being wheeled in for therapy and storage.

Waldemar himself has always been terrified of ending up like that, or that the child he and his wife never had would turn out that way. Maybe his fear of that explained why they never had any children?

'Shall we go in?'

Börje nods.

They press the button and the glass doors leading into the day centre slide open, and they go in. In a harshly lit corridor they stop a young blonde girl wearing a pink painter's smock.

They say their names, show their ID, and explain why they're there.

'I'm Petronella Nilsson, I'm an occupational therapist here. You're welcome to talk to me if you like, my art class doesn't start until eleven o'clock.'

They follow the girl into an art room with jars of brushes lined up on shelves along the walls, and a feeble light filters through the large windows facing a plant-filled internal courtyard.

Stained tables, no chairs.

They each sit down on a stool, and Waldemar notices the girl's freckles, and thinks how well they suit her snub-nosed, twenty-five-year-old face.

'It's all so awful. I can't understand it. We've all had the chance to get some counselling, but we still can't believe it. First Hanna's daughters, and now her. I don't even want to think about it.'

'Did you notice anything unusual about Hanna before the bombing? Did she say anything strange?' Börje asks.

'No, nothing. We've talked about that. But there was nothing. Why? Do you think the bomb was aimed at her?'

She doesn't know that Hanna was murdered, Waldemar

thinks. It's not come out in the media yet. And he isn't about to tell her.

'We're keeping all lines of inquiry open,' he says. 'What was she like as a person?'

'She was on compassionate leave after her husband's accident, of course. But things were getting better for her. She was actually the loveliest, happiest girl in the world. Our clients loved her, and she was so fond of them. And she adored her girls.'

'Did she talk much about her children?'

'Doesn't everyone?'

'Anything special?'

Petronella Nilsson thinks for a moment.

'No, just the usual, how they were getting on, that sort of thing. Things they'd said and done.'

'Did you know they were adopted?'

Petronella Nilsson looks surprised. Shakes her head.

'I'd never have guessed.'

'So you didn't know about that?' Waldemar asks.

'No. Hanna never even hinted at it.'

'Did she have any particularly close friends here?' Börje goes on.

'She was friends with everyone,' Petronella Nilsson says. 'Everyone and no one. She didn't see any of us outside of work. She pretty much stuck with her family. They seemed to be a very close-knit unit.'

Before they leave the Vidingsjö day centre they talk to another two members of staff who say the same sort of thing as Petronella Nilsson. Then they set off to drive the few kilometres to the North Wind pre-school.

Kids shouting and playing.

More brushes. More paint. Toys, and a headache-inducing volume of noise.

An older woman called Karin Kvarnsten, the manager of the North Wind, is standing in front of Börje Svärd and Waldemar Ekenberg in the middle of the chaos, grey-haired, with friendly eyes and round cheeks.

'So it's your turn now, is it? The Security Police were here yesterday. Aren't you working together?'

Börje and Waldemar look at each other, and they seem to be thinking the same thing: 'Are we following the same line of inquiry?' But that doesn't necessarily have to be the case, maybe the Security Police are doing the same as them, leaving no stone unturned.

'They like to do things their own way,' Börje says, and Waldemar pulls an annoyed face.

They go off to the nursery's kitchen, which smells strongly of curry, and a bearded man the same age as them is slicing a huge smoked sausage at the same time as somehow managing to pour couscous into a pan of boiling water.

The man introduces himself as Sten Håkansson.

'Tell us about the girls,' Waldemar says.

'The nicest kids in the world, best friends, very advanced for their age,' Karin Kvarnsten says. 'They didn't get the chance to come back after their dad's accident, so I don't know how that would have affected them. And now we'll never know.'

'No, we won't,' Börje says.

'It's so terrible,' Sten Håkansson says. 'It's impossible to take it all in, somehow, and we're all worried about what's going on in Linköping.'

'Did you know that the girls were adopted?' Waldemar says. 'Did the Security Police mention that?'

'Adopted? What are you saying?' Karin Kvarnsten exclaims. 'We had no idea, we'd never have guessed.'

Sten Håkansson stops stirring the couscous.

'Bloody hell,' he says. 'The Security Police didn't say a word about that. They just wanted to know if we'd noticed anything unusual about the family, which of course we hadn't.'

'Except that they seemed somehow happier than everyone else,' Karin Kvarnsten says.

Once they finish questioning the two nursery workers, Börje and Waldemar stop next to each other out in the car park.

Waldemar lights a cigarette.

'There's no doubt about it,' he says. 'No matter what happens, as long as it doesn't affect you directly, life goes on, doesn't it?'

'It does,' Börje says. 'It really does. Let's see if Malin and Zeke have come up with anything.'

Ronny Karlsson doesn't stop muttering as he leads Malin and Zeke through the cramped, dusty rooms of the district court archive, housed four floors below the red-brick building containing the county administrative headquarters, next to the library in Slottsparken.

They managed to find the details of the person in charge of the archive online, then called the reluctant bureaucrat, who had protested but eventually agreed to help them. He must have understood how serious it was.

'Can't it . . .?'

He abandoned his question halfway through over the phone.

No, it can't wait, there's no time to go through the normal channels with a load of form-filling.

'OK, come over in an hour and a half.'

And now he's walking ahead of them, in jeans and a red flannel shirt, and the archive smells musty and forgotten, and on tall metal shelving, painted bright blue, stand rows of files and boxes, identified by marker pen, beside piles of folders evidently arranged into some sort of system with elastic bands and Post-it notes.

'Most of the archive is available to the public,' Ronny Karlsson mutters, taking a long stride over a box in the middle of the passageway. 'But no one ever bothers with any of it. What you're after should be here.'

'We're bothered,' Malin says, and Ronny Karlsson stops beside a shelf full of black files.

'It ought to be here.'

And he reaches up on tiptoe with a frown as he reads the headings on the spines of the files, before pulling one of them out.

Ronny Karlsson leafs through it.

Reads, then holds the open file out towards Malin.

'Here,' he says. 'This is all I've got about the Vigerö girls.'

38

This world is overflowing with unwanted children, Malin thinks.

A planned adoption that never happened.

Who wants damaged goods if there's a choice? Sooner brown or yellow or red than someone with a damaged brain, a wrecked soul.

Malin looks out across the park towards the castle, sees the cherry and apple trees and magnolias competing to be the most beautiful, Miss Linköping Tree 2010.

It's a quarter to twelve, and Zeke is strolling slowly beside her, and behind the wall of white flowers they can just make out the castle, and the section of the park that's closed to the general public, and on the other side of them is the library, its huge glass windows glinting knife-sharp in the sun. In the passageways between the shelves, people are looking for books to read, and students are huddled over their computers at the desks.

The library.

Tove's favourite place. Malin and Zeke walk in silence towards the car, parked over by the cathedral.

Every corner of this city is so familiar to me, Malin thinks. Every stone of the cathedral's walls is in my memory, every tree, every nuance of the pink façade of the old gymnasium is part of me, every inequality between people, every injustice, every sorrow, joy, desire, and avaricious thought.

There was a name in the black file in the district court archive.

Not the name of the woman who gave the children up for adoption, nor the name of the father, but the name of a social worker who was involved in some way.

Swedish parents have no right to anonymity when they give children up for adoption. But in the case of the Vigerö twins, the biological parents were not identified.

Why not?

A bureaucratic mistake? Or something else?

The social worker was an Ottilia Stenlund, and six years ago she was working for Social Services in Norrmalm, office number four, at 13 Teknologgatan in Stockholm.

'We'll have to try calling Ottilia Stenlund,' Zeke says as they go around the big oak tree outside the old gymnasium.

The castle.

A grey box some hundred metres away. The residence of the district governor. Smart people get invited to official dinners there. And ice-hockey players from the Linköping team.

The cathedral.

Like a gigantic sarcophagus, it seems to demand the attention of Linköping's inhabitants, yet they still don't seem to care much about what happens in God's house. The mosque out in Ekholmen is bound to be better attended. Apart from when there's a bombing, or at Christmas, at midnight mass, when a thousand candles make the stone interior glow. Then the citizens of Linköping turn out to a man, and the churchwardens have to turn people away at the doors, and the collection boxes overflow with guilty consciences.

Bloody hell, Malin thinks.

In Springsteen's words: 'Still at the end of every hard earned day people find some reason to believe.'

She pulls out her mobile.

'I'll see if I can get her number through directory enquiries.'

'Shouldn't we call her at work?'

'That would take longer. Directory enquiries is quicker, and more straightforward. Let's give it a try.'

They reach the car. The white paint on the roof is covered with bird shit that wasn't there when they parked, and Malin sees Zeke look up at the sky, at the pale green oak tree that must have been full of defecating crows or ravens or some other urban refugees, and Zeke swears, but not very convincingly.

'Yes, we have an Ottilia Stenlund. Number 39, Skoghöjdsvägen in Abrahamsberg. Would you like me to connect you, and send you a text message with the details?'

The phone rings three times, then Malin hears a tired, hoarse female voice at the other end.

'Ottilia.'

Something in Ottilia Stenlund's voice makes Malin think she was expecting a phone call.

From us?

'My name's Malin Fors, I'm a detective inspector with the Linköping Police.'

She explains the reason for her call.

Apologises for calling her at home, but given the circumstances it couldn't be helped.

'I still work at the same office,' Ottilia Stenlund says. 'But today's my day off.'

Friday off. Malin remembers reading an article in *Expressen* saying that Social Services had started to open on Saturdays to meet the extra demand from people affected by the financial crisis.

'So do you have to work on Saturdays? I read about that.'

Show interest, build up trust, you never lose the habit, Malin thinks.

'Sometimes I have to work Saturdays, yes.'

Ottilia Stenlund breathes, long, thoughtful breaths, and Malin asks: 'I presume you've been following the case. And that you remember the girls.'

'I have to keep everything confidential,' Ottilia Stenlund says. 'I'd be breaching our code of conduct if I said anything,' and Malin feels a flash of anger as she snaps down the line: 'They were blown to pieces. Can you imagine that? Those lovely little babies you helped to get adopted grew into two beautiful little girls, and now there's nothing left of them but charred flesh, blood, and guts. So don't try it on with all that fucking—'

And Zeke has rushed around the car and is now yanking the mobile from her hand, and Malin feels everything going black before her eyes, and is having trouble breathing, and she reaches out for the roof of the car and can feel still-warm bird shit between her fingers as she hears Zeke say: 'I must apologise . . . my colleague is under a lot of pressure, we're in a tight spot at the moment, is there any way you could make an exception, getting a court order to get around the confidentiality legislation takes time, and time is something we don't have.'

The world grows clearer again.

Zeke, sounding resigned.

'So you can't make an exception? OK, thanks anyway.'

He clicks to end the call.

'She was scared,' Zeke says. 'Couldn't you hear it in her voice? She was absolutely terrified.'

It's half past four by the time Zeke drops Malin off outside her flat.

The pair of them, Börje Svärd, Waldemar Ekenberg, and

Johan Jakobsson have spent all Friday afternoon talking to people connected to the Vigerö family. Nothing terribly significant has emerged. The adoption seems to have been unknown to all of them, and the family appeared to have been impossibly happy.

And the Security Police have made their presence felt again.

On the same path as them? Not impossible. Sven Sjöman had taken care to keep them updated, as he had been instructed, and who knew what they might do with the information.

Ottilia Stenlund is my, our, best way forward, Malin tells herself.

The Pull & Bear has opened, and she stops outside the entrance to the pub, waiting for the urge to have a drink to wash over her, but as she stands there in front of the red and yellow paintwork she feels nothing. Just wants to get up to the flat, and a couple of minutes later she's sitting on the sofa in the living room, staring at the wall.

Tove is out at Janne's.

The bastard.

And then things start to move inside her body and she leaps up from the sofa. She needs to shake off this damn restlessness, can't bear the thought of just looking at the shabby walls of the flat any longer, listening to the ticking of the Ikea clock, and she pulls her running clothes out of the wardrobe, digs out her worn-out Nikes, and in just a few minutes she's running past the few people strolling along the path beside the river.

From the corner of her eye she can see the tall, newly built apartment blocks, which rumour has it are seventy-five per cent occupied by doctors. She runs past the new bowling alley, trying not to look at the other side of the river where the fire station, Janne's workplace, sits red and blunt, like a reminder of the unending meagreness of life.

How fast can I run?

How far?

Smart 1950s villas line the slope down to the river. She's been inside several of them in connection with other cases.

Her heart beating like a hammer inside her now.

Her field of vision reduced to a narrow oblong.

Move, get out of the way. And she feels her body working, obeying her, and the adrenalin pumps and she swings up over Braskens Bridge and runs on past Saab.

This was where Mum worked, she thinks. This was where she met the man who gave her her second child, my brother. This was where our lives, Mum's and Dad's and mine, turned into one big lie. Unless that had already happened before then?

I refuse, Malin thinks. It's not going to happen to me.

She's stopped outside the factory gates. Stands there panting, leaning over with her hands on her knees, catching her breath, then she runs back towards the city centre again, thinking: I refuse, refuse, refuse, and the word becomes a mantra inside her, carrying her forward, and she thinks, I'm thirty-six years old, I can't allow myself to be defined by the mistakes made by another woman and her husband, and by their inability to confront themselves. I've got the opportunity now to do precisely that, to look myself in the mirror and finally do something with my life.

I have to visit my little brother. For my own sake, for Tove's, for his. Have to conquer my fear. Because I am afraid of what might be waiting for me, aren't I?

Tove. She wants to go straight away.

Malin fights to suppress the dark feeling that grows in her stomach whenever she thinks of Tove, and she's aware that she's making the same mistake that she's always made.

But still.

Still.

First I have to finish this job. Put pressure on Ottilia Stenlund. Make her talk.

And Malin thinks of Peter Hamse. She hasn't spoken to him today. Even if I have a perfectly valid reason to.

Daniel and Janne. Bastards. And she forces herself onward, her surroundings become colours, sounds, pain, breathing, until finally she slumps in front of the door to her block as the bells of St Lars Church strike half past six. She feels her stomach clench and quickly leans to one side, spewing up all the bile from her stomach, and it feels incredibly good and her whole being is nothing but sweat and a chilly dampness.

She sticks her fingers down her throat.

Throws up the last contents of her stomach.

Sees her dad's face in front of her.

Dad, she thinks. How am I ever going to forgive you?

39

The car is pressing its way along the E4, heading north across the flat landscape of Östergötland.

It's only half past six in the morning, and Malin is glad that Zeke's driving, no coffee in the world could fight off the tiredness she feels, even though she got a full night's sleep.

She had to nag Sven Sjöman into letting them drive to Stockholm and put an extra strain on their already hard-pressed budget, to talk to Ottilia Stenlund in person rather than let their colleagues in Stockholm take care of it.

But she's sure that only she could do it properly, she and Zeke, and she really does want to follow up this line of inquiry, and Sven hadn't been able to resist the strength of her conviction.

Tired, so tired.

She hasn't caught up yet, the nights and days when everything seemed to be happening at once are still in her system, and she could do with sleeping for a week. But not now, there's no time at the moment, and she listens to the sound of the engine as she watches some white cows grazing in a meadow full of yellow flowers in front of a red-painted farmhouse on the edge of a dense forest of fir trees.

What's hidden among those trees? she thinks.

In those dark, in-between spaces?

What are we heading into, Zeke and I? Are we going to find anything new, or is the trail that leads to social worker Ottilia Stenlund a dead end? Are the lines of inquiry that Waldemar Ekenberg, Johan Jakobsson, Börje Svärd, and the others are following the right way forward?

Maybe the truth is to be found, if not in the Economic Liberation Front, then in some other militant organisation, Islamic extremists, biker gangs?

The pistol in the holster under her jacket presses against her body.

On the phone last night, when Malin insisted that they try to get Ottilia Stenlund to talk about the adoption them-selves, Sven told them to get to Stockholm as early as they could. He had told her that they still had no idea who the man with the bomb on the bike was, and that the interviews up at the University Hospital hadn't come up with anything. Nor had the forensic examination, so the field was wide open for Malin and Zeke.

'Do what you can,' Sven had said. 'Just keep going. We can deal with the financial consequences of the trip later.'

And Malin had felt that what he was really saying was: 'Keep going, into the darkness.'

And she looks out at the grey tarmac of the E4, reads a sign saying 'Norrköping 14' and thinks: I really am pushing into an unknown darkness now, I can feel it, but it doesn't frighten me, what I'm scared of is somewhere else. And Zeke reaches for the CD player and switches on the minor-key German choral music he's so fond of, but which has the ability to give Malin a serious headache when played at the wrong moment.

It's just right for this moment, though.

And she leans her head against the side window, shuts her eyes, and falls asleep.

* * *

When she wakes up again the car is rolling through the southern suburbs of Stockholm.

The brutal high-rises of Botkyrka seem to be bogged down against a receding horizon.

The hidden splendour of Mälarhöjden, the relative comfort of Midsommarkransen, where the functionalist blocks seem to defy the roar of the motorway and want to give their inhabitants a good hug.

Stockholm.

I moved here once, Malin thinks. With Tove, who was so young at the time, and it was almost impossible to reconcile life as a mother of a young child with studying at Police Academy. It worked, but only just.

Stockholm was like a piece of scenery for me, Malin thinks as they roll across the Skanstull Bridge and through the tunnel under the shimmering, ostentatious façade of the recently built hotel. I never found my way into the city, I never gained access, and why should I have? A single mother studying to join the police. Could there be anyone of lower status in a city completely obsessed with money and fashion, with everything just a bit beyond the ordinary?

I told myself that I wanted to stay, Malin thinks. But I convinced myself that it was impossible in practical terms, that I wanted to move back to Janne and maybe try again, but it was really something different. A strong sense of inadequacy, of not being good enough, and that's how you felt all your life, isn't it, Mum? The feeling that the world is so big, and you so little, and that others are important, while you're of no value.

When they emerge into the light again she can see the back of the parliament building, Riksdagshuset, and the water of Riddarfjärden, and she thinks: How could I ever have imagined that I could fit in here? How many people have succeeded with the journey I failed to make? Moving from a provincial city and making the capital their own? Succeeding, making something of themselves, astonishing the world, if only a very small part of it?

The München Brewery building rises from the water like a medieval citadel on Söder Mälarstrand behind them, the cliffs seem to be there to protect the bourgeois inhabitants from attack, and the tower of the City Hall on the opposite shore seems to warn: Feel free to come, but don't think you're anything special. The handsome functionalist blocks along Norr Mälarstrand are bigger than Malin remembers, and she wonders what it's like living there, waking up every morning to see the water and the Western Bridge. She remembers the flat she and Tove sublet out in Traneberg, a single room with an alcove for a bed, on the ground floor above all the bins, with a view of a car park.

But Tove was happy there.

With her pre-school.

With her babysitters.

Maybe because back then they both had a sense that they were actually going somewhere, and maybe that's why Tove has the nerve to take the next step now? Is that why the thought of her leaving makes me angry and panicky?

Janne. Daniel Högfeldt. They're on their way towards something new as well. But what about me, where am I going? And then she sees the boy in an anonymous hospital room. The way he's tried to suppress his mother's face, erasing it, and even though she knows that the boy is a man now, he'll always be a boy to her.

Sveavägen.

They emerge from the City Tunnel and get caught in the chaotic traffic beneath the blue façade of the Concert Hall. Malin watches young girls cross the road by the Adidas shop on the corner of Kungsgatan, and their

footsteps are firm, determined. I never had that sort of
step when I was your age, when I lived here.

They turn off into Rådmansgatan and drive up to the
spring greenery of Tegnérlunden, and the romantic statue
of Strindberg which seems to liken the old nutter to a lion,
and then they turn into a side street whose name Malin
doesn't know.

'Teknologgatan. It should be here somewhere,' Zeke says,
pulling up.

'Norrmalm Social Services, office number four. Let's
hope Ottilia Stenlund will see us, if she's actually working
Saturday this week. Otherwise we'll have to head over to
her home address.'

Hardship doesn't take weekends off during the spring of
2010.

The office is open, just as Ottilia Stenlund had said it
would be.

And she's there.

Malin and Zeke are asked to wait in a windowless room,
its walls painted an aggressive shade of yellow that makes
Malin think of Hare Krishna.

Ottilia Stenlund is willing to see them, but she has two
meetings with clients to get through first.

People scattered around the sofas and chairs.

Leafing through copies of the *Metro*, celebrity magazines,
or the interior design magazines that one of the staff must
have tactlessly brought in from home.

Some of the clientele look familiar. Alcoholics the same
age as Malin, but who look a hundred years older and stink
of piss and alcohol and dirt, and who are here to pick up
the weekly contribution to their drink budget. A skinny
woman who looks like she's in her forties, but is probably
no more than twenty. Malin can recognise a drug addict

from a hundred metres, the desperate pleading look in their eyes, yet still utterly focused. But there are also perfectly ordinary people in the waiting room, a smart mother with two young children, a man of about thirty in a blue suit and tie, a pensioner with a neatly pressed blue and white striped shirt.

Hardship is striking blind now, Malin thinks. Anyone can lose their job. No one's safe, and if you can't make your mortgage payment within twenty days the bank will seize your flat.

You could be out on the street in a month. Yet it's still hard to feel sorry for people who own flats in this part of the city. Highly paid toffs with luxury cars and runaway expenses. Now some of them are finding out what hardship feels like, and then a man emerges from Ottilia's office and interrupts Malin's train of thought, scruffy and dirty the way only the homeless can be, and suddenly a woman in her mid-fifties is standing in front of them, wearing a long, blue-flowered dress.

Her face is round, and a pair of deep blue, intelligent eyes peer out from beneath her blonde fringe.

'I can see you now,' she says, looking at Malin and Zeke. 'Come through, but I'm afraid I don't have long.'

Malin looks at the standard-issue clock on the wall of Ottilia Stenlund's office.

Similar to the ones Malin remembers from the rehab centre last autumn.

Twenty past nine.

They're sitting opposite Ottilia Stenlund, who is looking down at them from her elevated position behind a desk piled high with files and documents.

In front of her on the desk, face down, is a black folder.

She's got one hand on the folder, as if to protect it, before she lets go of it.

'I thought you might come,' Ottilia Stenlund says. 'What's happened is absolutely appalling,' and Malin feels her anger of the previous day flaring up again, and for a few short seconds she thinks that Ottilia Stenlund isn't going to say anything useful. But Malin manages to control herself, and her fears prove unfounded.

'It was an extremely unusual case,' Ottilia Stenlund goes on. 'Difficult. Unpleasant, very unpleasant. I've never experienced anything like it.'

Both Malin and Zeke can sense the fear creeping into the room, crawling across the floor like some ravenous, infected lizard, bringing with it an unshakeable stench of rotting flesh.

The woman on the other side of the desk looks at them.

'I don't see I have any other choice but to tell you,' she says. 'I'll tell you who the girls' biological mother is.'

40

Mummy.

You're not our mummy.

Not our real one.

We were confused at first, but maybe we had a vague idea already.

And now that this lady is telling you, Malin, we're wondering why you, Hanna, if you weren't our mummy, why you looked after us? Why did you want to look after us?

Because you loved us, that's why, isn't it? Because you needed something to love, and that's the way it should be.

Mummy!

We're calling to you, want to ask why you never mentioned anything to us, even though we realise you must have thought we were too little, that you wanted to protect us from ourselves, from what we are, from what we were.

Was that it, Mummy? Were you scared?

And Daddy wasn't our daddy either, and he isn't here either. We're alone, so alone, and we see Malin sitting in an office in a big city that we don't recognise, and next to her sits the bald man, and in front of them sits a woman, and we can see her mouth moving, but we can't hear what she's saying, and we know it's important. We know she's telling our story.

How we ended up with you, Mummy, you who aren't our mummy, and with you, Daddy, you who aren't our daddy.

But for us you have always been our mummy and daddy, and you always will be, the feeling of a love that can stretch *across whole universes, combining the sound of all roaring water, of all thunder clouds blowing back and forth above human beings, whispering to them: Love one another, love one another. And even if you can't manage that, don't abandon each other.*

Because we were abandoned, but we were also loved.

So who was it who abandoned us?

Who wasn't able to love us?

A mouth moving way down there. Is it saying a name?

Malin.

Can you get hold of a name? Can you get a description of abandoned love?

Can you tell us about Mummy and Daddy, the real ones, the ones who put us in a little reed boat and set us adrift into this wicked world?

Malin could see Ottilia Stenlund's mouth move.

Heard what it said. Felt that they were no longer alone in the room.

You're here, aren't you? she thinks. Can you hear what she's saying, what she's just said?

Ottilia Stenlund has told them, but she didn't look directly at Malin or Zeke as she did so, as if she were committing some sort of moral crime.

It struck Malin that the woman before her was actually breaching confidentiality laws when she told them what they needed to know, but to hell with that.

The woman who gave birth to the Vigerö twins was a Josefina Marlöw, and at the time she was thirty-three years old, a heavy heroin user, homeless, and was probably raped by another addict while she was high. At any rate, she didn't know who the father was, and couldn't actually remember having intercourse at all.

So she said.

Josefina Marlöw was the daughter of the financier Josef

Kurtzon, one of the richest men in Sweden, and the owner of a wide-reaching financial empire. The name Kurtzon seemed familiar to Malin, but she couldn't summon up an immediate picture of the man. It had been Ottilia Stenlund's duty as a social worker to ensure that the children were taken care of after they were born: the idea that they would be looked after by Josefina Marlöw, single, and a heavy heroin user, had been out of the question. Ottilia Stenlund confirmed what Malin had heard, that the natural solution in cases like that was to place the children with members of their immediate family, or find a foster home for them. Usually Social Services did everything they could to avoid going straight for adoption, there were hardly any Swedish infants adopted at birth any more.

But Josefina Marlöw had insisted on it, her family must never know that she had been pregnant, let alone that the children existed, or where they had gone. She had turned her back on her family and changed her name, and Ottilia Stenlund didn't want to, or perhaps couldn't, go into the reasons why.

Thoughts were bouncing around inside Malin's head.

So, even if the girls had been adopted, they were members of one of Sweden's wealthiest families?

What did that mean?

Could someone have wanted to get at them somehow because of money? And what could have turned this Josefina Marlöw into a drug user, so heavily addicted that it made her abandon her children?

Ottilia Stenlund went on.

'Josefina kept herself clean while she was pregnant, but no longer than that. She was adamant that the children should be adopted by a decent Swedish couple with no connection at all to her family, and that they mustn't be rich. Josefina was careful to stress that the adoptive parents should be ordinary people, as she put it. We did as she asked. There were no legal problems about not telling anyone else. The pregnancy and children were legally considered to be Josefina's private business.'

'What about her family, weren't they keeping an eye on her?' Zeke asked, and Ottilia Stenlund just shook her head and said: 'That family scares me. I've no idea if they knew about what was going on. Maybe Josefina just disappeared off their radar.'

'Why didn't she want anything to do with her family?'

'She didn't want to talk about it. But I got the impression that a lot of terrible things had happened in her childhood.'

'Her name wasn't mentioned on the adoption papers.'

'No,' Ottilia Stenlund replied. 'Information sometimes gets lost . . . Not even our system is perfect.'

'Where is she now?'

'Josefina is one of Stockholm's underground angels.'

'What do you mean by that?' Malin asked.

'She told me she lived underground. In tunnels and sewers, in the passageways of underground stations, and all she could think about was heroin. Don't ask me where she was getting the money, but she had no bank account, we knew that much. I assume she was prostituting herself, maybe stealing as well. Well, the way a lot of them do.'

'But if her family was so rich, why work as a prostitute?'

'She didn't want anything to do with their money.'

Malin nodded, then fell silent, and in that silence she now sees Ottilia Stenlund stand up and walk about the room, thinking before she says: 'I presume you'll want to talk to Josefina. I honestly don't have any idea of where she might be. She disappeared straight after the girls were born. She was exhausted when she left the hospital, and I haven't had any contact with her since then. That was six years ago . . .'

'How did you come to be involved in the first place?'

'I was her social worker when she returned to the city after she was sectioned for rehab up in Norrland. Long before she got pregnant.'

When Malin hears the word 'sectioned' the memories come flooding back to her, the disgust and seediness and shame, and the offensive intimacy she experienced when Sven Sjöman sent her to the rehab centre out in the forest.

But still.

Since then she's managed to stay in control of the urge to drink – but that wasn't thanks to any sort of fucking group therapy. That was down to me.

'So you've got no idea where we might find her?' Zeke asks.

Ottilia Stenlund shakes her head, but in her eyes Malin sees something that suggests that Ottilia Stenlund knows more than she's prepared to say about Josefina Marlöw's whereabouts.

She's just about to put pressure on Ottilia Stenlund when the woman raises her hand to Malin and says: 'I've already told you far more than I should. I've gone far enough. You'll have to ask your colleagues in the Stockholm force. If Josefina is still alive, they might know where she could be.'

Malin makes do with this.

Zeke shakes his head slightly, as if to say that this will do, that she's already given them more than they could have hoped, and then Malin asks: 'What about Kurtzon? What do you know about her father? The family?'

'If you google them you'll find loads of information. He's a bit like a latterday Wallenberg, only more secretive. You know, working invisibly behind the scenes.'

'I've heard of the name,' Zeke says. 'They have those investment funds, don't they?'

'Those, and much more,' Ottilia Stenlund says, going over to the door.

'If you'll excuse me, detectives. I've got a client waiting. I don't want to have to put in too much overtime on a Saturday.'

Do you know, Malin, do you know?

We floated down and were hanging in the air right in front of the woman's face, and we tried to read her lips when she spoke to you and do you know, do you know, Malin, we could understand, and we kept seeing the name Josefina. Josefina, is that the name of our real mummy, the woman who carried us and gave birth to us?

So who is she? Where is she? Shall we look for her together, Malin? We want to see her, want to read her lips to see what she says about us.

Does she think about us?

Do we exist for her?

But we do, we must. Maybe she's drifting here with us as well, even though we can't see her.

What about our real daddy? Who was he?

Maybe she didn't know anything about him, our real mummy. Things are coming together, Malin.

Can you feel it?

Spring is showing its anxious face now, and those are our faces you can see, contorted by grimaces, Malin, that's us you can hear calling: Mummy, Daddy, come to us, we daren't be on our own any more, we don't want to be frightened any more.

The other children, the ones who are locked up, they're shouting, just like we are. And we're wondering: Did we have to die so that they can live? Isn't that rather unfair? Isn't everything supposed to be fair?

How are we supposed to understand any of this?

★   ★   ★

As they're standing in the lift on the way down from their encounter with Ottilia Stenlund, Malin switches on her mobile.

Two missed calls. Two new messages.

Dad.

Don't call me.

Tove.

SHIT, shit, shit.

I forgot to call Tove and tell her I was coming to Stockholm.

Her stomach clenches.

Her heart turns black, the blood inside it congeals. How could I?

She brings up Tove's number, but there's no answer.

Instead Tove's beautiful, slightly hoarse voice, saying: 'I can't talk right now. Leave a message after the bleep and I'll get you back.'

Malin smiles, then she starts laughing, she'd forgotten what Tove's sense of humour was like, and she thinks she could stay in that lift for weeks, just listening to the message over and over again.

'What's going on, Malin?' Zeke asks.

She holds her hand over the phone.

'Nothing. I think I might be going a bit mad.'

She takes her hand away.

'Tove. I'm in Stockholm for work. I'll call you later.'

'You've been mad for a while now,' Zeke says, and they leave the lift and walk out of the building.

'What now?' he asks.

'Now we try to find Josefina Marlöw,' Malin says. 'Dead or alive, we're going to find her. This means something, it has to mean something.'

41

Who was our daddy, Malin?

Who was it who came to Mummy that night?

We know who our mummy is now, Malin, and she isn't here with us, we can promise you that.

You have to find her, Malin, only she can help you get any further, so that you find the other children before it's too late. You have to, because otherwise we'll never find peace.

Don't be scared, Malin, no matter where this story takes you.

This is the story of your life, and surely you can't be scared of your own life, can you?

It's very warm where you're going.

It's burning.

There's nothing but cruelty there, no hope, no singing, no mummy stroking her sleeping children on the cheek in the evening in a flat beneath pictures of a happy life.

The wind is rustling the treetops of Tegnérlunden, and up in the park Malin can hear children playing and shouting. She imagines she can hear something on the wind as well. Is that you, girls? she wonders. Are you whispering to me? But I can't hear what you're saying.

She and Zeke walk past a new building with a matt black façade and glass balconies, where someone has stuck up a huge silhouette of a leafless tree.

They walk down Tegnérgatan towards Sveavägen, and Malin's mobile rings as they are passing Rolf's Kitchen.

'Malin.'

'This is Ottilia Stenlund.'

Malin stops, and as she listens to what Ottilia Stenlund has to say, she looks in at the full restaurant, at all the smartly dressed, self-aware, Saturday brunch-eating types, the same age as her, the ones who made it in the big city.

What sort of jobs do they do?

Media. They look the sort. They probably work on glossy magazines, the sort Malin never reads.

And then she sees a man.

In profile.

And her stomach lurches, is that, no it can't be, yes it is, no, surely not? It isn't Dr Peter Hamse, but she can feel the tingling in her body. She wants to let go, just like Janne and Zeke and Daniel Högfeldt have let go, surrendering to their stupid masculine desires, and it occurs to her that that's what she usually does as well, and she knows she's going to sleep with Peter Hamse sooner or later, but when she connects the words with the doctor's handsome face it makes her feel sick, as though she's sullying something that ought to stay clean and pure and as sweetly scented as the spring.

'Are you listening to me?'

'I'm listening.'

'I saw Josefina six months ago. I didn't want to have to tell you, but I feel I ought to. Sorry. I bumped into her on a crossing outside Åhléns in the city centre. She looked wrecked, and she didn't see me, she was filthy and skinny and it looked like she'd reached the end of the road, to be honest.'

'Do you have any idea where she might be now?'

'Like I said, I've no idea.'

'Can you try to find out?'

'I can ask the people who work with addicts in the city centre.'

'Do you think she's likely to have heard what happened to the children?'

'Maybe. She probably tried to keep up with what they were doing. According to her own logic.'

'In that case she could be in a bad way. Grief-stricken.'

'That did occur to me,' Ottilia Stenlund says.

A shiny silver Jaguar glides past.

A young girl next to an old man.

'Bloody hell,' Malin says.

'Sorry?'

'I'm sorry. Something else just occurred to me,' Malin says. 'Something private.'

Tove.

You can't go to Lundsberg. You have to stay with me. I want you where I can keep an eye on you, don't even imagine you can go.

She forces herself back to her conversation with Ottilia Stenlund.

'She used to live in the underground. Various places. The central station, Slussen, Hornstull. There are loads of abandoned tunnels and passageways.'

'So Josefina Marlöw could be underground somewhere?'

Ottilia Stenlund falls silent, before whispering: 'That's where she's been for a long time.'

And Malin can hear the fear in her voice again.

The way it almost smothers Ottilia Stenlund's last words: 'I don't want anything more to do with this. Don't ever mention my name to anyone.'

At least you aren't underground, Malin thinks as she looks in once more at the people crowded around the tastefully distressed wooden tables inside Rolf's Kitchen. The diners behind the large windows seem to be making faces at her, and she feels scruffy in the dress she's wearing, feels like swapping it for something more chic, and sitting down in there as one of the successful people, and her distaste turns to envy.

'I'm hungry,' Zeke says.

'Me too,' Malin says.

'Let's go in,' Zeke says. 'They're bound to have a spare table for a couple of hungry cops from Linköping.'

'It's too expensive,' Malin says.

'We can afford it. We get a subsistence allowance.'

The people.

The food on their plates looks good, and they seem to be absorbed in incredibly interesting discussions about things that belong to life, not death.

'Let's find somewhere else,' Malin says, turning away and starting to walk down towards Sveavägen.

Big steaks, small prices.

Jensen's Bøfhus, a grubby steakhouse imported from Denmark. Lunchtime steak only sixty-seven kronor.

Perfect.

A different clientele here, even though the two restaurants are just a stone's throw from each other, and outside the windows the cars go back and forth along the broad, prestigious avenue, and people seem to know exactly where they're going.

'Looks good,' Zeke says, as a brick of meat arrives in front of him. Then he asks: 'What do we do now?'

'We eat,' Malin says, and sees the look of irritation on Zeke's face, so she forces a smile and says: 'We try to get hold of Josefina Marlöw. And we find out more about the Kurtzon family.'

'That sounds like the perfect job for Johan Jakobsson.'

'Is he working today?'

'Everyone's working every day until we solve this one.'

Malin pulls out her mobile, Taps in a message: 'Josef Kurtzon and family. Everything you can find, asap. Have you got time?'

The reply comes thirty seconds later, 'Weirdly quiet here. Info soon.'

What sort of trail has Malin picked up on?

Johan Jakobsson has googled the name Kurtzon.

Tens of thousands of results.

Head of the family, Josef Kurtzon. Born 1925. Started a finance company after the war. Said to have focused on looking after the fortunes of Jewish families saved from the Nazis. Also supposed to have managed the affairs of those who did well out of the war, stealing from Jews who died in concentration camps or getting rich supplying the German army with whatever it needed.

One article addressed the contradictions in Kurtzon's early activities. How no one seemed to care about ethics as long as their fortune grew.

Josef Kurtzon's own origins are shrouded in obscurity. As is the question of what he did during the war. One website has it that he's the child of a family that fled the Bolsheviks in St Petersburg in the early 1900s. Another says he comes from a family of sawmill workers in Sundsvall, a third that he was a junior officer in Mussolini's army, a fourth that he came from a Belgian family that made a fortune from rubber in the Congo. There seemed to be any number of stories about Josef Kurtzon's origins, but none could claim to be the truth. But after the war he was there, ready to double other people's money.

He was said to have sold his company in the fifties to manage his own fortune through businesses based in Jersey, Gibraltar, and the Caribbean. He was surrounded by rumour and supposed to be one of the richest men in the world.

Then, at the start of the sixties, he was back in business. He started a company to manage the fortunes of the very richest and most successful individuals.

Ten percent of the profits, year after year. International clients. Nobility, famous people. There were rumours that the whole thing was a big Ponzi scheme, a pyramid scheme. But no investigation ever found anything. Kurtzon was said to have invested in oil in Venezuela and Norway, and some claimed that the income from those investments saved the company.

But where did the money go?

In those days Kurtzon owned a large house on Lidingö, just outside Stockholm, but otherwise he kept a very low profile. He'd never given any interviews, and chose to contact potential clients through intermediaries. There were no photographs of him, he was said to have multiple citizenship, and wherever there was a krona or a dollar to be made, he seemed to be there. The money itself seemed to be the thing, rather than what he could buy with it. But maybe he was driven by the power that money brings? Johan thinks, as he carries on searching the Net.

A clear pattern is emerging: Kurtzon always seems to want more. He sets up a more public, accessible investment company, with no lower limit to deter investors in the so-called Kurtzon Funds. As if he is trying to get the souls of the entire nation.

He employs the best, pays the highest wages: guns for hire, the money-obsessed mercenaries that the financial world seems to be populated by, brilliant minds that are withered and burned out in the service of money.

Tragic, Johan thinks.

Then he pictures his own family's terraced house. The tired wood. The ceiling that needs painting, the ramshackle, old-fashioned kitchen, the feeble lamp in the ceiling, the lack of money that has led to a lack of furnishings. His wife is interested in design, but a policeman's wage and a teacher's wage have their limits, just like Ikea does.

And Kurtzon's mythical headquarters. A tall building by the bridge to Lidingö, entirely clad in expensive, shimmering white, ivory-like marble from Carrara. Johan knows the building, it's a well-known landmark, but he never had any idea what went on inside. Kurtzon is said to have his offices on the top three floors. And that's where he directs his primary business: managing the money of seriously wealthy people.

But the building has been sold now, and the business has moved to Kista, the core part of the company has been wound down, the money returned to the richest of the rich.

A lot of them moved their money to Madoff and Sandford when Kurtzon shut down.

A couple of articles, at VA.se and Swedish E24, deal with the mystery of Kurtzon.

No addresses listed in online databases.

The main Swedish business website. The *Financial Times*.

And then another rumour.

That Kurtzon doesn't think he has any worthy heirs. He married late, and his wife Selda died of cancer a long time ago. He's said to have withdrawn from life.

And that his three children, Josefina, Henry and Leopold, are all supposed to have fallen out with their father for reasons unknown. There's another rumour that a foundation in Switzerland controls the whole empire.

Eighty billion kronor. Two thousand billion.

Josef Kurtzon's fortune was estimated at each of these wildly different figures, and Johan can feel himself getting a headache just trying to work out how many zeros there would be if you wrote out eighty billion. Or two thousand billion.

No photographs, but on a website of financial profiles, Johan finds a sound-file that is supposed to be Kurtzon's voice. No information about where and when the recording was made.

The voice streams out of the speaker, rasping and dark, neutral, and in a tone that suggests it is conveying unquestionable facts: 'I have always wanted to uncover the very essence of what I am. And if I can do that, I will also understand what we are, and what we can be formed into.'

Johan plays the short clip again.

I? And who is this *we*? Johan wonders. His businesses? Human beings in general? Money? Who is to be formed? Us, human beings?

'. . .what we are.'

What we are?

Can be formed into?

Johan closes his eyes. Sighs. What a weird fucking bloke this Kurtzon seems to be.

I'm not like that. I'm not, am I?

Time to call Malin. Go through what I've found. Hope it helps her.

She's just paid the bill for their lunch when Johan calls.

She lets him talk, takes everything in, and thanks him, then checks on the situation back at home: nothing new, on any front.

Johan Jakobsson is curious. Asks how they arrived at Kurtzon, and she tells him.

Johan mutters something about taking responsibility for your children, then he ends the call.

She tells Zeke what she's just found out.

'The word rich has just taken on a whole new fucking meaning,' Zeke says when she's finished.

Zeke seems rather deflated at the thought of the Kurtzon family's wealth, even though he's close to money himself.

His son Martin is a millionaire ice-hockey star. But not a billionaire. Nowhere near. And definitely not a thousand times over.

No one needs that much money, Malin thinks as she gets up from their table and looks out at the half-empty restaurant. But greed is the worst virus a person can be infected with, and an awful lot of people seem to want more, that much she's learned over the years.

Is our truth hidden in money? she goes on to wonder. Is that what this Kurtzon stands for? and Zeke says:'Feels like it might be interesting to meet some of these Kurtzons. Do you think Josef Kurtzon knew about the twins?'

Zeke is entirely lacking in the instinctive respect and inferiority she feels in the face of people like this, this sort of naked power.

'I don't know,' Malin says. 'Why? Do you think it's important?'

'No, but you have to admit it's strange that she wanted to keep her pregnancy and the children secret from the rest of her family. And that she seems to avoid them like the plague.'

'We'll call Johan again, see if he really can't dig out the address of any of the Kurtzons. Preferably Josefina. But I don't suppose she's got an address.'

Then Malin's mobile buzzes.

A text.

From Ottilia Stenlund.

'Check the City Mission, at Slussen.'

'What was that?'

'Josefina Marlöw. Ottilia Stenlund thinks she might be at Slussen.'

* * *

Malin.

You're getting close to Josefina now.

Does she know what's happened to us?

Is she sad, grieving?

Is she as scared as we are?

Come to us, Mummy and Daddy, you're our real parents, aren't you?

Father, Mother, come here, to our domain.

They're crying now, Malin, the other children, the nasty thing is getting closer to them again. Full of fury. And the lizards that want to eat them up.

You've got to hurry, Malin. Hurry up and save them.

Before it's all too late.

42

Zeke and Malin manage to find a parking space close to the Katarina Lift.

It's already half past three, and Malin looks across to the round building sitting on top of the Slussen traffic interchange like a truncated, abandoned stump. Beyond it, the City Museum tries in vain to make itself visible in the urban confusion, pale posters for exhibitions about the city of the future hanging limply from its walls.

Who cares about the future? the people passing by seem to be thinking.

She turns to look back towards the commercial centre of the city.

The cars crowding along Skeppsbron seemed to want to spin out onto the quayside walk, where old, rusty ferries and a grey navy vessel are lying at anchor.

Across the water come shrieks and shouts from the Gröna Lund funfair, and the Djurgården ferries steam sedately back and forth. The air is thick with traffic fumes and pollen, and the heavy smell of diesel reminds Malin of the homebrew she drank as a teenager, and she remembers the wonderful sense of intoxication rather than the nightmarish hours spent vomiting over the rim of the toilet.

Red buses are driving on the carriageway beneath them, and a blue and grey train pulls out, heading for the suburbs, past the quayside where a Viking Line ferry is waiting to be filled with pensioners and booze-cruisers.

They head down towards the quayside and stop at a security booth at the entrance to a garage, and Malin leans forward and asks the skinny young guard: 'The City Mission's supposed to be somewhere around here, do you know where it is?'

And the guard stares at her, grins, then says in a hostile voice: 'This isn't an information desk. Get lost.'

And Zeke instinctively takes a step back, then two steps forward, and Malin realises what the guard thinks they are. Do they really look like a couple of homeless people? But even if they were, this bastard shouldn't be talking to them like that. Play the game, Fors, do it right.

'I was just asking a simple question. You've got no right to . . .'

And she can tell that Zeke has realised what she's doing, and is holding off behind her.

'Get lost. Or I'll call for reinforcements and arrest you,' the guard says. 'You shouldn't be hanging around here.'

'I—'

'And then I'll call the cops, so just take yourselves off somewhere else now.'

'You stupid little shit,' Malin says, pressing her index finger against the window of the booth. 'You sit there in your third-rate fucking uniform, like a little rat in a cage, and you have the nerve to think you can . . .'

The guard moves his hand to the phone beside him, and Malin yells: 'Now it's your turn to listen to me very fucking carefully!'

And Zeke steps up alongside her, presses his police ID against the glass, and Malin sees the guard's stubbly little chin drop as his mouth opens and closes like a fish, and he looks scared, his eyes flitting to the water behind them.

'Is that any way to treat people?' Malin says. 'You're

supposed to show them a bit of respect. You get that? No matter who they are.'

'Where. Is. The. City. Mission?'

Zeke's voice is as hard and hoarse and blunt as only his voice can be.

Bastard guard.

A minute later they're standing outside the unassuming, shabby doorway of the City Mission at the start of Stadsgården. There's a terrible racket from some air-conditioning pipes and fans mounted high on the concrete roof above them, and the stench of petrol fumes and rubbish is overwhelming.

A group of drunks is hanging around some steps, looking at Malin and Zeke, and one of them calls out through a toothless grin: 'So the city's finest have found their way here, then?'

A slender-limbed, middle-aged woman called Madelene Adeltjärn, dressed in a white blouse and blue jeans, is leading them through the shelter. The yellow linoleum floor shimmers under the dull fluorescent lighting as the empty dormitories are cleaned by cleaners, all of them black.

In the refectory, a man is picking at the last of the day's lunch.

'We're closed between lunchtime and eight o'clock in the evening,' Madelene Adeltjärn explains as she shows them into her cramped office, with a barred window looking out into a narrow internal shaft.

'Our clients are allowed in for dinner, then they get a bed for the night if they're sober, in order of arrival, until we run out. We're full every night.'

Madelene Adeltjärn sits down behind a tiny desk, and it's as if she can sense Malin wondering what a woman like her is doing here, in this setting, in this office.

There are no other chairs in the room, so she and Zeke remain standing.

'I know what you're thinking,' Madelene Adeltjärn says. 'I come from what you'd probably call a good family. We've got money. But there's nothing more empty than money. I'm a trained social worker, and I feel I can make a difference here, working with people who haven't had such an easy life as me. That's it, really. Money can ease your hunger, but it can't help your soul.'

Malin can feel her jaw dropping.

'I didn't mean . . .'

Zeke is grinning beside her, and says: 'Yes you did.'

'I'm no saint,' Madelene Adeltjärn says with a smile. 'I have very expensive habits.'

Then Zeke focuses, keen to make progress.

'What do you know about a Josefina Marlöw? Does she usually come here?'

'I'm not bound by any confidentiality legislation. But I'm very careful with our clients' privacy.'

'Please,' Malin says. 'We mean her no harm, we don't want to arrest her, we just want to ask her a few questions.'

Madelene Adeltjärn doesn't ask what it's about, and just nods.

'I know who Josefina is, where she's from. I can see myself in her, even if she's taken the act of running away to a far more extreme conclusion.'

'How do you mean?' Malin says.

'I mean there's a difference between working with the homeless in order to make amends, and actually becoming homeless.'

'Does she usually come here?' Zeke asks.

'Occasionally,' Adeltjärn says. 'A few nights a week for food, but she never sleeps here.'

'Where does she sleep?'

'I don't know. In the underground, maybe.'

'You said you knew her background. What can you tell us?' Malin says.

'Like I said, I'm very careful . . .'

'We're talking about murder here,' Malin says. 'That much I can tell you,' and she sees Madelene Adeltjärn's pupils contract as a shiver of fear runs through her.

'She's Josef Kurtzon's daughter. She's a heroin addict. I've seen her around ever since I first started here, and I have to say I'm surprised she's still alive. She's extremely run-down, quite possibly seriously ill.'

'And she's turned her back on her family?' Malin asks.

'I presume so.'

'Why?' Zeke asks.

'I don't know. I've got no idea, but environments in which life merely revolves around money can be fatal for the soul. Sometimes you just can't take any more, the greed and the lust for power growing bigger than love, and you try to find somewhere to escape to. And if you get your hands on heroin at that point, maybe that looks like a good way to escape.'

'Do you think she might be here this evening?' Malin asks.

Madelene Adeltjärn shakes her head.

'That's impossible to say.'

'Do you think any of the people outside might know where she is?'

'You can ask, but I doubt they'll be particularly willing to talk to you.'

Sure enough, none of the men or women outside the City Mission wants to talk to them, or even answer a single question about Josefina Marlöw, so they go back inside. Madelene Adeltjärn invites them to wait on the shabby sofas in the lobby, and she brings them each a cup of coffee before disappearing further inside the building again.

Posters on the walls.

About Aids and the risk of infection, about the symptoms of TB and the importance of seeking medical help to prevent the disease spreading.

Malin pulls out her mobile and calls Sven Sjöman, who tells her about the day's work, and how they still haven't come up with anything new with any of their lines of inquiry. They've checked Jonathan Ludvigsson's emails and phone log, but there was nothing to link him to the bombing.

They've had a visit from an expert in kinesiology from the university. He compared Ludvigsson's walk with the recording of the cashpoint, and declared almost instantly that he definitely wasn't the man with the bike outside the bank.

So in principle he's been eliminated from the investigation.

'Although we're likely to charge him about the weapons and making unlawful threats, and maybe fraudulent conduct as well,' Sven says.

They've also been in touch with the unit covering gang-related violence at National Crime. Although there were indications of an increase in tensions between the main biker gangs, there was nothing to suggest that the bomb was intended for Dick Stensson. So they've written off that line of inquiry for now.

And the Security Police hadn't been in touch.

'So we're pretty much stuck,' Sven says. 'We're carrying on, of course. Johan hasn't come up with an address for any of the Kurtzon family yet, but we're working on it. They're not registered as residing here, but they've got property here somewhere, that much is almost certain. We've tried Kurtzon's company, but they don't know where

Josef is, or they're refusing to say. What about you, how are you getting on?'

'We're sitting in the City Mission beneath Slussen. Waiting for Josefina Marlöw to show up.'

'OK. We haven't managed to find out anything else about the Vigerö family. We've taken a look at the car crash in which Pontus Vigerö died, but there's not much there. The car was scrapped a while back now, and the emergency services report is pretty thin, as is our own police report. Looks like he got a puncture and went off the road. There was no reason to suspect any sort of crime, and maybe there still isn't.'

'I'm not so sure,' Malin says.

'No, me neither.'

Sven's words confuse Malin.

Silence on the line.

'Are you staying the night in Stockholm?' he asks eventually, and through a small window looking out across the harbour Malin can see it's getting darker as a soft but somehow threatening twilight begins to settle over the city.

It strikes her that they haven't given any thought to where they might spend the night, but they'll certainly be staying, they're nowhere near finished with this line of inquiry, and she thinks of the bank card in her wallet, and how there isn't much left in her account, but enough to pay for a decent hotel room. She won't have to sleep in the street, or in some toilet, or in some smelly bed in a refuge.

'We're staying. We'll find somewhere.'

'Good,' Sven says. 'Everything OK otherwise?'

OK? Far from OK. Confusing, mainly, but maybe things are on their way to becoming OK.

'It's OK,' Malin says. 'We'll be in touch if anything happens.'

Beside her on the sofa Zeke has his eyes closed.

Malin can hear him snoring, and feels how much she'd like to drift off to sleep. She shuts her eyes, and in the theatre of her closed eyelids the boy, the man, the skinny body in the anonymous sickroom, comes to her and he's alone and she wants to go up to him and stroke his cheek but she doesn't dare, doesn't want to take the only thing he's got away from him, his loneliness.

Buzz.

She's woken from sleep by her mobile buzzing again.

A text from Johan.

She clicks to open it.

Josef Kurtzon, 42 Strandvägen.

How did Johan manage to get hold of that in the end? Never mind. Maybe he found a domestic residence attached to one of the businesses?

The clock on her phone tells her it's almost eight o'clock. The City Mission opens in twelve minutes, and there's a long queue outside the window. Stockholm's most rootless inhabitants have come to fill their stomachs and maybe sleep in a warm bed with clean sheets.

A few women.

Is one of them Josefina Marlöw?

Zeke opens his eyes, stretches, and says his back aches.

Madelene Adeltjärn comes into the room.

Looks out through the window.

'You're in luck,' she says. 'I can see Josefina at the back of the queue. Don't go out, wait until she comes in. Otherwise there's a high risk she'll turn on her heels the moment she catches sight of you.'

Malin looks at Josefina Marlöw.

At her big, dark eyes. So like the girls', but entirely lacking their innocence.

43

Börje Svärd and Waldemar Ekenberg are sitting together in Börje's kitchen, the seats of the black Myran chairs chafing against their buttocks. They're each sipping a glass of tepid whisky, their stomachs full of the sausage stroganoff and rice that Börje has just cooked for them.

After spending the whole day tugging at various lines of inquiry, following up on fruitless tip-offs from the public, they had both felt they'd had enough.

They had sat at their desks in the open-plan office, tired and smelling of sweat, looking at each other, thinking that Malin had better make some sort of progress in Stockholm, because how else were they going to get anywhere with this case?

And Börje had realised that he didn't want to eat alone, and that he could really do with a drink, but definitely not on his own.

And who was available?

Waldemar, and Börje had thrown the offer up in the air.

'How about dinner and a drink back at mine? To help us wind down?'

Waldemar had given him a broad grin.

'Sure. The old woman can pick me up when we're done.'

They'd prepared the meal together. Talked about anything but work. Drunk whisky with the food, along with low-alcohol beer, letting themselves get a bit tipsy. They had talked about dogs, car alarms, guns, and summer cottages. They had talked about children, and not having children. About grief, and the fact that it is up to each of us what we do with our single life.

Then they go out to the dogs in the garden.

And now they're standing there, patting the dogs in the mild spring evening, with the scent of dew-damp animal fur in their nostrils, and the promise of camaraderie that the smell seems to be hold.

'How do you think Malin and Zeke are getting on?' Börje asks.

'I'm sure they're doing brilliantly,' Waldemar says, and Börje can smell the whisky on his breath.

'What do you think about Sven letting her go off like that?'

'Might as well let her have her way,' Waldemar says. 'For a bird, she's a fucking good cop.'

A shadow of a human being.

The woman standing in front of Malin and Zeke can't weigh more than forty kilos. She's about ten centimetres shorter than Malin, her worn, stained jeans are hanging limply from her skinny hips, and her anorak, once white, is at least three sizes too big, her face partly hidden by its hood. For a moment Malin is struck by how much Josefina Marlöw resembles the figure on the bank video, then realises that it can't be the same person.

Josefina Marlöw is shorter, and her movements are jerky and irregular. Her hands shake, and she seems to have difficulty talking, as if her tongue doesn't quite want to obey the signals from her brain.

But the eyes . . .

The dark yet strangely colourless eyes sitting above the finely shaped, pointed nose are clear, and Malin can see grief and despair in them, and she realises that Josefina Marlöw knows what has happened to her girls.

From the refectory of the refuge comes the clatter of crockery and contented sighs.

'Fucking good, Manuel!' a male voice shouts, followed by a chorus of agreement, and Josefina Marlöw, who stopped when she caught sight of them and evidently wanted to talk to them, listened while Malin and Zeke told her why they were there, and now she gestures towards the door, saying: 'McDonald's up above, we can go there.'

Josefina Marlöw's mouth around a Big Mac.

Her jaws seem huge. Her two top front teeth have grown together.

She's starving.

Malin knows why she's skinny. That's what happens with heroin, the drug itself doesn't attack the body, but it dies anyway because you just stop caring about looking after it, and your body and soul gradually wither away in the face of the constant desire for more.

Malin has never tried heroin herself, but she's heard addicts talk about it.

The way the rush is like being completely enveloped by warm water, while you're raised up into a world where everything is good, and there's no need, no desire for anything. A world without cravings, where there's no avarice, no cruelty.

Malin can appreciate the appeal, how irresistible it must be, and knows she's had periods in her life when she would hardly have objected if anyone had insisted on her smoking a bit of heroin.

Josefina Marlöw takes another bite of the hamburger. Then she puts it down on the tray.

She's pushed back her hood, and her greasy, shiny hair covers an emaciated skull, and her sunken cheeks are covered with blemishes that look like Kaposi's sarcoma, a tumorous cutaneous disease common in people with HIV. Malin assumes that Josefina is in the advanced stages of Aids.

Josefina Marlöw looks out at Slussen, at the cars and buses passing in a steady stream on their way into the city centre, or up onto Södermalm, and when she turns around, the dusk light falls on her cheeks, accentuating the purity of her features, and neither Malin nor Zeke says anything, waiting for the person facing them, hoping that she will talk, tell them something important.

Malin has a hamburger in front of her. She hasn't touched it, isn't hungry, only bought it to seem sociable. She looks at Josefina Marlöw, wondering: How does anyone get to where you are, when every other option must have been open to you? The same question that occurred to her not long ago about Madelene Adeltjärn, but stronger now, and then the shadow in front of them starts to talk, saying: 'The girls. I know what happened to the girls,' and Malin can see that Josefina Marlöw is on the brink of crying, but it's as if her ravaged body doesn't contain enough moisture for tears.

'They were my girls,' and Josefina Marlöw's eyes turn empty and she falls silent.

'Why did you turn your back on your family?' Zeke asks, and Malin is taken aback by the bluntness of the question, but sees how the clarity, the absence of any hidden agenda, makes an impression on Josefina Marlöw, and she shakes her head and blurts out, whispers her reply: 'It was impossible.'

'What was impossible?'

'Living there.'

'Why?'

'There was no love.'

'In what way?'

'The idea of having us had nothing to do with love.'

'Having us?' Malin interjects.

'Yes, they were never interested in love. Just other things.'

'Like what?'

'Money.'

'They were interested in money?'

But Josefina Marlöw doesn't answer.

The dusk light slips away from her face, and her skin takes on the shimmering, mute hue that Malin recognises from dead bodies.

'And an image,' Josefina Marlöw goes on. 'They wanted to project an image.'

Mum, Malin thinks. The lack of love in you, your desire that everything should be something else, better than it really was. The way it shaped your life, eventually turning it into a lie. Is that the kind of image you mean?

'Tell us about the image.'

Malin can tell from Zeke's voice that he thinks her story is important, even if he probably couldn't explain exactly why.

But Josefina Marlöw drifts off, her hands start to shake uncontrollably, and the look in her eyes becomes clouded and unsettled, and she seems to want to get up, but it's as if her legs won't carry her.

'My mum,' she says. 'My mum.'

'Your mum?' Malin asks.

'Father. And my brothers.'

'What about them?'

Then Josefina Marlöw pulls herself together.

'There was no love in that home. And they were sadists, both of them, Mum and Father, but in different ways. I had to leave my family. You can't live in a world like that.'

'Did they hurt you?'

'They used to lock me up. And my brothers. But mostly

they just left us alone, when children aren't supposed to be on their own.'

'How did they lock you up?'

'In a cramped, dark room. A cold room. And they left us alone with the shame. I couldn't let them anywhere near the children, how could I have done that?'

Josefina Marlöw falls silent. Seems to think before going on: 'They didn't really care about me. And Father and Mum consciously messed up my brothers and made them scared and obsessed with money and everything that comes with it. They were to do whatever money demanded, for what they thought was Father's love.'

A couple of young Goth boys sit down at the next table.

'What happened to your brothers?'

Josefina Marlöw looks at Malin.

A sudden, boundless exhaustion in her expression. Her eyes turn black.

'Father tried to make them into the perfect businessmen,' she says.

'How?'

Josefina Marlöw shakes her head, says: 'By making them ruthless.'

'Ruthless?'

Then Josefina Marlöw closes her eyes, seems to disappear inside herself, shaking as if a powerful electric current were passing through her body.

She waves her hand, as if to fend off Malin's question.

'What did he do to them?'

No answer.

'Do you have any contact with your brothers?' Malin asks. 'Do you know where they are?'

'It's impossible,' Josefina Marlöw says in a weak voice. 'It's impossible.'

Then she manages to get to her feet, and Malin wants

to keep her there, wants to delve deeper into her story, but Josefina Marlöw turns her back on them, walks away from them, mutters something inaudible before stopping and turning around to look at them again.

'I didn't want the girls living anywhere near them,' she says. 'There has to be love. Otherwise life on earth is hell, isn't it?'

Malin and Zeke look at Josefina Marlöw. The way she could collapse at any moment, slump lifeless in front of them, and the clarity has gone from her eyes, and whatever it is she has to tell them, she won't be able to find it now.

McDonald's revolving door whirrs.

And the shadow is gone.

Swallowed up by Slussen's crowds.

The receptionist of the Hotel Tegnérlunden hands them each a key.

Malin looks at the receipt before slipping it into her wallet.

Three thousand, eight hundred kronor.

For two single rooms, one night.

So expensive! But Sven has authorised them to stay the night, and they won't find any cheaper rooms in Stockholm in the middle of the conference season.

'See you back here in half an hour,' Zeke says.

Malin nods and heads towards the stairs as Zeke presses the lift button.

It's nine o'clock.

Half past nine.

Is that too late to pay a visit to Josef Kurtzon? If he's actually at the address on Strandvägen. Of course it isn't. There's no reason to show any respect to money or age under these circumstances.

The room is small.

A bed.

A burgundy-coloured carpet, polka dot walls and a print of forest scenery above the bed.

Malin lies down, stretches out.

She can feel her mobile in the front pocket of her jeans, wonders about calling Tove, but feels she doesn't have the energy. Then she pulls herself together, takes the phone out and calls her daughter.

Five rings.

Then she hears Tove's voice.

'Hi, Mum.'

'Hi.'

'Are you still in Stockholm?'

'Yes, in some scruffy hotel near Tegnérlunden.'

'Where's that?'

'In the city centre.'

'I've got no idea.'

'We'll have to come up sometime. To Stockholm. Go to a few museums.'

'Sure,' Tove says. 'Are you getting anywhere with the bombing?'

'I don't know,' Malin says. 'You know what adults are like. All sorts of odd things can happen.'

Tove murmurs on the other end of the line.

Seems to be gathering breath.

Then an explosion in Malin's brain.

The monster with her hands around Tove's neck, the time she was kidnapped by a killer, and Malin looks out of the window towards the park, a tree, she concentrates on the tree, she can't see what sort it is – is it a chestnut, or lilac? – and the tree has the most exquisite white flowers she's ever seen, thousands of them, like an explosion of everything beautiful in the world.

Cherry blossom? A tree brought over from Kyoto?

'Did you want anything in particular, Mum?'

'I just wanted to hear your voice.'

And show that I care about you. To soothe my guilty conscience. But it isn't that easy, is it?

'OK, well, you've done that now. I need to get on with my homework.'

'Lundsberg. Shit. I forgot to email the headmaster. I'll do it as soon as I get home.'

'It's OK, Mum,' Tove says. 'I've already done it, in your name.'

'Tove, you can't do that.'

'I knew you'd forget to do it.'

What can I say to that?

'So when are we going to see my uncle?' Tove goes on.

'As soon as this is over.'

'OK.'

They hang up.

And I want to tell you how much I love you, Tove, Malin thinks. And I want to say sorry for not always being able to show it, sorry if my love for you has ever let you down.

44

The old, white, tar-scented boats anchored by the quayside along Strandvägen look as though they belong to the sea, rocking gently back and forth.

The building Josef Kurtzon is supposed to live in is halfway along Strandvägen, and Malin feels very small as she stands in the huge archway enclosing the doors that lead into this palace of wealth.

The flat she and Tove lived in out in Traneberg.

A rather different view from there.

Down on the quayside a flood of human flesh is moving, and the spring evening is mild and the avenue of lime trees rustles: the trees appear to be proud of their pale green chlorophyll costumes.

Kurtzon. The name on a small brass plaque next to an entryphone.

Not so secret that there isn't a sign.

A small camera lens next to the phone. The name Wallenberg on another sign. The logo of 'Economic Business Leadership'. Names like Brusser, Kviisten.

People good for billions, but how good are they?

Malin feels hungry and thirsty. Would love a drink, this evening was almost made for drinking beer at a pavement bar, and she presses the button of the entryphone and soon there's a crackle, then nothing but silence.

'Do you think he's here?' she asks Zeke. He had been looking more and more tired as the day had worn on, but now he looks alert again, ready to tackle whatever this evening and night might drop them in.

'We'll soon find out,' he says, and then there's a different sort of crackle from the speaker, and a female voice says: 'Yes, Kurtzon?'

How old? Thirty, no more.

Zeke explains why they are there and the woman asks them to wait.

Five minutes.

Ten.

Something in the woman's voice makes them wait patiently; they're sure she's going to come back.

'You can come up. Fourth floor.'

The woman sounds businesslike, and as the tall double doors of the apartment on the fourth floor open, Malin and Zeke are already astonished at the splendour of the stairwell, where a hand-woven rug forms the foundation for an orgy of expensively glossy stone, and the predominantly blue paintings of Leander Engström on the walls.

A man standing in the doorway.

Wearing a butler's outfit. Perhaps seventy years old, behind him a dark hallway where a fire crackles in a fireplace and damp heat rises towards Malin and Zeke, and they step inside the apartment, over the threshold, even though it feels like stepping into the open jaws of a predator.

The butler invites them to take their coats off, and takes them from them, saying: 'Mr Kurtzon will see you shortly.'

Then he is gone, as though devoured by the apartment's apparently endless confusion of rooms that all link back to the hallway. Malin can see how tasteful the decor is, a costly combination of old and new.

They are alone in the hall.

She feels like looking through the rooms, but can't bring herself to do so.

The humidity is making it hard to breathe, and she's starting to sweat as if it were a sort of tropical heat here, as if something more warm-blooded than human beings lived within these walls.

A woman in a white nurse's uniform appears out of the darkness from one of the rooms.

'This way,' and Malin recognises the voice from the entryphone shortly before, and they follow her down a dark passageway.

Real candles are burning in sconces as they pass closed doors, heading deeper and deeper into the darkness.

Light from beneath one of the doors. Is someone locked inside there?

How big could an apartment like this be?

Does it belong to a different world?

Then, just as Malin is starting to think it will never end, the passageway opens into a vast, rectangular, dimly lit room, with heavy velvet curtains behind which ought to be windows facing the water of Nybroviken.

In the middle of the room is a hospital bed.

The top end is tilted upwards.

Even more stifling in here.

There's a stuffed, two-metre-long lizard, its jaws gaping open, over by one of the panelled walls. Its teeth gleam yellow in the darkness, its skin shining with black and yellow stripes.

Malin feels like asking where it comes from, but manages to contain her curiosity.

An old man is lying on the bed under a white sheet.

The scene makes Malin think of her mother's coffin in the chapel.

The man's sharp, eagle nose stands out against the light from a simple standard lamp, and there's no other furniture in the room, not even a chair, just a peculiar silence that is broken every fifteen seconds by the man's strained breathing and a bleep from a machine.

It smells of death here, Malin thinks. I've never smelled it so strongly.

And loneliness. The same loneliness that surrounds Maria Murvall. The sort that surrounds people who have rejected the world.

'Mr Kurtzon is very ill,' the nurse says. 'But he wanted to see you. If you kneel beside the bed he'll talk to you.'

The nurse glides silently out of the room. Closes the door behind her.

The man's eyes are open. They're staring up at the ceiling, as if it were full of spiders and snakes and prehistoric flesh-eating lizards, all watching the scene from above and waiting to attack the two intruders.

They walk over to the bed and fall to their knees beside the head of the bed, so they're on the same level as the man's face.

Who is he? Malin wonders.

Where is he from?

From the depths of Congo's jungles? Treblinka? St Petersburg? Sundsvall? Is this what the *übermensch* I heard about earlier looks like?

What world shaped him? Mine? The world we share?

Josef Kurtzon moves his mouth, his voice is weak, and he doesn't turn to look at them, but evidently knows that they're there.

'You can't ask any questions,' he whispers. 'I don't want any questions.'

And Malin feels like saying that she'll ask whatever fucking questions she feels like asking, but she suppresses the impulse, looks at the sickbed, the man in it, and she thinks of her brother, alone in another sickbed in another lonely room, and then Josef Kurtzon starts to talk.

'I've disinherited my sons,' he says. 'They're not getting anything from me. I've put everything in a foundation that leaves them with nothing as things stand. Josefina is to be given control of the foundation, not them. I know she doesn't want it, that she might be dead, that she changed her name, as if that could make any difference, but when you have both lungs and your entire lymphatic system riddled with cancer like I have, you don't care about such things.

'Oh, the boys have money, I've given them enough money so they can manage, but they're not as rich as they would have wanted, and I tried, I tried having them in the business, but what were they good for? Nothing. In spite of my efforts to mould them. They were defective. It was as if they weren't mine. And what's a father to do then? Tell me that! I even tried various things on them when they were small, to make them more suitable, efficient, but unfortunately my method of upbringing didn't quite work.'

And Malin wants to interrupt.

Ask what Josef Kurtzon is talking about, why he's telling them this, and what sort of method of upbringing?

'No questions.'

And the weak voice is full of an icy chill and an authority that makes all questions unthinkable. This man is the opposite of my own father, Malin thinks. Yet they're somehow the same. Men who on some level take what they want.

'They came to see me. I told them about the foundation. That I had basically disinherited them. And that in principle they would never gain control of most of the money. They begged and pleaded, it was pathetic, and after that I was quite convinced, they aren't what we are. Out with you, I said, I don't want you anywhere near me again. I know it will hurt them when they find out that Josefina will get control of the money once the cancer finally finishes me off. Josefina is her own person. She's uncomplicated. We're the same, she and I.'

Thoughts are racing through Malin's head.

A multi-billion inheritance.

A daughter who's a heroin addict. A pair of sons whom the father seems to regard as defective.

What does all this mean? And how does it fit together with the bomb in the main square in Linköping, and the Vigerö family?

She opens her mind to the darkness of the room.

The lizard seems to be snapping its jaws. Staring at Malin with its artificial eyes.

So the real reason why you're handing control of your estate to Josefina Marlöw is to spite your sons, Malin thinks. Even though you must be aware that she's turned her back on you. Hates you, all of you. Because that's what I saw in McDonald's at Slussen: hatred and fear and loathing and hopelessness.

'Where—'

'No questions.'

Malin couldn't help herself. Wants to ask: Where are your sons? Where can we talk to them? Needs to make progress in this darkness, dissolve it, listen to its voices and save what good there is, or at least that's what it feels like even if she can't explain why. And the man before her slips into sleep, and she wants to shake him out of it, and says: 'Did you know about the girls? Her girls?'

And Josef Kurtzon turns towards her, and now she sees that his eyes are ruined by cataracts, that he must have been blind for years, and he waves his hand.

'My sons each have an apartment in the next building,

towards the Djurgården bridge. You can try looking for Henry and Leopold there.'

Josef Kurtzon turns his face away from Malin and Zeke.

Malin senses that all of this fits together: the Kurtzon family, the Vigerö family, the twin girls, the bomb, but she can't work out how, she doesn't know enough to tie the threads of the case together. She realises that Kurtzon is only telling them exactly what he wants to tell them, and that he's telling them for one reason alone, and he's playing with her, with them, in spite of his age and fragility. Malin realised that much from what she had read about the man on the Internet: he may well be one of the sharpest minds this country has ever produced, a sort of Ingvar Kamprad of self-interest and finance, with an equally murky past, and Malin can't help it any longer, she hurls her questions at the man in the bed, and she can hear how shrill her voice sounds, but can't control it: 'Why did Josefina turn her back on you all?'

'What did you do to your sons?'

'Why are you telling us this?'

'Did you know Josefina gave birth to twins and gave them up for adoption? Did you know they died in the bombing in Linköping?'

She looks around the big, muggy room, and notices a whirring sound, and only then does she notice the large humidifiers lining the walls, and assumes they're there to make breathing easier for Josef Kurtzon's decaying lungs.

'No, no, I didn't know anything about any girls.'

Then Josef Kurtzon loses his breath and gasps for air, and Malin is sure: he didn't know about the girls.

The nurse comes back.

She pulls an oxygen mask out from under the bed. Puts it over Josef Kurtzon's face, but he raises his hand and brushes the mask aside with remarkable force, before snarling: 'Terror. Terror at what people can do to each other. Leave a child alone with its terror and its shortcomings. And then every individual will be shaped with terror as their servant. To become as ruthless as necessary. That's what I wanted for my sons.

'What about you, Malin Fors? Is terror your servant?'

Then Malin hears a ringing sound.

A sound similar to the one in the main square after the explosion, when they thought there was another bomb in a rucksack outside the Central Hotel.

45

'What was all that, then?'

Zeke's voice full of uncertainty as he stands next to Malin outside the door of the building on Strandvägen. They can hear the cars in the street as if for the first time, as if their ears had previously been blocked with cotton wool.

It feels like I've just emerged from a dream, Malin thinks. The ringing in her ears is gone, it was just Josef Kurtzon's heart monitor starting to bleep for no reason.

'I don't know what it was,' Malin says.

'It feels like that didn't really just happen,' Zeke says.

The avenue of trees rustles from a gust of wind.

'How the hell does this all fit together?' Zeke goes on. 'I got the feeling the old man was in complete control of what he was telling us, and why he was doing it. Like he was somehow playing with us, and knew we were going to turn up. It was as if he was expecting us.'

'But how does this connect to the Vigerö family? The bombing? I'm quite sure he didn't know about the twins,' Malin says.

'Maybe we should start with the brothers,' Zeke says, gesturing along the road.

'Let's see if they're home,' Malin says.

The brothers Henry and Leopold Kurtzon not only live in the same building, but on the same floor, but there's no answer from either of the flats when they ring. No camera on the door either, and for a moment Malin thinks they ought to break into the building, then into the brothers' flats, just to see what they can find, but the path that has led them here is vague, so vague, a thin trace of human scent, a tiny hint, and they haven't got a shred of evidence linking the brothers to their investigation.

'We can't break in, Malin,' Zeke says, as though he could read her thoughts.

'No, you're right. What time is it? It's got weirdly dark, don't you think?'

'Quarter past eleven.'

'But it was only a quarter to ten when we went in to see Kurtzon. We weren't there that long. Were we?'

Zeke looks out across Nybroviken.

The water is black, and looks bottomless, and the sounds of the city are a gentle, sleepy rumble. The stars, thousands of them, seem to be burning in a sky where darkness is trying to take control.

'Don't think about it, Malin. Don't think about it.'

If she, Josefina, is our real mummy, then Leopold and Henry are our uncles. Aren't they?

Josef is our grandad.

Have our uncles got anything to do with this? Have they got anything to do with the captive children? Is that how those children are connected to us?

What do you think, Malin?

We can feel our space getting darker and darker, getting warmer, damper, narrower, and more cramped, and it's growing a roof of fear and screaming, which no person, alive or dead, should have to listen to.

You're walking down that smart street at night and you need to listen to the voices, Malin, you have to listen to them, you have to save them, just like you saved Tove.

Who is this man who's our grandad? Can a person be

*reduced to the acquisition, preservation, and expansion of assets?
And where does the rest of the person go?*

*And when the good gets lost, where is the evil then? That's
what you need to find out, Malin.*

That's the mystery you need to solve.

Who's killing prostitutes in New York?

Tove is sitting beside Janne watching a television
programme upstairs in the house in Malmslätt, she's got
a pink and purple blanket over her legs, and her back is
resting against a soft down pillow.

This film is shit, she thinks.

It's old and boring, but Dad seems to like it. Earlier in
the evening she told him about Lundsberg, and he was
pleased, not at all worried and angry the way Mum had
been at first.

Dad just seemed proud of her.

As if he knew how prestigious, and how expensive, it was
to go there. There are people living in places like Strandvägen
in Stockholm who go there, and even Dad knew that.

She'd wanted to ask him about what Mum had told her,
the woman she'd seen him with. Tove's curious, Mum had
said she was very young, and it seemed to send her a bit
mad, and Tove presumes it's made her feel old and abandoned and a failure.

Those are the feelings she's best at in the whole world.

Does Dad know about Mum's younger brother? Mum
will have to tell him that herself, and she can't have said
anything, because when would she have found the time?
Besides, she's probably still mad with Dad because of the
other woman.

Even so. I think she's going to be OK. That something
good is going to come out of all this.

'Dad,' Tove says after a while, 'Mum said she saw you

with someone else in the city. One evening. Outside Teddy's sandwich bar.'

Janne turns away from the film and looks at Tove, and the look in his eyes is tired, as if he'd rather not have this conversation now.

'She said that? Someone else? It sounds as if your mother's having trouble understanding that it's over between us.'

'She didn't put it quite like that, I can't remember.'

'Well, it's true though. There is a girl I've been seeing,' he says. 'She works at the hospital, she's a nurse in the X-ray department. You'll like her.'

'So you mean I'll have to meet her?'

'If you want, but it'll probably be hard to avoid, because I really do like her.'

'And you think I'll like her?'

'Definitely.'

On television a bearded man puts a noose around a woman's neck in a narrow alley. They watch the end of the scene before her dad asks: 'You're not upset that I'm seeing someone?'

'No. Not if it's what you want. I think it's a good thing. Then I know that you won't be alone.'

Her dad puts his arm around her and pulls her towards him.

'What have I done to deserve such a kind, considerate daughter?'

'I did think I might be jealous if either of you met someone, but it actually feels good. For your sake. I wish Mum could meet someone as well.'

'You know I'll always put you first.'

And Tove frowns, lets out a little laugh, then says: 'Sure, Dad. Same as ever,' and Janne knows he hasn't got a good response to Tove's quip.

They've never truly put her first, and she knows it, and

is having to live with it like an adult, and it's all wrong, so wrong.

'How old is she?' Tove asks.

'She's twenty-four.'

'But Dad, I'm almost twenty-four.'

Janne sits there without saying anything, feeling Tove's eyes on him.

'You know enough about love to know that you don't get to decide everything yourself,' he finally says.

The woman on the screen slips out of the noose onto the rain-drenched tarmac of the dark alley, and the man runs off towards the nearest subway station.

'What is it that you like about her?'

'Please, Tove, I'm trying to watch the film, I'm a grown-up, and grown-ups want someone to live with, to be with.'

'I realise that, but why her in particular?'

Her dad's reply comes in a flash.

Blows like a harsh wind through a wide-open teenage soul.

'Because she's the complete opposite of your mum.'

Malin.

Will you ever be able to forgive me.

Ever?

Åke Fors can't sleep, and the bedroom of the flat in Barnhemsgatan feels cramped and hot, the bed hard and lonely, and he thinks that he doesn't deserve forgiveness, and then he thinks what he has thought so many times before: Do I have a responsibility for the boy? Did I ever, right from the start?

No.

No, no, he wasn't mine, and I didn't want anything to do with him, but of course Malin had a right to know. And Margaretha had a choice, didn't she?

The flat in Tenerife.

Maybe it would be best just to leave, start something new, God knows, there are plenty of widows who would be only too happy to open their arms to him.

But this is where life is now.

Here and now, with Malin and Tove. This battle can't be avoided.

But there's something wrong.

And you know it, he thinks.

But time still passes, year after year after year, without you ever gathering your strength and doing anything about the mistake.

What does that say about us as people?

I ended up feeling scared of myself. Of what I'd become, of my own weakness. Are you scared of the same thing, Malin, and is it inside that fear that we're going to have to meet?

I was there when you tried to make sense of the world when you were small. I lifted you out of your despair, your shame when you'd done something stupid, comforted you when you were sad.

Together, Malin, we can put an end to each other's fear.

Like father and daughter should.

What could possibly have happened within the Kurtzon family? Malin wonders.

She and Zeke are in the car, on the way back to the Hotel Tegnérlunden.

Zeke behind the wheel, as usual, even though she could perfectly well drive now that she's always sober.

'So he disinherited his sons,' Zeke says. 'And told them. And probably also told them that Josefina Marlöw would end up in control of some sort of trust.'

Malin can feel how tired she is, she's having trouble thinking clearly.

'The brothers are the key to this,' she says. 'I can feel it. Why was Ottilia Stenlund so scared? I think she's scared of the family, of the brothers. Their father seems harmless enough in his current state, he could have been like that for years, he might have been blind for a long time. But, on the other hand, who knows how far his power stretches?'

'We don't even know who the brothers are,' Zeke says. 'Johan didn't mention them when he told us about Kurtzon, did he? And we've even less idea of where they might be.'

'And we don't even know if the Vigerö girls' background has anything to do with the bombing, or Hanna Vigerö's murder. Josef Kurtzon really didn't seem to know about them.'

'There has to be a connection,' Zeke says. 'We just need to work out what it is.'

As they drive past the NK department store, Malin thinks about how many of Stockholm's very richest inhabitants lend legitimacy to their ruthless capitalism by getting involved in the running of the City Mission and other charities.

But Kurtzon doesn't appear to give a damn about legitimacy, and for that reason money had always loved him.

She goes on to think about evil.

How she is sometimes inclined to think that it doesn't exist, because she can't feel its presence. Like when winter makes its last offensive against the spring, and one day the temperature plummets below zero and there's more snow and your whole body screams: 'Spring is an illusion. It doesn't exist!'

But at the same time Malin is sure: evil does exist, it's alive and flourishing wherever there are people, often where you'd least expect it, behind a thicket of goodness in a human soul.

'I'd like to talk to Josefina Marlöw again. Try to find out if she actually knows about her father's plans for his estate.'

'And the trust,' Zeke says. 'What's to say that the brothers wouldn't gain control of it and the money if Josefina Marlöw no longer existed? Do you think the old man considered that? That he might have put Josefina in danger?'

'He strikes me as the kind of man who thinks of everything,' Malin says. 'Maybe he's trying to manipulate yet another game from his deathbed?'

'What if the brothers knew about the daughters their sister gave up for adoption, and wanted to get rid of them to stop them popping up to claim any of the money?'

'No, we can't make that fit,' Malin says. 'We don't have enough to go on.'

And she thinks about the infamous Stenbeck family. How badly the siblings treated Jan Stenbeck's unknown son when he popped up out of nowhere after the financier died. They acted as if he didn't exist, even though he was their half-brother. But maybe that was only the distorted picture portrayed by the media?

Then Malin sees the man with the bike in the video in her mind's eye.

One of the Kurtzon brothers?

'Drive to the refuge,' she says. 'I'd like to try to talk to Josefina Marlöw this evening. Something tells me it's urgent.'

'But she never sleeps there?'

'Maybe there'll be someone there who can tell us where she is. Have you got any better ideas?'

Then she says: 'I'll give Johan Jakobsson a call. Ask him to see what he can find out about the brothers.'

'He'll be asleep by now. Or at least the kids will be, he's bound to be at home by now. Can't it wait till tomorrow?'

'No,' Malin says.

46

The day's spring warmth has been replaced by a damp night chill, and there's no longer any shouting or yelling from Gröna Lund.

It's almost eleven o'clock.

Johan Jakobsson was still up. He said he'd have a look on his computer at home and see what he could find about the brothers.

The noise of Stockholm's nocturnal traffic mixes with the rumble from the air-conditioners, and beside the entrance to the City Mission at Slussen sits a group of run-down men, passing bottles between them.

Malin and Zeke go up to them.

Malin recognises several of them, they were milling about outside the City Mission earlier, waiting to get in, but maybe they were too drunk, too high, or simply too unruly to get a bed.

Calm now.

No threat. Just cold and tired, and Malin asks, without looking at any of them in particular: 'Do you know where we could find Josefina?'

'What do you want with that whore?' one of the men snarls, but there's nothing threatening or critical in his voice, it's just a statement of fact.

'We're from—'

Zeke is interrupted.

'We know you're cops,' another of the men says.

'We just want to talk to her,' Malin says. 'Nothing else.'

The men stay silent, looking at Malin and Zeke, waiting for the inevitable.

Malin takes out her wallet. Holds up a five-hundred-kronor note.

'What do you take us for?' a third man says, and the others laugh.

Malin pulls out another five-hundred-kronor note.

One of the men takes the money.

'Try looking in Hornstull underground station. She usually hangs around there. One of the guards will be able to show you down into the tunnels.'

At first the guard was reluctant, but they managed to persuade him, and he said he knew where the junkies usually hung about, and that he and the other security guards usually left them alone, that they'd removed anything flammable from where they congregated, so that there was no risk of them causing a fire.

'Well,' the guard said. 'They've got nowhere else to go, and it gets bloody cold up here in the winter.'

And now Malin is following the back of the guard's grey uniform as they head down the escalator towards the platforms.

The underground station has its own microclimate.

A train thunders into the station.

People get on and off, and by the time the train pulls out again they've reached the end of the platform, and the guard leads them into the tunnel, where he opens a rusty iron gate and heads down a rickety galvanised metal staircase. They walk slowly and carefully along a narrow ledge into the darkness.

'OK, take it nice and slowly,' he says. 'If you stumble and fall, there are ten thousand volts running through those rails. Just so you know.'

The lights from another train approaching blind Malin, and her ears feel as if they're going to burst from the noise.

The guard stops.

'Stand still. Press yourselves up against the wall and it'll be fine,' he shouts, and as the train sweeps past, the lights disappear, and Malin can see into the carriages, people on their way home from work or an evening out.

Men on their own.

Groups of teenage girls, no older than Tove. Couples in love. Pensioners.

They all look tired. Eager to get home to bed.

Tough lads from the suburbs, wearing nothing but vests in spite of the cold. Gang tattoos. The sort of thing they never really see back home in Linköping. The level of crime there is tamer, even if it can sometimes get pretty violent between the various gangs of youths. Mostly they have to deal with solitary nutters.

There's a strong gust of wind and Malin thinks she's going to be swept away and fall onto the rails, dying from the shock from the conductor rail, burning and boiling from the inside as a punishment for all her sins, for her inability to deal with the things that really matter.

But she doesn't fall.

And soon the train is gone, and the guard carries on until he reaches a steel door that he opens with some effort, and inside the door is a ladder that leads down to yet another tunnel, and the guard switches on a torch.

They head down a flight of steps, then there's a long passageway lit up by intermittent lamps hanging from dusty electric cables.

'Who was it you were trying to get hold of?'

'Josefina Marlöw.'

The guard nods to them, and in the weak light of the torch his face becomes a skull with black holes for eyes, yet he still radiates friendliness, and Malin gets the impression that he's quite protective of his underground dwellers.

They carry on, turning off into an even narrower passageway, then the guard nudges a door open, and a strong smell of faeces and urine and dirt hits them. Malin fights an urge to throw up, and the guard lights the way into the cramped space.

Josefina Marlöw is lying on a filthy scrap of cardboard. The damp, dirty brown walls are covered in small, elegant chalk drawings of people.

She's asleep, snoring in that vacant, assured way that only a seriously high addict can, soft and self-contained, with a desire never to wake up again.

'I'll leave you on your own,' the guard says. 'You can find your own way out?'

Mummy.

What are you doing here, underground? In this room where nothing living should have to be. But you've chosen it yourself, haven't you? As protection against the cruelty. You wanted to withdraw, and you withdrew further and further, and you abandoned us because you knew there was no way back any more.

And now you're lying here.

In a sleep that's dreamless and vacant, yet still soft.

Hold on, Mummy.

You are dreaming, aren't you?

You're dreaming that you're dead, drifting here beside us and looking down on a different, much better world.

There's something you need to know.

We forgive you.
We want you to come to us. Together we shall exist as love.

Malin and Zeke wait. They've agreed not to wake Josefina Marlöw, and wait until she wakes up of her own accord.

Their nostrils get used to the stench.

They sink down onto the dirty stone floor. Illuminate the cave-like space with the light of their mobile phones. Look at the drawings, presumably made by Josefina Marlöw herself with some of the chalk on the floor. Stick figures, like letters in a foreign alphabet. They look like children playing.

Malin and Zeke are sleepy, it's almost midnight and they want to sleep, but can't yet, mustn't sleep here. Yet still, in spite of the hardness of the floor and the strange, damp climate, they both doze off.

Malin and Zeke sleep, and they both dream about a closed room, like the one they're in now, and in the room are two frightened little children crying for help, but there's no sound, just the children's lips moving.

'Here we are!' the children cry. 'Here we are!' and Malin can hear the voices now, and feels someone shaking her by the arm, someone saying: 'So here you are. How did you find your way?'

Malin opens her eyes. Zeke does the same, and they find themselves looking at Josefina Marlöw.

She's crouching in front of them, and the look in her eyes seems to cut straight through the weak light of a flickering candle, and they can see that she's clear and focused in the aftermath of her hit. Malin stares at her, tries to focus her gaze with groggy eyes, before saying: 'Your girls, we're trying to find out what happened to them, who killed them. You're the only person who can help us.'

Josefina Marlöw sits down on a piece of cardboard, looks

at them. Beside her are a spoon and a syringe, several blood-stained scraps of cloth, and the whole of her lower arms are covered with track marks.

'I know,' she says, 'that Father, Josef, has written a will giving me control of everything. He got some heavies to come and pick me up and take me to Strandvägen a few months back, I think it was. He's going to die soon, I know that. Maybe I've been back there since. I'm not sure.'

No shakes now.

No stammering.

More an assured flow of words from a well-brought-up girl.

No grief in her voice or eyes.

But possibly relief. The same relief that Dad seemed to feel at Mum's funeral, Malin thinks. The same relief I felt.

'He told me he'd disinherited my brothers, Henry and Leopold. That I'd be given control of a foundation in Switzerland in which he'd placed all his assets. He lay there in bed smiling when he told me. What was I supposed to do? Say I wasn't interested? He knew that. Maybe he just wanted to upset my brothers. I'm not interested in his games.'

'You don't remember anything else from your meeting with him?' Zeke asks.

'He said that if I died before him he might leave everything to the State Inheritance Fund instead. Or appoint some sort of independent management. Money for money's sake.'

'Why do you think he's made you his main beneficiary?' Malin asks as she feels an icy chill spread through her stomach.

An inheritance, billions managed by a foundation, or lost to the Inheritance Fund. Two disinherited brothers. This could be the motive for the bombing, for the girls' deaths.

Josefina Marlöw is silent for a while, then says: 'He wanted to give me the poison. His poison, instead of my own. He hates the fact that I turned my back on him and live a life of my own choosing. However fucked up that life might be. He wants me to become like him. But at the same time he loves the fact that I am who I am, and don't hold back. The way I inhabit my life so perfectly.'

'Why do you think he doesn't want to give your brothers any money?'

'They didn't turn out the way he wanted.'

'The way he wanted?'

'Yes. He used to experiment on them when they were little. Wanted to turn them into the perfect, greedy, ruthless businessmen.'

'What did he do to them?'

'He tried to get them to feel special, chosen, gave them power over various pets he bought, guinea pigs, rabbits, a golden retriever puppy, and he taught them that animals can be tamed through beatings. He gave them large sums of money to spend even when they were children, let them experience what it was like to have power over assistants, and traders, to have people fawning over them, so that they'd end up obsessed with the possibilities that money offers, the power. We had servants at home, and he put my brothers in charge of them, but they were also allowed to punish the boys. He never comforted them, he would hit them and yell at them, punishing them whenever anything went wrong, all to encourage them to be ruthless.

'He had a lizard. Sometimes he used to tease it, then set it on my brothers. To scare them, put them in their place.'

The stuffed beast in Josef Kurtzon's sickroom.

Josefina Marlöw falls silent and closes her eyes, then goes on: 'And he'd get them to beat me,' she says. 'He had them beat me in the cellar, and if they didn't, because they didn't want to, he'd give them electric shocks. So they beat me. Gave me electric shocks. He wanted to make them understand the meaning of consequences, of brutality.'

Malin feels the contours of the little room wavering before her eyes.

Nausea rising from her gut.

Then she forces herself to focus.

So Josef Kurtzon tried to turn his sons into psychopaths? Some sort of warped characters, perfect for business: was that what you tried to shape your children into, Josef Kurtzon? And Malin feels a sudden urge to go back to the apartment on Strandvägen and crush the old man's blind, cataract-damaged eyes into his skull. And the Kurtzon brothers, what would they be capable of as adults? Murder? A bomb in a city square?

'Father always despised them,' Josefina Marlöw says, opening her eyes again.

'Why?'

'Because the strength and business success he hoped to instil in them ended up as weakness and failure. He sometimes supported their business ventures, but in the end I think he only did it to play with them, to mock them with their failures. But at the same time he despised them for wanting to see themselves reflected in wealth.'

'Reflected in wealth?'

'They enjoyed showing how rich they were. But Father thought that money itself was what mattered. Buying status and boasting about your wealth disgusts him. A truly great man is above that.'

'So they like showing off their wealth?'

'Yes. Just like Mum. For Mum the most important thing was showing off a perfect, extravagant façade.'

Josefina Marlöw falls silent.

'That was what Mum tried to teach them,' she goes on after a pause. 'That a person's true worth is measured by how much money they have. And to do that, you have to show off your wealth, because what else is it good for? Mum was crazy about money. We had a toilet with a gold seat at home.'

'She and your father seem to have been very different?'

'Yes. But there were similarities. Money meant everything, love nothing.'

'Tell us more about your brothers,' Malin says.

'What else is there to say? Henry's the oldest, two years older than me, and there's a year between him and Leopold. Leopold's the dominant one, even though he's younger. Henry mostly follows his lead. At least that's how it's always looked to me. But in Father and Mum's eyes they're united by weakness.'

'They must have been confused by the conflicting attitudes of your parents?' Malin asks. 'That she wanted to show off her wealth, and he loathed that sort of behaviour?'

'No matter who talked to them as children, the result was always the same: money. Money, and still more money. Take away their money, and the promise of inheriting money, and you take their lives away from them.'

Malin feels the icy chill in her stomach growing as she hears Josefina Marlöw say those words.

'Where are your brothers now?' Zeke asks.

'They've both got flats on Strandvägen. I was given one as well, but that went in here a long time ago.'

Josefina Marlöw points at the track marks on her arm.

'They're not at Strandvägen,' Malin says. 'And we haven't managed to find any other addresses. Do you have any idea where they could be? Does either of them have a house anywhere else? A summer house? Something abroad?'

'I've got no idea,' Josefina Marlöw says, the light in her eyes gradually fading. 'It's a long time since I cared.'

She looks as if she wants to vanish from the face of the earth, but if that were really the case, why not jump in front of an underground train, or off the Western Bridge, or just pump yourself full of heroin? Malin wonders.

Why drag it out like this?

She realises how impossible it is ever to understand someone like Josefina Marlöw, what drives her, why she's ended up like this, what fears she carries within her.

'But I have done one thing,' Josefina Marlöw says. 'If I get Father's inheritance, then the girls will get everything when I die, which probably won't be long now. Even if I hate money, the girls can have some use out of it. I've sorted it all out officially with a solicitor.'

She falls silent.

'Would have got,' she whispers. 'Even if the money could have harmed them. It doesn't matter what you do, it never ends up right, does it?'

'Could your brothers have known about that?' Zeke asks.

'How would they have found out?'

'Could your father have known about it?' Malin asks, and now she can see Josefina Marlöw starting to drift away, and she looks down at her spoon, her syringe, the little bag of white powder in the far corner of the room.

'No,' Josefina Marlöw says. 'Father didn't know. I'm sure he didn't know about the girls.'

Or so you reckon, Malin thinks.

'So you don't think your brothers could be behind the explosion in Linköping that killed your girls, as a way of somehow getting their hands on the inheritance?'

'When people are put under pressure they're capable of anything,' Josefina Marlöw says. 'Who knows what my brothers might get into their heads? What Father could come up with? What he said about the trust and the State Inheritance Fund could have been rubbish.'

Malin and Zeke look at each other. Surreptitiously, without nodding or saying anything, they exchange a glance of confirmation in an attempt to hold something frightening, unknown, at bay.

'What's the solicitor's name?' Malin asks after a pause.

'Jörgen. Jörgen Stålsten. I was . . . at school . . . with him.'

'Where can we find . . .?'

Josefina Marlöw is no longer listening, and is scrabbling feverishly for the bag of white powder.

Malin sees her thin fingers searching, and Josefina Marlöw grunts, letting out small pained noises, as if ravenous lizards have appeared inside her, snapping at her with scalpel-sharp teeth.

Malin turns to look at Zeke.

He nods.

And they leave the room, leaving Josefina Marlöw in the flickering light of the candle.

I'm going to work out how this fits together, Malin thinks. I have to.

47

What's she getting close to?

The phone call from Malin hadn't woken his family, thank goodness. Johan Jakobsson himself hadn't been asleep, he'd been lying in bed reading an old copy of *Wired*, and managed to answer the call on the second ring. His wife had been asleep beside him, the deep sleep of an exhausted mother of small children, and the children had been snuffling noisily in their own rooms.

Malin had been brief when she asked him to dig out everything he could find about the brothers Leopold and Henry Kurtzon, if there was anything out there.

When he had sat down at the computer that was set up on a small oak desk in a cramped corner of the hall, Johan had realised how tired he was, how this case had almost poisoned him, how the fruitless search for connections and contexts, the digging into people's lives and opinions, had almost made him lose his grip on what he himself felt, what he actually thought about anything.

Then, once he'd switched the computer on, all his negative thoughts had vanished. He had started his search on Google, typing in Leopold Kurtzon and getting two thousand, one hundred and fifty hits, most of them in articles about his father, Josef Kurtzon.

One result led to the *Wall Street Journal*, and he clicked

the link but found himself on a page for paying subscribers only, thirty-five dollars for a month of access.

Two hundred kronor.

This'll make Sven groan, Johan thought, as he went to get his credit card from his wallet in his jacket and paid up.

The article was from 1998, from the paper's Sunday supplement, and was entitled 'Inheritance of misfortune'. It was about heirs all around the world who had struggled, usually in vain, to find a place in their families' businesses – usually their fathers'.

There were a few American examples, including Bernard Madoff's sons. And Ingvar Kamprad's boys. And then a long piece about someone depicted as a dark horse: Leopold Kurtzon, son of the mysterious financier, Josef Kurtzon.

The journalist had persuaded Leopold to agree to a lengthy interview, and the article was illustrated with a picture that looked as if it was taken on board a yacht. You couldn't see where in the world the picture was taken, and it wasn't made clear in the article either: the open sea in the background could have been anywhere.

Leopold Kurtzon's father was said to have tried to raise his son to take over the role of financial leader after he and his brother Henry had attended 'Sweden's most prestigious private school'. After they left school, scholarships to Harvard Business School were arranged for them, but the brothers evidently had problems with their studies and preferred to spend their time partying like idiots. A fellow student talked about 'the Swedish maniacs', and after a year there Leopold and Henry Kurtzon were thrown out. At that point Leopold Kurtzon was said to have returned to Stockholm and taken up a 'minor, junior position' in one of the many companies in his father's empire.

His brother was said to have done the same.

According to Leopold Kurtzon himself, his father had kept an eye on him but gradually lost interest in both him and his brother Henry when he decided they weren't capable of reaching the very highest level of business.

'I, or rather we, tried to prove to him that we were good enough. But it was impossible. He'd made up his mind.'

When he'd finished the article, Johan couldn't help thinking that the reporter had evidently been bewildered by Leopold Kurtzon: in the article itself he actually wondered why Leopold Kurtzon had agreed to the interview. Perhaps, he speculated, it was an attempt to get closer to his father. The whole time the reporter had a sense that he was part of a plan, a pawn in a game beyond his comprehension: 'Because why else would Leopold Kurtzon tell me all this?'

He described the way Leopold Kurtzon leaned back in his armchair and confessed that he had always wanted to get married, that he'd had hundreds of women but never managed to connect with any of them, none of them had been good enough.

'My brother Henry hasn't got a family of his own either,' Leopold Kurtzon said further down in the article. 'Maybe that's our way of getting our revenge for Dad's miserliness towards us: by not giving him any heirs, a next generation.'

The reporter said that Leopold Kurtzon had laughed at his own words, an uncertain, lonely laugh.

A finance company that the brothers had set up in Luxembourg was said to have gone bankrupt, then their father had apparently given them some property and homes in Sweden, and a yearly sum large enough for them to live in what most people would consider luxury.

After that Leopold and his brother were said to have set up everything from a chain of sweetshops to a business importing exotic pets.

When the reporter asked Leopold Kurtzon about his childhood, he turned aggressive for the first and only time, and told the reporter 'in a scary, ice-cold voice' that he shouldn't 'poke about in his childhood like some fucking therapist, those fuckers are completely useless'.

The reporter described leaving Leopold Kurtzon sitting alone in his armchair on a terrace overlooking the sea, and how he seemed to personify the loneliness and bewilderment that can be one of the consequences of money. The reporter described how unnerving it had been when Leopold Kurtzon's mood changed, revealing 'almost desperate chasms of darkness and boundless rage in the young heir'.

The article concluded: 'It was a relief to get away from Leopold Kurtzon.'

And Johan felt much the same as he carried on surfing the Net, felt like leaving this case behind, and not have to read about people like the Kurtzons, and their evidently totally dysfunctional lives. Then he heard a familiar sound behind him.

A child's footsteps padding through the dark. A little girl's voice saying: 'Daddy, I'm thirsty', and he got up and went over to his daughter, who was standing in the hall in her pyjamas, rubbing her eyes. He took her into the kitchen, got her a glass of cold water, tucked her up in bed again, then went back to the computer, only after he'd held her tightly and felt her heart beating steadily and reassuringly.

Henry Kurtzon.

What was there about the other son?

Nothing in the *Wall Street Journal*.

Barely five hundred hits for his name.

One result took him to a gossip site with pictures of parties on the Riviera, Saint-Tropez in July, and there was a picture of Henry Kurtzon on his own in the bar of the

Hotel Byblos, as if slightly removed from the hedonistic spectacle in the background.

'Mr Kurtzon enjoying the party,' the caption said.

But you don't look like you're having fun at all, Johan thought as he looked at the face, dark rings under watery, grey, alcohol-soused eyes.

His cheeks were red, soft from too much champagne. And in his mind's eye Johan could see Henry Kurtzon and his brother Leopold drifting from party to party, alone, unwanted by anyone, yet not quite banished from the world they ought to fit into.

He went on to check the property register to find anything in the brothers' names. Nothing.

He took a look at the register of companies, and found a number of defunct businesses. The Sweet Shack. Exotic Animals. L&H Financial Services. L&H IT Solutions. And plenty more.

None of the businesses had gone bankrupt, and the last of them had been closed down three years ago, wound down in what looked like an organised manner. Presumably your father tidying up after you, Johan thought. So what have you been doing since then? Have you been employed somewhere?

He looked up Henry and Leopold Kurtzon in the records of the Tax Office. They were registered at a PO box in Östermalm in Stockholm, and had registered zero earnings for the past three years. No income from capital. Nothing.

Did your father remove his protective hand? Did he stop supplying you with money?

Johan tried to conjure up an image of the brothers again, to understand who they are and where they're from, to understand how demoralising it must feel to have a father who seemed to be able to conjure gold out of thin air, yet apparently never be able to succeed at anything yourselves, never finding any lasting love, and possibly also being incapable of recognising it.

Johan found nothing more in any registers, and now he is sitting with his face too close to the screen, feeling how dry his skin is getting and how tired his eyes are.

But he doesn't want to stop yet, he has a feeling that he's getting close to something that might somehow be important.

He types the boys' mother's name into Google, Selda Kurtzon. He comes up with an article from an old celebrity magazine from the late seventies that a blogger had found in the toilet of his country cottage and scanned 'because it was so crazy'.

The pictures show a woman dressed in what is evidently a very expensive leopard-skin outfit from Roberto Cavalli. The woman is leading a large, yellow and black striped lizard around a garden with a view of the Lidingö Sound.

'This is my husband's pet. He's very fond of it.'

The woman is said to speak with a Polish accent, but any further details of her background are kept hidden, and instead she talks about her cosmopolitan lifestyle and her trips around the world.

In one picture she's sitting with her children on a gold-embroidered sofa in a huge sitting room with leaded windows in the background. Henry and Leopold, about twelve and thirteen respectively, are wearing pale blue suits, pink shirts, and white bow ties, their hair has been neatly combed, and their eyes are utterly blank.

On the other side of Selda Kurtzon sits a little girl. Josefina Kurtzon, according to the caption. Younger, smaller than her brothers, and when Johan sees the look in her eyes he feels a jolt of horror. He sees panic, restrained and controlled, yet unmistakeable, he sees pure and utter panic, as if this little girl wants nothing more than to escape from the picture.

What do you want to escape from?

What are they doing to you?

'I teach my boys to love money,' Selda Kurtzon says. 'I teach them that greed is good, because what is anyone without money? I know that from my own childhood. You're nothing. Absolutely nothing. A person has no value without money, it's better to be dead.'

The reporter from the magazine suggests that Selda Kurtzon's comment is a joke, and describes how they both laughed, but Johan can't escape the feeling that it really wasn't a joke at all.

Selda Kurtzon seems to enjoy having her picture taken, presenting herself to the world. She certainly doesn't give the same conflicted impression as her son in the *Wall Street Journal*.

Josef Kurtzon is only mentioned briefly in the article, as one of several people in a series called 'Swedish *Dallas* Lifestyles'.

Johan goes into the national population database.

Selda Kurtzon died just a few years after the article was published.

The boys couldn't have been more than about fifteen at the time, the girl even younger.

A fucking lizard as a pet? But it takes all sorts. So, how the hell does this have anything to do with their case, if indeed it actually does? What line of inquiry is Malin following? Rich people behaving badly is nothing new. It doesn't even count as tragic, it's only when poor people do eccentric things that it becomes tragic.

He goes back the *Wall Street Journal* article.

Looks at the picture of Leopold Kurtzon.

Those eyes. They look as if they're trapped in themselves, that he's trapped inside his own ego. Someone unable to do anything, yet capable of everything.

Who are you? Johan thinks before he gets up and heads towards the bedroom. A failed creation? At least in your father's eyes.

He stops at his daughter's bedroom. Looks in at her sleeping form.

Listens to her breathing.

Thinks: If I teach you anything, it'll be that money isn't the most important thing on the planet. It doesn't even come close.

Then Johan gets into bed beside his wife. She's warm and familiar and the very smell of her body makes him feel calm.

I'll call Malin first thing tomorrow morning, he thinks. Tell her what I've found out about the brothers.

48

It's as if oxygenated blood is once again flowing through her veins when her body returns from its visit to the dead.

Malin greedily gulps air into her lungs, and even though the night traffic at Hornstull is heavy, the oxygen still feels as if it's caressing her airways and lungs.

A large advertising hoarding covers an entire wall.

A woman in a bikini on a beach, palm trees in the background.

They head back to the car, parked outside a Chinese restaurant in the next block.

The pavements are practically empty, the restaurants have all shut for the night, and there are lights on in just a few of the apartment windows. Malin feels the tarmac almost swaying beneath her feet, as tiredness and confusion threaten to take over.

Zeke is walking silently beside her, and she knows his brain is working, trying to tease out the core of this investigation and find its innermost truth.

Piece by piece we're putting it together, the truth, Malin thinks, and they stop by the car, and the evening feels warmer again now. Above them the sky is clear and starry, and she thinks that it's a fairly decent night for the men outside the City Mission, and everyone else who doesn't have a bed of their own.

Zeke settles into the driver's seat.

Slowly they head along Hornsgatan, stopping at a red

light at Zinkensdamm, and there's a queue outside the bar on the corner, and Malin thinks she sees a famous singer, Ulf Lundell, go past on the other side of the street.

'Soon the angels will land'.

She and Janne used to dance to that song when they were young, just after Tove was born, before all the problems. I hope he's right, Malin thinks.

'I can't make any damn sense of this,' Zeke says, drumming the wheel as if to keep himself awake. 'Can you?'

And Malin forces herself to put the pieces together inside her head, making them form some sort of picture.

'If the brothers had anything to do with this, surely they would have murdered Josefina Marlöw first?' Zeke says. 'She's the one standing between them and their inheritance, isn't she?'

'I'm not sure that's right,' Malin says. 'After all, Josef Kurtzon told Josefina that he'd leave the money to the National Inheritance Fund if she died before him.'

'But why would the brothers kill the Vigerö girls, and Hanna Vigerö? What do they stand to gain from that?'

'Maybe they reasoned that if Josefina Marlöw inherits Josef Kurtzon's wealth and then dies, and the Vigerö girls are already out of the picture, then they'd stand to inherit everything from their sister as her only living relations, and get their hands on the money that way?'

'But Josef Kurtzon had arranged things so they wouldn't get anything?'

'Do we know that for certain? Who knows what he's decided should happen to the trust when Josefina dies. Maybe the brothers would inherit control of it? Either way, I don't think Josef Kurtzon knew about the girls.'

'So Josefina Marlöw's life is in danger?' Zeke asks.

'No, if the brothers' plan is to get hold of the money, they need her to stay alive until their father's dead. Because of his threat to leave everything to the Inheritance Fund.'

Zeke seems to consider this, letting Malin's reasoning sink in.

'That solicitor Josefina mentioned. We need to talk to him.'

Malin nods.

'He might be able to clarify things. If the brothers knew about their sister's adopted children, and her will, then it makes sense. Because if they did know about the Vigerö twins, they would have wanted them out of the way, to stop them inheriting anything from either Josef Kurtzon or their mother.'

'But surely Josefina Marlöw can still arrange things in such a way as to stop her brothers getting control of the money if she were to die now? She can leave most of it to other recipients?'

'You saw her just now,' Malin says. 'She certainly didn't seem to be in a fit state to plan anything that calculated. Whatever she arranged with this solicitor, Stålsten, I'm sure she wasn't thinking about what would happen to the inheritance if her twin daughters were dead. She doesn't even seem able to absorb the fact that they're dead.'

Silence descends upon the car, the only noise the monotonous growl of the engine.

The Kurtzon brothers are there in the darkness with them, in their thoughts of what they might have done: wiping out an entire family in order to get their hands on a fortune.

'Maybe Johan's managed to find out a bit more about the brothers,' Malin says. 'I'll give him a call.'

'He'll call us tomorrow,' Zeke says. 'Let him sleep. Not everyone's as manic as you.'

'Me, manic? What do you mean?'

Zeke grins, and in the gloom of the car his mouth

becomes a clown's smile, friendly but with a hint of horror.

They carry on down Hornsgatan, and as they pass the City Kebab restaurant Malin remembers dragging Tove halfway across the city just to eat there, and get a decent bit of junk food at a reasonable price. Imagine, it's still there . . .

'So the man in the video from outside the bank could be one of the Kurtzon brothers?' Zeke asks.

'Maybe,' Malin says. 'Or they might have hired someone. They're not short of money, even if they do want a whole lot more.'

'But all this? Killing children for money? And their parents? Who could you hire to kill a child? I don't know a single thug in the whole country who'd do a thing like that.'

'Money,' Malin says. 'Money, Zeke, you know there are people who'll do anything for money. And their father chased them with a lizard when they were little. What else was he capable of doing to them to turn them into the perfect businessmen? Who knows what sort of people they've become?'

'The sort of people who kill children? I don't want to believe that, Malin.'

The look in Zeke's eyes changes.

Becomes hard and cold.

He puts his foot down.

But killing your own nieces? Malin wonders. Is that realistic? She doesn't want to believe it, but it could be true. This investigation could be leading her into a darkness of unimaginable depths.

'I can see why Josefina Marlöw gave the girls up for adoption,' Zeke says.

Malin nods.

'I wouldn't want any children to have to grow up in the atmosphere we felt in Josef Kurtzon's apartment.'

'No, definitely not. But do you really think he didn't know about the girls? With all his power and influence?'

'I honestly don't think he did,' Malin says.

They find a vacant space outside the hotel. Before they get out of the car Malin says: 'We'll have to talk to Josefina Marlöw's solicitor tomorrow. Stålsten. It's too late now. If it turns out that the brothers did know about the children, and that Josefina's will left everything to them, we could be on the right track. Almost certainly.'

Zeke nods, says:'Follow the money. Always follow the money.'

It's half past one by the time Malin sinks onto the bed in her hotel room.

Her clothes are in a heap on the floor and she's completely naked. She's taken off her pants so they wouldn't get dirtier than necessary, she'll have to wear them inside out tomorrow, she doesn't have any fresh ones with her.

Killing your nieces.

Malin's hands are shaking. What sort of monsters are they dealing with?

The brothers. Who are you? My brother. Who are you?

She closes her eyes and soon the dream descends, like a black core, glowing orange, firing out a constant stream of faces, and all of those faces carries a story.

First Tove.

She whispers: 'I'm leaving, Mum, but I'm not going to abandon you.'

Dad.

Smiling.

But I can't smile back.

Then Peter Hamse, wearing his white doctor's coat, and she feels her crotch contract, but he's soon gone, and those feelings with him.

Daniel Högfeldt.

Janne.

They come together. They wave goodbye to her, and she feels like running after them but can't, doesn't want to, feels it's time to let go, that the struggle to keep alive that love, those desires, is over.

Mum.

Her face a mute mask. Where's my grief? Malin wonders.

Karim Akbar, Sven Sjöman, Johan Jakobsson, Waldemar Ekenberg, Zeke, Börje Svärd, Karin Johannison. They march past, smiling at her, stroking her on the cheek, wishing her well, and she wishes she could just sink into that feeling.

Karim's happiness with his new, unappealing woman.

Karin's longing for children, written all over her. Suddenly flaring up, but there the whole time, coming as a shock to her.

All the good people, wishing her well. And then Malin sees Maria Murvall's face.

Her eyes are full of longing. And Malin can see the person inside Maria, the person who has shut herself away inside room after room after room, until there is only a white room left, entirely devoid of ill-will and fear, and therefore also entirely free from memories and emotions.

I'm going to find my way into that room, Malin thinks. I'm going to take you by the hand and lead you out of there, Maria.

Then she sees the girls.

Their faces from the photographs in the flat in Ekholmen, and they're smiling at first, but then they start to scream, and in the shadow of their screams Hanna Vigerö and Josefina Marlöw's faces emerge, and they're calling out to Malin, but she can't understand what they're saying.

Am I dreaming now? Maybe.

Then two different faces.

Two men with prominent chins and almost identical straight noses, and neat, slicked-back hair with a side parting. One face is slightly fuller than the other, but they're both chiselled. Their blue eyes anxious but harsh, full of desire and greed, and Malin tries in vain to find any kind of warmth in their eyes.

You're the Kurtzon brothers, aren't you?

But they don't answer, they say nothing, and disappear into her darkness, and then another man's face appears, contorted in a terrible grimace.

'I'm doing what you did for Tove,' the man says.

'You feel love?' she asks.

'You saved Tove,' the man says. 'When she was in mortal danger. Now I'm saving my children.'

Then he's gone.

Am I alone now?

No.

But I'm asleep. Tell me I'm asleep, dreaming.

I'm in a different room that stinks of death, but also of stubborn life.

I'm not alone here.

I can see two little children.

I can see them, but I don't know who they are. They want me to rescue them.

I have to rescue them.

And now they're screaming. They're screaming with terror, and I want to reach them, but where are you?

Where are you, children?

Black water lapping against broken reeds in the darkness.

Then Malin slips deeper into sleep, taking the two abandoned children with her into her dreams, trying to comfort them, tell them that everything will be all right, that everything will be fine, and in the dream the children turn into her own brother, into a dream within the dream that in the end people get to rest in a shimmering all-encompassing whiteness.

Who arranged for us to be dead?

Was it a longing for money that killed us? A longing to be like a father, to be good enough in his eyes, or just a longing for the power that comes with wealth, the power that allows you to own anyone, to get anyone to do anything at all?

Or was it a desire for power over other people's lives? Over children's lives? Over your image of yourself, of your own life?

Or are you on the wrong track, Malin?

Does the solution to this mystery lie somewhere else entirely?

You're sleeping now.

But don't sleep too long.

The other children, the captive children, the ones who aren't dead, are still waiting to be rescued. Did we die for their sakes? If we did, then you have to rescue them, don't you?

The clock is ticking, the time has been set, but you don't know that yet, Malin.

49

It's just gone nine o'clock. The solicitor, Jörgen Stålsten, is standing behind his mahogany desk with his back to Malin and Zeke. He's loosened his pale pink tie and is looking out across Odenplan, where blue city buses are parked by the entrance to the underground station, and people are going in and out of the same chains of shops that can be found in every town in the country, open all weekend in the service of commerce.

Johan Jakobsson called earlier that morning. Told them what he'd found out about the Kurtzon brothers and their mother, and Malin felt her skin break out in goosebumps when Johan talked about how lonely Leopold and Henry Kurtzon seemed to be, and their elusive yet somehow unmistakeable personalities: how the two brothers seemed to have been raised and moulded from the start to become perfect greed-machines, with no desire for love.

Malin and Zeke are waiting for Jörgen Stålsten.

They managed to get hold of him at his Östermalm address, and he agreed to see them even though it was Sunday.

He didn't ask what they wanted, and Malin could hear the fear in his voice.

He invited them to take a seat when they came in, but they declined, preferring to remain standing to indicate that the reason for their visit was pressing.

Jörgen Stålsten is the same age as Malin.

Handsome, with chiselled features framed by fair hair that's slightly too long, and he doesn't look much like a solicitor. Maybe his hair is why he doesn't work for one of the more uptight companies down near Stureplan, she thinks. That sort of hair wouldn't fit in there, in the conservative Stockholm business world.

They've explained why they're there, told him what they want to know, and now they're waiting for his response.

Jörgen Stålsten doesn't turn around. The look in his blue eyes just now was incisive and free from fear, like someone who's committed a crime and is about to confess, and isn't ashamed of what they've done. Like someone who knows that time has caught up with him.

'I went to school with Josefina,' Jörgen Stålsten says. 'Lundsberg. She used to go through hell at home during the holidays. I know that much. Even the bullying at school was better than that.'

Lundsberg.

Bullying.

The words splinter into jagged lightning in Malin's brain, and she realises she can't let Tove go there, can't send her through the forest to some stuck-up school full of rich-kid bullies. But that debate, that anxiety, doesn't belong here, so she rationalises it away, listens, lets Jörgen Stålsten talk.

'She started back in year nine. With hash. There was loads of it going on in the school. Maybe she started with more serious stuff back then as well.'

'What was going on at home?' Zeke interrupts.

'She used to talk about her mother. She said she was mad. She used to drill them, making them march around the dining table, forcing them to wear particular clothes, forcing them to eat only the food she thought suitable, and beating them and locking them in a closet when they didn't do what she wanted.'

'Were you close friends, you and Josefina?' Malin asks, thinking that it's best to let Jörgen Stålsten tell his story in his own way, not steer him into any dead-ends by asking specific questions.

'Close friends? I'd say so. Well, no, actually, not really, Josefina didn't let anyone get very close. But sometimes she would talk about her family, and her mother came to school on open days. In a chauffeur-driven limousine. She used to totter about in her vulgar Italian clothes, showing off. Everyone used to laugh at her, but she obviously thought she was royalty.'

'What happened to Josefina after she left school?'

'She didn't come back to Lundsberg for the sixth from. I thought she'd started somewhere else instead, I only found out much later that she'd already fallen into addiction.'

'Why do you think she did that?'

'She probably had a predisposition towards it. And that home. Her father didn't seem to care at all about his children, except as a sort of social experiment. Their mother treated them as accessories that had to perfectly match the image she wanted to portray of herself. The brothers were a few years above me, but I got the impression they were under a lot of pressure, and had had serious problems at their previous school. They were the worst bullies of all, capable of extreme violence in the most unexpected situations, but in retrospect I've come to realise that they were probably just doing to other people what was being done to them. They were extremely aware of the power and status of money: in their world money meant everything, tradition and family nothing, and they never even spoke to anyone they knew wasn't rich. At the same time they seemed ashamed that they had money, and yet they couldn't help flaunting it. It was like they had some massive internal conflict going on which could make them perfectly harmless one minute, and dangerous the next. They beat up one of the scholarship kids once in the gymnasium storeroom. He could do more pull-ups than them. They tied him to a pommel horse and gave him a serious kicking. The whole thing was hushed up because the boy refused to identify them. But everyone knew.'

'Do you think their father beat them?' Zeke asks.

Jörgen Stålsten turns to face them.

'No, but I think he encouraged them, right from the start, to care about money and nothing else, to think that wealth has an intrinsic value, that the important thing is to keep getting more and more, that you can never have enough.

'I think Josef Kurtzon is only interested in money itself. But their mum, Selda, managed to make them completely dependent on a lifestyle that only money can buy, with all the trappings, and I think they ended up dependent on the power over other people that only money can give. And when they failed at pretty much everything they tried, their father mocked them for their lack of confidence and ability. When they were older I heard he threatened to deny them access to the family fortune.'

'That all sounds pretty sadistic,' Zeke says.

'It is sadistic. They failed at most things, and when they were grown up they never earned any money, which meant they were good for nothing in their father's eyes. And they were no good to their mother either. She wanted them to be perfect so she could show them off. No matter what they did, they were never good enough.'

'How do you know all this?' Malin asks, unwilling to think of the brothers as victims. They could be killers. Child-killers.

'I knew them back then. And I've heard all the stories over the years. From other people we were at Lundsberg with, who in turn had heard rumours about the Kurtzon brothers. We had a reunion at the Grand Hotel back in the early nineties. They showed up together, suntanned in the middle of winter, I seem to remember they'd been somewhere in Asia, and it felt like Leopold was dragging Henry around. It was as if nothing had moved on for them. Everyone knew they hadn't got anywhere in their father's business, that he'd given up on them, a bit like Kamprad. They kept boasting about their own businesses, but if you looked below the surface it was pretty obvious it was all hot air.'

'That fits what Johan said,' Zeke says.

'Sorry?'

'Nothing. Please, go on,' Malin says.

'Then, later that evening, when someone had had enough of all their talk and said they were lying, Leopold flew into a rage, and there would have been a big fight if Henry hadn't stepped in and pulled him away. I remember Leopold screaming something like: "Just wait till we get our inheritance. Then I'm going to buy your fucking arses and stick dynamite up them and make you run until you blow up. And the lizards can eat what's left of you."'

Expectation of inheritance, Malin thinks.

Desperate people. Lonely people. Despised people.

'When did you last see Josefina?'

'Two months ago, maybe. I was really shocked by the way she looked, I mean, I'd heard about her, but I still didn't think it was possible to look that terrible and still be alive.'

'And that's when you drew up a will for her?' Malin asks. 'Leaving everything to the daughters she gave up for adoption?'

Jörgen Stålsten turns away again, and looks out towards the pointed spire of Gustaf Vasa Church.

'Yes.'

'Are the brothers mentioned in her will?'

'No.'

'What about any provision for what would happen to the money if the girls died before her?'

'No.'

'And Josefina didn't sign any other will that disinherited her brothers after her death?'

'No.'

'The brothers came to see you, didn't they?' Malin asks. 'Those frightened, confused brothers that you hadn't seen since the reunion and presumably never wanted to see again. Did they put pressure on you to reveal the contents of the will? Did they threaten you?'

Jörgen Stålsten takes his eyes off the church and fixes his gaze on Malin.

The confidence in his blue eyes replaced by fear, the same fear she saw in Ottilia Stenlund, as if the Kurtzon brothers were physically present in the room.

'They haven't been here. I have a duty of confidentiality, and I would never . . .'

'Of course they've been here,' Malin says, trying to convey both icy detachment and sympathy in her voice. 'I can understand if you were frightened,' she goes on. 'You must have been more than aware of what they're capable of.'

'I've got a wife and two young children,' Jörgen Stålsten says. 'What could I do? They came in here in their bespoke suits, those reptilian eyes, and showed me pictures of my children that they'd got some photographer to take. That was enough. I knew what they wanted: the details of what was in Josefina's will. I got the feeling that was the first they'd heard about the existence of the girls in Linköping. That Josefina had given birth to twins. And now she was planning to leave everything to the girls, everything that she was going to get from her father, and they weren't mentioned at all.'

'Don't blame yourself,' Malin says.

'Why are you asking me about this? Do you think the Kurtzon brothers are behind the bombing, and the murder of the girls' adoptive mother? That Henry and Leopold would be capable of doing anything like that?'

Neither Malin nor Zeke answers at once, just look at each other first, before Malin says: 'That's one of the theories we're taking into consideration.'

'What do you think?' Zeke asks. 'Could they do something like that?'

'I can tell you this much,' Jörgen Stålsten says. 'I got the impression that they were capable of anything when they were here. They seemed to have crossed some sort of boundary. That when it comes to protecting their money, and making sure they get their hands on the family fortune, there was nothing they wouldn't do, because without money the very foundation of their lives would vanish. You know, like Karl Vennberg wrote, "Deep inside the darkest gloom . . ."'

'". . .you have to fight for your life."' Malin completes the quote for him.

'And losing control of the billions they've spent their whole lives looking forward to, that was their . . . I've done a bit of thinking about this. You know Juha Valjakkala, who killed his whole family up in Åmsele. He was overpowered by a woman who fled into the forest, where he eventually shot her. Then he dragged his girlfriend to the body so she could watch while he cut it up. That was his way of restoring his self-image. And it's the same for the brothers with their father's fortune. It has to be theirs, otherwise they lose sight of themselves, and their self-respect.'

'What are they like, the brothers? As people, I mean,' Malin says.

'Leopold's the confident one. Henry's weaker, less confident. Or maybe just more reserved.'

'So Henry could be influenced by Leopold?'

'No, I don't think that's it. They're just different sides of the same coin. They influence each other.'

There's anger in Jörgen Stålsten's eyes now.

Determination, like light forcing the darkness back.

'Most of my work is with charities,' he says. 'I thought I was strong, but when the brothers showed up here I caved in to their demands straight away.'

Jörgen Stålsten blinks slowly.

'Believe me,' he says. 'Henry and Leopold Kurtzon could have done anything. They could still do anything. If it's in their interests. But don't try to understand what they are. Because you'd never get a good night's sleep again.'

Grilled sausages, lukewarm prawn salad, warm mash, sweet mustard, and ketchup that sticks to the side of your mouth, the fatty food doing good, all the way to the soul.

Malin and Zeke are both eating flatbread wraps. They're standing in the sunshine beside the hotdog kiosk in the middle of Odenplan. Breakfast wasn't included in the price of the hotel rooms, so they're having an early lunch instead.

Inside the Tranan restaurant, media types are eating brunch with their families for four hundred kronor each.

Pushchairs everywhere. It's as if the happy and successful inhabitants of this part of the city are literally popping out child after child, presumably hoping that they will be just as bland and middle class as themselves.

'So, the brothers knew about the girls,' Zeke says.

'And it could have spurred them into action. They made

a start just by threatening Jörgen Stålsten. That in itself is a serious offence.'

'We're on the right track,' Zeke says. 'I'm sure of it. Follow the darkness.'

'He was just as scared as the social worker.'

'Wouldn't you be, Malin?'

'Maybe,' she says, thinking: No, I wouldn't be scared, I'd be furious, and I'd protect what's mine no matter what it cost. Then she goes on: 'We have to get hold of the brothers. Johan will have to spend today trying to dig out some more addresses.'

Zeke nods.

'What I don't understand,' he says, 'is how Josefina Marlöw was able to keep her pregnancy secret. Surely a family like that, with so many tentacles, would have been keeping an eye on her?'

Soggy flatbread.

A pleasant sensation turning into something disgusting in one and the same mouthful.

'She must have got very good at staying out of the way over the years,' Malin says. 'Good at staying hidden, not really existing. Maybe she disappeared to a different city.'

'But you have to look after yourself while you're pregnant.'

'Life's stronger than that, Zeke. Do you have any idea how many mothers with addictions give birth to completely healthy babies? You'd be surprised.'

Then her mobile buzzes.

A message from Sven Sjöman.

A video clip.

She clicks to start it. And looks for the first time straight into the face of the killer.

50

Brothers

Mother is calling us in to dinner.

It's being served in the large dining room, we'll be sitting on the Josef Frank chairs around the Swiss dining table.

Mother has got the cook to measure out exact portions of cod and perch with Iranian caviar, precisely as much as a seven-year-old and an eight-year-old need for their physical development according to the latest dietary research.

The housekeeper washes our hands, takes off our jackets, and leads Josefina in, she's five, and her portion is smaller than it should be because little girls have to be kept thin, there's no clearer sign of bad character than a couple of extra kilos.

If we squabble at the table, Mother hits us on the knuckles with a fork. We both have scabs on our knuckles, and so does Josefina, she gets hit if she so much as opens her mouth.

I, Leopold, get into more trouble than Henry, but I still want to do what Father wants, I want him to love me most, and sometimes I hit Henry to make him stop talking, to get him to follow Father's example the same way I do.

But Mother hits us most of all.

On Father's orders. And I can see that she enjoys hitting my brother, and she hits hard.

You shouldn't talk while you're eating. And if only pain

can stop someone talking, then pain is what you have to use. That's a perfectly rational conclusion, and in the end we believe it, we believe Mother, we believe in punishment as the path to proper behaviour, we believe in silence. But sometimes we can't help ourselves, because after all we're two little boys, and then she gets the housekeeper, sometimes with the gardener's help, to lock us inside the empty storeroom in the cellar, and we get to spend the night in there. Father tells us to mock the servants, then lets them punish us, beat us, and lock us up.

We talk.

Regain control of ourselves. Grow bigger the more frightened we get. Often Josefina is with us, and I remember the stink of excrement. Sometimes she sits alone in the dark, empty, cold room, because it's different for Josefina, it's as if Mother thinks she's inferior by nature and that her very existence is enough for her to deserve punishment.

We are given animals.

A grey rabbit, a brown guinea pig, a puppy.

Father encourages us to torment them even though we don't want to. He hits us until we hit the animals.

Learn power, he says, learn to be ruthless. You're the ones in charge.

Father travels to the Congo.

He brings home a large, live lizard that becomes his very own pet. He takes it for walks in the garden, on a leash, then sets it loose on us, and we run down into the cellar, to the storeroom, and he locks us in, and has the beast scratch at the door, scratching after us, hungry and starving, as if we are its prey, and I hug Henry, hugging away all his fear and anxiety, promising never to abandon him, promising to help him become like Father.

Sometimes we creep down into the cellar when Josefina's there alone.

We stand outside the storeroom, listening to her cry the way we usually do when we're locked up, when the lizard comes. We could open the door, but we don't. We whisper cruel things to her through the door and she tells us not to, and that drives us mad. We chase after her when she's been let out, hitting her, kicking her.

The contented look on Father's face. Mother's laughter.

We learn to believe Mother, we believe she's right, because pain is always right, it comes from logic, or rationality, as Mother says. She uses that to justify everything, even though there are no logical reasons for her outbursts and material vanity.

We merge together. Try to be what he wants, she wants. Those we love. We don't know any different.

Mathematics. Logical thinking.

All we have, Mother says, comes from mathematics, and that isn't governed by emotion. What your father knows is how to count, and how to turn that into business into an empire. He was the most talented student of mathematics ever at a university in a faraway country.

Father is seldom at home.

In the garden, with a sated and happy lizard on its leash beside him, he encourages us to take risks. And when we don't dare he drives us on, to do things like climbing the wall facing the Lidingö Sound, the one with the twenty-foot drop down to the rocks and the water, and he laughs at us, calls us *cowards*, and goads the lizard to chase us, and then Mother locks us in the cellar because she saw us climb the wall from the window.

You're not to climb the wall. What would people say if you fell off and killed yourselves?

And Father laughs as the gardener, or the housekeeper, takes us off to the cellar.

To the darkness.

And we believe in both the mocking laughter and the justified anger, we believe in mathematics, in always acting rationally.

But what does that mean?

Sitting quietly beside Mother on a gilded sofa while she shows off what she's got, what she's acquired since she arrived here from the country where no one was allowed to have anything? Smiling when the photographer tells us to. Smirking at our little sister, who's never learned how to smile, or even how to pretend to. Hitting her to show our strength, her weakness.

Does it mean hitting other children who think they're better than us? Who know things we don't?

You have to protect what you are.

At any cost.

Mother teaches us that.

Father teaches us that.

They teach us what it means to be human.

They teach Josefina.

Being human means being beaten by your seven- and eight-year-old brothers. Watching them get electric shocks if they refuse. And it means getting locked up in a dark room and accepting that this is right, because someone who knows best has decided that it's right, and if you're lucky you'll learn to come to terms with your own fear, your own terror, you'll learn to conquer it and grow fond of it, desire it, and without you even being aware of it you start to look forward to the moment when you get to set the rules, to your chance to be in charge.

It might mean being fourteen and lowering an eight-year-old pupil at the same school head-first into a crack in the ice when the teacher isn't looking, with your brother's help, even though he's pleading for mercy on behalf of his friend.

It might mean tying another pupil from a poor family to a pommel horse in the storeroom of the school gymnasium.

It might mean smashing a bottle of champagne over the head of some stupid bitch from the suburbs in Café Opera the day your father laughed at your latest business proposal.

It might mean hitting a secretary in your New York office and drawing blood because she's forgotten to book a restaurant for that evening.

But deep down you know all about your own shortcomings.

It might mean when your chain of sweetshops goes bankrupt and your father pays off your debts. Or when he laughs at your presentation at one of the management meetings of the family business, and sends you from the room in front of everyone else to do it again, like a naughty child who hasn't understood his homework or is too stupid to be able to do it.

It might mean when someone sees your weaknesses, and points them out to you at a school reunion. It might mean when all the women you've ever met who have been worth loving turn their backs on you because you radiate the same smell as damaged, defective goods.

It might mean when you know you wouldn't hold back from killing your own flesh and blood if that was what mathematics, rationality, demand. If that was what it took for you to save yourself.

You can't run away from rationality like Josefina.

Or hold back and try to be nice, like Henry. Trying to pretend there's another, gentler option.

There's no such option.

All the beatings, all my failures and shortcomings have convinced me of that.

And what would be the point of trying to find a more lenient path?

You have to live in the present, in this suffering. Otherwise you'll never be anything, and being anything at all has to be better than being nothing.

Archaeologists have found caves with paintings by those who came before us.

A different species' pictures of their lives.

Dark, lonely places with pictures showing how they beat each other to death with sticks.

And beyond those places, those pictures, there are even darker places.

Where they eat their own children, in pictures made from paint mixed with blood.

And it was the strongest members of that species who slowly, slowly developed into human beings.

51

Images.

From a surveillance camera outside the bus terminal next to Linköping railway station.

Sven Sjöman is leaning forward in his office chair, almost pressing his nose against the screen, trying to get as close as possible to what he's watching.

It took a long time to get hold of the images because the hard-drive they were on had crashed, and the junior officers in charge of getting hold of surveillance recordings hadn't made it a priority, seeing as none of the other security cameras in the city had captured anything of interest on the day of the explosion.

But one of the technicians working for the regional transport company, Östgötatrafiken, had made it his mission to fix the hard-drive. He'd worked overtime for days, and all weekend, laboriously restoring the binary code.

Then he had looked at the restored recording.

And saw the bomber with his bicycle. He had personally brought the recording to Sven just half an hour ago, in a state of some excitement, aware that his hard work had paid off, and Sven had thanked him, said he'd be rewarded somehow, and now Sven sits back, double-clicks with his mouse, and watches the recording again.

The same man as outside the bank. The man with the bike.

No question.

He's just sent the clip to Malin, and has summoned the others. The door opens and in come Johan Jakobsson, Börje Svärd, and Waldemar Ekenberg.

'Come over here,' Sven says. 'I've got something to show you.'

And the three of them go and stand behind him, in silence, not even Waldemar comes out with any sort of crass comment, they all seem to have noticed how serious Sven is.

He clicks to start the clip.

They see the man on the screen, at some distance from the camera, removing the bike from a cycle carrier on the back of a black Volvo, then gently taking the rucksack from the backseat and carefully fixing it to the parcel rack of the bike.

Then he leads the bicycle past the camera at close range, and you can see his face. He has thin cheeks, a long nose, and cropped black hair, and a thin scar above his right eyebrow.

Sven thinks the man looks Slavic, and you can make out his eyes on the black-and-white pictures, the look in them determined, but neither enthusiastic nor scared.

Your whole being gives a professional impression, Sven thinks. You're acting as if this is just one in a succession of jobs. Is this your job, blowing up little girls? Murdering people in hospitals at night? In which case, who are you? Or am I wrong, are you just concentrating on the task ahead of you?

'A fucking professional,' Waldemar says.

'Definitely,' Börje agrees, and Sven thinks the two of them sound tired, almost hungover.

'Doesn't he look familiar somehow?' Johan asks.

You might be right, Johan, Sven thinks. I recognise him as well.

He freezes the clip.

'So, who is he?'

'No idea,' Börje says.

'Hang on,' Johan says.

'Fuck me, I think I do recognise him,' Waldemar says.

The phone on Sven's desk rings. A mobile. Must be Malin. Sven wonders how she's really doing, but brushes the thought aside. No time to think about that now.

'We've seen the clip,' Malin says as she moves into the shade of the budding lime trees at Odenplan, past the little fountains next to the market stalls. 'Bloody hell, do the Security Police know about this?'

'No. The technician from Östgötatrafiken came straight here and handed over the recording in person.'

'Zeke and I both think we recognise him,' Malin says. 'But we can't place him. He moves like a professional, it's more obvious here than up at the bank, where he was presumably making an effort to look as natural as possible. But it looks like he knows what he's doing, doesn't it?'

'Definitely professional,' Sven says. 'A hired thug, military maybe, possibly even police. The way he moves is extremely focused.'

A group of children goes past. A school class? No. Not on a Sunday. The children are shouting.

No, they're not shouting, they're singing a song that echoes right across Odenplan before it gets drowned out by the noise of the traffic.

'What are you thinking of doing with this?' she asks.

'We're about to have a meeting. Then we'll circulate these images to our colleagues throughout the country, get a warrant out for him, and if that doesn't come up with anything, we'll release the pictures to the media. Obviously we'd prefer to avoid that, because then he'd know that we're on to him and maybe go to ground, or flee the country. If he's even still here, of course.'

'It looks like he's working alone.'

'Yes, it looks that way.'

'Then he must be a professional.'

'That seems pretty likely.'

'In which case he could have been hired by someone.'

'What are you thinking?' Sven asks, and Malin tells him what they've found out in Stockholm, about the Kurtzon family, the brothers, the complex game surrounding the inheritance and control of a family fortune probably worth over a hundred billion kronor.

'That could fit,' Sven says. 'But there could be an entirely different explanation.'

'We'll carry on digging,' Malin says.

'You do that,' Sven says. 'I'll update the others on how you're getting on.'

'Any other news?'

'No.'

Malin looks out across Odenplan again.

For a few short seconds it's completely free of cars and buses; the pedestrians and cyclists are in sole charge, and she feels a sudden desire to live in Stockholm again, to be part of a larger, less inbred city, where she would have a greater number of more interesting cases, and where she could live anonymously but still feel at home.

In Linköping everything is too small.

Everyone knows all about everyone else. Or at least that's the way it sometimes feels. Even if no one really knows anything about anyone. She often feels that she's been recognised, that people are staring at her. There she goes, Detective Inspector Malin Fors, the one we've seen in the *Correspondent* and on telly.

Here, celebrities get to go about their business

unhindered. People who've really achieved something are left in peace, here their faces are just part of the everyday scene.

But actually moving? Would that work?

'I think I recognise him,' Sven says, and Malin is dragged back to the present. 'So do Johan and Waldemar. So who the hell is he?'

Malin can hear the others in the background.

'It'll come out in time,' she says.

'Do you think it could be one of the Kurtzon brothers?'

'No,' Malin says. 'It's neither of the brothers, judging from the pictures Johan found. But if they're behind this, they may have hired someone. Or else we're on the wrong track. We'll have to see what these pictures lead to.'

'If what you're saying is right,' Sven says, 'do you think this Josefina Marlöw is in danger? Do you think we should try to dig her out from the underground again and put her under protection?'

'I think they need her alive for a bit longer,' Malin says. 'She's OK.'

'You're sure?'

'There's no real danger until Josef Kurtzon dies,' Malin says.

So that's what he looks like.

The man who hurt us so badly.

And we know where you are, you, our biological mother.

You're in your own dark room down in the underground. With your lovely drawings on the wall.

The syringe slips from your hand.

Your world is a white blanket now, everything is goodness and warmth.

You're turning your black room into a white one, Mummy, and we're with you, and we can feel that the mummy and daddy you gave us instead of yourself are here as well, but we can't see or hear them.

We can't.

But we'd really like to, because even if your room is white and soft and warm for you, it's really horrible for us. It's so nasty that it's making us cry.

We're running away now.

We're running away from the underground to the paved square where Malin Fors is sitting on a bench. She's looking at pictures of our uncles. Trying to make sense of what she sees.

A few alcoholics are drinking an early lunch on a nearby bench.

Malin and Zeke are still in Odenplan, now on a bench in the shade, the spring sunshine got too hot.

They let the images of the brothers scroll across the screen of the mobile phone. They look very similar, but there are differences. Leopold's face is sharper, with dark, thick eyebrows that lend almost unreal force to his long, pointed nose. Henry's face is slightly rounder, more friendly, but his blue eyes have a hunted expression, and the look in them seems completely vacant, doesn't contain any sort of desire.

Neither of the brothers resembles the bomber, they look far more Scandinavian. They've both got thinning hair, which makes them look older than their forty-two and forty-three years.

Leopold's eyes.

The expression in them both vague and focused at the same time. Cold, as if he were caught in a state of permanent calculation and consideration.

'They look ordinary,' Zeke says. 'If they did hire an assassin, how the hell would anyone from their background go about it?'

'You're being a bit naïve, Zeke,' Malin says. 'If you've got money you can do anything.'

Zeke rubs his nose with one hand.

'Show me the clip of the bomber again.'

Malin plays the recording, angling the mobile to stop the sunlight from making the man invisible.

The man moves towards the camera.

They see his face.

'Stop, right there,' Zeke whispers. 'Can you zoom in?'

'Yes,' Malin says, and zooms in on the man, and they see the scar running above one eyebrow, like a line drawn with eyeliner.

Zeke's eyes are burning with concentration, he's breathing heavily. Don't blow up now, Malin thinks.

'Fuck it,' Zeke says. 'I know who that is. I recognise him.'

52

'That's Jokso Mirovic,' Zeke says.

Opposite the bench he and Malin are sitting on, the doors of Gustaf Vasa Church open up.

An elderly black man in a priest's collar steps out onto the stone steps, followed by a thickset woman, also wearing a collar.

The priests embrace, say goodbye, and the black priest disappears back inside the church again.

'Mirovic was a heavy in the Yugoslavian mafia at the end of the nineties. I remember him from a case I worked on with Crime in Gothenburg. He was famous for being very intelligent, an academic. He's supposed to have got that scar fighting in Sarajevo.'

Sarajevo.

Bosnia.

That was where Janne fled when he couldn't face playing happy families any more, after Tove had arrived, unplanned, and he hadn't been anywhere near ready for that sort of responsibility. Other things had been going on in their relationship then, things that belong to nightmares. How could we possibly have managed to live together then, when we haven't even managed it as adults with more experience?

We were never going to manage it.

A bus blows its horn.

A mother with a pushchair, crossing the road on red.

'I remember he was granted asylum around the time of the Balkan conflict, then he got Swedish citizenship. I think he vanished off the criminal map sometime just after the millennium,' Zeke says. 'But I'm sure it's him. He looks older, but it's definitely him. A hard bastard. He's supposed to have been behind the unsolved murder of that businessman in Malmö ten years ago. The one where the victim was stabbed in the stomach a hundred times with a blunt knife. And they reckon he killed a paedophile by cutting his balls off and stuffing them down his throat so he suffocated.'

'Sounds lovely,' Malin says.

'Paedophiles. It's hard to feel much sympathy for them.'

'Humanity has no place for people like that,' Malin says, then feels alarmed by her own honesty.

She pulls out her mobile and calls Sven Sjöman, who tells her he'll put out a national alert and inform the others.

'Keep digging,' Sven says. 'We can't let child-killers go free in our society.'

Harry Karlsson looks at the queue at Entrance B of Terminal 5 at ArlandaAirport. Newly built and very nice it may be – the ceiling must be twenty metres high – but there are far too few security desks, and there's always a queue at busy times.

Like now.

It's just after one o'clock.

The queue snakes all the way back to the SAS check-in desk, and people are getting impatient and annoyed, and there's a stink of perfume from the new duty-free shop.

He's worked for the airport authority for over thirty years. Now he's supervisor for the main security checks, and it's a hell of a job trying to organise the second-rate people he has to work with.

The guards from the companies under contract are supposed to be friendly but tough. Make people feel happy about travelling, while still making them feel safe. Not a job for thickos, basically.

Harry Karlsson looks at the people he's got working for him. Young security guards, he knows many of them want to join the police, just like the two heavies in attendance today. Apparently there's some sort of national alert out for the man who set off that bomb in Linköping.

Two cops seconded to the airport. Just in case.

But what are the odds of the bomber showing up here?

Low, but not impossible.

They haven't been shown any pictures of the man, but evidently the police have been told what he looks like.

Why don't they want to show us his picture? Or even give us the name of the man they're looking for? Because they don't think either we or the security contractors are reliable, that's the reason, in which case they have to appreciate that we can't do as good a job as we could.

They want to keep the information confidential.

Bleep.

Check that a pensioner isn't carrying weapons on-board inside his shoes. Sometimes the harshness of the new security directives is absurd.

Then Harry Karlsson sees a change in the eyes of one of the policemen, and they both stiffen, and one of them gestures discreetly at Harry Karlsson, who goes over to them. The policeman says: 'That could be the man we're looking for. The one who's just putting his toiletries in a plastic bag.'

Harry Karlsson looks over at the table with the bags.

A man maybe ten years younger than him, around forty-five.

Harry Karlsson is looking at him from the side, but he

can still make out a scar above one eye. In spite of the scar, the man doesn't look particularly tough or hard, but Harry Karlsson still feels the adrenalin coursing through his body, the way it does whenever a known criminal wanted by the police shows up at the security control, even though he must have been through dozens of similar arrests by now.

'We'll pick him up once he's gone through the gate,' the policeman whispers. 'My colleague's already called for back-up.'

Harry Karlsson looks at the other policeman.

He must have whispered into his headset without him noticing.

'Don't do anything, just keep the security guards calm, OK?'

Harry Karlsson nods, knows that at this moment police officers will be covering every exit from the airport, every escape route, ready to draw their weapons and fire.

The man, the suspect, has reached the metal detector now, he's taken off his jacket, put his bag on the belt to go through the X-ray machine, then he walks through without any fuss.

Nice and calm now.

Calm, calm.

And then the policemen move towards the man.

It looks as if they're about to draw their pistols.

Harry Karlsson catches their movement in the corner of his eye, and now watches as the man suddenly explodes, one leg flying out in a martial arts move, knocking the two policemen backwards, and the people in the queue scream. Harry Karlsson's guards throw themselves to the floor to take cover, or simply out of panic, but there haven't actually been any shots, have there? And Harry Karlsson leaps towards the man, but he skips aside, and Harry Karlsson feels his two top front teeth push into his jaw and break as he lands on the floor, chin first.

Shit, he thinks.

Shit.

This is going to cost a fortune in dental fees.

When Jokso Mirovic saw the policemen move towards him he realised instinctively that they had been waiting for him, that they wanted to get hold of him. He'd had a feeling that something was wrong the moment he checked into his flight to Phuket, but dismissed it as his own paranoia, he was used to situations like this, but the feeling only grew stronger as he was standing in the queue and caught sight of the police officers. He knew from experience that there weren't usually any police at the security check.

But he had still dismissed it as paranoia, even though he knew he shouldn't, knew you should always trust your instincts, but not this time: he simply had to get on this flight at any cost, there were no other options open to him. He had to look for the children now, and that trail began in Thailand, where they were kidnapped, the children's passports had been left in the house, so maybe they were still in the country. But how the hell did the police know what he'd done, they couldn't possibly have tracked him down, could they?

The metal detector.

And the old, overweight bloke in plain clothes who seemed to be the supervisor had looked nervous.

Sweating, and then everything happened very quickly, as usual, the policemen tried to draw their pistols when they got close to him, and he raised one leg high and then kicked out with his trainer, and twisted with his right foot, and the policemen, clumsy idiots with bulletproof vests under their shirts, collapsed unconscious to the floor as Jokso Mirovic watched.

Their pistols were still in their holsters.

What next?

Run.

If it wasn't already too late. The place would be crawling with cops any moment, and now he's running through the main hall that forms the heart of Terminal 5, rushing past tourists on package tours on their way to the sun, businessmen on their way to what they presumably believe are important meetings.

Which exit?

Keep running straight ahead, then into SkyCity and into the hotel there, then the exit to the garage where you can steal a car.

He turns his head.

Three cops, maybe fifty metres behind him, and there are two rushing towards him up ahead, they must have come from Entrance C.

I can't get caught now, I mustn't, otherwise this whole idiotic business has been in vain.

No guns drawn.

But he's still back in the trenches.

Pursued by machine-gun fire and hand grenades and the cries of the Croats, and it's as if everything is transformed in a split second to a single explosive present, a present that demands just one thing: freedom.

He goes into a slide when he's five metres from the cops, gliding on his smooth cotton trousers, knocking them to the ground, and it works.

They fall.

Groan.

And he quickly gets to his feet and rushes on, but the little manoeuvre means that the other policemen are twenty metres closer now, then he's out into the glazed open space of SkyCity, and the light is harsh, and there aren't many people about now, just after lunchtime.

He swerves off to one side.

Takes the escalator up to the Radisson Hotel and races for the lift.

Inside.

Presses the button to close the doors.

And he leaves the cops behind him, they're ten metres away as the lift doors close on him, and when they open again one floor below he runs down one, two more escalators, then catches his breath, sees his two children in front of him, Daddy's on his way, Daddy's coming, and he sees the Vigerö girls playing in the square, the other children, and he feels like screaming, howling, but he knows he can't give in now, no matter what he feels, and then he stops.

Fuck.

Shit.

There must be at least five police officers barricaded behind the sofas in the lower lobby of the hotel.

Guns aimed at him.

He's unarmed, ditched his pistol out in the car park earlier.

Shit.

'Hands up!'

'Down on the floor!'

Various options run through Jokso Mirovic's head.

Carry on going forward, get shot, die, or get away and do what he has to do.

I'd never get past them.

It would be like running straight across no-man's land towards an occupied enemy line.

And the police would shoot.

They know what I've done.

I'll have to hope that someone else can do what I ought to.

But is there any police officer who could pull it off?

He remembers his friends in the war, the ones who died, the ones who had shown a courage he would never have thought them capable of.

Then he raises his hands in the air.

Shouts: 'Don't shoot, don't shoot!'

53

The underground is lit by cold, white strip lights.

A constant attack on the eyes.

The interview room is on the third basement floor of Police Headquarters, beside the lush green of Kronoberg Park in the centre of Stockholm. Even when she was at Police Academy, Malin thought the building was ugly: brutal 1970s architecture with tiny windows set tightly together in a façade of orange panelling.

They did their swimming tests in the Kronoberg pool. Struggling with heavy, waterlogged practice dummies, length after length, and there were several of them who couldn't do it and had to leave the course after almost a year of study.

Harsh.

But not as harsh at this interview room, which is unbelievably shabby, the paint peeling from the yellow walls, the black plastic flooring has deep gouges in it, and from the ceiling hang fluorescent lights that give off an offensive glare, not the trust-inspiring, warm, soft light from the halogen lamps they have in the interview rooms of the station in Linköping, the sort of light that's so good for interviews.

The wall mirror.

A few colleagues from Stockholm behind it.

Sven Sjöman called when they were on their way back to the hotel to change clothes. Malin and Zeke had both bought new underwear and white T-shirts from Åhléns, and Malin is now wearing them under her increasingly filthy dress. Sven told her that Jokso Mirovic had been arrested at Arlanda and was on his way to Police Headquarters in Stockholm.

They'd gone straight there, and to begin with the duty officer had been dubious about letting them conduct the first interview with Jokso Mirovic.

Surely the Security Police ought to do that? Or at least Stockholm themselves, seeing as he'd been arrested in their district, but Malin had given him an outline of their work so far, emphasising how keen they were to solve this case as soon as possible, to make sure the public weren't put in any unnecessary danger, so the best solution would be if she and Zeke spoke to Jokso Mirovic straight away.

Now. Not later.

And the duty officer had backed down. But only after consulting the head of the Crime Unit over the phone.

And now Jokso Mirovic is sitting opposite them in the interview room, and the scar above his left eye is glowing pink. He seems to be waiting for Malin or Zeke to say something while he looks at his reflection, inspecting his thin face, as if someone else were sitting in this room, caught by their own actions, and not him.

Malin reaches for the tape recorder on the table.

Clicks to start it, then says: '16 May 2010, time ten past four. Interview with Jokso Mirovic regarding the explosion in Linköping on 10 May and the murder of Hanna Vigerö in Linköping University Hospital in the early hours of 13 May.'

Malin pulls out her mobile.

Plays the clip from the surveillance camera outside the bus station, and Jokso Mirovic sees his face and smiles, then Malin shows him the recording from the bank, and this time Jokso Mirovic doesn't smile.

'That's you in both clips. We know that,' Zeke says. 'So you might as well confess and tell us how this all fits together, OK?'

Jokso Mirovic looks at them. First at Zeke, then at Malin, and she tries to catch his gaze, make sense of what she sees there, and she manages it, and finds a gentle desperation, the same desperation she felt the time Tove was in the hands of a killer and she was racing through the forests of Östergötland in her Volvo to save her.

The sort of desperation that knows calmness is vital. That knows panicking equals death.

He must feel like shit, Malin thinks.

As well he might, considering what he's done.

But he's tough. If he's done what the rumours suggest. A hundred stab wounds, and testicles rammed down a paedophile's throat.

He hasn't been registered as living in Sweden since 2004, when he lived in Gothenburg. Since then he's had Thailand listed as his place of residence.

'Tell us,' Malin says. 'That's the best thing you can do now. For your own sake.'

'Don't give me that bullshit. I'll talk.'

Jokso Mirovic takes a deep breath, then he starts talking.

He leans closer to the tape recorder, to make sure that every word is clearly captured.

He doesn't seem to want to put any emotion into what he says, just lets his mouth and tongue move, moving things forward. He talks with a slight accent.

'I live, or rather lived, with my two young children in Phuket. As you know, that was where I was heading when you picked me up.

'I've withdrawn from my earlier life. The children are three and six years old, a boy and a girl. The boy's name is Marko, and the girl's is Elena. Their mother's dead, she died in a helicopter crash when our son was a year old, so I look after them on my own.'

Jokso Mirovic falls silent. Takes a deep breath.

'You should have seen my children swimming in the pool of the house we live in on Phuket. They used to spend all day in there. You should have seen Marko the first time he dared to jump in on his own, you should have seen Elena. She was even happier than he was.'

Jokso Mirovic collects himself before going on in a more factual tone: 'On New Year's Eve a year and a half ago I met the brothers Henry and Leopold Kurtzon at Sri Panwa, a smart resort close to where I live. We got on well and spent a bit of time together. They were a bit like the sort of carefree people I used to deal with, and seeing them was almost a form of nostalgia for me. We seemed to have things in common, somehow.'

'Go on,' Malin says.

'I'm just pausing for breath,' Jokso Mirovic replies, and his eyes are empty and cold now, but deep down there's a hint of something pleading.

'Six months ago the brothers came to me with a plan. They were aware of my past. They must have got the impression I was capable of anything. Maybe they'd heard rumours about what I did during the war.

'They wanted me to kill some children and their parents in Sweden. They said they wanted help and that I would be perfect for the job. I asked why they thought I'd be good, why I would do something like that, and they said they'd checked me out. I told them I'd given up any sort of criminal activity, and that I'd never killed anyone. And certainly not any children.'

Jokso Mirovic pauses.

Looks up at Malin and Zeke, and his eyes say: I've killed plenty of people, you know it, and I know it.

'They refused to tell me why they wanted me to kill these people. They offered me two million kronor up front, and another two million when the job was done. I turned them down.'

Sudden irritation in Jokso Mirovic's voice. Restrained anger, and he clenches his fists so tightly that they turn white, then he lets go, as if remembering that he can't allow himself to get angry right now.

'What happened?' Malin says.

'I told them to go to hell.'

'And then?'

'Then one day my children were missing when I went to pick them up from the art class they sometimes go to where we live. Some men claiming to be from Interpol had turned up to get them, and the staff at the school believed them. They left a letter for me.'

The light in the ceiling flickers and everything goes dark for a few seconds, and when the light comes back on it's not as bright. Malin gets the impression that the room's shrunk.

'What did the letter say?' Zeke asks.

'It said they'd taken the children. That they were holding them at a secret location. That they'd kill my children if I didn't help them with the murders. That I should follow their instructions, and come up with my own suggestions of how to kill the family in Sweden.'

'And you didn't go to the police?'

'To the Thai police? No. They had Elena and Marko. I knew this had to be about a huge amount of money, that was the only reason the Kurtzons would have wanted that family wiped out. I realised that if I did anything to try to find my children, they'd get to hear about it and kill them.

'So I set to work. Suddenly I had two million in my account for expenses, transferred from a bank in Antigua. I started with the father. I shot out one of the tyres on his car, and he died in the following crash, and none of your lot had any suspicions at all.

'It was harder with the girls. Two six-year-old girls don't die just like that, and the bank was the brothers' idea. They called me and explained their plan: they wanted me to detonate a powerful bomb, far more powerful than necessary, outside a bank, so that it would look like the family had been the victim of a terrorist attack.

'I told them they were crazy. Then a month ago I was sent a recording of my children sobbing with terror, calling for me, screaming that a big lizard was trying to eat them up, screaming out loud.'

'Have you still got the recording?' Malin asks. 'That would make it a hell of a lot easier for us to believe you.'

'It's on my iPhone. The one you seized when you picked me up. I've got pictures of Elena and Marko on there as well.'

Jokso Mirovic falls silent.

Stares straight ahead.

'Can we have the iPhone in here? Now?'

They sit in silence in the room for something like ten minutes before the door opens and a uniformed officer comes in and puts the iPhone on the table without saying a word.

'Go ahead,' Zeke says.

Jokso Mirovic takes the device and brings up pictures of two young children playing in a sparkling pool, a little dark-haired boy with big brown eyes swimming without armbands, with a slightly bigger girl behind him.

'That's Marko and Elena.'

Jokso Mirovic closes his eyes. Composes himself.

Malin looks at the pictures of the children. They're young, their eyes open wide, their whole lives ahead of them.

Are you still alive? she thinks. Are the Kurtzon brothers holding you somewhere?

Jokso Mirovic picks the iPhone up again, clicks a button, then puts it back on the table.

Malin closes her eyes.

Listens to the clear sounds that start to emerge from the device.

> 'Daddy, where are you? . . . where are you, I'm scared . . . Daddy . . . [crying, sniffing] . . . Daddy . . . Daddy . . . we're locked up, you've got to come . . . they're going to hit us . . . Daddy . . . where are you? . . . rescue us . . . there are monsters here and they're trying to bite and . . . they're screaming, Daddy . . . [howling, screaming] . . . now I'm screaming . . . Daddy . . . Daddy . . . where . . . where are you?'

The children's words take hold of Malin, their fragile, infinitely terrified voices strike like a red-hot spear right into her very core.

That's Tove screaming.

Malin's own younger brother.

If my life has any meaning, she thinks, it's to save these children from that.

What sort of person would I be otherwise? What sort of pit would I belong in then?

Next to Malin, Zeke is noticeably shaken as Jokso Mirovic goes on: 'You heard them. What was I supposed to do?

'The mother used to go to the bank at the same time every Monday to withdraw money before she did the shopping. So I detonated the bomb by remote from the other square, I could get a good view from there. The mother survived because she was bending over.

'But the girls died.

'Just like they were supposed to.'

What's that I can hear in your voice? Malin wonders.

Remorse. Bitterness.

Is your story true?

Could that recording be fake? And those pictures of entirely different children? No, no, no.

The children's fear, their utter dread, was real. Mirovic is telling the truth, she's never been more certain of anything in her life.

And why would you be lying? You're confessing.

The children.

Marko and Elena.

You want us to rescue the children.

Me to rescue your children.

And Jokso Mirovic looks up at her.

'I know they're still alive. My children. You have to find them.'

'How do you know they're still alive?' Zeke asks. 'The Kurtzon brothers might have got rid of them.'

'I know they're alive. I can feel it. The brothers have still got them.'

'What about the brothers? What sort of people are they?' Malin asks.

'Leopold's the decisive one. Henry's more reserved. But they complement each other. Make up a sort of whole.'

'Hanna Vigerö,' Zeke says, his gaze and voice perfectly steady.

'I killed her at night. It was easy, I just had to sneak into the hospital and put a pillow over her face. I switched off the alarm on the monitor she was attached to. My wife was hooked up to a similar one after the helicopter crash, so I know how they work. I switched it off for a few minutes, then switched it back on again.'

'And then? What were you supposed to do after that?'

'The brothers told me to lie low. I protested, said I'd done everything they asked, but they said I wasn't finished yet, so I went underground. But after a while I couldn't do that any more, I had to get to Thailand, and find a way of getting to Marko and Elena, try to find them. Otherwise it would never end. I had to take the chance.'

'Do you know where they are at the moment?'

'No. The brothers were renting a villa at Sri Panwa for a month when we first met. But that's a long time ago now. They're not there. Maybe they're in Thailand. That's where the trail starts, that's why I had to get back there. But they could just as easily be in Sweden. I've been watching their flats on Strandvägen, but they weren't there, and they haven't been back. I haven't managed to get hold of any other address.'

Jokso Mirovic falls silent.

Malin looks at Zeke, who looks back at her.

Is he telling the truth? Zeke seems to be wondering, as if his system is refusing to take in the terrified, tormented children's voices on the phone. Are the Kurtzon brothers really holding two little children captive somewhere? The boy and girl from the photographs. Are they in Thailand? Sweden? Are the brothers torturing them? Are they really making them scream in terror?

'Every word I've said is true,' Jokso Mirovic whispers. 'The recording is genuine. You have to rescue my children.'

And Malin looks at him again, meets his pleading gaze.

Thinks about the parents at the gates of Nazi concentration camps, and later those run by the Serbs, forced to choose between their children, which one they took with them into the camp, and which one died at once.

Then she shakes her head, and fixes her eyes on Jokso Mirovic's face.

Sees his scar almost vibrating in the cold light.

'Daddy . . . *where are you . . . where are you . . . I'm scared . . . Daddy . . . [crying] . . . they're screaming . . . Daddy . . .'*

Malin takes a deep breath, and thinks: I would have done the same as you. I'd have done the same as you.

So we died so you could save your own children? Our lives in exchange for theirs. How are we supposed to understand that?

Mummy and Daddy died for their sake as well.

Do you think that makes us feel less afraid, that we'll forgive you?

You killed us, and that guilt is yours, no matter what your excuse is.

We're close to you now, Jokso Mirovic.

We're the draught you can feel on your neck.

We're whispering: 'So you didn't kill us for the money? Do you really care about the children, about Elena and Marko, in their dark, stinking, damp room of fear? You did it for the money, didn't you, you're the lizard, the spider, the snake, the vicious, hungry beast's sharp teeth, aren't you, you are greed itself, aren't you?'

Malin watches as Jokso Mirovic stands up in panic.

He starts waving his arms about, shouting out: 'I didn't do it for the money. I didn't get any money. I'm not a monster.

'Do you hear? Leave me alone. I'm trying to save my children. You can understand that, can't you? I killed you for the sake of my children.'

Then Jokso Mirovic falls silent, slumps down onto the black floor of the interview room and covers his eyes with his hands.

Malin knows what he can see, knows what he can hear.

She feels a draught against her ear, hears two girls' voices singing.

You have to find them, Malin. They've been locked up by our uncles, you have to save the captive girl and boy. Otherwise it's all been for nothing.

54

Malin can see Elena and Marko Mirovic in front of her.

Little huddled-up creatures shaking with fear.

Locked up in a dark, cramped room.

A chamber.

A chamber of darkness.

The room stinks of excrement, urine, and fear. It's a room where all empathy has been replaced by the logic of evil, the children will die in that darkness, and I have to help them, because no one else is going to.

'Do you think he's telling the truth?'

The man sitting on the other side of the table in the cafeteria of Police Headquarters in Stockholm is called Conny Nygren. Malin is taken aback by his words in this depressing room furnished with pine trellis panels covered with plastic plants snaking their way up to the ceiling. The panels divide the long grey laminated tables with their uncomfortable metal chairs. A clock on the wall says it's a quarter to eight. A quick evening coffee, black, with a dry pastry. The hours since the interview have been spent bringing Linköping up to speed, and dealing with paper-work.

Conny Nygren is a detective inspector with the Crime Unit of the Stockholm Police. His face is furrowed and grey, and he's thin as a rake, apart from his stomach, which sticks out like a cannonball above his belt. His nylon shirt stretches tightly across his gut, and he ought to be tired and lethargic, Malin thinks, but the detective opposite her possesses an energy that she rarely sees in fellow officers, even recent graduates.

'I think he's telling the truth,' Malin says. 'The photographs and the recording of the children are genuine. No doubt at all.'

'I agree,' Zeke says.

'I believe him too,' Conny Nygren says. 'And I think the recording's genuine. His story is improbable, but just improbable enough for it to be true. There's nothing new in this job, is there?'

'Money,' Malin says after a brief pause. 'Does it ever do any good?'

Conny Nygren laughs.

'I won seven hundred and eighty-nine thousand on the horses once. Which meant I got to see the Caribbean,' he says. 'Can't think of anything negative to say about that.'

'We can regard this case as solved now,' Malin says. 'Jokso Mirovic is responsible for the bombing in Linköping and the murder of the Vigerö family. He did it to save his own children, blackmailed into it by the Kurtzon brothers. If Mirovic hadn't been caught, the brothers could have just waited for their father to die, then got Mirovic to get rid of Josefina Marlöw. Seeing as she didn't have any other family, the money would probably have gone to them without anyone suspecting a thing. Now we just have to focus on catching the brothers and rescuing Mirovic's children.'

Zeke nods slowly.

Conny Nygren shakes his head.

'If they haven't already killed the children. To stop them being able to testify against them.'

'We have to assume they're still alive,' Malin says. 'That the brothers are holding them somewhere. They must have heard that we've got Mirovic by now, and are probably getting pretty desperate. That makes me even more worried about the children. Up until now they've been holding them so they could blackmail Mirovic. Now the only reason for the brothers to keep them alive is that they might need them as hostages if they try to make a run for it, or have to negotiate. We have to find the brothers and the children as soon as possible. It could soon be too late.'

She doesn't want to say what she's thinking: that it could already be too late.

'The Kurtzon brothers' plan is shot to hell, and they know it,' Conny Nygren says.

'So where do we think they are? Sweden, or Thailand?' Zeke asks.

'Well, they're not at that place he mentioned, Sri Panwa, at any rate,' Conny Nygren says. 'We made a call, and they've confirmed that the brothers did rent a villa there, but that they're not there now.'

'They didn't have any other address for the brothers in Thailand?'

'No. And we haven't got any in Sweden apart from Strandvägen. No summer house owned by the family, nothing,' Conny Nygren says. 'But that doesn't necessarily mean they haven't got a place here where they're holed up. We're keeping an eye on the apartments on the off chance that they show up there.'

'But where are they right now?' Malin says.

'They must live somewhere,' Zeke says.

'Mirovic was on his way to Thailand. Do you think he knows anything he's not telling us?' Conny Nygren asks.

'He's got no reason to lie. We're his only hope.'

'Is there any point issuing an international alert?' Conny Nygren wonders.

'Yes,' Malin says. 'It's a long shot, but it might help.'

'Do you think Josef Kurtzon and Josefina Marlöw are in danger?' Conny Nygren says after a pause.

'I don't think so, the brothers have nothing to gain from harming them now,' Malin says. 'And now that we've got Mirovic behind bars, they probably haven't got anyone they could send.'

'So what do you think we should do?' Zeke asks, and Conny Nygren looks at Malin as well, as if they're both waiting for her next brilliant idea.

'Can we get a search warrant for the brothers' apartments on Strandvägen? We've got enough to justify that now, haven't we?'

'I've got good contacts in the prosecutors' office,' Conny Nygren says. 'I'll get the warrants,' and he digs his mobile out of his trouser pocket and calls straight away, and Malin thinks that she likes him, he doesn't drag his feet, and Conny Nygren is off the phone a minute later.

'All sorted.'

'Great,' Malin says, and Zeke mutters:'Damn good job.'

Malin stands up.

'Time to pick up the pace,' she says, her body racing with adrenalin, and she looks at the clock on the wall. Quarter past eight now, and outside darkness has nearly taken over.

'Have you got your pistols with you?' Conny Nygren asks.

Malin and Zeke open their jackets, showing the weapons in their shoulder holsters.

'You might need them. I'll get you some bulletproof vests.'

Conny Nygren smiles again, a crooked smile that reminds Malin of Waldemar Ekenberg's.

Do you have a penchant for violence as well? Malin wonders, but at the same moment she realises that she'd be only too happy to blow the brothers into tiny pieces.

* * *

Malin leans her head against the side window, closes her eyes and thinks about her brother, wants to see him, and he's already real inside her, in her heart, as yet another reason to go on fighting.

It doesn't matter if he can never know who I am.

Or recognise me.

Conny Nygren at the wheel.

He says: 'Malin, you know I remember you from when you were at the academy? But I don't think you remember me, do you?'

Malin is wrenched back to the present, and opens her eyes just as they're driving past the aquarium façade of Kulturhuset.

'Sorry,' Malin says. 'So when did we meet?'

'I was in charge of the shooting exercises in an authentic environment. You got to play at being tough cops, making your way into buildings and rooms where there might be armed suspects and hostages.'

'I don't remember you being there for that. But I remember the exercises.'

Maybe that training's about to come in useful? Malin thinks. It has done before.

Conny Nygren's voice again, a note of amusement in it: 'I remember you, it was like you were possessed. I don't think I've ever seen a student with such drive and determination, so much aggression, yet still under control.'

'Now you're definitely joking, it's not nice to try and ingratiate yourself!'

'You can laugh, but it's true!'

A minute later Conny Nygren pulls up outside the building on Strandvägen that houses the brothers' apartments, gets out and waves to the officers in the surveillance vehicles.

The officers wave back. Seem to be wishing them luck.

* * *

Malin picks the three locks.

The stairwell smells of mothballs and rat poison as they stand in the darkness outside Henry Kurtzon's door.

The standard lock takes her three seconds, the two 7-level tumbler locks take a quarter of an hour each. There's no sound from inside the flat, and there were no lights on in the windows.

No alarm connected.

In all likelihood, no one here.

But they can't be sure, and Zeke and Conny Nygren are standing beside the door with their pistols drawn, and Malin tries to shield herself as best she can, but can't manage to keep her body entirely out of any eventual line of fire.

Are the children in there?

Is that whimpering I can hear? Elena and Marko? No, it's just the background noise of Stockholm, isn't it?

Then the third lock clicks and she pushes the door open and Zeke and Conny Nygren rush into the darkness, weapons drawn.

Empty rooms, an empty kitchen with glistening green units, empty cupboards, empty shelves, no lamps to switch on, nobody here, unless there is someone here? Children?

Malin searches deeper inside the flat, heading for the rooms that look out onto the inner courtyard. First an empty bedroom, then a bathroom, then another door on the other side of the bathroom.

Darkness behind it.

She hears a scratching sound. I'm coming, she thinks, as she turns the key that's sitting in the lock.

Someone's coming.

Daddy, is that you coming? You have to come soon, and now the men are coming and I take hold of little brother and pull him with me into the corner because then they might not find us.

Stop it.

I don't want to.

No.

It's horrid.

What are they going to do now?

I'm hungry, and little brother's crying, and you have to come, Daddy.

Is that you coming?

The door's opening now, it mustn't be the men. They mustn't be angry. They just mustn't. Are we going to be lizard food now?

Now we're screaming.

We're screaming so we don't realise just how scared we are.

55

Empty.

An empty cupboard.

Shit.

And the scratching?

A grey-black mouse runs between Malin's feet and out into the flat, and Malin watches it run off, then goes to find Zeke and Conny Nygren standing by a window, looking out at Nybroviken, their weapons pointed at the parquet floor, hanging heavy in their hands.

There's a thick layer of dust on the white marble window-sill.

Malin runs her finger through the dust and comes to think about her mum and dad's flat on Barnhemsgatan in the years she spent looking after it for them while they were in Tenerife and never came home.

She'd had grand ambitions to start with, to keep the plants alive, hold the dust and cobwebs at bay, but gradually, as she realised that Mum and Dad were going to stay away, she gave up caring.

She let the plants die.

The dust settled in a thick layer, and when Mum died, just before Dad came home, she had cleaned the flat with a frenzy that surprised even her. It had been like a session in the gym, and the sweat had poured off her and she couldn't think about anything but the dust, about making sure the flat was spotless for Dad's sake.

But it wasn't for Dad's sake that I started cleaning.

It was for yours, Mum.

But you never came home. And I can promise that I'm never going to clean anything ever again for your sake, you're not going to follow me through life making remarks the way you used to when you followed me around the house out in Sturefors whenever I wanted to try vacuuming when I was little.

I was five years old, Mum.

And all you did was complain about the Hoover hitting the furniture, scratching the paint, as if that little house was some fucking huge palace.

And all the while you knew about your betrayal of me, of my little brother. You withdrew, but you never realised that you were withdrawn, did you? Do you have any idea what effect that had on me, do you have any idea how hard I've had to fight to maintain a presence in Tove's life? Do you have any idea? That I haven't managed to be there for her, and how that fills me with sadness and an unbearable sense of shame?

The way I've struggled to give Tove the mother I never had, and whom I spent my whole life longing for. And in spite of all that, I actually failed.

I don't feel any vacuum now that you're gone, Mum. No grief. I see your face in the darkness and feel relief that you're gone. And now I know that I might finally be able to live my own life, a life without secrets and desires that need to be suppressed without me having the faintest idea why.

You died, and I found myself, Mum.

I shall take nourishment from my unlove for you.

Does that make me a bad person?

Then Malin hears Zeke and Conny Nygren talking, but can't be bothered trying to make out the words, feels tired, is tired of this, but wants to push on, has to.

'Come on, Malin,' Zeke says. 'This one's empty. Let's try next door, Leopold Kurtzon's flat.'

When she opens the third lock on the door of Leopold Kurtzon's flat an angry ringing sound starts up.

Loudly, stabbing at her consciousness.

An alarm?

Or is the door booby-trapped? Is it about to explode?

And she sees Conny Nygren run into the darkness of the flat.

He opens a cupboard door in the hallway and finds what he's looking for.

The ringing stops.

'Alarmed,' Conny Nygren says. 'The security companies usually put the control panel inside the nearest cupboard.'

Malin carries on into the flat.

She holds her pistol out in front of her, and the adrenalin is rushing through her veins again, her recent tiredness has vanished, along with all her thoughts, and they spread out, shouting: Clear, clear, clear.

This flat is furnished.

In a pompous, nineteenth-century British style, and the walls of the rooms are lined with bookcases full of leather-bound volumes.

The same dust.

The same mustiness, yet there's still a feeling that someone has been living here.

They gather in the kitchen, and Conny Nygren says: 'We need to see if there's anything that can give us any idea of where they might be.'

They switch on all the lights.

One of Anders Zorn's paintings of girls in traditional dress.

A Carl Larsson.

Art for people who want to show how important they are.

Who want to show that they themselves represent the nation's cultural inheritance, and Malin finds it all rather tasteless, and thinks the entire flats reeks of insecurity.

They move from room to room. Opening drawers. Rifling through receipts and documents, pulling sheets and towels out of the wardrobes.

We have to find something, Malin thinks as she enters what looks like some sort of office.

A desk, but no computer. The walls empty, except for two large portraits in oil. One is of a young Josef Kurtzon.

Next to him a woman with thin lips and piercing blue eyes beneath perfectly bobbed hair. A blue Chanel dress.

The woman is standing in front of a leaded window. Water in the background.

It must be Selda Kurtzon.

Wife. Mother.

Malin looks at the portrait. So these were the people you couldn't deal with, Josefina. What did they do to you, what did their way of seeing the world do to you?

And Malin thinks about her own addiction, her longing for alcohol, and about her mum, and she thinks about her flat, and it dawns on her that she was relieved when her parents moved such an inconvenient distance away, that her drinking is a sign of exactly the same desire to run away that has characterised Josefina's life.

The difference is just a matter of degree.

And events and genes, coincidence and chance and fate, giving things a direction, and then there's a momentum that no one is able to stop, or wants to stop, or has the energy to stop.

Tove.

I haven't ruined you, have I? and she looks away from

the portraits, sees a folder on the desktop, opens it, but the folder is empty.

She yanks the desk drawers open.

Empty.

Nothing.

The last drawer.

A single photograph.

An aerial photograph of what looks like an island out in the archipelago. A large house, painted white, that looks as if it's been built into the rock. The house looks new, and there's a bridge leading to the mainland. Several rectangular white outbuildings down by the water. The picture was taken in the autumn, the woodlands on the island and those around it are glowing like fire, as if flames wanted to devour the buildings in the picture.

Why is this photograph here? Does the island belong to the brothers? Is that where they are?

Malin holds her breath.

Turns the photograph over.

Blank. Nothing. It could be anywhere.

She calls Zeke and Conny Nygren in.

Shows them the picture.

'What do you make of this?'

'Could that be one of their houses?'

Conny Nygren is animated, alert even though it's starting to get late.

'Impossible to say,' Zeke says.

'Could that be where they're holding the children?' Malin asks.

'It's a picture of a house, an island a hell of a lot further north than Thailand,' Zeke says. 'And the Mirovic kids are supposed to have been kidnapped from Phuket. Why would they be in Sweden, on an island, if this photograph is actually anywhere in Sweden?'

'They could have brought the children to Sweden,' Conny Nygren says. 'Either on a regular flight, or by chartering a plane.'

'The problem is that we have no idea where this photo was taken. Even if a long shot like this turned out to be true,' Zeke says. 'We haven't found any property registered under the brothers' names in any database.'

Just as Zeke finishes this last sentence, Malin's mobile rings.

Johan Jakobsson's name on the screen.

Couldn't bear to go home.

Couldn't bear to see his own children when others are in such obvious danger, and maybe, just maybe he can do something about it. So Johan Jakobsson has been sitting at his computer in the police station, tired from a day of paperwork and meaningless interviews with left- and right-wing activists whose names had been mentioned in anonymous tip-offs.

He's searched through the property register again, cross-checking transactions against each other, typing in the names of all the companies the Kurtzon brothers have been involved in, any name he could think of that resembled the names of those companies.

Nothing.

It was as if the Kurtzon family, the brothers, didn't exist as anything more than shadows in Stockholm, as ghosts wherever there was money to be found.

Then he remembered something he had read in a profile of Josef Kurtzon in *Svenska Dagbladet*, about the man being eccentric and keeping large lizards as pets. And there was that picture of Selda Kurtzon taking a lizard for a walk in that old gossip magazine.

Surely you need an import licence for large lizards?

Johan wondered. Assuming that they were actually legally allowed into the country at all.

One last chance.

The characters on the computer screen were starting to blur, and he had three messages on his phone from his wife, presumably wanting him to go home.

But he logged into the website of the Customs Office, and the only existing import licence for live lizards had been issued to a company by the name of Exotic Animals ten years ago.

One of the brothers' companies.

Exotic Animals went out of business in 2003. But there was an address on the licence that hadn't appeared anywhere else.

Number 37, Lundviksvägen.

In Norrhammar.

Where's that?

He looked it up on Google Maps.

Norrhammar council district, one hundred and sixty kilometres north of Norrtälje, almost two hundred and fifty kilometres from where Malin is. That's north of Stockholm, isn't it?

No match for number 37. But the satellite image of the road ends with a small island in the archipelago, with a large white building in the middle of the island, and outhouses down by the water. The island ought logically to be number 37, seeing as number 35 lay some two kilometres back through the forest.

And who owns that property now? Johan logged back into the land registry and typed in the address, but there was nothing registered at number 37 Lundviksvägen, it was as if the address had ceased to exist, or had never actually existed.

But the house on the satellite picture in front of him had to be number 37. Didn't it?

Can a property simply vanish from every register? From reality? Possibly, if you really want to be left alone, and if you bribe the right officials.

That picture of Leopold Kurtzon in the *Wall Street Journal*. It had looked as if it had been taken in warmer climes. Johan clicked his way to the picture again.

Studied it carefully. Sure, it looked like the Caribbean, but it could have been anywhere, with a bit of retouching.

It could be the Swedish archipelago. In soft light. And the reporter who had agreed not to reveal the location for the interview. The photographer's name, Swedish: Stefan Björck.

The telephone directory.

A minute later he was talking to the photographer. A pleasant, helpful man, who said: 'I remember it well. I took the pictures on some island north of Norrtälje. They retouched them. I got the impression that they owned the place. Leopold Kurtzon and his brother. They treated me like I didn't exist. And there was something really weird about it. Of all things, they kept big lizards on the island.'

Johan hung up, stared out across the almost deserted open-plan office, thinking about Jokso Mirovic and the fact that the Kurtzon brothers might have his children. The way Jokso Mirovic had actually murdered other children in a calculated effort to save his own.

I would have done the same, Johan thinks, if it had been my children.

Leopold Kurtzon in the picture.

His brother in Johan's mind's eye.

Those children have to be rescued. I don't give a damn about what happens to you.

Then he called Malin, noting that it was already eleven o'clock.

★   ★   ★

'That's the best I can give you,' Johan Jakobsson says. 'A property that doesn't exist except in a photograph, and the photographer's statement that it might belong to the brothers. They could be holding the children there.'

Zeke and Conny Nygren are sitting silently beside Malin.

Johan has just given her directions of how to find the island, and Malin has a feeling that this could be right, the brothers could have brought the children to Sweden, they could be holding them in a house that doesn't exist, yet still exists.

The lizard in Josef Kurtzon's room.

The import licence.

More lizards.

The peculiar logic of evil.

Are there lizards on the island now?

'We'll set off at once,' Malin says. 'It really is our only hope, it's all we've got, isn't it?'

Johan mutters in agreement at the other end of the line.

'Good work,' Malin says. 'Damn good work.'

'I'm going to head home to the kids now,' Johan says, and hangs up.

56

Leopold Kurtzon's mood sinks slightly as he sees his own face reflected in the screen of the laptop; his thin, pointed nose seems to dissolve in the reflection, as though his time is running out. The computer is sitting on a desk in a room on the second floor of the house.

Jokso Mirovic has been caught. So the police probably know everything by now.

Jokso Mirovic.

There's an archive picture of him halfway down the main page of the *Dagens Nyheter* website, under the heading: Hitman caught at Arlanda. Suspected of Involvement in the Linköping Bombing.

Leopold reads on.

'Unconfirmed sources suggest that Jokso Mirovic carried out the job on the orders of two brothers in financial circles . . .'

Even though he suspected that the police were onto them now, it's still a shock to read it on the *DN* website. It feels like being hit twice, once in the gut, and once in the heart, and now he knows for sure that everything has gone to hell, that Jokso Mirovic has told his story to the police, and now it's only a matter of time before they find their way here, isn't it?

Before they catch us. And we'll get life imprisonment. Thirty years. I'll be an old man by the time we get out.

But then his mood rises again, he pulls a face, as

energy and determination reassume their places inside him.

Because how could they find us here?

No one knows we've got this place.

By putting money in the right pockets, absolutely anything can be erased. A patch of land, a house? No problem. Father sorted that out, wanted to have a place that existed yet didn't, and he let us take it over, ordered us to get hold of monitor lizards from Asia, to keep the beautiful, prehistoric creatures on the island. Try to breed them. 'Maybe you can succeed at that, even though you've failed at everything else.'

Leopold goes out onto one of the house's terraces.

Looks down towards the outhouses where they keep the animals.

He hates going down there, even when the creatures are full and sluggish and resting in their cages under the light of the heat-lamps. When they're hungry they gnaw like mad on the bars of their cages, trying to get out.

They bought them in Thailand and Indonesia, set up a company purely for the purpose, and got hold of an import licence. Then they shut down the company, claimed that the creatures had been put down, and no one seemed to care.

They take turns feeding them. That was a while ago now, because neither of them wants to go down to the lizards in the outhouses, neither of them wants to see the snapping, greedy jaws.

And the man who helps them with the creatures when they're away, often for long periods, he stays quiet, is so well paid that he never says anything to anyone, and he seems scared of the brothers. They've told him not to come back again until they call him.

Then Leopold suffers a moment of doubt again.

Who knows how the police work, who knows what they might dig out, and how, when they really have to and want to?

We're responsible for four murders.

We're pariahs.

The money won't come to us. We can never show ourselves in public again.

And the police must know about the children, and kidnapped children are top priority.

Like murder.

They're not going to drop the case.

Everything's fucked. What are we going to do now? What the hell are we going to do now?

Leopold doesn't want to think about it, but knows he has to.

Think logically now, Leopold.

Rationally.

He feels the chill from the sea and the surrounding forest, but it doesn't take hold; as usual it's warmer here than in most other places, a peculiar microclimate.

He looks down towards the buildings where they keep the lizards again, and suddenly the thought of them makes him feel safer, knowing that Father is aware that they've got the creatures here, and that they've actually succeeded in breeding them, even if all the female lizard's young had died after just a week or so.

Then Leopold suddenly hears the lizards hissing and banging against their bars.

And he is filled with terror.

Are they about to gnaw their way out? Creep about in the forest, find their way up to the terraces of the houses and attack them?

But they can't get out.

Can they?

Leopold tries to forget about the lizards and looks at his brother Henry lying on the sofa, listlessly drinking a glass of Coca-Cola, and Leopold calls him over.

Reluctantly his brother gets up.

They go off to the kitchen, and as they stand beside the Gaggenau units Leopold tells Henry what he's seen on the Net, then says: 'We have to kill them now, then we get away from here.'

At first Henry feels scared by how cool his brother seems, then he realises he's right, his conclusion is the logical one. Kill the children, bury them, or give them to the lizards, let the carrion-eating creatures do the work, two small children could disappear without a trace here. Or just blow them up. Simple, so simple.

They were frightened when he last went down to them. Screaming.

As if to drown out their fear.

To get the better of it.

Both he and Leopold have already felt anger building up inside themselves. Who do these kids think they are? The sort of people who can get the Kurtzon brothers to back down and go soft? Huh? Whatever gave them that idea? Do they really doubt that we're tough, efficient?

We have to get rid of them.

But still Henry says: 'Do we have to kill them?'

Leopold's face contorts into a grimace, his eyes take on that focused look they always get when he's convinced of something, as he often is, much more often than Henry, who is occasionally doubt personified.

'Have you got a better suggestion?' Leopold asks. 'OK, we might need them as hostages, but they're still more of a hindrance alive.'

'But do the kids have to die? Isn't everything pretty much lost anyway?'

'We play this out to the end,' Leopold says. 'Do you want to spend thirty years in prison?'

'No. No. It was a stupid plan from the start,' Henry says, and sees his brother's eyes boil with fury and frustration.

'We knew exactly what we were doing when we kidnapped them on Phuket and chartered the plane to bring them up here. Didn't we?' he screams. 'It wasn't a stupid plan. Should we just have given up? You knew what you were doing when you sedated them before the flight and paid off the pilot.'

Henry stays quiet.

Then he says: 'And now we're going to end up with nothing.'

'But we can show Father how strong we are,' Leopold says.

And in what ought to be a moment of panic, a sense of calm settles, rather like the stories he's heard about the sinking of the *Titanic*, when the passengers calmly awaited their fate and let the ship sink without panic breaking out.

Or the *Estonia*.

Similar stories when that sank.

'We could let them live,' Henry says. 'Just let them go. Leave the house, let someone find them. They're three and six years old, we can't kill them.'

'We have to.'

'Why?'

'To show how strong we are. How powerful. Show the whole world.'

And Henry looks at his brother, at the unshakeable clarity in his eyes, and his reasoning does seem to hold a certain cruel justice.

No one ever gets out of their own cramped, dark room.

No one who has been there will ever raise their eyes to the sky again.

Instead there is the desire, the greed for something else.

'So where are we going to go afterwards?' Henry asks.

'We clear out. Let the timer count down. Wipe out everything that could prove we were ever here.'

'Where do we clear out to?'

'We'll take the motorboat to Estonia. Straight across the Baltic, the boat can go much further than that on a full tank. Then we sort out a flight to South America. Or Asia. The world's a big place. We've got enough money here to last a long time.'

'OK. We'll do as you say.'

'Good. But first we have to kill the kids,' Leopold whispers.

'Can't we just leave them to die in the explosion?'

'Now, we have to do it, you have to do it, so we know they're dead. Those kids down in the cellar have to die, and we have to do it.'

Henry finally nods.

He raises and lowers his head over and over again, and they go up to the next floor, to the unused fourth bedroom, open the wardrobe and take out the pistols and sub-machine guns.

They stand there with the guns in their hands in the dim light of the bedroom.

They look at each other.

Have only each other.

Are each other.

Hug each other, and feel their blood flow become one and the same, and doubt and determination, love and hate, good and evil, greed and generosity all melt together into a single quality that has no name, running through them, quick and clear.

And then the brothers pull free of each other's arms, go down to the bottom floor of the house, the one that's half-hidden below ground, dug into the rock of the steep slope the house is built on.

They open the door that leads to the room where they've got the children locked up.

They hear the ticking.

Have to sort that out.

They made a fuss to start with. In spite of the crayons they were given.

But we put a stop to that, Leopold thinks. Almost, at least. We knew how to do that. They got to experience our fury.

It's quiet in there now. They're not even whimpering. They can't have any screaming left in their lungs. Just mute fear.

The brothers release the safety catches of their guns.

And open the final door.

The one that leads into the chamber of darkness.

The door that leads to the children.

57

There's a faint, almost rumbling sound from the car's engine.

They're already past Norrtälje, and are driving straight through the deep forests that skirt the coast, and the trees become ghosts in the night, seem to be smirking at Malin even though she can't see the faces of the trunks.

Zeke behind the wheel.

Focused. Conny Nygren has gone home, she didn't want him to come with them, and he protested at first, but eventually gave in. It's unlikely that the brothers and children are even at the property north of Norrtälje. The most likely reason the property isn't listed in the property register is simple administrative error.

I want to do this myself, Malin thinks. I have to. And if the brothers are there with the children, it would be better to creep up on them under cover of night. Wouldn't it?

Zeke appears to think the same.

Malin shuts her eyes.

The explosion in the square has thrown me into the air, she thinks. The pressure wave is carrying me deep into the darkness of Sweden: at first everything expanded in volume, spreading out, and now it's contracting again.

What are we going to find? Are the brothers even there, and do the children exist at all?

But she knew that Jokso Mirovic was telling the truth about his children.

The desperation in his eyes couldn't be fake. The recording was genuine.

'Daddy . . . Daddy . . .'

But Elena and Marko could be absolutely anywhere in the world. Maybe Thailand? Still out there somewhere? Or dead, dead for several days now.

In this short space of time they haven't been able to find even the smallest electronic trace of the brothers. No email traffic, no mobile calls, no credit cards in their names had been used.

Nothing.

Try to sleep, Malin. Get an hour's rest before you get there. Make sure you're alert then.

Zeke's hands firmly on the wheel.

Silence in the car. They should get there just after midnight.

Sleep soon comes to her, and the reclining seat brings the strangest dreams, streams woven by the chill of the spring night.

The faces of the Vigerö girls.

White, pure, guiltless, and they talk to her from the darkness of the dream.

Is it too late, Malin, is it too late? We know, but we daren't say.

'It isn't too late,' Malin says, but her voice isn't her own, it's Tove's.

'It isn't too late,' and the girls laugh and then they vanish and are replaced by two silhouettes in a dark room, stretching their arms out towards her.

'Where are you, where are you?' and she can see Josefina Marlöw in her underground room, and in the dream she's stretching her arms out towards her father, and towards her mother, and they respond, but their embrace is made of red-hot metal in the shape of rose thorns.

Are there actually any children?

Do Elena and Marko exist?

And Hanna Vigerö is there, a man beside her who must be her husband, and she says: *They exist, Malin, they exist, but where are they, we haven't found the girls, and we desperately want to.*

Isn't that what death is supposed to be, a place where only love exists?

Then her sleep turns black, and she shouts into her own dream, has to find out before it's too late: 'What about my brother? Is he OK?'

And the girls, and the pale, faceless children whisper: *He's OK, but he's alone, and he's waiting for you to go to him.*

Börje Svärd is pacing up and down in his kitchen.

Johan Jakobsson called him half an hour or so ago to tell him that Malin and Zeke were on their way to an island in the archipelago where there was a small chance that the brothers were hiding, and that they might be holding Jokso Mirovic's children there.

The whole of the investigating team has been informed about events in Stockholm, and he has a feeling the case is moving towards its conclusion.

And it turned out to be nothing to do with Islamic extremists, political activists or biker gangs.

His first reaction when he heard about Malin and Zeke's nocturnal excursion was that it was madness to head out there alone, without back-up, but then it occurred to him that it was very unlikely the children and the brothers were actually there, and if they were there, maybe a small-scale operation made more sense, just two officers who could get on with the job calmly and quietly.

And he knows Malin. Knows her well enough to know that she would want to do something like this herself, she's almost obsessively independent, and Sven Sjöman has a tendency to let her have her own way on occasions like this. Sven evidently thought it was OK for them to head out there tonight.

But still.

He can't help feeling worried. Whatever he may think, there's a chance that Malin is getting close, and that might mean it gets dangerous.

The house feels empty without Anna.

But her spirit hovers over the decor, a hundred times more tasteful than anything he could have come up with.

Then his phone rings.

Waldemar Ekenberg's name on the screen.

Waldemar Ekenberg is standing in the kitchen, smoking a cigarette under the extractor fan above the cooker, trying to let what Börje Svärd is saying calm him down, but it's not working.

'Shouldn't Stockholm be sending back-up?'

'You know what Malin's like.'

'Shall we get in the car and go after them?'

'It's too late for that, isn't it? Anyway, it's probably a dead end.'

'The Kurtzons are rich fuckers,' Waldemar says, taking a last drag on the cigarette. 'If they get a whiff of money, or even worse, get it into their heads that they're going to lose their money, then anything could happen, you know that as well as I do.'

'They can handle it,' Börje says, sounding as if he's trying to convince himself. 'Zeke's a tough bastard.'

'Let's just hope they kill them if they manage to find them,' Waldemar says, hoping that Börje is going to contradict him.

'Yes, there won't be any witnesses, after all,' he says instead.

'You're pretty hard,' Waldemar says.

'And unlike you, I'm properly hard,' Börje replies. 'And that means I can afford to be soft sometimes.'

'So you're a philosopher too?'

'Have a whisky.'

Waldemar grins.

'Listen, my head's still thumping from last time.'

Malin wakes up to hear her mobile ringing.

She might have been asleep for an hour or so in the reclined car seat, and before she answers, it occurs to her that they must be close now.

Tove's voice.

'Mum, where are you? I've been trying to call.'

Malin tells her what she's doing, that the investigation has led her north, out to the archipelago. But that she should be home tomorrow.

'I miss you,' Tove says. 'And when you get home we're going to Hälsingland. To see my uncle, your little brother.'

'Yes, we are,' Malin says.

'You've got to let me go with you.'

And Malin detects a lack of trust in Tove's voice, and it strikes her that she's heading out into the night, possibly putting herself in mortal danger, without sparing a thought for her daughter, and that she'd be motherless if anything happened. But Tove isn't a child any more, she's probably more grown up and sensible than I am.

'Of course you're coming with me,' Malin says. 'I'd never go and see him without you.'

Tove hangs up.

And Malin feels her anxieties about going to Hälsingland to see her brother fading away. Thanks to hearing Tove's voice just now.

Tove sounded as if she doesn't really care about where I am and what I'm doing. But of course she has her own life to live. Presumably she hasn't got the energy to feign a load of feelings just to show how worried she is about her mum. She didn't even seem to consider the possibility that I might be heading off on a dangerous job.

Another car comes towards them.

The driver leaves his lights on full beam, and Malin sees Zeke squint, but keeps her own eyes wide open.

Light.

Stronger light.

And then the solid dark of blindness.

And Malin feels it, knows they're on the right track, they're going to rescue the children.

They're going to rescue Elena and Marko.

It can't be too late.

Terror, have you made it your servant?

Josef Kurtzon stares out into the darkness of his cataracts. Knows that everything has reached its endgame, knows that life is a game that you must never stop playing.

Weakness, what can we do with that? With uncertainty?

I toy with it, he thinks, as a jolt of pain hits his airways and his body is racked with coughs that almost burst the lining of his lungs.

I've never stopped playing. The pleasure has always been on my side, just like it is now, on this night when everything is moving towards its dark conclusion.

The stuffed lizard hisses by his side. He pats it in his imagination, stroking its cold skin, and looks out into the darkness.

His blindness is a white blindness.

He isn't afraid of the dark. He's sought it his whole life, made it his own.

Josefina.

Leopold.

Henry.

The twin girls, Tuva and Mira.

The other children.

Tell me, has there ever been a more grandiose game?

He closes his blind eyes. Tries to imagine what is about to happen. Takes pleasure in what has been his life's work.

58

It hadn't worked.

They had turned on the lights in the room where they were holding the children, saw the fuzzy drawings they'd made on the walls, saw them open their eyes in utter terror, heard them scream, saw them hold their arms up, then hug each other, and the brothers had aimed their guns at them, but they hadn't been able to shoot.

Henry and Leopold Kurtzon had yelled at each other. Their voices merging, impossible to tell apart.

'Do it!'

'Shoot!'

'This is your job!'

'Kill them, shoot for fuck's sake!' But neither of them had been able to pull the trigger.

Hiring someone to kill someone, to kill children, was an entirely different matter from killing someone yourself. Things that happened at a distance were strangely fictional. The reality was something else.

The children on their own inside the room. Silent. Somehow blind.

And Leopold and Henry had looked at the little bodies in the darkness, and then the brothers had started shouting again: 'You've got to shoot. We can't leave it like this.'

But then Henry had changed his tune, and said: 'We have to let them live.'

'We have to kill them,' Leopold had screamed.

'I can't do it. You do it.'

'If we don't kill them, we'll never be free of them.'

'Look how scared and lonely they are!'

'Then I'll kill you.'

'You can't. You know you can't. We'll leave them here. We can't abandon each other.'

And Leopold had looked at his brother, realised he was right, and then he had nodded, yes, we'll leave the children here, who could have expected anything different, I'm backing down, the way I always have, I'm nothing.

The brothers had slammed the door shut, leaving the children alone in the room, then rushed up to the terrace, throwing their guns on the stone floor, and looked out at the dark garden, the black, almost still sea, and down at the outhouses containing the beasts. They could hear a strange banging on the door of one of the buildings, and desperation had started to creep up on them, and for a few moments they were transformed into nothing but survival instinct.

What do we do now, should we leave, should we leave them here, but where are we going, should we shoot ourselves, let the children live, or should we shoot them first, and then ourselves?

Questions that go around in circles.

Everything they thought they knew just a few moments ago, down in the basement, returns in the form of new questions, impossible to unravel.

No matter what they did, however much they might try to eradicate their own capacity for empathy, a tiny fragment remained, infuriating them.

That's not who we are.

We are mathematics.

Rationality.

And the bomb ticking outside the room. The one they

had had made for them in Bangkok, before the kidnapping in Phuket, powerful enough to blow the whole house into tiny fragments. The pilot of the charterplane had no idea that it was in their bags. Kidnapped children are one thing. But a bomb?

They had landed at Gävle Airport, and then brought the children here. Back then the brothers had been exhilarated: We can do this, it's going to work.

They had more or less ignored the bomb for the past twenty-four hours, as if they couldn't quite bring themselves to think about it. Somehow letting the threat of their own and the children's impending death hang in the air.

Should they set the bomb off? Only another hour or so to go before the timer needs to be reset again.

'We're leaving now,' Leopold had yelled.

'Shouldn't we let the kids go anyway?' Henry had said.

'We have to kill them.'

'That's what Father would do, isn't it?'

And they had gone back down to the basement again, opened all the doors, pulled the children out, and dragged them up to the living room.

First they had checked the timer on the bomb, and put it back a bit, to give themselves some more time. Now that the sea was so calm, they would surely be able to make their way across the Baltic to Estonia.

The children had been silent.

Not even the three-year-old had made a sound, and maybe they were beyond fear, beyond life even before they died.

They stank when the brothers brought them out. Their bodies were covered in ingrained brown dirt, and they looked more like animals than small people.

'Shouldn't we take them with us?' Henry had asked. 'Use them as hostages?'

'Any benefit would be outweighed by the fact that they'd slow us down, and if the police catch us we'll spend a lifetime in prison,' Leopold had replied, and Henry had realised that his brother was right. They had to do what they had to do.

The brothers had each sat down with one of the children in their laps, hugging them to calm them down. And then they had aimed their pistols at the children's temples.

59

They turned off to the right, down towards the sea, which should be just a few kilometres away to the east.

Empty country cottages in among the trees. They pass a sign pointing to an old summer camp for children, fifteen kilometres away.

Their satnav is pointing them in the right direction.

Their movement into the darkness is being registered on the colourful screen lighting up the interior of the car.

'What do you reckon, then?' Zeke asks. 'Are they going to be there?'

Malin can feel the cold pistol against her chest. Says: 'I don't know, but it feels right.'

They drive past what should be the last house before number 37, the house that doesn't exist, yet apparently does.

The headlights shine into the forest, the vegetation thickens, becomes almost tropical, but surely there can't be palm trees here?

No: pine trees, firs, dense clusters of pitch-black ferns, and the sense of being in an ancient forest is tangible, then overwhelming, and they drive a few more kilometres before the road reaches the sea. It's lighter here, and Zeke switches off the headlights to conceal their arrival, just in case anyone is looking out for them.

They drive around a headland, then into a small inlet, heading slowly along the uneven gravel track, and then the island rises up in front of them, and the tall fir trees

surrounding the main house that they can just make out
deep within the woods become the turrets and towers of
an imaginary castle.

Lights in the windows.

Someone's there.

The brothers?

The children?

Human beings, imposing themselves on nature.

Tearing out the vegetation, setting down their roots, then
recreating the greenery they've destroyed in order to live
in close proximity to monsters.

There's something about this place. The vibrations the
island is emitting.

No one should have settled here.

Nature should have been left in peace.

Malin and Zeke have parked some two hundred metres
from the bridge leading to the island. Have crept up to the
two-metre-high gate, surrounded by barbed wire.

Malin peers into the darkness, looking for surveillance
cameras, but there aren't any there.

No signs on the gate. No letterbox. Nothing to suggest
who or what is hiding out on the island.

She can hear Zeke's breathing beside her. Heavy, almost
rattling, and if breathing can sound angry, then Zeke's does
now.

'Bloody hell,' he says. 'What a fucking place, do you feel
it, Malin? It's like the sea itself smells sulphurous, not salty
and fresh, but sulphurous.'

'It feels humid as well,' Malin says. 'And warmer than
it should do, doesn't it? As if the spring night is somehow
warmer here.'

The clock in the car had said a quarter to one as they
left it at the edge of the forest.

No sign of anyone out on the island.

No one.

Her pistol.

Am I going to have to use it? Malin wonders.

Maybe. The children are here. The brothers. I can feel it, and Malin and Zeke haven't discussed what to do, but without saying a word Zeke takes off his jacket and throws it over the barbed wire on top of the gate.

'Do you think the fabric's enough to cover the wire?'

Malin shakes her head, aware that they can't stay here by the gate, exposed, they have to move on.

'But we can't shoot the lock off.'

'Fuck it,' Zeke says, then swings himself up onto the gate, grabs his jacket, and he's lucky, there are no spikes where he puts his fingers, then he's over.

Malin follows his example.

Manages to avoid the barbed wire, and they press on, across the bridge, towards the large house on the island, it looks like a huge sugarlump that someone has rammed into a steep rockface.

A jetty.

A large motorboat rocking, pale against the dark water.

Is there rain in the air? The sky above them is dark, no stars.

Outhouses to one side of the main house. One door is open, and is that the sound of scratching coming from the oblong buildings?

They run across the bridge, then they're on the other side, on the island, Malin moving soundlessly behind Zeke, who's drawn his pistol and tucked himself behind a tree trunk, and she sees something coming towards them, a large, slithering creature, and she feels like screaming, and sees Zeke switch on the pocket torch she saw him tuck into his belt before they left the car.

The creature's red eyes burn in the night.

Its yellow teeth gleam.

Its striped body glistens.

She throws herself behind Zeke, and can feel how scared they both are.

A lizard.

A huge, live lizard with a black and yellow body, skin that looks impregnable.

And then another one, and the creatures hiss at them. Hungry prehistoric lizards. The brothers are here, Malin is sure of it now, and the animals move to attack them, and Zeke shines the torch right into the eyes of the largest lizard, and Malin wants to scream and run, but they stay where they are, stay silent, and Zeke moves the torch quickly, and a miracle happens.

The creatures' bodies quiver.

Turn around.

And they head off into the darkness. Find somewhere to lie in wait. Wait for the next opportunity to tear someone or something to pieces.

The torch goes out.

Malin and Zeke look at each other in the darkness.

Shake their heads, before Zeke gestures towards the house and they set off.

The brothers are sitting on the sofa in the larger of the villa's living rooms. Exhausted.

They've gathered their things, taken out the case with the money, and are grabbing a few minutes' rest before making their way down to the boat by the jetty.

They need to get going now.

The bomb.

It ought to go off more or less as they get on the boat. In ten minutes.

Not with a bang, but a whimper, Leopold thinks.

They've closed the heavy white curtains, turned out the lights, and darkness has taken hold of the room.

They've put their pistols down. They're shimmering blackly on the glass tabletop. They sit in silence, not talking to each other.

They listen to the room.

Was that something moving out in the garden just now? Have the lizards managed to gnaw their way out? God knows, they've tried.

And that light the brothers thought they could see has gone. Maybe it was never there?

They discussed whether to call their father, tell him everything, but is he even still alive? Or has the cancer taken him at last?

What have we done?

Who are we?

What are we?

They weren't able to shoot in the end. Unable to do what they had forced someone else to do.

While they had thought they were united in decisiveness, all they found was indecision, then a deep, all-enveloping sense of shame.

They had put the children back in the room. Now they'll be blown up along with the rest of the house. Buried among the rubble.

Then there's a muffled thud from the terrace, and the brothers stand up at the same moment, go over to the glass wall and push the curtain aside.

The lizard is almost two metres long from nose to tail, and it shines darkly as it forces its body across the white stone of the terrace. It must have clambered up the rock-face and somehow found its way onto the terrace.

It catches sight of them through the glass. Stops, turns

its head towards them, then it opens its jaws, and they can almost smell the stench of the creature's empty stomach, hear its claws scratching against the stone.

The creature remains motionless.

Stares at them with a dead look in its yellow eyes, and for a moment the brothers think it's their father's pet, the beast that used to scratch at the door of the cellar out on Lidingö, but they know that animal's dead, was stuffed years ago, that its open jaws are now an empty gesture rather than any real danger or cause for alarm.

The animals in their cages. In order to get their hands on this place, they had to have them. But here at the house, on the loose, dangerous – they're not supposed to be here.

'Fuck off!' Leopold yells.

'Go away,' Henry whispers.

And the monster crawls away, heaving its bulk over the edge of the terrace and down into the wilderness of the garden below.

Then it's gone, but at that moment Leopold Kurtzon sees a shadow, faintly picked out in the light from the windows.

The shadow of someone moving across the terrace. Isn't it?

But he can't see anyone. Has Father died and come back as a ghost? Is everything too late now? Is it too late to run? And the bomb. There can't be more than a few minutes before it goes off. We have to get out of here.

Get them now.

Kill them.

Wipe our horrible uncles and all that they bear within them from the face of the earth.

Complete our vengeance, Malin Fors, as you now approach the horror.

The core of cruelty.

The evil of evils, that which takes over when evil's attempts at dissembling come to an end, the evil created when children are abandoned to their pain.

But don't let yourself be content with that.

After you've destroyed them, dig downwards, dig out the truth.

Dig out the children, the goodness in yourself.

But kill our real mummy's brothers, Malin. Kill them, they're cruel, kill them for our sake, for Mummy's, for Daddy's.

Of course, perhaps they are to be pitied, but everyone has a responsibility towards all children, all people.

And be quick, Malin.

Because even if we're envious of the captive boy and girl, we want them to carry on living.

The clock is ticking. Time will soon run out. Hurry, Malin, hurry!

'They're coming,' Leopold Kurtzon whispers to his brother, 'they're coming. It must be the police.'

'What are we going to do?' Henry Kurtzon asks, nodding, aware that the animal-keeper would never enter their domain without ringing at the door first. And the gate on the bridge is locked.

It must be the police. Or someone else who wants to catch them.

Leopold whispers: 'We carry on to the end, just as we planned. We shoot our way out, then we head straight down to the boat.'

And Henry follows him as they creep deeper into the room, pick up their pistols, take the safety catches off the sub-machine guns, and barricade themselves behind the big white sofa and wait.

Then the shadow becomes a black outline through the white curtain. Something dark against the darkness.

One person, then another, and they aim their pistols at the shadows.

But they don't fire.

They feel their fingers on the triggers, but they can't fire, and then the first shadow comes back, or is it the second, and finally Leopold does squeeze the trigger, and the room shimmers with noise, and the glass in the sliding door shatters into a thousand splinters that rain to the ground.

Malin and Zeke had crossed the plot, creeping from tree to tree, peering up at the light coming from the uppermost of the house's two terraces, and trying to keep an eye out for the nightmarish lizards that had appeared out of the darkness a short while before.

As they got closer they could see the splendour of the house in spite of the darkness.

It was built of concrete, cedar wood, and marble, a freeform style, with a number of subterranean levels blasted into the steep slope the house was built on.

Single-storey white outhouses down by the water.

Is that where they keep the lizards? Malin had wondered.

They had crept up to the front door on the ground floor of the house. Locked. No cameras there either.

Then they had scrambled up the rockface, and from there dropped onto the top terrace.

Are you here? Malin asked herself as she landed as quietly as possible on the white stone of the terrace.

Marko and Elena? Are you here? Or is this just a dream? The sudden exertion on top of her tiredness was making her feel giddy, her brain seemed sluggish, and she could hear Zeke panting from the effort.

The villa must have a floor area of at least five hundred square metres, she thought.

'What do we do?' Zeke had asked as she was catching her breath.

They had crept across the terrace with their pistols drawn, looking through the windows into an empty kitchen. The sliding door was locked and they didn't want to make a noise trying to break in, or risk the sound of breaking glass. Then they had passed a glass wall covered on the inside by white curtains.

From there they had made their way down a flight of concrete steps to a second terrace.

More glass walls, curtains. A flowerbed some ten metres below them.

What's behind this glass wall? Malin had thought. Is this house actually empty, is there no one here? Then they had crept back under the protection of the shadows, whispering their doubts to each other, and made their way back up to the top terrace, having agreed that they needed to break into the house.

As they were passing the white curtains a second time, the world exploded, and Malin felt bullets flying past her temple, then she heard Zeke cry out.

In the darkness, Malin can see Zeke lying on the white stone of the terrace, blood pouring out of him, but she can't see where from, and she snakes her way towards shelter as bullets fly above her head, above Zeke, and she looks in past the shredded curtains, through where there had been glass just moments before, and sees a table, and a white sofa about twenty metres long lining the wall of the room.

They're hiding behind it.

It has to be the Kurtzon brothers, and she empties her clip towards the sofa, then pushes a new one in as Zeke clutches his arm.

Has his artery been hit?

If it has, he'll die here.

In which case he doesn't have much time left.

And Malin fires off two more shots before leaping up in a flash and rushing towards the sofa, and she sees two figures dressed in black race towards a staircase, and she fires at them, one, two shots, but they disappear down the stairs, and she rushes after them, past an open case full of green dollar bills, and notes in currencies she doesn't recognise. She tries to present as small a target as possible, she can't get hit now, and the stairs lead towards the lower terrace, and she sees the brothers over by some steps that lead further down, and screams: 'Stop, or I'll shoot!'

And one of the brothers turns around, raises what looks like some sort of automatic weapon towards Malin, and is just about to fire when she squeezes the trigger of her pistol, praying that it's not too late, either for her or Zeke or the children, the missing, lonely children who could be here somewhere.

They might not be dead.

Please, let them not be dead.

Zeke holds his arm as he hears shots from an automatic weapon down by the lower terrace.

Did I hear pistol shots as well?

Malin.

Did they get you?

I have to save you.

Shit, I'm bleeding badly.

The tops of the firs and pines sway in the wind. He takes a firm grip on his arm. Can I stem the blood somehow?

If the bullet hit my artery, I'm finished. But I have to save Malin.

He gets to his feet.

Picks up his pistol.

Hurries over to the far end of the terrace, towards the place where the gunfire came from.

He fell.

Whichever one of the brothers was holding the sub-machine gun fell, firing up at the sky as she hit him in the leg, and now he's lying on the terrace clutching one of his knees, without making a sound, as the marble under him turns red.

And now the other brother slowly raises his pistol towards her, and Malin can't see his face, which one is it, who am I about to be shot by, or who am I about to shoot?

She hesitates.

Then she fires, but her pistol clicks, and now she can see the man's face, he's smiling, his finger stroking the trigger, and Malin is sure she's about to die, but then a shot rings out, and she sees the man fall backwards over the low railing of the terrace, down into the garden, landing in the flowerbed ten metres below.

She hears Zeke call in a weak voice: 'Are you there, Malin? Are you OK?'

'I'm OK,' and she rushes over to the other man, who has let go of his knee and is trying to crawl forward to reach the machinegun a metre or so away from him.

One of the Kurtzon brothers.

A pointed nose. She can see that from his profile. Leopold, this must be Leopold Kurtzon.

She kicks the gun away from him, leans cautiously over the railing, and ten metres below she sees the man she presumes must be Henry Kurtzon, his body like a crushed flower among the plants.

His eyes are open.

Lifeless.

And one of the huge lizards is eating his leg, tearing at his body, silently but with a frenzy the like of which Malin has never seen before.

More lizards appear.

Their jaws open. Their bodies move. They rip the human body apart, hissing with delight and fury.

Malin turns away.

'Are you OK?'

She hears Zeke's voice behind her.

'Yes,' she shouts. 'How about you?'

'At first I thought the bullet had gone through the artery, but it hasn't. I can stem the bleeding if I put enough pressure on my arm.'

'Keep an eye on this one,' Malin says, kicking the man at her feet. 'I'll check the house.'

The man on the ground looks up at her.

With a peculiar smile that looks like a grimace in the darkness.

As if he knows something she doesn't.

'Which one are you, Henry or Leopold?' Malin hisses, her voice ice-cold. Wants to know for sure, even though she recognises Leopold Kurtzon from his passport photograph.

'Leopold. Does it matter?'

'I'll take care of him. Go and find the children,' Zeke says. 'Find them.'

60

Malin rushes through the house, searching every corner of every floor.

Zeke has called for back-up and an ambulance.

Minutes pass.

I have to find Elena and Marko.

Take their fear away.

She makes her way downwards.

The bottom floor of the house, dark and gloomy and lonely.

Another little terrace, two shovels discarded on it.

Recently used?

Impossible to say, and she doesn't want to believe the worst, but feels that the children are here somewhere.

Beneath the soil by the terrace? Or behind the door straight in front of me, which seems to lead straight underground?

She yanks the door open.

Behind it is a sequence of rooms lining a damp, dark corridor, and she must be moving deeper into the rock face now, surely? To where the chamber of darkness might be found?

She opens door after door. Empty, windowless rooms and storerooms.

She switches on the lights as she gets deeper into the building.

Moves further and further into the darkness, closer to what must be the rock face itself.

She is holding her pistol out in front of her.

Silence. Or is it actually silent? She listens. Hears whirring, ticking, and light breathing.

What's making the ticking sound?

A white door leading into a storeroom. Malin turns on the light.

And at the back of the storeroom is another door that leads into yet another damp but oddly warm room.

She turns on the light.

Another door, and she can hear something behind it. Breathing? Life?

Is that you? Is that you, tell me it's you?

The ticking.

Voices behind the door, she can hear them now, weak and scared:

'Daddy . . . where are you? . . . where are you? . . . I'm scared . . . Daddy . . .'

But the ticking. Louder here. What does the ticking mean?

Is that you? Are you there?

Light filtering in under the door.

Someone's coming.

Not them again.

Is that you, Daddy?

'Daddy . . . where are you? . . . where are you?' Are they going to kill us now? You have to rescue us, Daddy, tell us what's going on, take us away from here. You mustn't abandon us. Is that you out there?

They took us out, pointed their guns at us, at our heads, and they screamed and shouted, but then they shoved us back in here again, so no one would find us.

Those words, those actions will live on inside us forever, even if we can't put words to them right now.

Light.

Darkness before the light.

And then a whole lot of light. As someone opens the door to our dungeon.

The children.

Naked.

Dirty. Smelly.

But it's them. It's Marko and Elena.

And their room stinks, and they're skinny, and they screw up their eyes as they peer in her direction from where they're huddled on the floor in their own excrement and urine. They can't see me, but there, in my shadow, there they are.

Malin sinks to her knees.

Never mind the dirt and the smell. That doesn't matter. The children are alive.

She crawls the few metres to the figures in front of her.

'Now, is your name Marko? And you must be Elena?'

Drawings on the walls. Strange symbols made with crayons. Characters, like a strange, alien language, brought here by spaceships from a distant future.

'It's all right now,' she whispers to the children, hugging them, feeling the warmth of their skin. 'It's all right now, Marko and Elena. You don't have to be frightened any more.'

And then she hears a voice, and seems to feel four small, white bird wings flapping above her head.

'We're not frightened any more either,' the birds whisper, and Malin holds the children tightly, feeling the warm blood coursing through their living bodies, as the ticking in the room that led to the children's cell is replaced by a ringing, and Malin doesn't want to let go of the children, wants to hold them, fill them with love, but she has to deal with the ringing.

She picks up the children and carries them out of the room. Can't leave them in there.

A large white box in one corner. She lets go of the children and they scream. She crouches down and crawls over to the box, and opens it.

Fifty-five.

Fifty-four.

Wires and transparent metal tubes. A digital counter, numbers, a speaker spewing out the ringing sound, and the children, silent behind Malin.

Explosives.

At least ten kilos. A detonator.

Fifty.

No obvious switch to stop it.

Should I pull out that wire, that cable? The black one, or the white one?

Red?

Green?

Sweat breaks out on her forehead.

Forty-five.

If I touch the bomb anything could happen, I'd set it off. And that fucking ringing sound.

Forty, and Malin turns around, tucks one child under each arm and rushes out of the underground, through room after room, through the corridor and up into the light, out onto the bottom terrace, counting inside her head the whole time, as the ringing disappears behind her.

Thirty-five.

Thirty-four.

Up on the other terrace. Zeke catches sight of her, he's covered in blood, and he smiles, and the children scream, and she tries to calm them as she runs. Zeke's alone, where's Leopold Kurtzon? And Malin sees Zeke point towards the railing, and he says: 'He fell when I was trying to help him up,' and Malin realises what's happened. Zeke didn't back down. And she can hear the lizards grunting and roaring and hissing as they tear Leopold Kurtzon apart.

Twenty-two.

'There's a bomb!' she screams, passing the little girl, Elena, to Zeke. She knows he can carry her in spite of his injury, she can see it in his eyes. 'It's about to go off, we have to get out of here,' and Zeke shouts: 'That's why he was smiling, the bastard . . .'

He runs after her with the girl in his arms, and they run up the steps towards the entrance hall.

Ten.

Nine.

Out through the door, out into the garden. The lizards can't be anywhere close, they're busy elsewhere.

Eight.

Seven.

How powerful is the bomb? How far do we have to run to avoid being turned to ash?

Six.

Five.

Four.

Fifty metres from the house now, on dew-wet grass, on their way to the sea and the bridge, then out onto the bridge. Is the world about to end?

Three.

Two.

Malin and Zeke stop, panting, hugging the children.

One.

How far away do we need to be?

Zero.

61

A rumble.

The island seems to vibrate behind them, and the house shakes, the bridge lurches violently from side to side – just let it stay up.

The air thickens, and Malin's whole body seems to be sucked into a furious vacuum.

They're standing in the middle of the bridge, trying to stay upright with the children in their arms, watching the brothers' house shake, the arched roof twists this way and that, as an invisible force seems to rip the trees and bushes apart, and the bridge beneath them is shaking even more now.

Then the roof of the house disappears, blown out into the night sky.

A dark grey cloud of smoke is rolling towards them from the island, and the world vanishes into a cloud of ash, smoke, and dust.

Malin sinks to her knees, feels the thick oak planks of the bridge protesting, puts one hand over the boy's mouth to shield him, help him breathe, and can see Zeke doing the same before the smoke envelops him.

Are you about to die, Zeke?

Small, green, poisonous fragments fly through the fog.

Where's Zeke? Gone. The girl in his arms.

Then the smoke eases slightly.

She sees Zeke, the girl. Their chests heaving up and down, up and down.

The boy in her own arms. Gasping for air.

They're surrounded by poisonous smoke.

But it doesn't stop the children breathing.

Epilogue

Hälsingland, June

Mummy's here.

And Daddy.

We're together again as a family.

There's no pain any more, Malin. No desire.

Just a moment in which we can be together.

Who was our real daddy, Malin? Our biological daddy?

He isn't here, even though he should be. But who is he? A shadow, a tree in a forest, raping a young woman?

Our real mummy is still in her home in the underground. Her father and brothers are even further down, in places that can't be described.

In a cell inside the prison next to Kronoberg Park, Jokso Mirovic is playing with his children. He's allowed to have them with him, and they'll have a loving home with their aunt, where they can live and grow up during the years their father is locked away.

We see them playing, laughing and having fun, bubbling with life, and we can understand him. We can see their mummy too now, she's close to them, but in the same realm as us.

Your mummy was with us once, Malin, and she was wondering if you're OK, and you are, aren't you? You're finally happy now, aren't you?

Your mummy didn't want to, or couldn't, or didn't dare to get any closer to you, any of you.

We're going to go now, Malin Fors.

It's time. We're going to pretend we're real people, doing the things that people do.

This is the last time we'll see you, Malin.

Thanks for everything.

You're walking towards a bed now.

And in that bed lies your brother.

Malin is holding Tove's hand.

The room around them is furnished like a teenage boy's bedroom. A desk, a bookcase with ornaments and a few videos.

Children's films, as far as Malin can make out.

A Swarovski crystal bear, posters for some hard rock group from the eighties on the wall, and for the Finnish group Lordi.

Through the open window, summer is streaming in.

Outside, the sun is pouring its light onto a garden where microscopic apples are starting to form on the branches of the trees.

Norrgården Care Home.

An old works-manager's house, beautifully situated on the edge of the village of Sjöplogen in the heart of the Hälsingland forest.

They have been shown to the room by Britta Ekholm. She was pleased to see them, said: 'He's having his nap at the moment. But I'm sure he'll be pleased to see you when he wakes up.'

There was so much Malin wanted to ask.

What should I be expecting?

How is he?

But she didn't ask anything.

Instead, she and Tove went into the room, and when she hesitated Tove took her hand, pulling her mum in with her.

In one corner of the room, beside the window open to the summer, is a hospital bed. And in that bed a thin man is sleeping. Beside the bed is a wheelchair.

They approach the prone body.

He's resting quietly, and Malin can see her little brother's face from the side. His chin isn't very pronounced, and his nose sort of juts out between his cheeks, and Malin wonders what she's feeling, then she puts her hand against her brother's cheek and slowly strokes the warm skin, and his warmth becomes her own, and she knows that she has arrived somewhere, at a place she's been longing for.

You've got my cheekbones, she thinks, my fine hair, my prominent nose. Tove's delicate forehead. You are me, she thinks, stroking his cheek again.

She met up with Peter Hamse when she got home from Stockholm.

They went for a meal at the Aphrodite restaurant, talked remarkably openly, and then he went back to her flat with her, and it was all that she had been longing for.

He seemed utterly present in the moment as she gave herself to him, and afterwards she asked him to stay. And he had done so, and they spent all night talking, and in the morning he stayed until Tove got back from Janne's, so he could meet her as soon as possible.

He spends almost every night in her flat now.

She's seen both Janne and Daniel Högfeldt with their new girlfriends. And she accepts their choices, their love, wishes them well.

Tove's school holiday has begun. In August she'll be moving to Lundsberg.

Malin often asks herself how on earth she is going to cope. But it will work. It has to work. I can always curl up in Peter's arms when anxiety starts to eat away at me from the inside.

Zeke's gunshot wound turned out to be superficial. And the injury has healed, and he is still seeing Karin Johannison, Malin is sure of that.

But Karin is longing to have children. Malin can see it in her, and Zeke is the wrong man for that. He'll never leave his wife, and Kalle, her husband, wants to cling to his 'freedom'.

Zeke hasn't said outright that he pushed Leopold Kurtzon over the edge of the terrace of the house out in the Norrhammar archipelago. But Malin knows he did, and is full of silent admiration for him. Child-killers have no place among us. Just as little as predatory paedophiles.

Johannison Ludvigsson was given a three-month sentence for possession of illegal firearms. His invented Economic Liberation Front never made it to court: his confused behaviour was written off as a work of artistic creativity by the prosecutor, the career-minded woman to whom Karim Akbar, increasingly cocky and self-satisfied, has now got engaged. An investigation into Dick Stensson's affairs was started, but soon dropped.

'He's sound asleep,' Tove says, and Malin replies: 'He sleeps like a child,' and she enjoys the feeling this moment is giving her, doesn't want to let her mum in here, never wants to let her in anywhere again, she's been eradicated now, hasn't she?

Her dad's back in Tenerife.

He gave up in the end when she didn't answer any of his calls.

And then, one day, he was gone. He'd put a letter through her door, saying he thought he might stay on the island for a while, that he had taken his flat there off the market, and had arranged for a friend to take care of the flat on Barnhemsgatan for him. He was planning to scatter her mum's ashes on one of the island's golf courses: 'That was where she was happiest.'

Happiest.

Tove strokes the cheek of the sleeping man who looks like a boy, and in that moment Malin feels a wave of pressure ebbing away.

'I'm here now,' Malin whispers. 'We're here.'

'I'm here now,' and a warm breeze comes in through the window, and she can feel tears on her cheeks.

I'm here now.

Sorry it took me so long.

Sorry, that's all I can say.

In the best books, the ending often comes as a shock.
Not just because of that one last twist in the tale,
but because you have been so absorbed in their world,
that coming back to the harsh light of reality is a jolt.

If that describes you now, then perhaps you should track down
some new leads, and find new suspense in other worlds.

Join us at www.hodder.co.uk, or follow us on
Twitter @hodderbooks, and you can tap in to a
community of fellow thrill-seekers.

Whether you want to find out more about this book,
or a particular author, watch trailers and interviews, have
the chance to win early limited editions, or simply browse
our expert readers' selection of the very best books,
we think you'll find what you're looking for.

And if you don't, that's the place to tell us what's missing.

We love what we do, and we'd love you to be part of it.

www.hodder.co.uk

 @hodderbooks

HodderBooks

HodderBooks